Jani, whose full name is Zahid Dara Abro, is a romantic at the quintessence with skills in painting, poetry, and prose. He predominantly expresses himself in his mother tongue, Sindhi. Jani writes about the remnants of life's carnage, yet at the same time he draws inspiration from the garbage where life crawls. His aesthetics are abstracts like reverse tenses. His analytical side, coupled with an immense attention to detail, is evident in his work. Jani has viewed life through various lenses, including rural and urban perspectives, the developing and developed world. Over time, he has honed the ability to capture subtle nuances and reveal their true meanings.

His novel *Those Trees Outlive Them* is a rolling tale of how five generations search for meaning and find the object of life itself, their overlapping narratives bridge the gaps between poverty and wealth, past and present, east and west, and good and bad.

Jani is a trained physician, working as a neurophysiologist (an allied health technologist) in New York/New Jersey since 1999.

Dhayani Alam Abro

Jani Abro

THOSE TREES OUTLIVE THEM

Stories from the banks of
Sindhu (River Indus)

AUSTIN MACAULEY PUBLISHERS™
LONDON * CAMBRIDGE * NEW YORK * SHARJAH

Copyright © Jani Abro 2024

The right of Jani Abro to be identified as author of this work has been asserted by the author in accordance with sections 77 and 78 of the Copyright, Designs and Patents Act 1988.

All rights reserved. No part of this publication may be reproduced, stored in a retrieval system, or transmitted in any form or by any means, electronic, mechanical, photocopying, recording, or otherwise, without the prior permission of the publishers.

Any person who commits any unauthorised act in relation to this publication may be liable to criminal prosecution and civil claims for damages.

This is a work of fiction. Names, characters, businesses, places, events, locales, and incidents are either the products of the author's imagination or used in a fictitious manner. Any resemblance to actual persons, living or dead, or actual events is purely coincidental.

A CIP catalogue record for this title is available from the British Library.

ISBN 9781035820252 (Paperback)
ISBN 9781035820269 (ePub e-book)

www.austinmacauley.com

First Published 2024
Austin Macauley Publishers Ltd®
1 Canada Square
Canary Wharf
London
E14 5AA

I want to start by bowing and prostrating in sheer respect to the aura of wise individuals, thinkers, and writers who shared awakening with their works, they have shared objective knowledge and truths that resonate with us all. While it is challenging to name them all, a few immediately come to mind: Latif Sarkar (Shah Abdul Latif Bhittai), Fariduddin Attar, Immanuel Kant, Giordano Bruno, Anton Chekhov, Shaikh Ayaz, Noon Meem Rashid, and Sherwood Anderson.

I owe a debt of gratitude to Mohammad Ali Mahar, Nadeem Iqbal, and Hasan Mujtaba, who meticulously reviewed every scrap note and rough draft, encouraging me to pen this book.

I also extend my appreciation to Dr. Atai Khan Yousufzai, Tariq Iqbal Soomro, Akhlaq Ansari, Inamullah Sheikh and Kehar Shaukat, who have been significant milestones in my learning journey.

Special thanks are due to Emily Hauze, whose efforts made this book more accessible to a broader audience than it would have otherwise been. Emily not only provided invaluable assistance with meticulous line editing and manuscript checks but also ensured that ideas were presented clearly to readers. She consistently highlighted Sindhi terminologies that required simplification for better comprehension by the audience, dedicating extraordinary time and care to its development.

I am deeply grateful to my wife, Uzma Kazmi, whose unwavering inspiration has been the driving force behind the publication of this book.

Without the support of all these individuals, this book would not have been possible.

This book is based on legends, stories and real-life experiences of Dhayani Alam Abro and Zaib-Un-Nisa Alam Abro, heedlessly heard by me as a child.

Table of Contents

Foreword	13
Chapter 1: He Was Afraid of Riding the Train	14
Chapter 2: Googling a Cluster of Stars	18
Story I: Fakeer	21
Chapter 1: Mehann-Jee-Khaahee (Drigh)	23
Chapter 2: Millions of Purple Flowers	32
Chapter 3: Distress Calls of a Lonely Titihar	42
Chapter 4: Unwanted Tour of the City	53
Chapter 5: Morr Tho Tilay Rana (Peacock Is Displaying, My Love!)	56
Story II: Alam	85
Chapter 1: Dharamsala	87
Chapter 2: Cosmogonic Hymns	92
Chapter 3: Roopee for Life	98
Chapter 4: A Man Who Took It on His Chest	101
Chapter 5: The Task of Living in a Synthetic World	104
Chapter 6: Do Not Move or Blink	108
Chapter 7: Lonely Dead Goose Feather	114
Chapter 8: Chinkoo Bhangi Doing Autopsies	119
Chapter 9: Throwing Flowers Like Cupid's Arrows	136

  Chapter 10: A Heart That Stopped Beating, but Was Still Saying,
    'I'm Fine'   *143*

Story III: Ali Gohar   **147**

 Chapter 1: So It Begins   *149*

 Chapter 2: Two Sugar Dolls   *156*

 Chapter 3: People of the Unseen   *170*

 Chapter 4: Showering Moonshine   *185*

 Chapter 5: The Sweet, Biting Smell of Wild Cannabis   *207*

 Chapter 6: A Rotten Breeze Blew By   *213*

 Chapter 7: She Looked Almost Like Oriana Fallaci   *221*

 Chapter 8: Map of the Atum-Bom   *234*

 Chapter 9: Idling for Thirty-Five Years and Counting   *247*

Story IV: Jani   **249**

 Chapter 1: Pineapple of White Marble   *251*

 Chapter 2: Medium Rare, Almost Bleeding   *257*

 Chapter 3: Agrasen Ki Baoli   *261*

 Chapter 4: Kali Masjid   *264*

 Chapter 5: Apollo Command Module   *267*

 Chapter 6: Jumping Like a Grasshopper   *272*

 Chapter 7: Whose Funeral Are You Crying Over?   *285*

 Chapter 8: Tiffany Bow   *295*

 Chapter 9: A Mass Panic of Thoughts   *299*

 Chapter 10: Darvaish-Geologist   *303*

 Chapter 11: Wrinkled Photograph of Tolstoy on the Wall *307*

 Chapter 12: A Writer Who Rode to Rob a Train   *310*

 Chapter 13: A Romantic Account of Death   *314*

 Chapter 14: Magnificent Ray of Divine Truth   *319*

Chapter 15: Back under the Gulmohar	325
Chapter 16: Winds Avoiding Him	329
Chapter 17: Stupid Monologue	333
Chapter 18: Seven Days and Six Nights	338
Chapter 19: He Who Used to Manufacture Time	342
Story V: Kabeer	**345**
Chapter 1: "If You Are Sad, You Go Hug the Tree, You Go Fit!"	347
Chapter 2: Dying Freshness	356
Chapter 3: Solid-Looking Body of Liquid	362
Chapter 4: The Rest of the Journey Was Dust Grey	368
Chapter 5: Guy with No Glitter	382
Chapter 6: Crowbar Clanging Noise	385
Chapter 7: "Physical Inventory of Giggles and Acrid Sadness"	394
Chapter 8: "Qalandar! Mast Qalandar. Qalandar, Lal Qalandar!"	405
Chapter 9: Is That the Place?	411

Foreword

This is a rolling snowball story of five generations interwoven in a long tale; which runs simultaneously between 1875 and 2012. It explores the land of Sindh and its people in many layers: their socio-political situation, their five-thousand-year-old civilisation, their enduring Sufi attitudes, and the Indus River, which is a vital part of this civilisation—but due to several dams and barriers upstream, the river has dried up, just as its mystic trends have evaporated with time. The narrator wanted to share his pathos with his readers.

First generation: a self-made entrepreneur who became an orphan the day he was born.

Second generation: a flamboyant character who ran away from home at the age of 12 and came back as a young man of 25.

Third generation: an upstanding, hardworking, ambitious man, who started out in the Sindhi countryside and ended up in New York City.

Fourth generation: a poet, who is the narrator of this story. He wonders, *How do I know all this?—it must come* partly from stories that I heard from my grandmother*, and partly from my own imagination*. Later in his life he became a physician by profession.

Fifth generation: An American Sindhi who loves his heritage, but can't go back, and is still trying to find his way.

Chapter 1
He Was Afraid of Riding the Train

He is walking along with three other astronauts—ironically he's known all of them since high school—one is Ronak Patel and the others are Ben and Sid. He had this weird feeling that something wasn't right, and that Ronak shouldn't be there, even though Ronak had been his best friend all along, and is an extremely kind-hearted person. But he knows Ronak had also failed to get a high school diploma and had ended up doing a GED just so that he could get into community college, so how did he become an astronaut overnight?

All four of them are wearing full gear though it's still several hours till the launch. The rocket is encased in a temporary scaffold, with a hoisting elevator to traverse from top to bottom. They get into that elevator with two of the checkout crew and rise from the launch floor, 337 feet up to a walkway bridge near the top of the 36-storey high Saturn rocket, a vessel carrying five and a half million pounds of liquid explosives in the form of hydrogen and oxygen and everything in between.

The check-out crew is there to assist them in opening the elevator door, getting into command module, making sure that astronauts won't touch anything, and minimising—he'd like to say, preventing—the risk of their astronaut-suits' getting even a pin-hole puncture.

They reach the top level and the assisting crew opens the elevator doors; from here they cross a walkway bridge to get into the command module. They settle into their cockpit seats, and the checkout crew buckles each astronaut tightly in place by putting one foot on his shoulder and then pulling the belt straps. The hatch is shut and they are left strapped vertically to their seats, waiting for lift off.

He sees a solitary cloud drifting freely in the sky from one of the triangular windows, which gives him a sense of serenity. Though he has not been anxious at all—the time for getting worried had long passed. He hears the voice of Matt Lauer from NBC's Today Show, who is saying in his ever-soothing tone, which has the quality of a gentle touch of a priest's hand on a confessing sinner's forehead, bestowing the approval of a whole nation—he is saying, 'T minus 20 seconds, T minus 15 seconds and counting, 12, 11, 10, 09 ignition sequences start…01 ignition. And we have a lift-off, people, of this NASA Mars pioneer human mission. It reaches mark one altitude in 64 more seconds, all four boosters are going to burn off, and the rocket boosters are about to pierce the heavens, and they are going to be on their own from here onwards,' and he starts to think, what the hell is Matt Lauer of NBC doing in NASA's mission control center?

While doing the all-system check-up, he looks at his fellow astronaut's glass helmet and sees the face of his great-great grandfather, who died more than half a century before even he was born, but that doesn't bother him, and all of sudden, part of the cockpit panel looks like an old locomotive inside, with small and large pipes bent in loops and making U-turns, and he somehow can see this rocket from outside while still strapped onto the seat, and this rocket looks like a steam locomotive in the dark with hot water dripping from its holes and steam leaking from its vents.

And this surreal thought comes into his mind for just a fraction of a second: that his great-great grandfather walked hundreds of miles from Larkano to Karachi because he was afraid of riding the train. And all of sudden, one of the alarms goes off, and he keeps switching it off but it's not responding, rather its intensity increases, and the arousal of a strange sensation wakes him up, and he turns off his alarm clock.

Back to reality, Kabeer woke up and hit the snooze and threw his head back on the pillow for another few minutes. He came out of his bed eventually and tried to find his shorts that he always threw aside before falling asleep and never knew where they went. He located them and pulled them on and emerged from his room, descending to the first floor living space of his parents' upscale three-story rental townhouse. They lived in one of the most financially conservative counties of New Jersey—in other words one of the poor towns, that's what he always thinks—and his parents love this place because it's away from city and tucked into Schooleys Mountain ridge of northern Jersey and they have their small business there, which he never thought of as being either good or bad.

He came downstairs from his bedroom and went straight to the patio to smoke a cigarette. And he shut the patio door hard, which moved the frame of his great-great grandfather's only known black-and-white rough-and-tough photograph in sepia tone, which his father realigns pretty much every day and then always asks him to shut the patio door slowly. Kabeer had seen this photograph so many times but never understood what the big deal was.

It was just an old photograph that looked like it came out of the classic pictures from one of Life magazine's special editions, a picture of an old Indian man, with bare shoulders and a big white turban and a long malnourished wrinkled face, with lines of loose skin, and tired eyelids which barely could hold his intense, shouting eyes, even though it was a still photograph, and saying, *"we have seen all,"* just above sagging and drooping cheeks, with a folksy beard which looked like a country man's, and a long moustache with pointed tips but not like Dali's, and a slightly wavy nose. That whole photograph was falling apart, faded with oxidized yellowish grey colours, maybe because of its age and sepia.

But today, Kabeer was more concerned with making it to a meeting with one of his grumpy professors about his paper on the effects of long-term data on real-time voting behaviours. In which he had explained the blanket effects and in fact adverse effects of collecting data from voters. And in which he wanted to showcase the thumbs-down effect of a 22-year-old female malaiseing with a cold who got a telemarketer call regarding a survey from a conservative political think tank.

He was a fresh social sciences graduate from Rutgers and wanted to work in a field with advanced research applications, so there was nothing more attractive to him than joining the Democratic National Committee as a junior data analyst, where he could do real-time political data collection for the forthcoming presidential elections. It all came naturally to him, just like being a liberal did, though he always wondered why that was.

And then he would wonder about the problem of how the talented analysts tended to lean toward the left, and the biggest technically and conceptually minded scholars regularly collaborate with interest groups on the left, which resulted in a generational loss to conservative ideology, and the right failing to keep up with its own invention of voter targeting. All this was spinning in his young Democratic brain.

His grades were average, because he always studied at the last minute, still thinking he'd get good grades, but then settling for B's and occasional A-minuses. This was his last year and he was very eager to get into the field. One of his friends who was doing his bachelors in computers had already gotten a 120K offer. His father kept telling him, *"you should become a physician!"*—but he never forced him to do anything.

His father wanted him to go into medical profession to gain a strong financial footing, but he would support his argument with lofty reasons, saying that the true, noble healer hardly existed anymore. And in these conversations, his father would always find a way somehow to bring in one of his favourite reasons, which he would always introduce in the form of a question. "Do you know why a physician, a medical practitioner"—and he would always say both of these together, physician and medical practitioner—"is called a doctor? Doctor is a Greek word."

Kabeer knew that it was actually Latin, but his father thought all knowledge and complex reasoning came from the Greeks.

"The meaning of doctor is, 'one who knows and who could explain.'"

"But by that logic, why is this not the word for a teacher as well as a doctor?"

Then his father would always to bring in the whole kitchen sink of reasoning.

"That's why they refer to PhDs as doctors," he would say. And also that, "a doctor has 28,000 more words in his vocabulary than any other science graduate," without any explanation of where he had read it, or how he calculated this 28,000 more words thing, or what difference it could make.

Once when Kabeer's father was reasoning to convince him on that same topic, his grandfather, who was in his seventies, was also sitting with them and listening to Kabeer and his father very carefully. But then Kabeer's grandfather said a weird thing: "There used to be a boy, Maadho!" Then he paused and made a humming sound before continuing, "Humm...with me in Qamber, in my schooldays, long time ago. He too wanted to become a doctor, but was too poor and couldn't become one. Then he memorised the entire dictionary and went insane."

Chapter 2
Googling a Cluster of Stars

It was dark and cool—one of those dreary December nights. He went outside to smoke. Television lights were flickering in windows, and the sidewalk outside their condo was an arch between two dunes, like a long smile. He was taking those fast puffs that he always did, and while blowing one of those he looked up and got lost in that beautiful sky for a moment or two, and he was happy he could still identify that Big Dipper, along with the belt of Orion the hunter—his father had taught him that years back when they used to live in Plainsboro. He also noticed a small cluster of stars joined together, but couldn't name that constellation. "Oh well," he said to himself, and went back in. After a while, he googled that cluster of stars and found that it's called the Seven Sisters, but they were not just seven stars in close proximity—actually, these were a cluster of over half a million stars, though only seven of them could be seen.

His father always told him that life was somewhere out there in the void, in that unexplained emptiness that is probably not empty at all. Then he would look to Kabeer's right or left and tilt his head a little, like he wanted to look at something behind him, into invisibility, into some kind of cuckoo world where time is irrelevant—as if by looking to his right and tilting his head his father could see into the past—and he would say, "try to see into another dimension, behind the obvious."

His father was one of those in between ones, neither a Sufi nor non, one of those people who always try to find an ingenious excuse to get his bank overdraw fee waived, and at the same time could talk about transcendental aesthetics for half an hour before taking his first real good pause.

And Kabeer looked at the tilted frame of his great grandfather's photograph, which his father had not yet corrected, and thought about that long unending walk that his great grandfather did somewhere back in time, in fact in another millennium. He kept his eyes shut, wanting to enjoy that thought for a little longer.

Story I: Fakeer

Chapter 1
Mehann-Jee-Khaahee (Drigh)

It was a dark and cold night; he was lying down next to railroad tracks in the middle of nowhere. God knows what was cooking in his mind while he gazed absently into the sky, not even paying attention to that breath-taking, moonless night or that tilted galaxy, which looked so clear that one could reach out and grab that cloud of cosmic dust like cotton candy. Perhaps he was looking at the Big Dipper and Orion the hunter, or maybe trying to make triangles out of those stars, like a kid, or maybe he used the star from the Big Dipper's handle to find the North Star, or perhaps he got entangled by that concise charm of Seven Sisters, which he probably mistook for Scorpio, because that's how that small cluster of stars is known in Sindh. Or maybe he paid no attention to all those celestial wonders, just focusing on keeping his feet and legs in the direction he had to walk tomorrow, and worrying about his court appearance hundreds of miles ahead in the completely foreign and unknown city to which he was heading. Slowly his vision began to blur and he drifted into sleep.

    He was an old man with all the essentials of old age: tall and thin, with deep triangular cups over both collarbones, wrinkled sagging dehydrated skin like a swag valance window draping under both eyes, and those big deep-set eyeballs with grey cloudy halos around those dark brown centres, eyeballs which were pushed back into the bony orbits of his eye sockets. He had prominent cheekbones and caved-in cheeks, and around his lips there were sagging thin muscles stretched down to his chin, but all that was mostly covered under his henna-stained red beard and proportionally long moustaches.

    With one distinction, a crooked nose for which he always blamed himself while sparing the actual culprit, his elder brother, whom he always called by the respectful title *Ado Saeen*. Many years earlier, Ado Saeen had thrown a hard leather shoe at his crawling baby brother to stop him from eating dried chicken shit. It stopped him for sure, but also broke his nose.

His mother had died giving birth to him. His elder brother was just ten or so years old then; their father was already dead.

So he started his life, like from the deep pits reminiscent of a scene from a Dickens novel, in a dusty hamlet called *Mehann-jee-khaahee,* right across from Lake Drigh. There was a three-span arch masonry bridge made of red bricks crossing the centre of the lake, and that bridge led to Mehann-jee-khaahee village.

No one called it by its full name; usually they just said, "Khaahee." It was a place enveloped in dirt and barely breathing, suffering its last throes, somewhere in Northern Sindh. It was not an island in the middle of that lake; rather that lake formed an odd-looking 'U' shape. There were date trees, but most of them were infertile, bearing instead only colonies of bats that live in them. There were also a few huge *aa-sirheen*[1] trees spreading their branches horizontally, reaching twice the length of their height, making canopies of deep cool shadows in the hot and punishing summers of Sindh.

Once a year, peculiar spherical headed flowers sprouted out of the branches of those aa-sirheen trees. They looked like pom-poms or old-fashioned shaving brushes, made up of thousands of white tentacle-like stamens. At flowering time, the trees exuded a fragrance—calling it merely a scent wouldn't do it justice—which was, in a word, intoxicating.

Because that enchanting smell has everything in there, in layers: an appealing top with a strong, floral smell, enveloped in dry leather, which jolts your senses like a dead beloved calling from a distance. Then comes the middle part of the fragrance, like an anxious aching heart who never said what he had really wanted to say. That scent stays a little longer with you. And in the end arises a steady, residual perfume that lingers in your memory slots, scenting them forever and ever.

So that's what aa-sirheen flowers were like. Gradually those stamens would die and fall to the ground, making a soft padded rug of tired saffron colour there.

Most of the mud houses in Mehann-jee-khaahee were built up on dunes, because every few years the village would be flooded during the monsoons, and only a home on dunes had any chance of not being washed away completely.

---

[1] *Aa-sirheen*: *Albizia lebbeck* trees.

That bridge, that red brick bridge, was at the loop of the 'U' turn in the lake. Just beyond the bridge there was a two-story farmhouse of colonial appearance, made up of the same red baked bricks. In fact, that farmhouse, that bridge, that entire lake, and the thousands and thousands of acres of land around the lake were all owned by some antediluvian feudals who had owned everything in and around Mehann-jee-khaahee since forever. In colonial times, those landlords used to host a hunting event each winter to please the imperial British bureaucracy. That hunt would last for days.

There, in Mehann-jee-khaahee, his elder brother raised him, although he was a child himself. He would ask the nursing mothers in their village to feed him. And they would oblige, placing their own child at one breast and latching him onto the other and thus feeding him like their own. And so he survived through those women who held heaven under their feet without even knowing it.

As he grew, those same mothers, like mother nature herself, would sustain them with *ribbaa*,[2] and unyielding life kept moving relentlessly forward. Ado Saeen learned to become a barber, and it was the barber's duty to cut around and remove the foreskin of the penis. But he had no interest in his brother's profession, so he kept roaming around those same two and a half streets of Mehann-jee-khaahee, where there was no one to teach him anything. But he kept his flame alight, and became teenager just by following every day with a night and every night with a day. Neither he did anybody else knew his real age; the only record of his birth was what Ado Saeen always told him: "I myself was too young when you were born."

But one day they came, the mystics in their long black cloaks, holding *bairagi-riyoon*[3] in their hands, and wearing *zeher-mohra* and *feroza kuntha*[4] around their necks, and singing hymns and spiritual psalms.

You are the art and creation, you are the friend,
You are the remedy of every pain;
You are the true meaning of every word

---

[2] *Ribbaa*: thin rice porridge.

[3] *Bairagi-riyoon:* talisman sticks, which take their name from the sad and reclusive '*Bairaagi*', restless souls who are cursed to wander, never to find what they are looking for, wishing to become invisible.

[4] *Zeher-mohra… kuntha*: *zeher-mohra* is aquamarine and *feroza* is turquoise; *kuntha* refers to a necklace that would feature these sorts of real, rough gemstones.

You are the cure of my aching heart;
I wanted to listen to your unheard silent voice,
The only cure it is for my pain,
The reason I call for you
Is that none could cure the ache of my soul
But you.

This brought the listeners to tears, and he followed them into oblivion, into the transient restless lust of *musti-o-baykarary*,[5] singing with them.

With pity hear, Tahmineh is my name!
The pangs of love my anxious heart employ,
And flattering promise long-expected joy.
My voice unheard, beyond the sacred screen.
How often have I listened with awe?

So with no worldly belongings he followed these *Fakeers* into insensibility, begging from town to town and village to village. Three Fakeers in that group wore multiple rough iron bands on their right arms, and they would bang against them rhythmically like chimes, using a chopstick-length stick that they held between their thumb and index finger and moved with the remaining three fingers.

Others had a *yak taro*[6] and they kept plucking its single string, which resonated in their weeping souls, singing hymns, *dohas*,[7] and verses of Latif Sarkar and Saint Kabir;[8] and sometimes they would sit and recite the long tale of

---

[5] *Musti-o-baykarary*: 'the intoxication of restlessness'.

[6] Yak taro also known as Gopijiantra, Ektara, Iktar, is one of the oldest stringed instruments of India. The use of a stringed drone instrument to accompany the voice in religious settings can be documented in images as far back as the 4th-5th century when the singer was painted in the Ajanta Caves. It is used in parts of India, Nepal, and Pakistan today by Yogis and wandering holy men to accompany their singing and prayers.

[7] *Dohas*: couplets, typically rhyming. The word descends from the Hindi *do hara* meaning 'two greens'—in other words, two living lines.

[8] *Latif Sarkar and Saint Kabir*: The great Sindhi poet Shah Abdul Latif Bhittai (1689–1752) and the Sufi saint Kabir (c. 1440–c. 1518).

Rustum-o-Sohrab from the *Shahnameh Ferdowsi*,⁹ which they had memorised. And sometimes they would go to a village and only say *aahay ko Allah!*—is there a god?—contrarily, reiterating divine promise. All this fascinated him. The new influx of mystic knowledge tickled his mind.

He became closer to two of the mystics in particular, Kalb Ali Fakeer and Lal Fakeer. They both used to recite *dastaans,* which were stories enveloped into stories. Most of them came from Sindhi oral traditions, and some of them came from *Attar.*¹⁰ Kalb Ali Fakeer and Lal Fakeer would often switch characters back and forth.

One day, while roaming around they ended up in Qamber, a town bigger than a village but much smaller than a city. Fakeer had not seen this place before. A town with a downtown!—which had rows of shops on both sides of a narrow alley. Qamber could offer only a distant glimpse of suburbia, but that was enough to tickle young Fakeer's heart. And he loved it.

They roamed streets of Qamber for a while. They wandered around the central market place, the Shahi-bazaar, where young Fakeer saw shops of *mahajans*—jewellers—for the very first time. The word *"mahajan"* is made up of two short words that literally mean 'great people', but God knows why that word was dedicated to people who dealt in gold and silver. There were other shops where people sold fresh produce, live poultry; there were grocers with stores full of all sorts of grains, spices displayed as colourful mountains of cayenne pepper, turmeric, and coriander in jute sacks with necks like rolled-up sleeves. And there were all sorts of other things.

There were other shops filled with bolts and bolts of raw fabric sold by the yard. For the very first time, Fakeer saw shops selling flowers, mostly garlands of roses. There were also women sitting on ground right outside the shops selling balls of churned butter, which were floating in glazed soft clay pots filled with cloudy sour-smelling water and fruit flies. But Fakeer was not interested in curd butter; he had seen that often enough. He was eager to see other shops.

Eventually, they settled down and sat in the cool shadow of an old *tahli* tree next to a stream at the base of the Norang Wah levee. God knows why tahlis

---

⁹ *Shahnameh Ferdowsi:* the epic poem *Book of Kings* by the Persian poet Ferdowsi (c. 940–1010).

¹⁰ *Attar*: the Persian Sufi poet Abū amīd bin Abū Bakr Ibrāhīm (1145–1220), known by the pen name Farīd ud-Dīn-Attar.

have such cool shadows. This tree threw its shade on the corner of *Suantak-Sir*, an old Hindu monastery. And Lal Fakeer began to narrate a story. He spoke loudly, almost shouting:

"There was a prostitute in a place sieged by moving sand dunes called Bhaloo-paar[11]—*"*

That captured audiences! Lal Fakeer continued:

"—and that woman's entire stock in trade was villainy, immorality and perversion, though she was independent like a queen and very proud of her profession. Whenever someone sought debauchery, she would offer herself as their partner. She had a melodious voice, was graceful in her movements and pleasant of speech, and there was never a moment when she was not singing."

When Saghoro[12] *went to the city named Bhaloo-paar, and war and hate were changed into love, belief in a singular God prospered, Faith was strengthened, and Unbelief was overthrown. When none of the wicked was left, having been scattered on every side, that woman went to Bhaloo-paar in a state of great poverty. Sore of heart, she approached the Chosen One. The Chosen One said: "Tell me, how is it that you have come? As a fugitive or to ply your trade? Have you come here for the sake of the Faith, or have you come to sell you wares?"*

The woman said to the Lord of both worlds, "I have made the journey neither for this reason nor for that. I have come hither because I heard tales of your generosity. Wretched and forsaken as I am, I have travelled this long way in the hope that you will give me a present."

Said the Chosen One: "Bhaloo-paar is full of young men: it would be more fitting for you to ask them."

"Because of your wars and battles," said the woman, *"the fear of your dagger and arrows, the fame of your strength and might, the greatness of your miracles and your renown, the horsemen of Arabia have lost their strength. How then should anyone go to the singing-girls?"*

---

[11] *Bhaloo-paar:* 'Prosperous bank'. This is a Sindhi nickname for the city of Mecca, translated roughly as 'prosperous bank', 'utopic prairie', or 'perpetual other end'.

[12] *Saghoro*: 'Flawless'. This is one of many names for the Prophet Mohammad in Sindhi, who is also called 'the proclaimer of the will of God'.

The Chosen One was pleased with her words and gave her his only cloak. And he said to his companions: "Let all of you who are my friends give her something from what you have." The Companions gave her a hundred different kinds of presents, and she became a person of wealth.

Lal Fakeer paused there, like he was allowing his audience to cherish the climax. Then he added his own thoughts about divine intervention into Attar's story.

"A lost woman was honoured by the Chosen One of God. Even though she had fallen to polytheism and depravity. Just because she once uttered a word or two in Your praise—"

Kalb Ali Fakeer plugged in, "*Your* praise, Mehboob Saeen!"[13] Reminding everyone that all the praises are His and His only.

Lal Fakeer carried on, "she became, by your generosity, the owner of great riches. You did not cause her to despair; you did not deprive her of your endless favour."

Kalb Ali Fakeer's voice interrupted Lal Fakeer with a rhyme: "*Jay key mungh jahan, tagay say thunjay.*"—*Whatever is glowing, it's your glitter, you own it all!* "All the pleasures are yours. Don't judge me please, as I'm the sinner, as I'm in it to my eyeballs, just let me walk away with it."

Lal Fakeer continued the dialogue, addressing the divine directly. "You know that, in praising You, I turned many times upon you! On you Mehboob Saeen; you my maker, like a compass. If I could just receive as reward a handful of the dust of your Chosen One's street, it will be as if I have received a new glorious sun in every tiny grain of it. Because, Mehboob Saeen, my heart is telling me you had praised the Chosen One's soul with the dust of your astral street; admit me to it if you can. As I cannot do without you, do not disappoint me; take my hand as the one who has fallen."

And Kalb Ali Fakeer interrupted, having been waiting for his cue, overriding Lal Fakeer's unsolved mystic riddle, in which all nouns, verbs, and tenses had intertwined and switched places with each other, leaving nothing but only Mehboob Saeen in the end.

It seemed that everyone, every member of the audience, had heard and understood that unsaid part of the story. So Kalb Ali Fakeer just brought the performance to a close, saying, "There is a chasm of fire, and Mehboob Saeen

---

[13] *Mehboob Saeen*: 'Divine Beloved'—a typically Sindhi-Sufi way of addressing God.

is on its other end. You have to cross it on a bridge of string made up of a single hair."

And he pointed both of his index fingers up toward the heavens, as if to poke the skies, and he craned his tilted head up with peacefully shut eyelids and lips dripping with saliva, and said: "*I want love; I want you; I want God.*" And a baker came in running with his hands full of bread loaves, which he placed on ground and dropped his head in front of Kalb Ali Fakeer to seek his blessing.

He learned their trade and eventually started telling stories himself. And one day Kalb Ali Fakeer and Lal Fakeer left on their journey of no return, a journey that would absorb them. Fakeer knew from Sufi traditions of that there is no schedule to start an end, and that his masters were invoking that starting of their end. They would keep walking and burning, and walking and burning, and finally they would sit somewhere and burn and burn and burn until either their consciousness became impure ashes or the subject of their awareness became object of the same and they might meet Mehboob Saeen.

On that day, you could see the searing heat causing distant trees to flicker in pools of mirage. The sun was so hot that a steamy haze filled the skies with a dominating muddy purplish tone. Fakeer could smell heat combining with his perspiration. He walked alongside his masters for a while, and then Kalb Ali Fakeer asked him to stop, and, before telling him to go back, they gave him their *kashkul* to keep. The kashkul was half of a split-open sea coconut that they used to beg for food. This was the only kashkul they had between them, which they had shared. They would eat from it together, alternating boluses between them, and they would take turns drinking from it as well.

Fakeer held that charred dark shell in both hands like a trophy. And then Kalb Ali Fakeer and Lal Fakeer left him and went on alone. Fakeer's lower eyelids filled, and then one of them gave in and a teardrop rolled down fast across his cheek and then waited for few moments at his jawbone before falling into that kashkul, which he was still holding in both hands, close to his chest, and his own teardrop became his first taking of his own offering. Fakeer kept looking at them as they got farther and farther away in the heat of those mirrory-mirage illusions of simmering pools of water, which were slicing Kalb Ali Fakeer and Lal Fakeer into horizontal gleams.

Fakeer kept looking at them as long as he could, until they became a thin point, and he had to strain to keep focused on those two tiny black and saffron orange specks. That was the last image of Kalb Ali Fakeer and Lal Fakeer that he remembered. He never ever said to anyone that he had to wipe his eyes quickly several times to keep his gaze clearly focused for as long as he could on those two diminishing dots, which appeared and disappeared again and again before completely dissolving into the limitless hazy purplish-blue horizon.

Chapter 2
Millions of Purple Flowers

Fakeer kept gathering stories, and after some years he began to tell them on his own. They were legends and folklore, stories of wounded wisdom wrapped in rags of simple words, or stories of love-madness that rarely had a happy ending, or stories of valour and tragedy. He didn't want to sit where Kalb Ali Fakeer and Lal Fakeer used to sit, because his heart told him, *cut them lose, let them go, you are no match to your masters, so how can you sit at Suantak-Sir, where they used to recite their long tales?*

He chose to roam the streets of Qamber and sit under the calm shadows of any old tree, though the best were always the cool round shadows of big aa-sirheen trees. Or sometimes he would go to the outskirts of Qamber and sit next to the tilting mud wall of any of the dilapidated sad mosques of those small hamlets. To gather an audience he would hum a few couplets of Latif Sarkar.

Once he had grabbed their attention, he would pull any story from his memory sack, mostly long rhyming poems. Without thinking about it, he might switch the format of the story, sometimes starting from the middle or narrating backwards altogether, putting the climax first. Or he would make mortal characters immortal by letting a killer be killed at the hands of his victim.

Once, sitting under an old aa-sirheen, Fakeer started his story thus:

He was old, but a master of tricks. He was a Persian gladiator. That day he was having the fight of his lifetime with a young and ruthless gladiator who was probably half his age and was known to crush his opponents' skulls slowly by gripping his five fingers around their heads and squeezing them like half of a split lemon. On the western banks of the river Amu-Sind, in that vast valley of plains, two armies were waiting to collide head-on, surrounded by fields of millions and millions of purple saffron flowers swinging their heads in the gentle winds and waiting for their own tragic destiny of being plucked by their necks.

Their frail beauty blended tragedy and romance; they were decadent in their lavish glory and impermanence, lasting only a few days before they withered and died.

The generals of those two armies decided each to send one of their best gladiators to fight in single combat, and that the winner of the fight would secure the victory for his entire army. The general of the Persian army called upon his seasoned hero who had never lost a one-on-one fight. The other army sent their young gladiator who was also undefeated in fights. The air was filled with that ineffable scent of saffron flowers, that undecided smell which gave them a bitter sweet and intimately earthy, dry-leathery-dusty fragrance.

The fight began. The old gladiator was slippery, a master of tricks. He yielded no ground to his opponent, fatiguing the young gladiator by making him circle around him. After wrestling long and heavily, the old gladiator began to feel weak, and, fearing for his reputation, prepared to stab his dagger into the young gladiator's heart.

But just before he could complete that final blow, he noticed a necklace around the young gladiator's neck, the same necklace that he once gave to his own beloved, who gave it to their son to keep him safe in war. And in that fraction of a moment of perception, the old gladiator's son came into his mind and he lost his focus. And in that same moment the young gladiator grabbed the dropped dagger and jabbed it through the old gladiator's ribs and into his heart.

The old prize-fighter fell from standing height like a sack of grain. A dust cloud rose when he hit the ground, and the young gladiator was yelling and squeezing both eyes shut and opening his mouth wide, revealing all of his upper and lower incisors and canines. He was making a wild cry by moving his lower jaw, and he was forcefully kicking his feet on the ground, causing more dust to rise.

Like always, everyone was looking at victorious young gladiator, and no one was looking down. Then the young gladiator placed his feet on broad chest of the dying old gladiator, who was now lying in a pool of blood, but still alive, breathing shallowly, trying to move his lips to say something but mustering only a few aching sounds from his mouth, which was filled with blood and he was drowning in it. He was rapidly exhaling air from his nostrils, parting a bit of that dust cloud hanging around his face. That enabled him to see the victorious zeal in the hot burning red face of the young fighter.

The old gladiator wanted to live a millennium in that single moment. He wanted to remember one more time that princess who loved this gallant warrior and to whom he had given that necklace for his unborn child. But even a millennium can't last forever, so the old gladiator died with open eyes and kind of a frail smile, without saying that he enjoyed losing a winnable fight.

When Fakeer finished his story there was an audience of six or seven people crunched down, sitting in a crescent formation in front of him—*in complete silence?* He marvelled—looking at him with their eyes popped wide open and mouths ajar. But the winds of Qamber did applaud him by rattling the dried seedpods of the old aa-sirheen tree in an ovation.

He gathered a few coins and put two bowls worth of wheat berry into belly of his *jhool*,[14] and someone else gave him a chunk of curd butter as his appreciation, which he swallowed right there.

One of the affluent landlords of Qamber became Fakeer's admirer, and every now and he would send one of his servants to summon Fakeer to him. And every time he would ask Fakeer to recite the same story again and again, and almost always he would weep at the end of it.

It was the story of a rich merchant of Baghdad, in a millennium when Baghdad was the centre of knowledge and wisdom. This merchant was a dealer of expensive perfumes, which he would concoct by grinding scarce rare herbs and real pearls. All day, this merchant would sell his hypnotic and alluring fragrances and compounds from his holistic pharmacy. Every evening, he loved to count his money from his daily sales, and he would count it all twice to make sure he had the right number.

Then one day, by the deed of Mehboob Saeen, a gaunt beggar, as dirty as one could be, came and stood in front of his shop. The strong stench of his body odour could be felt from quite a distance. The devils of his smell were terrifying those elfin fairies of delicate perfumy air roaming among the merchant's wares. Indeed that smell was working like a wrecking ball in a mirror shop.

At the end of the day, the beggar shouted, *"aahay ko Allah!"*—*is there a god?*

The merchant, who had been completely absorbed in counting his money, was extremely irritated by the beggar's plea. The Merchant ignored beggar and held his focus on counting the gold and silver coins. The beggar then cried, *"Haq*

---

[14] *Jhool:* a sling bag of looped cloth.

maujood"—God exists! *"Dhay kujh un' a jay naau"*—give something in his name.

That made the Merchant forget his count. He became angry with the beggar and yelled at him: "Don't you see I'm doing something very important? You are bothering me. Sit there on ground. Let me finish what I'm doing and then I will give you something."

The beggar complied and sat there outside merchant's shop, crunched down on the dirt, clenching his hands together at his chest like he was asking for forgiveness. But after a few moments the beggar again cried out, *"Haq maujood!* Give something in his name."

Again the Merchant's count was spoiled. Exasperated, he turned again to the beggar. "I ask you to sit there quietly. But you keep repeating, is there a God, is there a God, give something, and give something! Yes, there is a God I know, and yes I will give you some money, but first let me finish this very important work!"

The beggar answered, "Why you are hesitating to give? Because you can't give what you don't have! There is no room in your heart for me or for God or for anything else. Your heart is filled with your love for gold and silver. That is the meaning of life for you. You can't even die peacefully because you love your wealth, and how could you leave your beloved! And there is no meaning in your death! Because there is no meaning of your life."

Angrily the Merchant said, "And what is the meaning of your filthy and useless life? You are begging me for money to live."

The beggar smiled and said, "yes, but I don't need it. My Mehboob asks me to do that, so that the needle of sharp words from good people like you will keep deflating the balloon of my self-worth and my want."

"Enough of all that talk, can you die for your Mehboob Saeen?" And the exasperated Merchant turned away and went back inside without waiting for an answer.

Nonetheless, the beggar did reply, with a glad tone, "Yes I will." And then he lay down on the dirt in front of the merchant's shop, and he took a deep breath, and said, "Haq maujood." Slowly his chest deflated and that deep breath gently left his body.

The Merchant finished his count and secured the gold and silver coins in two small sacks. And went back outside to give him some money, but the beggar was long gone.

You wouldn't have seen any change in the Merchant at that moment. Only that the two coins he was holding in his hand for the beggar got loose and hit the dirt. But that set the course, and he began to change. He gave up all of his wealth and abandoned his business. He even left his family and became a beggar—but all he begged for was forgiveness. The strangers he approached would reply, "We forgive you," but his restlessness only increased with each new forgiveness.

The landlord's eyes glistened every time Fakeer finished this story. And this even though he was a despot, a man who would trap his workers in a web of complex compound interest loans designed never to be paid off. He would beat his peasant farmers and rape his cleaning women and maidservants at will. One of his loyal servants once mistakenly dropped and broke a piece of fine English crystal, and as punishment, the landlord commanded him to grind whole dried cayenne peppers into a fine powder, and then take his pants off in the centre of the town square and stuff the ground pepper in his rectum in front of everyone.

But the same landlord was also fond of mystic tales of love and selflessness. So he gave Fakeer a small room to live in, somewhere in that very Shahi Bazaar that Fakeer had enjoyed such a long time ago, and where he was still roaming and telling his stories. It was a dingy room, but then, beggars can't be choosers. At least, there was a place to keep him safe from the elements. Slowly that room became a centre for meetings for all sorts of beggars, and also transgenders and a few hermaphrodites.

Some of them even joined Fakeer and started living there as well, in that small dark dingy room, whose mud walls exhaled different smells in different seasons. In humid summers, those walls emitted an acrid odour of old dirty socks. But in dry winters those same mud walls could arouse the soul with their earthy petrichor scent, like the first raindrops hitting the cracked dry earth, and then those raindrops would strike notes in low registers to form melodies from the freshness of the ozone.

Every evening, right after sunset they would gather there. And they would take their offerings out of their sling bags and put them in a *pa'tra*[15] and then eat together. Those offerings were usually hard mouldy pieces of bread, overripe and spoiled fruits, and frothy lentils days past their prime. Those were the offerings that the God-loving people had given them in the name of Mehboob

---

[15] *Pa'tra:* a big clay pot for sauces and stews.

Saeen himself! But they were good enough for Fakeer and his fellows, in any case.

After eating, they would pull their daily experiences out of their memory sacks. Sometimes, they would share virgin stories about those same old dreaded exploited themes of love, hate, and betrayal, and somehow those stories always felt new.

One of the beggars in Fakeer's brethren was *Sanwal'o*[16] *Fakeer,* a quiet old man who didn't say much. While the other beggars shared their tales of the day and chewed opium as if it were bits of dark chocolate, he would simply sit in the back and listen to them. If someone asked him to tell his story, he would laugh, a short shallow laughter. As the evening darkened, and others slowly became numb and passed out, he would keep sitting in that corner until all the others fell asleep. Then he would count his offerings.

Sanwal'o Fakeer was the only one in Fakeer's group who had actually walked to *Lahoot La-Makan.* This was not an ordinary destination, but rather the mythic place where the bodily world ends and the conceptual world began, a place where you are almost there, yet nowhere near, even though Mehboob Saeen is just a breath away! But then you become short of that very same breath! The mystics believed that this was the first place to come into being in the entire universe.

Once, Fakeer asked him, "Sanwal'o, what you have seen at Lahoot La-Makan?"

Sanwal'o looked into Fakeer's eyes for longer than usual, and then said, "*Kujha bi na. Ka shaia na!*"—*There was nothing there! Nothing at all.*

Then Fakeer asked, "Why do you count and save coins? To whom are you going to give this?"

"I will buy a piece of land and have a family one day," he answered. Then Sanwal'o secured his small sacks of coins, stretched out his body from sitting to reclining, and fell asleep. But Fakeer stayed awake, thinking. Could a storyteller, a beggar, actually buy a piece of land? Could someone who did nothing but roam suddenly stop, and become settled, and have a wife? There was an uneasiness and anxiety in the banality of this new thought, but Fakeer still wanted to ponder

---

[16] *Sanwal'o*. Literally this word translates to 'monsoon', but it carries many resonant connotations. This one word contains the entire idea of a maddening, all-consuming summer of love.

it. So he didn't throw it away; rather he kept it in some corner of his mind, so that he could become familiar with it later.

The next morning when Fakeer woke up, most of his fellow Fakeers were gone. A few of them were still there, coughing and twisting on the rags where they lay. After a while everybody went on their way, and Fakeer was left alone with Sanwal'o, who was still sleeping. Actually, Fakeer realised, Sanwal'o was motionless, lying on ground, face up. Fakeer approached where Sanwal'o was lying, clenching his small sack of coins in both hands, holding them against his chest and still not moving. Looking at his washed out face, Fakeer felt sure that Sanwal'o had finally left. He had gone to make his last pilgrimage to Lahoot La-Makan, once and for all.

Sanwal'o Fakeer's eyes were still closed when he spoke: "I'm still here."

Later that day Sanwal'o left and then never came back.

Soon, Fakeer was again roaming the streets of Qamber. At his side was a newly bought sack for collecting coins. He found himself keeping track of things, like shadows to tell him time of the day, and of seasons to remind him of things past and his years advancing. He counted his coins into set of tens, where ten set of tens could be a hundred. For his storytelling, he tended towards those places that had produced generous offerings before.

On one day Fakeer was passing by Suantak-Sir, that place where Kalb Ali Fakeer and Lal Fakeer used to please their crowds with a tale about the hair-thin bridge on a chasm of fire that one has to walk to meet Mehboob Saeen. Someone called out to Fakeer and asked for a story, brandishing an offering even before Fakeer could begin. He accepted the offering and thus broke his vow not to tell stories in the places where his mentors had entertained their crowds. Fakeer began:

In the land of moving hills of sand, a long time ago, there was a needy man. But his need was not material; his need was for a child of his own. So whenever he saw the Adored One who went to the mountaintop to speak to the Divine Lord (indeed, he was called 'the One with whom God spoke'), Needy Man crumbled and melted in selfless humbleness, always imploring Adored One to talk to God and ask God to give him a child of his own. And Adored One always replied, "I will."

Months and years passed, and the poor Needy Man eventually stopped asking Adored One, and life kept moving on like it always does. But then something amazing happened. Adored One was walking towards mountain. It was evening and the sun was about to set, and effervescent bubbles of joy were popping in his heart because he was going to meet his Divine Lord. All of the sudden, he saw Needy Man carrying a giggling infant coming his way.

In sheer veneration, Adored One asked Needy Man, "Whose child is this that you are holding?" And he was locked into the certainty that Needy Man would reply that the child was not his.

But Needy Man replied, "The child is mine."

Adored One said, "It can't be—the Divine Lord Himself told me that you had a childless destiny. It was written in your fate."

Needy Man, holding his child, said, "I asked *Baalow Mast*[17] if he could pray for me, and he did." Then Needy Man turned his face away and went on his way.

What had been a tingling fizz of joy turned into the boiling of his blood, and Adored One climbed faster, thinking, *how come Baalow Mast, that naked man who's always rummaging in the trash hoping to find something of value, and who eats the stale and mouldy food that he finds there, who smells like a dead animal—how could he do that?* Stewing in these thoughts, he reached the mountaintop and said to Divine Lord, "Needy Man had a child. I was asking you for years and you kept saying it wasn't destined for him."

There was an utter quietness. Adored One then said many things that he shouldn't have, and lastly he said, "My people and I bow only to you, love you, and believe in your oneness. I need a reasonable answer for me and for my people."

A mysterious nocturnal voice, a telephonic voice, appeared from all four cardinal directions simultaneously, filling everything with its presence, and said, "Go and ask your people to get me a piece of human flesh and I will answer your question."

The mysterious voice disappeared and everything turned dark. Adored One was shaken and profusely warm, like a towel right out of a hot dryer.

Adored One went down to his people with the same speed with which he had climbed up, thinking that any one of his people would be more than glad to give just a small piece of their flesh in the name of Divine Lord. But he roamed there for days, asking everyone he came across, and everyone replied, "We are your followers, we believe in your God, and we bow to him, but to cut a piece of flesh

---

[17] *Baalow Mast*: the name hints that the man is autistic, but also is more literally what the name translates to, which is 'intoxicated with God'.

to show our affection is illogical—only a lunatic would do that. No God wants to hurt its followers."

Sad and dejected, Adored One returned to his home, wondering, *what face am I going to take back to mountain top? How am I going to explain to God that everyone I spoke to believes in His oneness, but no one wants to give piece of their flesh.* Walking in his thoughts, he came upon that part of town where people throw trash, and sure enough Baalow Mast was there, digging around and trying to find something. Baalow Mast was a concomitant, his soul always drowning in his own love for Mehboob Saeen; externally he looked lost and disoriented in a heaping pile of filthy trash, but at the same time he was 'intoxicated with God himself'. He had trashed his existence for that divine fragrance that he called Mehboob Saeen.

Baalow Mast looked up and asked Adored One, "Why you look so worried?"

Adored One told his whole story to Baalow Mast, who was already intoxicated with God. And Baalow Mast responded, "That's it—Mehboob Saeen just asked for a piece?"

And he asked for the knife the Adored One had been carrying all day long and cut a chunk of his thigh and gave it to Adored One. And as he was about to leave and run to the mountaintop, Baalow Mast called out to ask which part of body's flesh had Mehboob Saeen asked for. Adored One replied in confusion, "The Divine Lord never said which part."

Baalow Mast asked him to come back. He cut a piece from every single part of his body and gave it all to him. Adored One climbed back up to the mountaintop holding different pieces of Baalow Mast's chunky flesh.

That nocturnal-telephonic voice appeared again, and said, "You are holding the answer of your question in your own hands. Don't ask ever again why Needy Man got a child. You are my servant and you call me Divine Lord. Baalow Mast calls me Mehboob Saeen; he calls me his beloved. You asked for a reasonable answer earlier, and here it is. You and your people are caught between reason and logic. You could have given a small piece of your own flesh."

When Fakeer finished his story, one young man in the audience, who had probably not heard such a love-madness story before, shouted *"Ba'-lay!"*[18] In astonishment. There was a floating glaze in his eyes, like something had touched him, like he was almost able to understand part of that riddle. That young man

---

[18] *Ba'lay!* "Wow!" An expression of astonishment and admiration.

stood and walked away, looking at the ground, shaking his head slowly and repeatedly saying, *"ba'-lay, ba'-lay,"* again and again. He hadn't left any material offering for Fakeer, but it felt like the young man had thrown his heart into Fakeer's kashkul. And right then Fakeer could sense some inner disruption, the way a worn and dry wooden mine truss can suddenly fracture. It felt to Fakeer that his own passion, his soul had left him and walked after that young man into oblivion.

Other people did throw coins in the kashkul, which he took out of there and placed in his small drawstring pouch. As he walked back, those coins where jingling so merrily in the pouch that Fakeer stopped and pulled the strings to open the pouch's mouth so that he could look at them. He unloaded the pouch into one of his palms and closed his hand back and fell the crunch of the somewhat faded rubbing coins. He opened his palm and counted them: they were two annas short of a rupee. He decided that tomorrow he would save two annas and make it a rupee. Thus started his lust for money.

Chapter 3
Distress Calls of a Lonely Titihar

It took him twenty-two days to reach Karachi. He walked across fifty-seven railroad bridges, some small and some long, and several villages and a few towns. He would walk all day long and rest after sunset, usually spending his nights close to some dwelling or in a place of worship, either a mosque or a temple, whichever came first, or at a shrine of any small village, or even on the platforms of railway stations.

One morning, about a week into his journey, he found himself thinking about an old woman he had met the night before, an old woman with two little children whom he met the previous evening at the platform of Dadu Station. He had arrived there before sunset and settled under the porch next to waiting room. He took his *trapri*[19] out of his *gundri*[20] and laid it on the dust floor. He began to take off his turban, which he unwound slowly; bending his head and neck as each twist came off, gathering the spiralling folds in his lap. When it was off completely, he shaped it into a coil and placed it on the floor under his head for a pillow.

The sun was all but gone and the birds were making their return commute in the gigantic pipal trees. The sky turned amber first for a short while and then fog took over with darkness, and he saw her. That old woman with two children appeared out of the darkness. She was carrying a small bamboo ladder on her shoulder. The young boy was carrying a canister of oil, and the little girl following them empty handed.

---

[19] *Trapri*: a small quilt.
[20] *Gundri*: a hand-made sack like those you would see on a hobo stick—a square piece of cloth whose four corners are tied into a bundle.

He asked the woman, *"Ammari khush aan?"*[21]

The woman, who looked old beyond her years, replied, *"ha ada, toon khush aahiyan."*[22]

He asked her out of curiosity, "Why you are carrying that ladder?"

And she replied, "I light street lamps every evening."

"—I guess you are alone?" He asked before she had even finished her sentence.

"I'm a widow and these are my grandchildren, my daughter's kids. She and their father have also passed away. Now the children live with me." And after a quick pause, she spoke again: "The union council gave me this work."

"So they are orphans," he said.

"Why do you say they are orphans? I'm still alive," she replied with distaste. She turned away and went on with her work.

He kept looking at her and her grandchildren as they placed the ladder against each pole and then took out the glass chimney, spitting in it first and then wiping it clean, and then put it back. They lit the wicks of each oil lamp one after another, each lamp adding a tiny spot of brightness. He watched them slowly drift back into the darkness of night.

The next morning he continued the same long walk along the tracks. Dawn had just broken amidst a thick, low-hanging fog. In the distance, he could see a golden dome with four minarets sticking out above the fog. Birds as usual were trying to explain the mystic riddle in their predawn chirping hymns, but he kept walking next toward the railway tracks.

Now he could see that golden dome fading at the top, with four thin minarets, and a tall crimson *alam pak* of Ghazi Abbas[23] which was tilting a little to one side, supported by long ropes, equally spaced and tied to neem[24] branches.

The day grew a little more, the fog had all but gone, and he was walking into a huge jagged rock, split open by nature, creating a natural passage for railroad

---

[21] *Ammari khush aan?* "How are you, my mother?" The question is formed more literally as, "Are you well, my mother?" In Sindhi, all women, including strangers, are addressed as *Amma* (mother) or *Ammari* (my mother) as a form of respect.

[22] *Ha ada, toon khush aahiyan:* "Yes, brother, are you well?"

[23] *Alam pak of Ghazi Abbas:* An oriflamme—a long banner with pointed ends—representing the one carried by the martyr Ghazi Abbas, who did not let the banner fall even in his death. He and the banner are symbols of loyalty and valor.

[24] *Neem*: the neem tree is *Azadirachta indica*, also known as 'Indian Lilac'.

tracks to pass through. He walked into that snake-curve alley, a cool breeze blowing into his face, and he looked at the high cliff walls of *Kirthar Jaba*.[25]

The sound of his footfalls disturbing the gravel echoed louder with each step within that ravine as he continued toward Laki Shah Sadar.[26] Soon, he emerged, with the long valley on his left, and at the end of valley he saw an immense sheet of glittering silver, unbelievably smooth, and he realised, that's the great *Sindhu*—the Indus River. He wanted to see him up close, so he approached his right bank, and soon he was standing right next to his *lackoo*,[27] where pure clay and layers of sand make it treacherous. He treaded carefully alongside its, edged bank until that edge washed into a smooth shoreline. "*This is enormous*," he said to himself.

The river was vast, but calm. Its surface was oozing in swells, and he felt a humming noise from the giant's depths. He sat there on the bank in the reflection of sunlight, and the breaking waves around him induced a calming trance, and the wind had a muddy humid smell. He could feel the gentle touch of the wind on his eyebrows, and he spoke to river, saying:

"*Darya shah badshah jo khair.*"[28]

And Sindhu replied nothing.

Or maybe he did! By pushing a gentle wave towards him in reply. At least, that's what he thought. He knelt down into the thick dark grey wet sand, and made a bowl by joining his palms, and filled it with that ever-nourishing water. And he drank. Some of it was dripping back into the river from his elbows. He kept looking at it and could feel that brisk yet profound roar of the great body of tranquil water flowing. He wanted to hear, he wanted to tell, he wanted to know the story of this river. From this river! He felt that he was almost there, one more step and he could enter and cross that chasm. That dimension where he could hear this river and the river would listen to him.

But then reality cut into everything, and the entire trance fell apart. Fakeer settled with a deep, long sigh. It was late afternoon, so he decided to stay by the

---

[25] *Kirthar Jaba*: Kirthar Mountain.
[26] *Laki Shah Sadar:* this town's name derives from the word *lackoo* (see next note).
[27] *Lackoo:* the pure, highly slippery, layered clay on the banks of the Indus.
[28] *Darya ... khair:* "Peace to you my King River, my river of rivers." In Sindhi, rivers are address as male.

riverbank that night. Evening turned into night. He lay very close to the riverbank on his short travel bed. He joined his hands together at the fingers and placed them behind his neck. The winds were tricking him, making new sounds with the river surface, and those utterly gentle sounds of breaking waves at the riverbank reminded him of an infant tasting something sweet again and again.

The next morning he strode into the unknown. He returned to find the railroad tracks where he left them to see the river yesterday, but today, he was heading south, and on his right there was an endless sequential series of mountains, which were blocks of rocks trampled over each other, making piles of brittle limestone sheets crumbling down. And on his left was Sindhu. He couldn't see him all the time because of the levee, but from a higher elevation the sparkling glare of the sun dancing on his surface was unavoidable.

The town of Kotri was still far ahead, and he saw a row of elephants crossing river, but then he said to himself, *this can't be elephants—that's too big to be even a row of elephants*. As he slowly approached, this thing began to look like cages joined together, and then he figured out that it was a huge bridge. Finally, he reached at Kotri, where the railroad tracks forked. One track went over the river to the other bank through an immense grey bridge, stretching six spans long, which from a distance he had mistaken for elephants in a row. He kept walking and this bridge kept getting bigger and bigger until finally he reached it.

The gigantic structure had a single railroad track in the centre flanked with paved roads left and right. There were loops of approach roads on either side just going up to its starting end. He walked up following one of those roads in a hairpin turn.

He reached the top, which was several yards high and level with the top of the levee. Some bull carts followed by pedestrians were already ahead of him, and he followed them with this amazing feeling that was causing him to smile on his own, and he could feel an unexplainable tingling radiation in his heart. He had never before seen such a structure, made up of diagonal iron beams, high up and joined together with thousands of fist-sized rivets.

When he was almost in the middle of that bridge, he could see the horizon, as far as any eye could see. He was standing at top of this giant river, looking at its fast-moving surface with its swells like boiling water, which he had never thought he could see even in his wildest dreams, and he said to himself: "So recently I saw Sindhu for the very first time, and I'm glad that I rightfully called him *'Darya shah badshah'*."

That same happiness was still flowing over and spilling from his eyes. He could see both its banks, where big trees were looking like small green peas, and there were several boats with their open topgallant sails swelling with the air, and that fullness of sails revealed odd-coloured patches on them. He had never seen a panoramic view from such a height before. He held the rail firmly and looked at the serene tranquillity of nature.

All of the sudden, he felt slight tremors in both hands—there were vibrations in the rail pipe under his palms, which soon became violent, and the wind started blowing. He knew it was the train, and he didn't like trains at all. Everything started shaking, and initially there was a distant sound of *woofs-woofs-chou, gurgle; woofs-woofs-chou, gurgle-goo,* accompanied by bells, which very soon turned into the piercing cry of screeching metal, and he saw that beast of a locomotive making violent motions, and a long iron rod spinning like crazy but somehow keeping all the throttling wheels together, blowing thick smoke through its chimney. And it passed, and every single small pebble and rock on the road shook, and there was a flashing noise of several passing bogies.

After few moments, all that shaking stopped and things went back to normal, other than the lingering smell of that thick smoke. And he started walking back with haste, not paying any more attention to the serene panoramic view, and that unexplainable smile from before had turned a frown of displeasure.

He was off the bridge and now walking towards Kotri railway station, but still could taste that bitter smoke in his mouth. There was a shrine near the station, under the shadow of a huge pipal tree which was several times larger than the shrine. He went and squatted down under that tree in a *kanbh'a*[29] position. He wrapped his *bochan*[30] around his back, twist-tied it in front of his knees, and swayed his chest to and fro in a gentle, rocking motion.

At this point, it had been several days since he left home. All along he had been striding, walking and sometimes even dragging himself along the railroad tracks. He had left Kotri yesterday and had slept that night next to the tracks at a place that was just like so many others on this monotonous path, with a flat view of a row of telegraph poles and wild shrubs distantly spread. There were two

---

[29] Kanbh'a: a seated position in which a person wraps a long piece of cloth around his back, knots it at his knees, and thus creates a swing-like seat, in which he can rock peacefully.

[30] *Bochan*: an oblong piece of cloth carried by men on their shoulders, used for multiple purposes.

railroad tracks that looked annoyed with each other, maintaining a gap between them like a difference of opinion, running parallel for immense distances and stopping together at several destinations, yet never meeting one another.

On this day, he was heading towards the town of Jhampir. He came across a small valley covered with oval-leaf milkweed shrubs, with lobes of greenish white and pale purplish buds waiting to bust open and bloom. And he saw thousands and thousands of monarch butterflies, a whole sea of them. He didn't think much of them; he'd seen them all his life, with their yellow-orange and black wings like stained glass along with white oval dots on the edges.

But some of these were big, almost the size of an open palm. He lay down, trying to flex his feet, but his toe joints were cracking on their own. Slowly dusk turned into night, and what a night it was, with inescapable cool moonlight spreading everywhere, over everything, every single cobblestone was granted a shadow that night by the immense cool moon, who himself had a halo as big as if he had stretched both his arms out to mark the halo's boundaries. And he was listening to the invisible, snivelling calls of the lonely *titihar*[31] who had lost his way home and even the moon couldn't help him.

They say the titihar has been making these lonely calls from beginning of time because he can't find his way back, and around this people have woven stories that grew into legends: that the titihar procrastinates and keeps gathering food for his chicks, thinking that there is be enough time and sunlight left for him to find his way back home, but then it turns dark every day and he can't find his way back. What a romantic tragedy—even the moon with all his immense brightness can't help him find his way.

He was grooming his moustache by holding its tip with his pointer finger and thumb like a pen, and pulling them together and spinning back and then rolling the base of his palm over it. He was staring into the skies and listening to the sobbing calls of the titihar until his eyelids became so heavy that he couldn't hold them back. He drifted into sleep, and just before losing consciousness he felt a cheerful smile, which assured him of his purpose.

Fakeer was thinking about this beautiful morning, flambéing with light. The morning seemed to have a face, which was glowing like the face of God himself!—the face in which divine light lives. The hidden part of that morning

---

[31] *Titihar*: Red Wattled Lapwing.

felt like a reward, like the mystic love of Mehboob Saeen bouncing in within the hearts of his selfless devotees. What a day it was.

He was walking between the railroad tracks and Keenjhar, a big lake with even bigger stories. Fakeer's mind was mostly fixed on what was to come, and that uneasiness of explaining things. But still, the turquoise waters of Keenjhar were unavoidable. He sat on the pedestal of one of the limestone columns of a railroad bridge. The cool breeze whispered something in his ears. He enjoyed those whispers but had no desire to understand them, because he knew explanation is digging, and digging makes things dirty.

But then he digs himself into his gundri to find a piece of homemade cookie that his wife had baked for him. There were only a few broken pieces and crumbs left of it. He gathered those crumbs in his palm first and left the bigger pieces in sack. Their taste was a mix of cookies and dirt and the smell of his own perspiration.

It was a winter mid-day, of nineteen hundred and something; he didn't keep track of calendars. He just knew what he had been told by the person who had brought him the court summons: "Fakeer'a,[32] you have to be physically present in court on January 14, which is 41 days from today, in front of the honourable judge." So it took him 10 days to prepare, 28 days for this long walk, and now he had been in the city for 3 days, so all together there were 41, which makes that day January 14, and January 14 it was, of year nineteen hundred and something, Fakeer didn't care what year.

He was waiting in the veranda in the building of high court of Sindh, Karachi. He had never before seen such a marvellous building, which he entered by climbing two flights of twenty or twenty-two steps, heading to the platform in front of that majéstic row of tall straight slender red stone Roman columns, with their scroll-like flourishes at the top and huge looping bands of stone at the bottom. He managed to hide his continuing astonishment as he heard his name called out loud by a bailiff who was wearing a blood red robe that went down to the knees, and a slim brown belt around his waist, and a huge red turban.

When he heard his name, he stood up, grabbed his gundri and his walking stick, and stepped into the courtroom. It was huge, with walls of limestone and a very high cathedral ceiling. He took few more steps and there was an

---

[32] *Fakeer'a*: The Sindhi language treats most of its nouns with a complex system of final vowels, which are altered given their function in the sentence. In direct address, male names are appended with an 'a' sound.

unexplainable damp smell of ageing paper combined with rotten dust, pigeon droppings, and old furniture, smells which were unfamiliar to him apart from the pigeon droppings. A soft gust of this air hit his face periodically with the strokes of the *jhalla*.[33]

He was brought in front of the honourable Judge, and the bailiff spelled out charges. "My Lord, Sheer Muhammad Fakeer attempted to kill a monk of Qamber Shewalo[34] by throwing—I'm sorry, correction: by *dropping* a hard baked brick on his head from his roof top."

"How do you plead, Fakeer?" the Judge asked.

The bailiff translated into Sindhi, and Fakeer replied, "Tell My Lord that I kept asking those Shewalo people not to urinate on my wall because my *niyariyoon*[35] often pass by there, but they never listened."

The Judge interrupted, "But Fakeer, you are not supposed to break people's skulls open by dropping bricks on their heads. This is a serious offence. You are accused of attempted murder."

The Judge began to write out his ruling, and the bailiff tried to translate it and explain it to Fakeer.

"So My Lord thinks it's my fault, and Shewalo people are innocent?" asked Sheer Muhammad Fakeer.

"Yes," replied the bailiff.

Fakeer rose onto the tips of his toes in sheer anger and the muscles of his forearms protruded fiercely at his cuffs.

But then he relaxed his feet and stood with both heels touching ground. He spread open his dhoti, tilted his groin a little forward, and proceeded to urinate in the courtroom. A pin-drop silence fell over the room, and time seemed eternal before the Judge, who was still writing, lifted his head in response to the splashy ringing sound of urine hitting the ground.

In pure disbelief, the Judge tried to beat his gavel onto the sounding block, but the gavel was hitting the desk directly. He yelled at top of his lungs, "Order! Order! Stop this man, Bailiff, stop him!"

---

[33] *Jhalla*: a manual ceiling fan consisting of a long hanging cloth attached to a wooden frame, operated by a complex crisscrossing pattern of rope pulleys which pass through a wall out to the veranda, where a fan operator would pull the ropes with both hands as if he were ringing a church bell. It is a grueling and undesirable job.

[34] Qamber Shewalo: a Hindu monastery.

[35] *Niyariyoon*: unmarried young daughters or granddaughters.

The bailiff scrambled towards Fakeer, mumbling in Sindhi, *"Fakeera cha payo kareen, courat saghori jee beizati."*

Fakeer replied reluctantly, his voice calm, *"Courat saghori aa, jetha rogo murda betha aahyoo ain muhnjay gharjee betha, jetahn muhnjiyoon nindryun potiyoon, niyariyoon guzran thyu sa saghori nahay, puch sahib kha cho."*

"Bailiff, again, what is he saying?"

The bailiff replied in a thin and faltering voice, "I told him, Your Honour, that he is purging himself and therefore is to be held in contempt for dishonouring this respected court. And he replied"—here the bailiff took a deep breath before continuing. "He then said, Your Honour, is this court honourable? Here, where we are all males present? Meanwhile the outside wall of his house, where his innocent granddaughters pass by, isn't honourable? And he asked why that is."

The bailiff stopped there, ushering an airy silence into the courtroom. Only the squeaky pulleys of the jhalla kept up their noise. After a pause, the Judge said, "Sheer Muhammad Abro Fakeer, this court finds you guilty as charged and sentences you to two years' imprisonment and an additional two months and fifteen days for contempt of court."

Fakeer stood there looking undisturbed, hovering in some neutral space between agreeing and disagreeing with the ruling.

They handcuffed him and placed him on a bench in a corner of the veranda, where he was to wait to be sent to jail. He was thinking merely that these two years will pass, like so many years before them.

He had wondered aloud to his wife and his children, "Could I be sent to the gallows?" Because Moolchand Waqeel, a local claims solicitor in Qamber, told Fakeer that his summons was for an attempted murder charge, and that Fakeer should avail himself of Moolchand's legal help. Of course Moolchand wanted Fakeer to hire him, rather than finding some other real attorney, since Moolchand was a pretender and had worked for years as an orderly.

At the barrister's office in Shikarpur and had not actually read law; rather he had just heard it, or really, overheard it—listening to what barristers would say to their clients and fellow lawyers. The irony was that the entire town of Qamber knew that Moolchand Waqeel wasn't a real lawyer, but still they called upon him as if he were. And so did Fakeer himself.

A few steps away from where Fakeer was waiting in that veranda, there were two middle-aged men engaged in a discussion. The first was tall, with a slim face and very prominent cheekbones, and a white turban on his head; the second appeared to be a lawyer like any other. The lawyer said, "The British parliament has passed the legislation; Sindh is now completely separate from Bombay residency."

The lawyer was looking up eagerly for a comment, but the tall man kept thinking. The lawyer couldn't wait longer, and asked the tall man, "Mr Shahani, what do you think?"

And Rishi Dhayaram Shahani replied with smiling eyes, "You have remembered all those section and clauses!" And after a pause, he said, "Yes it's good for Sindh, but it doesn't seem to me that it's going to benefit the common man of Sindh. On the one hand, since this legislation passed, all the opportunistic *waderas*, *pirs*,[36] and feudal lords are trying to secure their territories by determining and holding their constituencies."

By now, the smile on his face had turned grim. After a short pause, he said, "But then, I think, there are all these different political parties—federalist, nationalist, some solely provincial, but still they are there…" And the conversation faded as the two men went on their way.

But Fakeer had not been paying any attention to their conversation as he sat picking his nose with his index finger. For hours, he waited for the court official to transfer him to jail. Day turned into late afternoon, the shadows of the stationary roman columns moved on the ground from one side to the other. Still he kept sitting on that bench with both feet up on the seat board until finally that same bailiff came back and said, "Follow me."

Fakeer grabbed his rough leather shoes that he had placed on the bench next to him and banged them together like he was dusting them—they were already dirty and worn-out, but he did that out of habit—and then he dropped them on the floor and guided his feet into them hastily. He hugged onto his gundri with his one arm and grabbed his stick with the other. He followed the bailiff down those majestic winding hallways of the court building until they ended up outside two heavy-looking, beautifully carved, closed wooden doors.

"Wait here," said the bailiff, who then went inside, and shortly thereafter asked Fakeer to come in as well. Fakeer paused to get a close look at the glittering brass doorknob, and then entered. It was a huge room and cooler than outside. The bailiff signalled for him to stand there quietly. There was a grand table with a blanket-like dark green cover on it. Fakeer had never seen such a big table

---

[36] *Waderas, pirs*: landlords and holy men, respectively.

before. One of the walls of that room was made up of identical thick books in a dark red colour with golden words written on them, all looking the same. He could only relate the colour of those books to dried blood. And Fakeer said to himself, *these books look like they're all the same, but they must have different things written in them.* Just looking at those bookshelves was making him anxious—how had he missed so much? How could people read all that, and what has been said in them? But then he didn't want to pay any more attention to those damn books.

That same Judge was writing something, but now he was not wearing fake curly hair on his head. The Judge lifted his head and said something in English, which was Greek to Fakeer, so he kept staring at him until he finished. The bailiff translated, "Mr Sher Mohammad Abro Fakeer, he says that he hereby commutes your sentence and pardons you from any and all charges against you in case file number… You are free to go." Then he added, "That was an official commute of your sentence that the honourable judge has written on your file, but His Honour wants to tell you that when he sentenced you earlier this morning he was angry at your behaviour. Which he still is, but he thinks that the way you acted in courtroom was the only way you had to make your arguments, and your point was considered by His Honour's honourable court. But don't ever try to take law in your hands and harm others to justify your legal point of view."

Instinctively Fakeer joined his hands together and raised them to his forehead in order to thank the Judge. "*Lakh thora sahib'a,*"[37] he murmured.

The Judge didn't even look at Fakeer, and Fakeer didn't expect him to, either. As he walked out of there, Fakeer remembered one more thing that Moolchand had said: "Have no fear—the British Judge will do what is just!"

"And so he did," Fakeer said to himself, and he strolled out of there and went on his way. Little that he knew there are going to be more complaints, trials and litigations, lawsuits and court proceedings against him in future and he will not be this lucky to walk away. After literally peeing in a full courtroom!

---

[37] *Lakh thora sahib'a:* "Many thanks, sir."

Chapter 4
Unwanted Tour of the City

That was it—he was free. Now he could go see more of this incredible city. Actually, it felt to him more like a duty. He chose to stay there a few more days, knowing he might never come back here again. He would spend the nights at the *serai*.[38]

Karachi was a metropolis, with huge stone buildings, some of which were even two or three stories tall, the likes of which he had never seen before. It was full of buildings of all different sorts, apartment blocks, offices, markets, town halls, and several of them had clock towers.

There were asphalt-paved roads flanked with concrete sidewalks on either side. But Fakeer was more comfortable walking on the road than on the sidewalk. The roads were full of something he didn't like: tram cars. To him, these were smaller trains wreaking havoc in the middle of streets.

There was one huge building, which initially he thought must be another court, but when he asked someone he was told that it was a market, a kind of bazaar. He circled around that building, which covered a couple of city blocks, with extended paved sidewalks on all four sides. Just within those sidewalks were the short walls of a compound, about chest high, made up of chiselled blocks of limestone, and then there were gardens all around with palm and *chikoo*[39] and mango trees. Just beyond the garden there were long and wide corridors with fourteen stone carved arches each, and each corridor ended in a square tower with three more arches, of which the middle arch was bigger than other two. But the entrance was from south corridor, where there was a huge

---

[38] *Serai*. A cheap travelers' lodge with beds in the open air and rows of clay pots filled with drinking water.
[39] *Chikoo*: sapodilla, a fruit-bearing tree.

three-story central tower with a wider central vault entrance big enough that five grown adults could cross at the same time without hitting each other's shoulders.

On the second story of that tower there were three smaller arches, but the central arch was still bigger than the other two, and on top of it on third story there was a clock tower. He entered into the main vaulted archway, which led him to the great open court of the bazaar. Here he saw rows of shops all of same size, all with the same folding wooden doors. For a while, he wandered these hallways, underneath a ceiling of angled timber beams holding baked red clay bricks, and then he circled back out the south corridor towards the colonial buildings in the streets of Karachi.

The air was thick and salty, brushing his face and plugging his desire in his heat to go see the ocean. He was not comfortable asking people where to find the sea, because the people here were different looking and taking circuitous paths to avoid him on the sidewalks. Probably, they didn't want to bump into him. He found a dark-skinned man wearing clothes pretty much like his, who was sweeping the sidewalk with a large broom.

Fakeer said, *"Bhaoo khush aan?"*[40]

The man with the broom gave Fakeer a disdainful and cosmopolitan look, and responded, "What?" Simply by raising, rather twitching his eyebrows.

"Brother, do you know where the ocean is?"

"Go straight," said the man with the broom. "There is a red stone bridge. Go past that, and after few miles you'll be there."

Fakeer thanked him and followed the instructions. He reached a handsome stone gazebo on a pedestal, with a dome perched up on five pillars. From there, the view of the ocean seemed like a work of fiction, yet somehow it was real.

Fakeer thought of that cast stone gazebo as *hawai thaloo*, a 'windy porch', not knowing that he was standing at the Lady Lloyd Pier. The thick air blew persistently in his face, and he could smell the salty dampness of the ocean, but he couldn't identify that alien fragrance. He continued along the pathway, a long staircase made up of cobblestones, which brought him to the beach and as he left that path way and stepped into sand, he saw wet sandy shoreline, divided from the horizon in the distance by an utterly light blue line, so it was almost impossible to grasp where that limitless sea ended and the unending sky started. Harmless Clorox-white clouds bulged in patches on those skies. Fakeer could

---

[40] *Bhaoo khush aan:* "How you doing, brother?"

see their reflecting silhouettes on that wet sand. He liked that, but was hesitant to say that it was amazing.

There was an overwhelming sound of waves breaking with a crash, one on the top of another. He looked into the distant horizon. He was reminded of the legend of that quiet man who, if he wanted to, could grab and carry the entire ocean on his bare back.

It did not occur to him that there might be another world beyond those waters. But it sure did look pretty to him. The wind was constantly blowing in his face, and he looked back at the 'hawai thaloo', which seemed very small from here. He walked close to the edge of the waves in that soft, grey sand and was looking down at his footprints, but every few moments a new wave would erode and wipe out his footprints completely. Seagulls hovered around, doing nothing other than just being bothered by every new wave, which would cause them to fly a few feet up and then come back down again.

And so many different shells lay scattered. He grabbed one that was smooth and the size of his palm, curling inward, with milk chocolate brown pigments on it. The other side of the shell reminded him of the folds of the hard palate. He held it to his ear just to experience that legend that an ocean is hidden in every shell. Sure enough, he did hear a roaring ocean in that shell. A delicate smile spread on his face. He gathered few more shells there before turning to leave.

It took him even longer to walk back to Qamber, and the experience was completely different. Now he was free of that anxiety, that burden of being accused and put on trial.

He strode along the railroad ties with a uniform pace so that he won't miss his step. Slowly the city disappeared, and Fakeer reappeared in his own domain, in that open space where time is shelved like a reference book—an important book, but used only occasionally. Most of the wooden ties beneath his feet were worn, cracked, and stained with everything including dried faeces.

Chapter 5
Morr Tho Tilay Rana
(Peacock Is Displaying, My Love!)

It didn't matter whether that day was beautiful or not. He was almost narcissistically happy. He was about to get married, but then again it was a marriage of necessity. He was alone, without any close or distant relatives other than his elder brother, and no one had wanted to give him their daughter. So he had purchased a weaver's daughter from Bhattiyain-jo-Shehar, a small village fourteen miles north of Qamber.

Social class didn't matter to him because he was an orphan and orphans were children without legal legitimacy. There were no orphanages in Qamber then, and, even now, there aren't any! Such children had and have no chance in society. Those unfortunate children usually roam around, sleep on the streets, and end up as sex slaves or slaves of society period.

But Fakeer had broken that spell of deprivation by turning to the mystics, because they were in search of nothingness itself. They wanted to reach a transcendence state where pleasure and pain became the same, and where it would be acceptable for distance and destination to switch places with each other. Their objective was to step out of their real being and look at themselves from outside. But then, Sanwal's seed of an idea also stuck in his mind. He had taught him how to love Sufi teachings and keep singing hymns and keep telling those mind-boggling stories and become a worldly person too! "Who is stopping you from doing both?"

So Fakeer did that, and became an entrepreneur who sold mystic tales. He considered wealth to be of highest importance as an entrepreneur and paid no attention to class or religion as a mystic Sufi. And he became a regular, multifaceted human being.

His expression was unwary as he looked out to horizon over the domed tops of the baburs[41] at the horizon. His rough, raw leather shoes made a crackling noise against the path, a combination of dry parched grass and salt-drenched earth, as if he were stepping on crushed light bulbs. The peelu shrubs gave off a smell like rancid oil, with just a hint of hidden, elusive freshness. There were sounds of singing and crying birds coming from the mysterious long branches of the big aa-sirheen tree, and those echoes were skating along the calm muddy surfaces of springs and watercourses.

His one foot slipped when he jumped to avoid the *drewseerh'a*,[42] but he regained balance, accidentally crushing several wild daisies on the edge of the path under his shoes. He took a quick peek at spoiled petals of the smothered daisies before moving on, all the while entertaining those teething desires of infantile grooms in his heart.

She was supposed to be fifteen or sixteen years old, but it turned out she was a child of only nine. Her name was Sharma Khatoon, which translates to "shy lady." Her uncle had lied about her age to Fakeer and had given her for 123 rupees, as was the social norm. In Sindh, the bridegroom traditionally bears the entire financial burden of the wedding, and pays a considerable chunk to bride's parents as well. At this time, it was not uncommon for a girl as young as nine to be given up for marriage, either.

Fakeer arrived at the home of his bride. It was getting dark, and unexpected grey clouds with pregnant bellies gathered from who knows where to ruin his wedding. The bride's uncle, who had brokered the deal, greeted Fakeer with the traditional long, squeezing hug, which was associated with a long standard greeting narrative, which flowed almost like a poem:

Are you happy and well-off?
Strengthened and
Healthy; in your
Will and vigour
Stronger than strong?

---

[41] *Babur:* the *acacia arabica* tree.
[42] *Drewseerh'a*: a fine, powdery, talc-like mud.

I guess,
Your kids and parents,
Your cows and cattle,
Your land and fields,
Your trees and shrubs,
Your joys and pains,
Are all well too.

"All together, all are well," Fakeer replied, hardly even listening to him, even though in reality, other than a little joy and pain, he had none of the above to account for. Then Fakeer reiterated the same monologue, which all Sindhis know by default from the time even before they can speak.

Then the girl's uncle asked Fakeer to make himself comfortable and sit on any one of several well decorated *Khata'oon*,[43] which were covered with untouched, virgin quilts of shocking colours, the kind of *ralli*[44] that takes several women working for months to stitch the patchwork for a single one of them. Those women didn't just stitch tiny bits of otherwise scrap fabric together; rather they sewed mandalas, dreams, as if stitching together the universe of a dreamer in search of completeness.

Fakeer sat on one khaata and dropped his raw leather shoes on the ground. He kept flexing his toes, moving them as if to ask them to forget the exertion of his long walk, and at the same time swinging his head, panning left and right, completely ignoring all that beautiful patchwork with perfect half-squares, triangles of radiant lemon yellows followed by bottle green, orange chrome and blood-crimson, though he could sense that new fabric smell rising from them, as if those quilts were breathing.

But still he paid no attention to them, instead looking horizontally into a huge backyard fenced off with thorny hedges. He saw a big pile of dry thorny babur branches stacked one on the top of other, and heat of Northern Sindh had turned those thorny branches into bones, dry bones, and every few inches down those branches grew a pair of thorns, joined at the base like Siamese twins, thorns making victory signs.

Those beautiful perfect thorns, like ivory needles, became more cunning stabbers as they got drier and drier. People who got stuck by them would usually

---

[43] *Khata'oon*: four-legged wooden cots. The singular form is *khaata*.
[44] *Ralli*: traditional Sindhi quilt.

end up with a fever for a day or two, or, if they were lucky, they walk away with a sweet pain lingering in their flesh for days on end.

A raindrop hit one of his eyelids, soon accompanied by several others, fat droplets which were absorbed by the breast of his *hirko-aachee*[45] shirt. But then that pregnant cloud's water broke, and she poured, as they always say in Sindhi when talking about rainclouds. Fakeer helped the uncle to wrap the quilts, and they ran inside under the shade of small straw-top porch of their two-room mud hut, and they spread one of those cots and waited for the rain to stop.

But it didn't—rather it kept raining all night and into the early morning. And Fakeer and his bride's uncle kept talking on useless topics, as they had nothing in common. The uncle was a weaver and a part-time thief, but Fakeer was a beggar, who would rather ask than steal, and who sang mystic hymns explaining to everyone that it's all short-lived and transient anyway.

Occasionally as they spoke he could hear light laughter, which was sneaking to his ears from holes in the wall where clay plaster had eroded a long time ago, leaving behind only straws and sticks.

The rain had stopped by early morning. That's the time when Sindhi wedding vows take place, right before daybreak, looking at low hanging North Star just above horizon. Too bad the clouds didn't let Fakeer and his bride see North Star that day. To perform the vows, all the elders would gently touch the foreheads of the bridegroom and bride. Some wicked aunts would bump them rather hard. And the head-touching ritual would continue until every elder present had performed it.

The stream of well-wishing elders would cycle around the couple as if through an open drawbridge, going crazy and coming midway and then going back again, while the bride and groom would keep pouring dry grains of rice into each other's hands, like an hourglass being repeatedly flipped. And that all did happen with Fakeer and his wife Sharma Khatoon, a child, a baby, a kid whose aunt stacked pillows under her to raise her head up to Fakeer's level. And she was giggling out of happiness for getting married, as the weight of sadness had not yet settled in. She would soon have to go with this stranger, who was the same age as her father, leaving everything behind forever.

Coming back, the entire wedding procession consisted of Fakeer carrying his nine-year-old wife on one of his shoulders, and holding two folded quilts which

---

[45] *Hirko-aachee:* chalky-white colour.

were her dowry, as he walked back fourteen miles from Bhattiyain-jo-Shehar. She sat perched on his left shoulder as if on a saddle, and she held on with both arms wrapped around his turban. Occasionally he could hear her sniffle, and her left arm would slip down and block his view, and he would have to push it back up again to see clearly. He looked at his distorted reflection in the wavy puddles of rainwater.

While he was walking, he had to face the disappointment that his wife was a child, and those desires of brand-new grooms, which are always beautiful to do and embarrassing to say, could not be actualised just now. Those thoughts drew him into extreme solitude, and he didn't say or hear anything, though his wife's occasional low feeble nasal sounds were stirring that quiet.

The sun was rising, bathing everything with its distilled soft satin light. Sitting up on Fakeer's shoulder, Sharma was sniffling. Teardrops were rolling on her cheeks, but pausing there for a moment, allowing sunlight to make a heiligenschein, a glow that would make the glittering of every precious gem look like tartar compared to that sparkling tear, for that infinitesimal moment before Fakeer's tramping gait made them fall.

The sunlight was perfectly clean, as if freshly laundered. There was clamour of birds coming from those same mysterious branches of the tall aa-sirheen tree, vehemently shouting about the last night's rain, which had probably shattered their nests. And he saw a strange splashy arrangement of white clouds as if the sun had ejaculated on the belly of the sky.

So Fakeer got married to Sharma, a heavenly sweet cupcake. At the time, he was not yet aware that in the recipes of some sweet cupcakes, a pinch of awful bitters are essential, but those bitters are only there to enhance the ultimate sweetness. And his marriage to sweet Sharma brought a number of other characters into Fakeer's life, such as Chacho Momdali Pathano and Mamoo Siddique Jogi, who were bitter folk indeed, but they were there, mixed into that otherwise heavenly dessert.

Chacho Momdali Pathan was a tall man with chiselled features. His real name was Muhammad Ali Kori, and he was one of Sharma's first cousins. He had given up weaving and become a dacoit.

He was fond of cast-iron axe heads. On one occasion, the blacksmith had just moulded a new cast-iron head for his axe and mounted it on a long hard oil-soaked wooden grip. And he was itching to make sure it could kill. As he was coming back from blacksmith, passing through the woods close to his village, he saw a member of the Brohi caste walking in the same direction and munching on toasted chickpeas. And he thought, *if I curse him he will fight back, and then I could try my new axe head.* So he took some fast steps to catch up to him, and when he had come up right behind him, he said, "*Chud'a ja, bhugrda kharaija*"—*give me your chickpeas, you motherfucker.*

Instead of getting angry, that poor Brohi said, "Have some, brother," and offered him the chickpeas earnestly.

Momdali kept walking behind him for a bit and then cursed him again, "I'm cursing you! Don't you have shame? Why don't you fight!"

Brohi said, "I'm a poor man. I don't want to fight with you, brother."

He raised his new axe head and said, "But I do." And he hit poor defenceless Brohi with such a vicious blow to head that his skull split open like a walnut shell in a nutcracker. He pulled his new axe head from poor Brohi's skull, wiped it clean and walked away.

The next day his father mentioned that someone had killed a traveller few miles away in woods.

Momdali always said he had been cursed by an old woman. He blamed her for these maledictions which made him kill his pregnant wife along with their unborn first child, and his sister, and his brother's wife, and his aunt, all at the same time, with the same axe. All those killings, he would say, were the fault of the damnation of that old woman—whom he had also killed—as he tried to drown out those crickets of guilt in his own head, which kept gnawing his mind till the very end of his life.

Legend had it that the curse happened during a cattle-raiding trip he went on with two other partners in the middle of the night. They had rounded up three bulls and everything was going clock wise, smooth as silk. They went quarter of a mile out from the village to round up bulls. He saw a shadow following at a little distance. He asked his accomplices to continue on while he hid behind an old peelu tree.

In a few moments, the shadow revealed itself to be an old woman who had been following them. He came out from behind, withered and complexly corded peelu trunk. Even before Momdali could say anything, the woman spoke: "*Abba, muhnja, dhaga motaye day.*"—*Son, return my cattle! which belongs to me.*

"Go back," he said. "We have nothing of yours to return. Why didn't you wake them up while we were there?"

But she was not listening and kept asking the same thing. She had been following them for hours. Dawn was about to break and another small village was approaching fast, and he repeatedly asked her to go back. He even took his turban off and placed it at her feet and begged her to let them go. But kept insisting that they give back her livestock. In desperation, he yelled, "I'm going to hurt you, you are my mother's age, for heaven's sake, go back!"

But then he snapped, and he entrenched that axe of his in her forehead, telling himself that he had killed before in his life and at least he had given this old woman enough warning. But from her dying lips there came a whispered curse whose words would turn into the constant and gnawing crickets of his mind. "May you put this in your own…" she mumbled, and then she died.

Years later, when he was married and his wife was expecting their first child, the curse returned to him. He was sipping tea at the village teashop, same as always, when he heard the voice of Sumar, whose name literally translates to Monday. Probably, he was born on Monday and his parents didn't bother to think of something else, or maybe they were grateful for that day of week on which their wishes came true. Momdali had known Sumar since childhood and there had always been friction between them.

Sumar was taunting him. "For others, you kill their Karo-Kari."[46]

But then Sumar stopped short and left his sentence unfinished with a murky smile. Momdali smelled that hint of doubt, and he thought in his heart, *maybe he's talking about my woman.* He called after Sumar, "Wait, just wait there!"

He came home yelling his wife's name at the top of his lungs. He hit her on the head, missing the line where her hair parted by a fingerbreadth. His sister and his brother's wife came in running. He killed his brother's wife, but his sister grabbed his axe grip firmly and he couldn't pry it loose from her. She looked into his eyes and said, "Assan kayoo cha?"—*What have we done?* "Just tell me."

---

[46] *Karo-Kari*: Words used to describe an adulterer and adulteress, who could both (but especially the woman) be subject to 'honour killing' in some Sindhi traditions. The words themselves, Karo-Kari, refer to the tainted man and his stained woman, both of whom are likely to be victims of the honour killing. However, in some particularly cruel cases, the structure is used to seek revenge in other spheres, where no adultery is actually occurred. In a case like this, a person might first kill one of their own sisters or daughters or aunts and then kill the person they have their grudge against, claiming *karo-kari*. Usually, the killer will pick one a female family member who is autistic or physically challenged, considering her useless to begin with.

"Nothing," he said.

She released her grip from his axe handle and said, "Go ahead." And she let him kill her.

Then he killed a fourth time—his elderly aunt who had come to visit, a witness to his murderous rage. Still not satisfied, he headed back to the teashop to kill that person who had started him on the rampage—but Sumar had already gone. Eventually, Momdali tracked him down and killed him, too.

So that was the mad house that Fakeer married into.

Mamoo Siddique Jogi was a dark-skinned man with typically Sindhi facial features: joined-together eyebrows sitting on his unsophisticated doe-eyes, revealing his yellowish, veiny jaundiced eyes. He had a traditional Sindhi beard that was trimmed from the neck and cheeks to make his jaw appear squarer and his cheekbones more prominent, and he had long tipped moustaches. All in all, his face seemed to have been moulded from same cast as that of the King Priest of Mohen-jo-Daro.

He too was Sharma's distant cousin, a small leaflet on her complexly knotty family shrub. Why shrub? Because nothing was clear. There were no primary, secondary and tertiary braches of her family tree. Here's one small example of her Byzantine family chart:

One of her cousins married a widow who had a daughter from her prior marriage. By the will of God, her cousin's father, who was Sharma's uncle too, became interested in his wife's daughter and married her. From that day, her cousin's wife became his father's mother-in-law! Not long thereafter, the daughter of Sharma's cousin's wife, who had married her stepfather, gave birth to a child. That child technically became his cousin's brother because that child was her father's son!

But on the other hand, that child was also Sharma's cousin's widowed wife's grandson too. That made her cousin his own brother's maternal grandpa. After a while, her cousin's wife also gave birth to a baby, which made her cousin's stepmother his baby's stepsister! But she was also the grandmother of that baby because she was married to baby's grandfather! Who was also Sharma's uncle!

So Mamoo Siddique was that first baby who was born to her cousin's father, who had married her cousin's stepdaughter.

Sharma herself never showed a great deal of interest in straightening up that family chart. She just let it be a simple family.

Mamoo Siddique's real name was Muhammad Siddique Kori, but to keep his family affairs separate from his business, he had given himself a different last name, Jogi. With that name, he had unwittingly made a great ecumenical example by joining these three names together, Muhammad, Siddique, and Jogi[47]. But no one bothered him about combining water and fire in that peace-loving place called Sindh.

He was initially just a casual thief, but then it became his profession, out of necessity and probably for the adrenal rush too. He became a master in a method of theft called *khata*: robbing someone while they slept. The first step was to pick a wealthy target and learn everything possible about the target's home—how many rooms, what time they slept, where their valuables would probably be stashed. The burglars made all their plans orally, or at the most they would sit crunched down and draw little lines in the dirt to make things clear.

Their informants were beggars or imposters disguised as Jogis or roaming fortune-tellers. They knew how to get into those homes in the middle of day by charming the naïve women of the house, and by telling them solutions for problems those poor women didn't even have, and while they were inside they could sneak around enough to get a rough idea of the place. And they would pass all that information along to the thieves, who would then pick a moonless night for their silent entry. They would dismantle an accessible part of the wall using a single wooden tool that looked like a drumstick with a pencil-sharp head, which they called a *naanga muhoo romboo*.[48]

In the second part of the night, they would remove the mud plaster around a single brick. That first brick would be the linchpin, because once that came out, the rest could be removed in no time. Then the thieves would enter, passing several sleeping members of the household, to get into that room where the owner himself was sleeping. That's where they would find the keys to the vault safe, usually under the owner's pillow. After that, all the thieves needed to do was to open the vault's rusted iron door, get the valuables, and get out.

But Mamoo Siddique Jogi didn't trust others and didn't have any partner. He was master of his gig, and pulled his acts all alone.

Someone once asked Siddique Jogi what had happened to the three fingers of his right hand, which had frozen like hooks. He replied, "It was long ago." He had waited till the second part of the night and then climbed up to the roof like a

---

[47] *Jogi*: a follower of Shiva.
[48] *Naan'ga muhoo romboo*: literally, 'snake-head pick'.

chameleon and stayed little longer, lying there in anxiety and perhaps uncomfortable because of those fast moving white clouds, thinking they might reveal his cover, even in that moonless night.

There was no chance of that, really, but still his was a thief's heart. He started undoing mud around clay bricks very gently, camouflaged in black. He said, "Those first one or two bricks always take an eternity to undo. But that Hindu Mahajan had lots of gold and money. I was almost there, but to get the first brick out I had to pass my fingers through it first, in the darkness, as if blind folded."

But his prey was waiting for him to do that. The moment he passed his fingers through, his prey hit them with a vicious blow, and what was left was this!—and he lifted his three crooked hook-like fingers again and laughed.

Fakeer was living in the *otaak*[49] of a well-off landlord, who had offered it to Fakeer because he was touched by one of Fakeer's mystic stories. Though Fakeer had also sung him hymns and told him those unending stories that start from the middle and end in the middle and carry along another sequel, there was just the one particular story that the landlord loved, and it was enough to inspire him to lend Fakeer his otaak.

So this otaak was a large room hidden in one of the back alleys of Qamber, secluded from the thorny hedges of family dwellings.

Fakeer had left his nine-year-old wife with his elder brother's family some six miles from Qamber at Mehann-jee-khaahee to become ripe and enter childbearing age.

Five-years passed, and spring came five times in those five years, followed by five rainy seasons, each one more soaked in love than the last. And the number of times full moon had lollygagged aimlessly through the nights! A few times in those five years, the moon had gotten so big that it had almost fallen on earth. But apart from that, everything stayed the same as it had been. Except that Fakeer grew a little older.

His brother's wife called for him, so he went and she told him, "*Sharm saamaee aa, gul'aa aya thass.*"—Sharma has come of age and is bearing flowers.[50]

---

[49] *Otaak*: From the Persian word for 'room' or 'chamber'. In Sindhi, an otaak is usually a sort of a guesthouse belonging to a wealthy family, set at some remove from their main house; a sort of getaway location.

[50] *Bearing flowers:* in other words, menstruating. (Similar antiquated expressions exist in English, as well.)

So later that day he saw a young Sharma. Just as it is promised that beauty will come to everyone, so it came to her too, she had turned into an appealing young girl.

He brought her to Qamber to live with him in that one-room space, which was virtually a revolving door for hermaphrodites and beggars who later became Fakeers, for Fakeers who used to be beggars, for folk singers of both genders and also one transgender, Nan'goo,[51] who had chosen to be silent and banish his voice, as he didn't need it anymore, after he had felt the divine presence of Mehboob Saeen.

Sharma Khatoon had learned to get along with all of them, and they all respected her as Fakeer's spouse. And in that room, though it was more like a lobby, she gave birth to her first child, a baby boy and the antithesis of Fakeer, and they called him 'Alam'.

They would have known the obvious meaning of the Arabic word *alam*, which is 'universe'. But there are many other meanings that Fakeer and Sharma may or may not have been thinking of, such as 'knowledge of another'. Fakeer's first-born son was raised by his parents and by countless beggars and some hermaphrodites.

Living in such close proximity with these different people and their distinct raw psyche, Sharma Khatoon instinctively developed the skills of a female bartender in an all-male bar. Her earthy nature allowed her to become people of many different walks of life. From the midwives she learned, at a very early age, the art of breech tilt or baby spinning to bring foetus head down, using magical finger massages on the domes of the bellies, which succeeded in delivering the baby most of the time.

And she became friends with Jeevini Bai, a folk singer who had reached stardom. Columbia Gramophone Company, Ltd. had released her records, which used to play in every teashop, even though the warning was clearly printed on each record that "This copyright record must not publicly performed without licence." And then it had first line of lyric on it printed in Sindhi:

"Look! Spring just stepped into this desert of loneliness." Jeevini Bai was originally from a place that was perpetually drowning in sand. She always asked Sharma, to give her son Alam to her so that she could make him a singer, but Sharma would always spin that conversation into something else and then leave

---

[51] *Nan'goo*. The name means 'unraveled'.

it with a little laughter, because she knew that Jeevini Bai had a thing about young boys, and in the past she had a few boy students who disappeared into thin air.

Years later, Jeevini Bai was travelling in a train, sitting in the women's compartment, and there were some other women travelling with their young children in that same compartment. Those women appeared to come from a very wealthy family, and Jeevini Bai liked rich and beautiful people, like everybody does, so she chatted with them, and their young girls opened some of their suitcases, which were filled with silk and chiffon dresses, and some older woman among them were wearing *'Duhreeyoon'*, seven-strand accented round gold beaded necklaces, having a pendent at the centre of each layer with red and green and blue gems. These are the necklaces traditionally worn by wealthy married woman, along with *'Nathoon, Thako'*, and heavy gold bracelets worn above the elbow.

When these ladies came to know that they were speaking to Jeevini Bai, some of them became apprehensive, because back then all performing female were considered prostitutes, but some of the younger girls kept chatting with her. Eventually, they got off at some station or other, and after a while another female passenger noticed a leather suitcase—a beautiful one, with two brasses latches and handles and an empty rectangular luggage name label tag and three leather belts with brass buckles and those shiny cups like knee-cap covers on all eight corners—placed right above where those women had been sitting.

She shouted out that they left their suitcase and tried to call to the roaming police constable. But Jeevini Bai stepped in and said that the suitcase was hers, and she cursed and yelled on that poor woman. Everything fizzled out and the matter was settled a little later when the train stopped at the next station. Then that woman snuck out and told the whole story to ticket collector, who went to police constable, and after few minutes everyone was swarming in the compartment around that suitcase.

Jeevini Bai was furious at all of them, wanting at first to intimidate them with her femininity and then with her stardom, but the woman whom Jeevini Bai had insulted was adamant that this suitcase belonged to someone else. But the police constable, a dark-skinned short chubby fellow wearing a deep blue uniform, promptly suggested an easy solution. He asked Jeevini Bai to tell everyone what was in the suitcase, and just as promptly she responded: a few silk and chiffon dresses.

And they said, fine, let's open it. At first, Jeevini Bai didn't have the key which she claimed to have misplaced somewhere there, and that increased the curiosity? So the ticket collector and police constable waited till next station stop where some higher police officials could look into the matter.

The next train stop would be Jeevini Bai's destination anyway, because when they cut open that suitcase it was filled with sugar or salt like granular material having chopped human body parts in between. That was end of Jeevini Bai, she broke down in tears, that it was not hers, and yelled and cried and mourned and begged for mercy, wailing that she had gotten greedy and she was sorry, but no one listened to her lament.

Fakeer was becoming more impetuous, succumbing more and more to his desire to ride that golden horse called success, which makes people jump impossible obstacles of risks in a blink of an eye. Sharma Khatoon encouraged Fakeer in his business ventures, especially his idea to establish a livery stable close to the grain market at the southern outskirts of Qamber. So he inverted all of his pockets, dusted and combed through all his possessions, and gathered every single penny he had to purchase a small piece of land.

And on the land he built a straw-top mud hut, which became their home. He started a livery stable to board villagers' horses and keep carriages. And soon he added bull carts for hire for those farmers and other villagers who needed to visit the grain merchant's property, which was on the edge of town. So it goes: aano, tako, paiso, where aano was six cents, tako was three cents and paiso was one cent. For one tako, you could board your horse for whole day, and it would be fed grass and kept in the shade; an aano could get you an ox-driven cart with the same deal, and a paiso for a donkey with the same.

This innovation brought Fakeer much success, so much that he soon needed a bigger lot to accommodate higher traffic. He started expanding, encroaching onto the adjacent land most of which was government own lands so no one said anything to Fakeer. But one side of his property was next to a Hindu monastery. This led to a long fight, literally a fist fights as well as civil litigations, and he fought them very sincerely. "From beginning of time, success only belongs to those who walk away with it," he would say, and he genuinely believed in that philosophy.

Having been a beggar, a day labourer, he knew well how to make clay mud walls. He would make a huge pile of cob mix in the courtyard of his house, and he would work all day outside his property wall, coating it with a thin mixture of straw paste to make it the whole wall seem wet and new. But then after dark, he would start erecting a new wall, ten or fifteen feet out, and have it finished before the break of dawn.

Inside those expanding outer walls, life brewed on with its usual variety. It was not only Fakeer, Sharma, and their son Alam who had moved into the hut. They had brought along with them a truckload of other Fakeers and transgenders, beggars, and also a loyal friend named Shehoon.[52]

Shehoon was a pale-cream and brownish-yellow mutt, maybe a Labrador retriever breed with some other mixed canine heritage too, who knows what. It didn't matter who that puppy was in the moment when Fakeer pulled him by a back leg, a fraction of a second before a standing oxcart started moving backwards—its bull had gotten irritated for some reason—and the wheel would have crushed Shehoon's head. Fakeer had no interest in pets, nor did he take any interest in Shehoon, but Shehoon chose to follow him. After a while, Fakeer's wife named him Shehoon because the golden fur around his neck reminded her of a lion's mane.

The livery stable business caught on quickly. There was no one else around who could offer an organised well-groomed stable, with straw canopy top shades, or cater food and water to the boarding animals. Fakeer soon found himself every evening counting canisters filled with coins, which left a sour metallic smell on the fingertips of both his hands. He was becoming rich, and at the same time his fingers were losing that gentler sense of touch, that ability to feel utter softness of petals. He developed calluses very fast in this process of counting and filling and tying bags of coins, placing them in hard baked clay pots, and concealing them in mud walls, and then worrying, what if someone finds them and steals them?

His spiritual inclination grew sluggish as his house grew finer. Soon, he had built a stronger and more luxurious addition to his house, with a high ceiling and two new rooms and a staircase leading to the rooftop, and that rooftop also had a waist-high clay mud wall. Fakeer his wife and kids would often sleep up there during the warm, stagnant summer nights of Qamber. And by the time all these improvements were finished, everyone—all of his friends, accomplices, fellow storytellers—had left him, all except for Nan'goo Fakeer and Shehoon. Nan'goo

---

[52] *Shehoon*: a male lion (with a mane).

Fakeer still quietly roamed around all day long, carrying Alam on his shoulders through the streets of Qamber.

Nan'goo Fakeer was a *Matheno Khadaro*,[53] a quiet eunuch, covered in dirty clumps of hair joined together into a thick wild braid. He had piercing eyes, but he tried to avoid inflicting them directly on people's faces; most of the time he keep them shut or cast down toward the ground. When he occasionally did he look into someone's eyes, they could never stand the warmth of his fixed stare. He wore rings, those wrought sterling silver rings holding Yemeni aqeeq in their clenches.

Aqeeq is the Darvaish of the stones. It was believed that Yemeni aqeeq had been the very first among all the rocks to accept the oneness, the omniscience of the sweet, almighty Mehboob Sain, and of Risalaat, and Wilayat of Mola-e-Kainat Imam Ali. It was said that only Yemeni aqeeq believed, and that belief could be unbelievably, beautiful, you could believe in his oneness without seeing him. He who doesn't want anything from you, rather only gives from his endless perpetual blessings, he does not look like you nor do you look like him, he who is made up of love, a commodity of which you have more when you give it away. So what the heck, just imagine that Yemeni aqeeq, a semiprecious stone, has a heart of its own, made up of stone. Of solid rock.

---

[53] *Khadaro*: a eunuch, which is to say, any castrated man or boy whose testicles have been crushed or removed or congenitally do not function. In era of the dynasties of Sindhi emperors, eunuchs were employed to guard the women of their palaces or as court officials. A khadaro was regarded as an ineffectual man because of his lack of sexual potency.

In Sindh, eunuchs are considered a member of a 'third' gender, neither man nor woman. Most are physically male or hermaphrodites, but some are physically female. Sindhi khadara usually dress as women and refer to themselves as female, but they are addressed by others as male. In Sindh, especially during Fakeer's time, but to a large extent still today, there were no resources for genital modification surgeries, so there is not a concept of 'transgender' in the surgical sense, apart from castration.

Sindhi eunuchs gather in communities with other of male transvestites and eunuchs, and they traditionally perform as singers and dancers at religious festivals and other special occasions like baptisms and weddings.

Socially they are considered harmless, and in general society carries an undertone of sympathy towards them, and at times eunuchs have been known to take advantage of that sympathy.

But Nan'goo Fakeer wore several other semi-precious stones on his other fingers, and each of those stones had its own set of beliefs, and years of dirt had petrified into black crescents on his nails right below his cuticles. And his feet turned light grey like cement, so there was no differentiation between his toenails and skin. Some people had noticed a rose-like fragrance emanating from his perspirations.

Others had seen him outside Qamber, at that part of the day, when daylight gives herself to darkness and both times meets in mysterious way, sitting in an upright position with his head erect and shoulders straight and both legs folded into each other with his feet touching his thighs, and his heart beat sounding from his chest like as if from subwoofers, and hitting them in their face, giving some of them chills. But for Fakeer and Sharma he was simply a friend, a person who had chosen to be silent a long time ago.

Sharma gave birth to three more sons. She turned out to be strong and cutthroat, but a people's person as well. She managed Fakeer's business single-handedly while Fakeer was busy expanding his property and dealing with legal skirmishes with his neighbours, who happened to be a Hindu monastery.

As time passed, Fakeer was gradually extending his property boundaries in all four directions, and one of those directions encroached upon the monastery's property line. Unfortunately for Fakeer, the monastery also had plans to expand. They changed their entrance location because they wanted to bring elephants into the monastery, and this put their entry on the side facing the grain market.

Fakeer's livery stable front opened in that direction too, so Fakeer's business had to share the entry way with the monastery, and nobody liked that, for good reason. Fakeer didn't like it because the elephants made noises that upset the horses and bulls and other parked animals in his stable. The religious Hindus of the monastery didn't like it because Fakeer deliberately asked his workers to leave horse shit and trash out front by that shared entrance.

In retaliation, the yet unwise young disciples of that monastery started urinating by the wall of Fakeer's stable, which happened to be his home entrance too. That urine worked like fuel on a fire, and Fakeer then encouraged local butchers to slaughter their meat in his stable, which was much closer to their meat market than the town abattoir was. So they would hang slaughtered animals upside down from the centre joist of the stable door and wash all that blood onto street, and the trickling blood would somehow find its way to the monastery.

Sometimes, Fakeer's Shehoon would roam inside the monastery in what Shehoon thought was a furtive and stealthy manner; in reality he always got caught banging pans in the monastery's *Rasoi-ghar*,[54] which started yet another fight between Fakeer and monastery. Shehoon liked a slow pace. He was a "been there, done that" kind of dog, nothing excited him, he enjoyed just hanging out, sitting and relaxing and watching life from a literally down-to-earth point of view, because that's where his head and chin rested in those three or four small trenches that he had dug for himself in the cool, moist soil of Fakeer's stable, which he rotated according to sunlight and seasons.

And he loved to sit in one of those trenches, where one of his eyelids and his snoring both fluctuated like peaks and valleys on a graph. He would emerge from sleep when he stopped snoring and try to lift one eyelid, which took forever, and then he would drift back and start snoring again, relaxed and not worrying about anything.

In that monastery there was a *purohit,* too. In timeworn days, there used to be two kinds of purohits: those who worked as priests in royal courts, and others who roamed in the wilderness seeking wisdom and then sharing it with those in need of it. But the purohit from monastery next door was neither of those; he was just a simple priest. Maybe it was the gold merchants of Qamber, who were also the patrons of that monastery, who had start calling their priests "purohits" just to make them sound more royal.

That purohit used to come sometimes and ask for Sharma Khatoon for drinking water, and she would pour water into his cupped palms, which he stuck up to his mouth while he kept looking at her. That purohit was a soft-spoken slim bare-shouldered man with a shaved head and a gazelle-tan complexion.

Fakeer woke up one night to find Sharma missing from her bed. He jumped up and rushed out and saw her pouring water out of a clay pot. Volatility was a vital part of Fakeer's grouchy nature. You could say that it cost him too much—he could be a very violent man at times. He would sometimes make up reasons to pick a fight with his wife. One day, he gave her a dead wasp, and by heaven and God's throne what a beautiful wasp it was: it had a metallic sapphire head which then dissolved into a turquoise and peacock-blue thorax, like an unbreakable illusion, which met up to its emerald green jointed legs, and an abdomen which held the secret of all colours, unbelievable pigments from fiery

---

[54] *Rasoi-ghar*: a kitchen.

yellow to shimmering amber to torchlight orange in the centre, enveloped into a hint of emerald leaving rest to parrot green. It was a Jewel Wasp that he gave her, telling her, "Keep it safe. I will ask you when I need it, it's my golden wasp."

She tied his 'golden wasp' with a knot to the corner of her *gandee*[55] corner and accidentally crushed it. When Fakeer asked her to give it back to him, she barely looked up from the food she was preparing. "It's lost, got crushed."

In anger, Fakeer grabbed her hair, which was parted like a banana leaf, so smoothly that her scalp skin had been shining at the middle line until it was disturbed by Fakeer's rough fingers. Then he get hold of the tail end of her hard wood scraping spoon from the pot of boiling stew and hit her viciously, which left a permanent scar, and she would never again be able to shut her left upper eyelid completely. And she sat there trying to stop the bleeding on her own by pressing her wet cheesecloth veil against it.

Eventually, when her bleeding had stopped for some time, she stood up walked over the stable shades and tried to see her reflection in the languidly calm and stagnant water that filled the big round baked red-clay tanks that dispensed water for the horses and bulls. She saw herself in the water's cool grey reflecting surface.

There were different shades of brightness, mediating the contours of her face. Her left eye was all closed-shut and swollen, but even in her lament she had a small smile, a facetious, wry smile, and she forcefully readjusted her reflection so that the softer and brighter light accommodated the smile. In that calm water tank, everything was dark other than a small part of her face and tip of her veil; everything was dark grey in that image. Then she felt that someone was coming, so she covered her left eye by pulling the veil a bit more towards the centre of her face, biting into it to hold it in place.

And she heard the purohit asking for drinking water in his ever-soothing voice with his quietly smiling eyes. She grabbed a small *gharo*,[56] and the purohit held his palms together to make a bowl and then and crunched his knees to sit, and she poured the cool water into his hands almost immaculately, without a single splash.

There was a stream between Qamber and Mehann-jee-khaahee called *Norang Wah*, which originated from the Indus River. After several branches, sub-branches and then tertiary branches, it seemed that Norang Wah itself had

---

[55] *Gandee*: A long soft cheesecloth veil, commonly used as a headscarf by Sindhi women.
[56] *Gharo*: a clay pot with a long neck.

lost track of its origin, but what was certain was that it ended next to Qamber. In reality it was a canal, but it had come to be considered a stream, maybe due to neglect or to its uneven banks or uncertain depths, in which a number of teenagers had drowned.

One evening Fakeer was coming back from visiting his ailing brother, who was ten or so years his elder and who had lived all of his life in Mehann-jee-khaahee. He had asked Fakeer to come see him so that he could consult in the matter of his only daughter's marriage. Obviously, it was just a gesture of honour extended by Fakeer's elder brother; that's how decisions were made back then. The Sindhi people are uncanningly loving.

At their simple marriages they have no banquet, no grand white table top lavish dinners; rather the linchpin of their occasion is for every relative, close or distant, to be present there. Usually, it would be the responsibility of the groom's father or grandfather to go to each relative's doorstep, literally walk to their homes—not just sending a message or written invitation but rather presenting themselves physically on the doorstep of those relatives who had become estranged for any reason, a prior ill word, or misunderstanding or anything else, didn't matter.

It might it take them several trips; sometimes the groom's father would carry holy scriptures on his head just to show the gravity of his gratitude. In some severe situations, they would bring along all of their *maayro,* that means all of their unwedded daughters and sisters, which is a big undertaking. Like in any ancient culture, Sindhi females are their honour, and unwed females are vestal. This gesture would usually tip the balance in the groom's favour, and the angry relative had to give in and make a truce and agree to attend the wedding.

That's the way everyone wanted their children's wedding to be, with everybody who is anybody in that family present under bride's rooftop, eating *bhatuu*—an early morning feast of rice pilaf, with broken unpolished rice and chunks of beef with potato cooked together with mild spices, along with a sweet pilaf in which raw dry sugarcane juice was boiled with the rice. All this would be served in a large baked clay pot. Small groups of six to eight people would gather around each pot, sitting on the ground or on dry date leaf mats to enjoy the feast. And each guest would take some of that feast back home. They would vehemently ask the person who served the food, *"Baadhi ba daay!"*—*wrap me some!*—and spread a corner of their shoulder cloth on ground, into which they would receive a few servings of oily wet cooked pilaf. They would tie the cloth into a small sack or lobe and carry it back home, and soon that lobe would become soaked with dripping oil, but they wouldn't mind.

There were no such ill feeling between Fakeer and his brother. For them, it was simple hug and his brother told him that he is getting his daughter married, and asked Fakeer, "What do you say?"

And Fakeer replied with utter humbleness, "You are my elder, your decision is mine."

And that was that.

It was a late morning, and while Fakeer and his brother were talking, Khawind'a-dino started to make noise. Khawind'a-dino was Fakeer's nephew, his elder brother's only son, who was in his early 20s at the time. And he was playing tricks with a wooden box with an acoustic brass horn called a *bhopu*. When he ratcheted into that wooden box, it caused a metallic arm holding a sharp nail to hit against a spinning ceramic plate, which was making the noises. In fact, he realised that it was not noise—it was singing like a human.

"Khawinda-din'a, what's that?" Fakeer asked.

His nephew responded, *"Phono aa, Chacha"*—It's a gramophone, uncle—and Fakeer said to himself in his heart, *when a clear human voice starts coming from a wooden box, that's the end of it, it's the apocalypse.* But he said nothing to his nephew other than nodding, "Hummm."

In the evening, Fakeer returned home, walking on the top of levee of Norang Wah, which was flowing quietly opposite to him but somehow seemed to be flowing with him. The levee surface was all ruined, uneven with ruts of heavy wheels of ox-driven carts. There were white patches of dry salty soil littered with golden rice husks. The sky had turn into a sad mild purple monotone, which then converted into a dull amber right above horizon before dipping into a different purple tone again.

On the water's surface it was all amber shades, with that inverted mirror image of dark brown distant trees. All of that was melted very fast, and the darkness of dusk gulped up all those chromatic tones, but Fakeer was angrier at the uneven path, and he cursed the oxcarts as he walked carefully to avoid spraining an ankle. He was walking on the edge of the levee away from the stream, close to the high shrubs and date trees, when there was a sudden commotion in the tall shrubs, like a bull or wild boar. And before Fakeer had even grasped all that, he heard a solid cracking sound, which was followed by pain in his head and numbness in his both hands and legs, there were several knocks after that.

Fakeer was not feeling a whole lot pain by then, and was trying to appear dead. Thinking they had beaten him to death, his assailants threw him into Norang Wah. Fakeer kept floating there; face down, barely breathing from his one nostril, floating on the slow-moving currents of stream, which were taking him back to Mehann-jee-khaahee. In that fearful discomfort, he still wanted to rationalise what had happened, and the thought of the purohit came into his mind from nowhere.

And at the same time his several secret vows broke loose and glided away on waves of Norang Wah and left his mind too, as he floated on with the currents, then the thought of Shehoon's snoring injected some happy adrenaline in his body, and he thought, if he'd had Shehoon with him, things probably would have turned out quite differently.

The floating was growing tedious, and his submerged eye was really bothering him now. But still he waited quite a while to make sure all were gone before he very slowly lifted up his head, then grabbed at the bulrushes and reeds growing by the banks to drag himself out of there. It was dark; crickets were inflating the emptiness of the night with their tweedle chirping rhythms. He saw a flickering frail light, of a lamp from some dwelling. It was a villager come to help him.

Loneliness tends to teach individuals how to do things on their own. As Fakeer was an orphan and a very quiet man, he tended to think through his projects in his mind and then undertake them all alone. He had dug a well in his backyard all by himself. There was no easy source of soft water around his home, other than one well, which was way past the octroi tax checkpost on the outskirts of Qamber. All the other wells had hard water. So hoping against all odds to find sweet soft water, he dug a well in his backyard single-handedly.

There was a holy ceremony, where his wife and daughter-in-law gathered a few women relatives to pray, to reach out to His sweet mercy to grant them a sweet water well. They cooked sweet rice pilaf and sang sweet wedding songs; in other words they did every sweet thing possible. And the next evening Fakeer started digging a *khu-hee,* which means female well, usually they are narrow wells, narrower than the span of two arms. The soil was so drenched in salt that it seemed more like a rock. It took him thirty-one days of working each morning to finish it. Before the dawn prayers, his wife would come and sprinkle holy rosewater in the ditch with the hope that every droplet of would make the earth ooze soft sweet water.

On the thirty-first day, he reached groundwater. It was deep enough to stack five adult males in it head to toe. Fakeer could feel his feet getting wet, and that wet soil aroused a cold shiver. Instead of enjoying that feeling, he deliberately ignored it, taking it for a weakness of some kind. He called out in a loud, graceful voice, "I got water," and everyone in around the home came up to the rough neck of the well.

He asked for a brass bowl, which Dhayani, his daughter-in-law, carefully dropped down without disturbing the yet-unpaved rough edges. Fakeer caught the brass bowl, knelt down to fill it and then waited for the mud to settle. Then he took a sip and said, "*kharo aa,*"—*it's pungent*—and those two words put an end to all the sweet prayers and droplets of holy rosewater.

But his wife didn't let the mood drop. Right away she said, "It's a blessing in disguise, something we can't see because we don't have that foresight. Let us give thanks to Mehboob Saeen. So what if it's pungent? It's still water from our own well." And her words buffered that hopelessness and somehow rekindled that joyful, festive mood. Her wisdom strengthened their trust. In all logic, the water had to be pungent in such salt-drenched soil. So the thrill and hope of sweet water ended and life again started dragging her feet.

Fakeer had to kick the bucket eventually—he was mortal, too. They say he died of *karo kamun,* cirrhosis of the liver. His wife used to say that his blood got parched, which could literally be seen on him: his skin looked like burned flesh. First chunky scabs appeared on his skin, which then turned into flakes of dandruff. Or maybe he died of virus-stricken, corrupted blood. Or was it sadness covering him in veils of doubts ever since the day he was born. He never asked his son Alam or his wife to take him to any kind of doctor, holistic or otherwise. He just waited and waited, and finally he died. What a trivial death it was, just like the death of god in the heart of an atheist.

This person who single-handedly used to erect clay mud walls as tall as a grown man between dust and dawn could no longer hold his neck up to take a sip of water. With every passing day, the wooden cot bed he lay on sagged in more, like a hammock. Even though he had lost much of his body weight and was shrunken to a skin over a skeleton, still his wooden cot sagged.

Sharma had placed his bed in a corner from which he could see his livery stable through the window. She had also placed a beat-up rusted tin canister filled with rice husks under his wooden cot, and loosened the strings of the cot right under his back where his bony hips were, so that he could relieve himself, because he was not able to walk. And he was so weak that he couldn't even brush away fruit flies that entered through the drooping lips of his open mouth and nostrils and sit on his eyelids where eyelashes used to be.

Sometimes, he would sit raised up against a pillow or rolled quilts behind his back, and he would lie there for so long that his perspiration gathered in small puddles in those triangular pits above his collarbones.

Sometimes, either coming back from school or in the evening, young Ali Gohar would come and sit beside Fakeer's bed. Just by looking at his grandson, life would silently rush in Fakeer's eyes, like high tide.

And when Ali Gohar would to ask, *"Tokhy cha thyo aa?"*—*what happened to you?*

Fakeer would reply, "nothing; I'm completely fine," knowing that he was dying, but not wanting to disappoint his grandson.

And then Ali Gohar always used to ask a silly question: *"Maa tokhay pyaro ta ahya na?"*—*Am I dear to you?*

And that would make Fakeer's voice crack, *"Aado saeen aa tu muhnjo"*— *You are dear to me like my fathers are.* And while saying this he would scramble to find a coin that he had kept under his pillow, to give it to Ali Gohar.

One day, Ali Gohar came early from school in the mid-afternoon and saw a young dark-skinned man in saffron robes sitting next to Fakeer's cot. He was reciting some tale, and humming some of it in rhyme. Fakeer's eyes were closed and his pupils were running around at breakneck speed under his calmly shut eyelids, like his own eyes feverishly wanted to find Fakeer himself in those rhyming tales, as he listened to this man in saffron robes.

Fakeer was gently moving his head in such a fashion as if to say he was agreeing with every single word the man was saying. When the man stopped, Fakeer gathered every single coin there was under his pillow and gave it to young man in saffron robes, and the man left. Fakeer's eyes were still closed when Ali Gohar asked his silly question, *"Maa tokhay pyaro ta ahya na?"*

Fakeer opened his eyes but didn't reply, just kept looking at him. Ali Gohar looked back at him for a few moments, and saw the distorting glaze of Fakeer's melting pupils bulging and gathering on his lower eyelids. Fakeer was swallowing because he was too proud to cry, and who else could have known that better than his own tears, who didn't give in, balancing themselves like tightrope walkers and somehow managed to stay on his eyelids until Ali Gohar walked away.

But death laid siege upon Fakeer's entire body. Life was reduced to his eyes only, which he would blink slowly, like a vintage blinking doll, taking all the time in the world, and eventually one day he stopped doing that also.

Sharma Khatoon was the person who found him. And she spoke to herself in her heart, saying, *"Naith piyalo pee-tuie."*—*Finally, you finished drinking your bowl.*

Fakeer was buried in the graveyard behind the dry pond, though he had always said he wanted to be buried at Mehann-jee-khaa-hee; who knows why that wish of his was not fulfilled. According to the decision of wise elders of family, he was buried in Qamber. Probably, they thought, *who is going to walk six miles to visit his graveside?* Hardly ten or fifteen people walked with his funeral procession. The whole thing wrapped up in three hours.

On sixth day after his burial, Sharma Khatoon and couple of Fakeer's other elder in-laws sat together and divided his wealth into three equal shares: one for Alam, one for Saleh, and one for Sharma Khatoon. Every piece of gold or silver jewellery was sold and converted into hard cash. Alam wasted part of his share of inheritance on an ornamental axe-head with real precious gems on its silver gilded grip, but he used the rest of the money to build a two-room house.

Saleh thought that an hourly bicycle-rental business was what he wanted to do. He had seen similar things thrive in Sukkur and Larkano, but no one had yet opened one in Qamber. So he used his cash to buy fifteen brand-new 'Humber gents roaster sports 24 inch frame bicycles' and five medium-size bicycles for young kids, and his business got started. Those bikes arrived in wooden crates via train from Karachi.

Saleh's friend, a bicycle mechanic who was the main inspiration behind this venture, assembled them. All came with small leather saddlebags hanging behind the seat and a light set of chain-case and wavy sport handlebars. Right under the handlebars each bike had a brass head badge which read, "By appointment to the late King George VI."

But Qamber was a small town surrounded by hundreds of small and tiny villages in all directions. Most people travelled on foot in Qamber, though a few of them had their own bicycles. Most of his customers were villagers. Initially, it worked, but after a few months he was left with only five medium size bicycles.

The large bicycles got stolen—people rented but never returned them. Some of them broke. And that was it. He closed that business and went back to his movie projection operator job. Over the years he would occasionally see some stranger riding one of his Humbers through Qamber, and instead of getting angry he would just smile.

Sharma did nothing with her money for five years. Then one day she announced that she was going on Hajj, the holy pilgrimage. The Hajj was a do or die affair back then. It used to take eight or nine months for a person to go and perform Hajj and come back: no passport, no visa, no ships or airplanes. You had to walk with a caravan, or if you were rich you could pay to ride on camel- or horseback, but people usually walked.

Many of them died of illness or exposure to elements either going there or coming back. Sharma was in her fifties and a tiny lady, but her confidence was immense. She made always talked seriously, looking directly into other people's eyes, without even blinking much.

She started making preparations for her journey, giving away her valuable possessions to those she thought were worthy of keeping them. Along with the few things that she was carrying with her, she kept three things that belonged to Fakeer. One was his 'kishtuo'—the kashkul bowl from his begging years.

Every Darvaish carries one, and to some those bowls are magical. Legend has it that once a Darvaish came into courts of an emperor, a king of kings, and asked him if he could fill the bowl. The king gave the beggar a disgusted look and said to his courtiers, "Look what this filthy beggar is asking of an emperor like me? To fill this little bowl!"

He replied to beggar, with the arrogance of gods, "yes." But the bowl was a magical bowl. Hundreds and thousands and millions were poured into it, but they could not fill it. It always remained half empty, its mouth wide open to be filled. When the emperor began to feel poor in filling the bowl, he said, "The bowl is magic. It has swallowed my treasures, and it is empty still."

The Darvaish answered, "Your highness, you king of kings, even if the whole world's treasure was put into it, it would still remain empty. Do you want to know what this bowl, this kashkul is? It's the want, the desire of men."

Fakeer's kishtuo, however, was an ordinary beggar's bowl. It could be filled with very little and possessed no magic.

The second thing that she took with her was Fakeer's *bairaagiin*, his "rod of dispassion." This simple metal rod was believed to protect its carrier from the influence of strong emotions, keeping him rational and impartial.

The third of Fakeer's possessions that she took with her was his *kantho,* the beaded necklace whose beads and stones he had been collecting for his entire adult life. That necklace was made up of nineteen objects, and in the centre there was a pendant of Yemeni aqeeq mounted in silver braces. All the other stones and beads were directly threaded onto the waxed string. It took him his lifetime to collect those mere nineteen beads and stones. Some of them were from *Chandi'ya jo Daro*, the ruined dunes of a lost civilisation close to Qamber.

For years, every monsoon and whenever it rained hard, he used to go to those ruins and wander around for days in search of a single bead or stone. Sufis wear these kantha because of Kabir Panth,[57] though it evolved way back as a symbol of Shiva, '*Satya-Purush*', the supreme lord who dwells within and who is above all else. The length of the kantho is supposed to make it level with the wearer's heart, the place in which God is said to reside.

Having those three things of Fakeer and a few other belongings, she left for the Hajj amidst hugs and kisses and tears. Months passed, and the caravan she had left with came back, bringing with it whoever survived. But she was not with them. They said she had run out of money, but that she had wanted to go and see the Karbala and other holy sites, especially shrine of Mosa-Ali-Raza, which she always called Mosa-Raza. So, they said, they had left her in Basrah on their way back.

After a few more months, the next caravan of pilgrims left, and there was no news of her. Everyone presumed she had died. But then, one day, against all odds, she reappeared—all by herself and bringing unbelievable stories, which made her uncomfortable to tell. made her uncomfortable to tell.

One night, many days and months after she came back, she started murmuring to her granddaughter Shamshad, whose real name was Shams-un-Nisa, and who used to sleep alongside her. Sharma started telling her story with a sense of immense emptiness.

"That journey was full of suffering no doubt, but with an immense hope and happiness that we would see the *Kabatullah*, the house of Allah," she said. "Though Mehboob saeen is in heart of every granule of sand, they say." That

---

[57] *Kabir Panth:* 'Path of Kabir', a religious community based on the teachings of the mystic Kabir.

was her mildly sophisticated way of saying that she felt presence of Mehboob Saeen much more right here in that dingy small room at the back of her home every morning; with her Bengali parrot saying repeatedly "*Haqq Pak Allah.*"

In other words, she wanted to express that after the arduous journey to the house of God, she had expected to find something in the Kaaba that might evoke a sense of magic or uniqueness. But upon arriving, it felt as ordinary as the dingy storeroom in her home. But after reaching there it was as ordinary as her home's dingy storeroom. But she didn't dare to say those real, almost existentialist observations to her young granddaughter.

Young Shamshad acknowledged her philosophical interpretation of the Divine by replying with a weak and reluctant, "yes." But she was a child, after all, so she was not interested in that prelude; she wanted to know the adventure of Sharma's journey.

"It began with unendingly long walks in scorching heat, and the monotonous sounds of the camel's bell, and whirls of fine sand pinching into your face like pricks of small needles. There were the miserably painful moaning sounds of mother camels who had twisted their necks back to find their cubs and then been beaten pitilessly by the caravan grooms and *their* drivers who wanted them to stay put and look straight."

"The camels in the caravan walked in a line like a train, all linked together with rope, dragging their feet. In the day, I use to take nap in the shadow of a sitting camel. They walk all night long between two resting spots, hundreds of miles apart. Those resting spots were nothing but a well in the middle of nowhere. Everyone filled their sheep stomach water-bottles with pungent and deplorably bitter water, and coming from a dry sheep's stomach makes it even more distasteful. We wore the same clothes for days, soaked in perspiration and dust. Day after day turned them into parchment, and our hair become one thick log hanging from our head."

She paused for a bit, but her granddaughter shook her quietly so that she would resume. "Only dried meat to eat and brackish water to drink. Occasionally they would give us a few pieces of dates, which tasted so sweet in comparison. There was a bare-shouldered and half-naked young camel driver boy who kept saying in his language, 'there is going to be a huge dune, in front of which this caravan looks like salt granules, and it will move across horizon in front of your eyes.'"

"Well, that never happened. We came out of the desert into a valley of big sharp-edged orangish-red rocks, which abruptly changed into a brown mountain looking like burned copper. Slowly the caravan came to a flat plateau of red stuff like ash surrounded by distant high cliffs; the fast winds caused those cliffs to speak in tongues. It was…" After a pause, she snored a tiny snore, and Shamshad nudged her again gently.

She woke up and said, "It was long." Then she patted Shamshad on her shoulder in half sleep, and said, "There is a lifetime waiting for me to tell you the rest of story. Go to sleep now." And she carried on with her tiny snores.

Story II: Alam

Chapter 1
Dharamsala

His heart was pounding. He could feel his throbbing heartbeat in his ears. His face turned copper hot. He was perspiring as he ran to the train station and boarded a train that was about to leave; it didn't matter where it was going. Slowly the train started moving into a new epoch, twelve years that were to influence his entire life.

Soon, the train had caught her speed, and he was looking out through tearful eyes to the distant trees and mud houses as they drifted back. He had no idea of the Laws of Motion, imagining that those trees were in motion and he was at rest, even though the train was taking him away from his whole world; and a frail whistle of the kerosene engine, which he had not even noticed, kept sounding.

Alam was in the train for hours; night was about to fall. Gradually the ticket collector was getting closer to him.

There were three Rishi Bhiksu sitting on the floor and reciting Vedic hymns. He moved closer to them, prompting one of them to ask, "Are you lost, child?"

He did not reply, rather kept staring at him. After a while, he moved through to the next car by following a vendor across the planks that spanned the two bogies. This whole passenger car was for women and children, and he felt a little more comfortable there.

He sat down, and soon a woman asked him, "Where is your mother?"

"I'm alone," he replied.

She placed her right thumb under her chin and said, "*Aaiee Ghoraa,*"—*I'll be darned*—and then asked him to sit closer to her. She gave him some food to eat. It was dark, apart from the flickering light of those tiny bulbs caged within iron bars, like eight segments of a peeled orange.

He slept a while, was awakened by a police constable nudging him with his long bamboo stick. He got frightened and shrugged his shoulders to hide his head, unsuccessfully. But he then realised that train was completely empty and not moving.

The policeman said, "What are you doing here, and who you are with?"

He replied truthfully but in a fearful voice, "I'm alone," thinking that this policeman was going to help him.

"What do you mean, you're alone? Where are your relatives?"

In a firm voice, Alam again said the same, "I'm alone," which he should have not said. All of sudden the whole car shook violently with a jolt and started moving and the policeman lost his step for a while. The policeman said 'humm' and looked around into completely empty train car, caressing his cheeks vulgarly. He put his bamboo stick aside and sat down right next to Alam, who could smell his sour breath blowing into his face. Fear clenched him completely; he was paralysed. The train had left this station now but had not yet reached full speed.

The policeman undid the fly of his khaki uniform pants with one hand, and with the other he grabbed Alam's small, childish hand and force it into his open fly—but then there was this another sudden shakeup of the train—probably it was shifting or shunting of railroad tracks, and in that fraction of a second he escaped, breaking himself loose from the policeman and running towards the door. Policeman lunged after him. The train had just left the platform and was picking up speed. Alam looked back at the policeman who was about to grab his collar, and he jumped from the moving train!

The train had not yet reached full speed. She was still moving slowly, just pretending to be fast, but her sheer volume and her hard and brittle wheels were forced to turn on cast iron rail tracks where making loud but muffled noise, as if those tracks and wheels were forcing sound to go through a meat grinder.

Alam's fall was perhaps not as perilous as it seemed to be, amidst that crushing noise, but still he got hurt very badly, and he passed out where he landed. When he regained consciousness and opened his eyes, he found himself under a low hanging tree branch near some fields.

It was already dusk, and the setting sun in his face was making everything look dark. He could still see shredded clouds in fiery amber colours; they looked like a pheasant's wing. He said to himself *titarkhararee*,[58]—that's what mackerel sunset clouds are called in Sindhi—but he couldn't think any more about it

---

[58] *Titarkhararee*: a scratched pheasant's wing.

because of the pain. He tried to crawl out of there, scared to remember what had happened. Those titarkhararee skies were of little comfort because he had seem them numerous times in Qamber, at home lying down on a cot in courtyard or from the rooftop of their house or from the gaps of the thinly gathered straw canopies of his father's livery stables.

But then he heard the sound of barking dogs, and started walking instinctively toward the barking. Shehoon came into his mind, and he wanted to bundle himself in the security of those barks as if they were Shehoon's. He ended up at a group of mud homes in the middle of fields.

The people who lived in those mud homes took him in for a few days and took good care of him. He came out of his shock and started making plans to go somewhere else. He learned how to hop trains and duck and dodge the ticket collector, and how to protect himself from perverted policemen. He found himself in Delhi with no money and no food for few days, but still he was reluctant to beg.

Wondering around in that city he saw a *naan wai,*[59] and the cook was baking naan in an underground clay oven. He was selling and keeping the good ones and throwing the few over-baked ones aside. Alam waited till very late, and when they had closed the shop and left for the day, he picked through those charred naans and scratched burned baked lumps of dough and ate their few good parts and drank water on top. And he rested in a kind of half-awake state on a long sagging bench made up of raw unfinished hard wood, parts of which had become so fine and glazed by mere friction over time, like someone had put multiple layers of clear lacquer on it.

When he woke up from that half-awake sleep, it was still very early morning. He started walking aimlessly and saw a big red brick mosque with three white domes, with a pyramid of stairs going up into it. He sat on the stairs for a while. The day had grown brighter now. A crowd of people had started to gather nearby, so he walked closer.

There were wooded barricades around a park, and in its centre there was a long hanging silky cloth draped to cover a black metallic figure, but winds were irreverent, constantly blowing aside the drapery to reveal a fat soldier holding a crown on the right side of his lap, mounted on a beautiful horse. This statue was already placed on a tall stone pedestal, waiting for its ceremonial inauguration.

---

[59] Naan wai: a street-side bread shop.

The festival lasted all day. There was a parade, and later someone in a red military uniform covered in golden medals and ribbons came forward and pulled a rope in a ceremonial fashion, while several others did the real work of pulling those long hanging flags to reveal the statue. Someone said, *there is the king!* But Alam did not grasp who that king was. Was it one of the men in red military uniform that pulled the rope, or the statue of fat soldier sitting on horse?

The day ended, evening turned dark, and little by little the crowd dispersed. He was again wandering on the street around that statue when two police constables spotted him and one of them asked what he was doing here. Alam told them that he had nowhere to go and that he was alone. And so they took him to the *dharamsala*.[60]

The people of the dharamsala took him to be a homeless child who had perhaps come to be their disciple. A middle-aged man wearing a white dhoti, with a shaved head and bare shoulders, placed his hand upon Alam's head in a gesture of deep humanity. Alam looked up to his face, which bore no expression at all, rather it gave a numb look like he had seen all and had come to know that there is nothing but sorrow.

The man asked him to follow, and they kept walking down the long veranda, alongside the central courtyard of this old building. The veranda culminated in a room with several large cooking pans. The man showed him where to wash his hands and asked him to sit, and then gave him white rice topped with lentils. Once he finished eating, the man took him into a room where several other kids were sleeping on the ground, and pointed to a place for him to lie down and rest.

He curled into a foetal position on a *taddo*.[61] He was so young that he couldn't even identify exhaustion. His lower legs and shoulders were aching, but he couldn't recognise this as a sign of being extremely tired. Sleep engulfed him; he had no choice. Everything turned grey. He smiled and the left corner of his lip was twitching.

He's in a murky dark street, littered with dry black mud on both sides that open sewer drains had dumped out for years. In the distance, he sees a beggar wearing black robes and looking at him with cunning half-closed eyes, which seem to tell him, *if you come close to me I will take you*. And suddenly he finds

---

[60] *Dharamsala*: literally a religious sanctuary, dharamsalas function as resting places and lodges for pilgrims and other religious travelers, as well as orphanages.

[61] *Taddo*: a mat made of strands of dried date leaves.

himself very close to this beggar, who extends his left arm and drags him into the darkness of his black robe, and he can't breathe.

With his mouth wide open, he woke up, inhaling with a cracking cry.

Chapter 2
Cosmogonic Hymns

He found himself surrounded by a number of shaved-headed boys looking at him. One of them said, "*Ka ray ghabarlas ka?*"—*Hey, you got scared*. He didn't answer; he was still trying to catch his breath.

The same man from the last evening reappeared and asked him to follow. They walked past the same long veranda, but it had a different atmosphere now: lots of different noises of children talking and giggling, finches and doves singing on their own and making those familiar mourning bird sounds.

The adjacent courtyard looked very big now. It had two huge banyan trees with roots hanging from their branches, and there was a small tree with several white flowers, and while he was spinning his head to get acclimatised with this place and looking at the black streaks where the walls were drenched with dead algae, while he still taking all in, they ended up in a room where an old man in saffron robes was sitting with both legs crossed, his hands joined together in his lap and eyes closed, his neck pulled upward extending his chin a little.

He realised that this old man was praying. The other man from last night placed his index finger on his lips while looking at Alam, meaning he should sit quietly. After a while, the old man in saffron robes opened his eyes and said, "Dharma.*"

And the man sitting with him replied, "Maharaj, this is the child who came last night, the one I told you about earlier."

They kept Alam in that dharamsala, and the monotony began. They shaved his head like all the others. He recited along with those tedious litanies of holy words, again and again. Alam told them his name, and they had probably figured out that he was a Muslim, but no one there asked him to follow the faith they were practicing. But it was after all a Hindu monastery, so they instructed him within the context that they knew.

He would live his childhood there, and see the naivety of life, the cruelty of time and nerves, and come to know more than what you are supposed to know. In his naivety he learned by heart beautiful rhyming hymns like 'Shiva is truth, and truth is beautiful'. He would sing these, every morning in the dharamsala's quadrangle, cloistered with two big trees and one smaller one.

Sometimes, he got to sit under that smaller tree during in morning prayers and watch its soft velvety flowers falling on the ground. The blossoms were yellow on the inside and they had a tingling and sinister potency in their fragrance, a blend of smooth earthy lilac and balsamic and spicy clove. To Alam it was simply a pleasant aura, and he did not need to know that the flower was called *champa*.

And he would experience the cruelty of time, when in the middle of the night some of the bigger teenage boys would climb on top of the younger boys' mats, and he could only hear muffled slit tearing noises, which were the voices of the younger boys. Scared to death, he awaited his turn every night, yet somehow he did manage to fall asleep each time.

Alam would learn *Atma-Budha,* the arcane knowledge of self, which circles around *Parmatma,* a constant, which is the essence of Shiva himself. It forms a cycle beginning with birth, the formation of organs, the feeling of existence; and from existence comes the devil of devils, the I, the ego, with its steep falls and depressions. And he learned about actions and their reactions in the form of *karma*, competition between desire and selflessness, worrying for nothing, ageing and ignoring death and disease, but ultimately dying of illness and again starting from birth. He would learn all this through long and painful repetitions and loud recitations of those holy words.

Adolescence was abrasive for him as it is for everyone. In the early part of his youth, he travelled with Yogi Maharajas to other ashrams of Banaras, and roamed around the Gangetic north learning the traditional holistic Vedas, and there on the banks of Ganges in Banaras he learned the Gayatri Mantra by heart, which is named after goddess Gayatri. It is believed that the Gayatri Mantra is one of most powerful and oldest human invocations there is. If you learn it by heart and cuddle it in your mind, it's a shepherd of happiness and brings herds of joy to your soul. So Alam use to sits behind his gurus and say:

"Aum
Bhuh Bhuvah Svah
Tat Savitur Varenyam."[62]

And in all this divinity and letting the light come into dark corners of his heart, he somehow developed an interest in photography, which has nothing to do with dharamsalas and ashrams.

A few years passed as he circling from one dharamsala to another, from one city to another, Delhi and Banaras and others along the Gangetic paths. It was in Delhi that he passed through the gate of adolescence.

He was still doing the same rituals, repeating them in same order, along with his fellows. Every morning before sunrise he went to the banks of the river Yamuna with the others. They would lower themselves into the river up to their waists and pray to the rising sun, singing the Gayatri Mantra while continuously filling their palms with the blessed muddy waters of the Yamuna, raising their palms to eye level, and then releasing the water back into the river, gazing all the while into the ever-soothing rising sun, which would melt the darkness of night.

The holistic teachers taught that the Vedas, which were Holy Scriptures, in some places said that the divine force gained its status, or even created the entire universe, through the power of its inner heat, called *tapas,* acquired through the rigorous practice of physical and spiritual self-discipline and mortification of the body. The term 'tapas' derives from a Sanskrit root meaning to heat up or burn, and it refers to any one of a variety of ascetic methods for achieving religious power.

In the Rig Veda, Indra is said to have achieved his divine place through the practice of asceticism and the generation of this powerful 'heat'. Elsewhere in that ancient work there are cosmogonic hymns that attribute the origins of the universe to the Primal One who creates by 'igniting ascetic heat'. The metaphysical qualities of both truth and order are said to have derived from ascetic heat, and the ancient Indian *rishis*[63] who had supernatural insight and could see visions of the future also were supposed to have achieved their powers through tapas.

---

[62] *Gayatri Mantra* ('*Aum…varenyam*'): Sanskrit: "O divine mother, our hearts are filled to the brim with darkness. Please make this darkness, distant from us and foster us with your divine illumination."

[63] *Rishi*: a sage or saint in the Hindu tradition.

This mystic philosophy was being chiselled onto Alam's impressionable mind, the waves of Yamuna kept floating just as time did, and after a few years he had mastered the Vedic scriptures and could recite the Gayatri Mantra by heart.

She was bathing in Yamuna, a short distance from their morning ritual site, and from behind the wild shrubs he saw her delightful womanliness. Her wet sari all but revealed her round and full breasts, which a sari should not, and her beauty rose with twists and turns from the Yamuna like fragrance rises from a flower. And there was a distant voice creating a soul-drenching *alaap*[64] and singing *bhairavi*,[65] as if giving permission to the sun to rise, and time was standing still, wrapped in the soft morning dew, and all this was with him, waiting for her to pass. He kept thinking about her and then trying to push those thoughts away by repeating cosmogonic hymns in his heart. But those holy anthems were ineffective when it came to banishing that wet sari from his mind as he eagerly waited for the next morning.

Somehow it took an eternity for that next morning to arrive. He tried to hurry his steps, but the rest of the devotees were keeping him slow. Dawn had not yet broken as they finally reached the banks of the Yamuna. They started the daily ritual. With the others, he lowered himself in the same blessed waters of Yamuna and kept reciting the empty phonetic shapes of the Holy Scriptures, only waiting to see her again.

The ever-warming sun rose like it has always done and will do forever, and he kept checking for her in that part of distant the river bank from corner of his eye. With the ritual completed, everyone started back toward the ashram. He waited until the last moment to see her again, but she did not appear. The next day he did the same, and the day after that, and days turned into weeks but he never saw her again. But she had ignited that spark in his heart, which resonates in his groin too, and he stepped into adolescence.

He started feeling this analogous dilemma inside himself, and he could not acclimatise to the parallel yet different mechanics of mind. He was being trained to tame the wild selfish instincts of desire with the heavy whipping from a righteous and selfless conscience. And his fragile teenage mind boggled with this universal complexity of good and evil.

---

[64] *Alaap*: The unmetered melodic improvisation that forms the prologue to a raga.
[65] *Bhairavi*: a raga for the morning.

And one day a Swami arrived, whose forehead was marked with three fat parallel lines of ash, and who wore heavy rings in both ears which always seemed like they were about to slit both of his ear lobes. He had an unmanageable bundle of hairs on his head, and his age seemed to have stopped somewhere along the way, and he looked neither young nor old. He had given up whatever he used to do and had no money and no worldly possessions. He had done this because money couldn't buy God, and he wanted to see God. So he had found a guru to teach him the path to enlightenment get him to God, and his guru did that! His guru took him to God.

That was a long time ago. Now, as a guru himself and a master of yoga Vida, Swami was taking his own disciples to meet God. And he came to Alam's dharamsala from Banaras, carrying a cloth sling bag.

Alam was sitting in the back of the group, far across the room from Swami Jee, but he was watching him intently while he did his yoga practices.

Swami Jee opened his eyes and looked directly at Alam, and his gaze passed through him an infinite number of times in that one fraction of a fragment of mathematical time. And Swami Jee said to him, "What's in your mind? Ask."

And joined his hands together with utter humbleness before replying, "Maharaj, I have learned that the meaning of 'vida' is knowledge, but what could the meaning of 'yoga' be?"

Then he sat still, holding his hands together and waiting for an answer from the wise one. After a long, gentle exhale, Swami Jee said, "The meaning of yoga is!"

Then he stopped and said, "Humm."

Then again he started to explain, "The meaning of yoga…"

He stopped again for a split second, but then started speaking as if he had just found the word. "Is not cheap, nor is it extravagant or costly. Yoga is the concept of oneness. It's to bring you out of yourself, and to unite you with your true being. It arises from the word *yuj*, which means unite. And it can simultaneously connect the beliefs of many and mean something subtly different to someone else."

Then he closed his eyes again and started raising his head up slowly, and undistinguishable minute noises started coming out from his closed thin lips. And he exhaled for some time, and began again:

"The meaning of yoga is that you leave sensation—*samadhi*—which is your body, and learn to perceive with your true mind, where true love is. The meaning of yoga is folded and rolled in layers upon layers, and you keep peeling them off in pursuit of finding something inside, but it's all the same layer after layer. And then you peel open the last layer—and there is nothing there! And then you will realise it's the same as what you already have."

And then Swami Jee stood up and slowly walked away toward his resting area. Alam did not understand what Swami Jee had meant, only barely grasping from Swami Jee's interpretation that probably the meaning of yoga is 'expensive'!

Chapter 3
Roopee for Life

It was the kind of day they called a *rugha*—an almost asphyxiating smoky hot day—in late July. There was not a shred of cloud in the dusty blue skies, whose looming purplish tint close to the horizon gave assurance of the suffocating heat of Northern Sindh. He was walking slowly and slowing even more before he reached home. He was perspiring. A drop of sweat rolled into his eye, which he wiped with the back of his hand. And he saw front door of his house, that very same awkwardly short old double-leaf heavy wooden door of hard *sheesham*,[66] which his father, Fakeer, had purchased from an old junk seller, just because it was made of hard wood.

It was already old then, but now it was almost completely faded to silver-grey from being bare-naked under the hot sun forever. Its right side was still sagging down more than the other, with the same bent central joint panel and cast iron metal straps on both sides trying hard to hold eight squares of rotten wood carving, which were time had gilded smooth to their decimation, and faded almost beyond recognition, so much that no one could say for sure whether it was a carving of Gautam or Ganesh-ji on each square. And there were those hanging rusted chain latches that never used to reach the upper knob, even before he left. Thirteen years had passed.

Alam approached the door full of thoughts of his mother and father and younger brother, Saleh, whom he had presumably killed before he left home.

Saleh was the reason Alam had run away. Once, when they had been playing on the rooftop, Alam accidentally pushed Saleh aside, and Saleh tripped and went tumbling down the long and awkward stairs, banging his head several times. Alam could remember that he had tried to wake Saleh, but he was not

---

[66] *Sheesham*: Indian rosewood.

moving, and a halo of crimson blood was getting bigger and bigger around Saleh's head. And so in his horror, Alam had run away, leaving him there, those thirteen years ago.

He pushed the door open stepped in. His mother was sitting on a khaa-ta, and there was no one else there. He approached her, and she was scrambling herself together, and was trying to find her cheesecloth veil to cover her bare head, and was on the verge of getting angry, but he kept walking towards her. And he said simply, "I'm Alam."

And she leaned her back hard against the wall with a sigh, still sitting on her khaata.

She was still absorbing the shock when his father came in from the veranda. Thinking he was seeing a stranger, he asked firmly, "who are you?"

And his mother replied for him, "He said he is Alam."

"Roopee aa charee!"—*He's an imposter, you silly!*—shouted Fakeer, looking at Sharma and disregarding Alam's claim right away, Then Fakeer looked at Alam and said, *"ninur heethann"*—*go away*—with equal vigour and distaste.

Fakeer went on to say, "People told you that I have wealth, and you've come here to claim it. You are a hoaxer after my money. Now *leave*."

But Sharma was like not listening to a single word her husband was saying; rather she kept looking at Alam, trying hard to find young Alam in him. And she said again, "Who are you?" Like her auditory abilities wanted to perceive it; she wanted to hear it again, from him, that he was Mohammad Alam, her elder son. The one whom she always called *"muhanjo kandhee":* my own who will carry me to my grave on his shoulders.

Sharma had made up her mind, but still there was a commotion because Fakeer wanted to brew his storm in a teacup. So Alam had to leave and had to stay that night at *Hundh-Khatoloo*, a bed-and-breakfast kind of thing. Actually it was only a roadside makeshift bed in the open, under panoramic skies, with no breakfast at all.

After that, there was more melodrama. Some elders got together to try to resolve the dispute. Fakeer was adamant that Alam was an imposter trying to inherit his wealth, and that his real son, the real Alam, was dead; whereas Alam was trying to convince Fakeer and the others that he was who he was. And the melodrama began when Sharma Khatoon, Fakeer's wife and Alam's mother, started telling her story.

She said that their son had been bitten by a horse when he was a few years old. There had been a merchant who used to come to Qamber on his **beloved** horse, and he would leave the horse at Fakeer's livery stable, and their son Alam used to give him grass and water and touch the horse's face, and the horse would caress him back with a loving brush of his horse's face.

But one day that merchant switched horses and brought in a wicked and cunning one to board at the stable. And when Sharma and Fakeer's son approached to this wicked horse and tried to touch his face, the horse started champing; it grabbed Alam and lifted him in its bite and threw him after a few swings.

And before Sharma could finish telling the story, Alam raised his shirt to reveal that scar, which had become little lighter and had moved little higher on his body. The dispute was resolved and the rest was history. But for the rest of his life Fakeer never quite got rid of that looming doubt, and every time he got angry at Alam, he would tell him, "You are not my son, you *roopee*."[67]

His mother approached Mohammad Suemar Khan Rajper, who was chairman of municipal-committee of Qamber, and asked him to give Alam a job. And Mohammad Suemar Khan made him the octroi-tax collector.[68]

His first day on the job was mainly just training, so he was surprised when, at the end of the day, his superior handed him some money, saying, "This is your share." Alam thought this must be something fishy, or maybe bait of some sort, and he refused to take it. Because his salary its self was forty rupees a month, which was a lot of money for a single person in the early 1930s.

---

[67] *Roopee*: impostor.
[68] *Octroi-tax collector:* the octroi tax covered local road tolls and other municipal taxes.

Chapter 4
A Man Who Took It on His Chest

Mohammad Suemar Khan Rajper was a retired deputy collector of the Indian Central Superior Services, a long name and a genuinely privileged designation: in those days it was extremely difficult to rise to such a high administrative position within the tightly packed imperial bureaucracy. At first, his title became a part of his name, and later it became his entire name. That is to say, in the end the only thing anyone called him was *Deputy Sahib*.

He had a crew-cut hairstyle, and round English Berkshire Chase turtle-shell handmade eyeglasses with dirty nose pads. He wore complete three-piece suits, some of them with thick charcoal grey-and-white stripes, with a watch on a gold chain tucked into his waistcoat pocket. Altogether, he had everything you could possibly expect of a retired Indian civil servant, even that damn chicken-pattern tea cosy on his teapot.

And apart from all those things, Mohammad Suemar Khan also had something special. Something that Indian poets had often disparaged a lot—to be honest, they had beaten the crap out of this thing—and that was a heart that was in fact beating beneath his chest, but loved someone he was not supposed to love. How could you trust your disloyal heart, who left you and became the lover of your beloved?

Mohammad Suemar Khan's heart had done that to him, and had fallen in love with a woman who was already married. How he fell in love and where it all happened is irrelevant. It lasted for a few years, and even though he was married and had children, he also fathered two sons out of wedlock with his beloved.

And then, coincidently, Mohammad Suemar Khan's lover become gravely ill. George Bernard Shaw thought coincidences make drama weak, but that's the way life is. She became mortally ill and sent for Mohammad Suemar Khan, and, just before dying, she brought it out into the open in front of all who were present there. And she gave the little hands to her two boys into Mohammad Suemar Khan's hands and said these are your sons.

So goes the legend. And Mohammad Suemar Khan raised those two kids, gave them his name and the best education possible. And Qamber looked on this all this tolerantly. Nobody made a fuss; rather as of today Mohammad Suemar Khan Rajper is known as a great man who took it on his chest.

Alam wrapped up those thirteen years of tapas, of dharamsalas and ashrams and shovels in into his memory dump, never to revisit them again. He simply peeled off those layers of his personality, as once a yogi maharaj had described to him. But instead of finding underneath the same as what he already had, as that yogi had predicted, Alam found a joyously unrestrained heart full of desires for fragrance, flesh and flamboyance.

So his life began anew in his hometown of Qamber. His forty rupee per month pay was more than enough to buy the posh clothing that caught the wandering eyes of the promiscuous women of Qamber—flashy items like his white cheesecloth turban with navy blue and orange chunri tie-dye at the top end. He grew his hair long and rolled it under his turban to make it look bigger.

His snow-white shirts gleamed with gold buttons, which matched his gold chains and the gold tooth that showed when he smiled.[69] Over this, he wore a rough homespun tweed jacket with two cuff buttons of imitation lion nails, which he always claimed were real, combined with a printed silk scarf. And he walked around on swanky all-leather monk-strap shoes with high-built military heels. Most of these items he bought via VP parcel from Bombay.

So Alam's visual aspect was crafted to dazzle. But the elite women of Qamber were also drawn to the more abstract refinements of his personality. His ability to produce translations of Omar-e-Khayam and Kali-Das into simple Sindhi in a single breath, perhaps varying the text slightly to please whichever woman he was romancing at the time. Thus he earned the attention of many women eager to help him quench his thirst.

And there was an aquifer of art inside Alam, the kind of aquifer that people usually don't even know they have within them until one day it finds an outlet and gushes forth.

---

[69] *Gold tooth:* having one's tooth or teeth coated with a layer of gold was (and still is) a cosmetic procedure in some parts of the world. Gold in one's mouth in this context is considered a symbol of wealth.

So, without being directly inspired by any painter—because there were none in Qamber in the first place—he started drawing. Perhaps there was also some inclination to this during his time at the dharamsala—God only knows. But Alam found this spontaneous urge to draw lines, which should make sense, too. Now he wanted his lines to bend and curve and go straight and then make full circles in a form that could be seen as a design. Perhaps he was recalling the contours, curvature, and cleavage of that young woman's body that had risen from the river Yamuna like a fragrance, which he never chanced to see again.

Those designs gave way to crude sketches of his own left hand and toes, which were meant to become finer and finer until those sketches were so real and soft that one would want to touch and hold them. He decided to become an art teacher, and fortunately the exam for that didn't require a high school diploma, so he passed it without any problem. Then that very same Mohammad Suemar Khan Rajper made Alam an art teacher in the municipal school of Qamber.

Chapter 5
The Task of Living in a Synthetic World

While all this was going on, his father's niece and his first cousin, who was also named Sharma Khatoon after his mother, started coming to their house frequently. Her husband Allah-Dino had recently died, and Alam's father, Fakeer Sher Muhammad, was helping her financially to fight a dispute in court with her in-laws, who wanted to take custody of her three elder daughters who were of age.

According to Fakeer's niece, her husband had been estranged from his extended family because they had deceived him by initially agreeing but later denying him a marital arrangement. He had married her nonetheless, and they had five daughters together. While he was alive, he kept a distance from his relatives and had only a shallow relationship with them. They keep asking him for his two elder daughters' hands for their sons, but he kept refusing. He was an old man and became ill, and in those days if an older person fell seriously ill, it was generally assumed that he would die.

So those same relatives started coming to see him quite frequently. He told his elder daughter, Dhayani,[70] "As long as I have a head on my shoulders, no one dare harm you. But after my death they will come like hyenas."

And Dhayani maintained a reassuring face, hiding her mortal fear of his death, and replied to her father as if he were not Allah-Dino but Zeus: "You are going to recover and live, and everything is going to be fine."

He looked at her with smiling eyes, and she squeezed his shoulder with both her hands, and there was a sense of assurance that has no accordance with the truth that he is dying. But then his cough filled the room and was bouncing back and forth against the mud walls. During the night it kept progressing and his

---

[70] *Dhayani*: the name means, "one who keeps her flock together."

condition worsened. And she saw him drifting slowly. First he stopped responding to her, and then his eyes rolled back. Time kept ticking, and finally his chest collapsed and he exhaled his last breath, and that was it. She had to start her Sisyphean task of living in a synthetic world, as a fatherless girl in early twentieth century Sindh, where women were treated as a commodity. She had to lookout for herself and her four young sisters and a grieving mother in a society dominated by men.

A few of Dhayani's paternal relatives were pushing her mother to give them two of her elder daughters, but she was adamant to follow her husband's will, and refused. Some well-wishing women told her that her in-laws were planning to sneak in while she was sleeping to get her thumb impression on a legal document saying that she agreed to give them these two daughters along with whatever little land her husband left to them. So Sharma stopped sleeping at night, and in daytime, during whatever distressful rest could get, she asked her daughters not to leave her side.

In Muslim culture, a grieving widow must stay in her late husband's home for a period of forty days after his death, literally confining herself to a room, and not come in contact with any male to exclude any potential pregnancy. So Sharma had to stay there for that period. And this gave her and her daughters the chance to up a plan to escape to her maternal uncle's town, some three miles away. When the forty days had passed, they went to pay respect to Allah-Dino's gravesite, and from there they walked onward to her uncle's place.

Eventually, the scheming in-laws found out where they had gone and came to take them back. And that's where legalities came into the picture. First, there was a local traditional dispute settlement via negotiations of the communal elder, which went in favour of the in-laws. In Dhayani's words, that decision was composed by her wicked relatives and narrated by communal elders, who had treated her and her sisters like livestock, giving them away without even asking their will. So they did not accept that decision and came to Fakeer to help them to get justice from the court of law.

And a period of legal dispute started in the Indian penal session Court of Sukkur-Larkano. They would come every few months and stay for a few days with them, and Fakeer would go to court with them for the hearings. Fakeer would leave very early so that he could walk the whole distance, twenty-three kilometres, because he was afraid of riding the train.

Ultimately, on a summary judgment day, the judge called Dhayani to the stand and to give her statement to the court, and her wicked relatives were expecting that a bereaved young woman like her would fall apart in front of their attorney's cross examination. But she did not; rather she stood her ground and accused the plaintiffs of embezzling her dead father's land and forcing her and her younger sister to marry against their will. The plaintiff's attorney reminded her of her oath to make her nervous and frightened, and then said, "You were and are married to this man." And he pointed a finger toward one of her wicked relatives and then forced her to answer.

"No I'm not," she replied in a weak and anxious voice. Then the attorney tried another tactic to confuse her, saying, "Both your ears are pierced, which proves that you are a married woman."

And she gathered all her strength to reply, "In our village, they pierce every new-born girl's ears on the sixth day after her birth. But they only pierce the nose when a girl becomes engaged." Then she collapsed in the courtroom, and her mother and sisters took her out to the veranda and tried to revive her by rubbing her palms and patting her cheeks.

The honourable judge gave his decision in their favour, concluding that Dhayani and her sister were not married to anyone, and that the court found no evidence of any prior marriages or any prior engagement. And because the court found Dhayani to be an adult, it gave her mother full custody of her younger sisters.

And furthermore, the court asked her paternal relatives to step back and not interfere in their lives, and gave Dhayani and her mother ownership rights of her father's small piece of land. But her father's wicked relatives had already taken over that land, and they didn't want to give it up. Dhayani and her mother couldn't summon the will to wage another fight, so they let it go.

So they came back to Qamber after winning the lawsuit. Fakeer's niece thanked him profusely for his help. But then she wanted to tell him something else, and her voice fell to a choking whisper, as if what she was about to say would let all hell break loose. And she told him that her brother, her real brother, who had helped her all along to go through these difficult time, now had a change of heart, and wanted to marry Dhayani to the local landlord in his town, and that he had probably already taken money from that landlord.

So she wanted Fakeer to take Dhayani for his son Alam. And Fakeer agreed to it, and he was glad for this new knot tied in a long string of old relationships.

And Fakeer's wife Sharma Khatoon was happy as well, or at least went along with this tying of the knot. This was in part because her own sister had deceived her previously by agreeing to give her daughter Gulab Khatoon's hand to Alam, and she had taken lots of money from Sharma and Fakeer, but then turned around and had Gulab Khatoon married to someone else.

Alam's mother told him that evening about his wedding with Dhayani. Alam's mother Sharma and her niece, who was Sharma Khatoon too, and was named after her, were sitting on a kha-taa in the middle of huge courtyard of their home.

Hearing this, Alam and was more interested in looking at Dhayani's expression, who was half hiding behind one of the dry mud pillars that supported the straw-top porch of their house. He could see three quarters of her face, and her stunning eyes, which was blinking slowly, as if her eyelids had all the time in the world to do that; and he could see half of her long joined eyebrows, and that flawless young skin of her cheeks, and several gold earrings in that lobe of her ear. She was playing with her *choti*,[71] into which were woven colourful bands ornamented with small silver bells.

She looked extremely pretty. The bells in her braided hair were chiming lightly. She was about to enter the love story of her life, which would later become a story without love, and everyday life would then become a miserable life, and later turn into a pile of memories she won't even want to remember.

---

[71] *Choti*: an ornamental cloth braid worn in the hair.

Chapter 6
Do Not Move or Blink

I never learned how to write.

Alam got an old beat-up minute-camera from Sukkur and started taking photographs in the streets and markets of Qamber. The camera was a square wooden box on three legs, joined together with tiny brass hinges on all sides. Its small window in the back was covered with a black hanging sleeve, which Alam always called the '*jorabo*'—the sock. And in the front it had a crystal covered with complex crescent brass rings, with all sorts of gauge lines between numbers, and pins and tiny spring clutches, all holding that convex crystal glass in the centre, which he called a lens.

With this blackish mahogany box on its tripod, and a black screen as a backdrop, he started making black and white postcard portraits. He would hang his black screen on any crumbling wall in the busy streets. He became Qamber's first street photographer.

A person had to sit stock-still on a box-stool looking into that crystal ball that lens, in order to have a portrait taken. All the while Alam would keep ducking behind that black box under a thick veil of black textured canvas, blindly adjusting the focus by moving lens on a rusty track back and forth, while looking at an upside-down image on a milky glass inside camera. And once he had finished focusing, he put the lid back on lens and loaded the negative paper.

He would keep ducking beneath a black cloth to ensure that the frame is up to the mark. Then he would move to the front and artfully remove that dirty cardboard lens-cover for a fraction of a second to capture the image. But before removing that dirty cardboard lid from lens he always barked firm and grumpy orders at his patrons: *pull your neck up, and do not move or blink your eyes or else I'll charge you twice.* Most of his subjects held their breath, and their pictures showed serious, grim-faced persons with protruding eyeballs ready to pop out.

There was a tiny inbuilt dark room at the back of the box, where he would dip the photographic paper in solution and hypo, the chemicals that would develop and fix the negative. The moment he saw those craned necks and protruding eyes on the negatives, he would always say to himself "*fuss class*," by which he meant first-class or perfect.

Then again the whole process was repeated to get a positive. In front of the same lens, he would place a wooden arm with a ledge, where that negative would be placed to get a positive copy. There were three size options for customers: a quarter size, a half size and a full size, which was postcard size.

Sometimes, Alam would forget to put lid back on the lens, and that lens would mesmerise whole world, dazzling with its fish-eye crystal ball. The entire sky with every single piece of cloud fit comfortably into its upper half, while the lower half held everything else: mud walls of cross-street buildings with canopies of all different colours peeping from under from purplish blue film like smudges of fingerprints.

He started coming up with new options. By manipulating the lens and altering the filters, he could take 16 very small photos all on the same card. Those became very popular when one of his customers got those stamp size photos and mounted them on cufflinks and on rings and on locket pendants.

He would bring this mobile Photoshop of his to different locations at different parts of the day. It was a lucrative business. He was charging a quarter for a small photo, half a rupee for the half-card size, and a whole rupee for the postcard size. On a good day, he was making 8 to 10 rupees. But his liabilities had mounted over the five years since his marriage. He already had four kids to support, plus his flamboyant nature compelled him to spend money gifts for various women.

Among them was that maternal cousin who had once been engaged to him but then got married to someone else. Nonetheless he carried on his affair with her, as well as with her brother's wife.

He was not just flirting with them. These were full-blown adulterous extra-marital sexual relationships, with everything rolled together: the tears of Dhayani, the moaning sounds of other women, mixed with the heavy breathing of Alam in the very late-night or early-morning hours. Grim faces with arguments about nothing.

Sometimes, Dhayani would catch them, hearing these noises in the middle of the day coming from that dark dungeon storeroom of their house. And she would wait, and wait, and wait outside that storeroom for them to finish, and after Alam would leave, looking at her shamelessly, she would enter the room and find one of those women rushing to pull up her *salwar*, or tying her *aagathou* with both hands, holding the long front part of their *kameez*[72] tucked up under her chin.

But Alam had already dipped his finger into that honeypot. He kept his extramarital relationship with Gulab Khatoon, and he carried on with her sister-in-law at the same time. They would come and stay at their house for months on end. Alam also fathered an autistic daughter from Gulab's sister-in-law. That autistic girl lived till the age of fourteen, and the only thing she accomplished in her short life was singing the wedding songs of Ali Gohar. She died as pure as the name of God itself.

It was daybreak. Slowly, a blend of soft aurora combined with the aerial sounds of birds and the birdlike whistle of a distant kerosene engine started filling the atmosphere. But she wasn't even noticing all that, or maybe it was just a nuisance for her. Anyway, she stuck to her prayer and kept saying, "*Haq pak Allah; haq pak Allah.*"[73] And her Bengali parrot, whose cage she was holding, repeated after her: "Haq pak Allah; haq pak Allah."

That's how she would pray, five times a day. She was illiterate and had no idea how to read and write her own Sindhi, let alone how to pronounce the Arabic verses of the Qur'an. But she believed in her heart that 'haq pak Allah' was the basic message of the Qur'an, repeated again and again in different ways. And what difference did it make? It was a mutual understanding between her and her God.

There was no window in that smallest room of Fakeer's home, and there was a reason for that, too. He kept his money in that room. Rather, he kept his money in small clay pots and stashed those clay pots in the walls and covered them with mud-plaster. His wife made a small hole in the west wall to let in the morning sunlight, and she covered it the rest of the time with half a brick. She would bring

---

[72] *Salwar, aagathou, kameez*: the parts of a typical South Asian suit. The salwar are the pants, which are light and loose but fitted around the ankles; the aagathou is the drawstring belt typical of salwar pants, and the kameez is a long tunic worn over the pants.

[73] *Haq pak Allah*: Arabic: 'true, immaculate God'.

her parrot into that room every morning. It was actually a green Indian ring-neck parrot; god knows why she called him a Bengali parrot. That parrot had an attitude, too. He would get upset and emotional and stop all his mimicry for days on end. She had to carry him with her and try to talk to him, for a certain amount of time every day, just to keep him happy.

She pulled that half-piece of brick from the hole in the wall. Sunbeams gushed in, giving existence to all those otherwise unnoticeable dust particles, like small threads doing their space-walk. In that blinding brightness of sunlight, everything else appeared darker. The moment when the brightness filled the room, the parrot started talking on his own, "Billundh'a-Billundh'a; oooooiee." This was how she usually called to her younger son, Saleh, to wake him up every day. It was his nickname that she always used for him: Billundh'a, which meant mighty, gracefully tall. 'Oooooiee' is not a properly evolved word in Sindhi, but rather an onomatopoeia associated with calling.

Saleh was a stout young man with a solid body. He didn't finish school; he was more interested in technical things, like making radios. He would get those make-your-own hobby kits from England. After a while, through friends of friends, he ended up with a job as the assistant to a cinema projectionist.

In those days, every cinema uses to staff a movie projection operator. That job was not always enough to sustain him, as Saleh was also a flagrant gambler and an occasional thief. But in any case, Saleh was not at home on this day; the parrot simply started calling "Billundh'a-Billundh'a; Oooooiee," out of his natural habit.

Slowly Sharma's vision acclimatised and she noticed that the wall in which Fakeer hid his money had been freshly plastered. Right away she went out to the stable to find Fakeer and tell him what she had seen. Not panicking, Fakeer went inside to see the wall for himself, and Sharma Khatoon followed him, still holding the cage of her Bengali parrot.

"It's not an outsider," said Fakeer. He tried to solve the riddle by saying, "Why would a thief put the plaster back? He could have taken the pot filled with money and run." After a pause, he said, "either it's you, me, or Saleh."

Fakeer set to work undoing the wet clay plaster to see if anything was left in there. And he was astonished to find that out of seven clay pots, only two were missing; five of them were still there. Actually, six pots were there, but the sixth was on its side and there were some loose silver rupee coins lying around it. Fakeer took the inventory. He found 64 loose rupee coins around the toppled pot, and all the other five pots appeared to be untouched, still holding their 100 silver rupee coins each.

All in all, there were only 136 silver coins missing. If Saleh had been behind this, he would have taken all of it, because he was a gambler. "This money was taken by someone who needed just 136 silver rupees," Fakeer mused, while Sharma's parrot was still alternating between its calls of "Billundh'a-Billundh'a; oooooiiiee," and "haq pak Allah; haq pak Allah."

Fakeer walked through the courtyard toward Alam's living quarters and asked Dhayani, "Amma, where is Alam?"

"Nana, Alam is gone to Shirkarpur," she answered. Then she asked, out of her own curiosity, "Why?"

"Just checking," Fakeer said, and he went back to his stable.

After a few days, Alam came back with a porter and a donkey that was carrying two wooden boxes on its back. One of them was a camera, and the other was a portable enlarger, though it was not actually 'portable' by a long shot. The porter placed the boxes securely inside, took his payment from Alam, and went on his way.

"Nana came few days back asking about you," said Dhayani. She was surprised that Alam didn't ask why. She added, "Nana looked little wrapped up in his thoughts." That's what she called Fakeer, "Nana."

Sindhi family relationships tended to be like tangled bits of thread looping around in coils, forming unwanted knots that were impossible to release; their family relationships were like that. That is to say, Fakeer was Dhayani's father-in-law, but at the same time he was also her maternal grandfather, because Fakeer was also the uncle of Dhayani's mother. It only made matters more complicated that Dhayani's mother was named Sharma Khatoon too, same as Fakeer's wife, having been named after her.

Alam sat there on the floor for a while, at times rolling his right hand on his face and squeezing eyelids of his both closed eyes with his thumb and middle finger. But then he stood up and went straight to the stable, where he found Fakeer sitting on the ground, crunched down in a squatting position and drawing lines in the dirt with a piece of straw. There was only one horse left in the stable, and Fakeer was probably waiting for his owner to come and retrieve him. Alam sat down on the ground near Fakeer. Fakeer looked at Alam and said, *"Kadaay wayoo ho-ain?"—where have you been?*

But Alam did not reply to Fakeer's question. Instead he said, "I took 136 silver rupees from your stash. I'll return it to you when"—then he paused like he wasn't sure what he was saying, but he finished his sentence anyway—"when I have 136 rupees."

Fakeer kept making lines in the dirt. After a few moments, he sighed and said, "I never learned how to write."

There was a blissful soft evening light in that partly shaded stable. Fakeer and Alam sat there quietly. Every now and then the horse broke the silence with a forlorn neigh, probably missing his owner.

One day, Maro decided to skip school along with her younger brother Ayaz. Maro was Alam's fifth daughter and sixth child. Instead of school, Maro took Ayaz to visit their maternal grandmother who lived some six miles away in the village of Mehann-jee-khaahee, which they called simply 'Khaahee'.

Chapter 7
Lonely Dead Goose Feather

Khaahee was also where Alam would go and take photographs of the elite class every winter. That was when the village's feudal lords would entertain British imperial guests. Usually, the invitees were from the third rank of bureaucracy, including civil servants, commissioners, and deputy commissioners. But one time they managed to invite the Viceroy of India, and that particular mid-winter saw festivities of unimaginable proportions.

The feudals orchestrated a hunt for the British officers, and to do this they filled Lake Drigh with northern geese. They sprinkled a whole *kharar*[74] of wheat onto the lake surface—that had to be done gently to keep it afloat—so that the birds would flock together, so that Sahib (that is, an English officer) would definitely be able to hit a bird even with blind eyes.

Alam was there that day on his photography assignment. In the sky were huge rolls of bulging grey clouds with swells of appliance-white rolls in between were crawling across the horizon like snails, giving the impression of a stationary fleet of medieval warships docked on the horizon.

A streak of geese arrived from north, which then turned into a wedge formation, and a group of local hired helpers orchestrated a series of high-pitched sounds to imitate the voices of female geese and the scratchy broken cries of distressed young geese using wooden reed duck-calls. Those sounds then mixed with sound of the actual low-flying geese as they descended toward the lake, creating a tremendous noise spreading outward from the centre of the lake like a symphony by Beethoven.

And all of sudden, a shotgun was fired. Its echo was more intense than its initial blow, like multiple slaps on the face in succession, and nothing

---

[74] *Kharar*: an ancient unit of measurement roughly equivalent to a ton.

happened—all the geese were still there flying. But then all hell broke loose. The holistic symphony turned into fireworks gone wrong.

Shots blared out and some geese dropped chaotically into the lake while others were hit but still trying and trying, failing to fly, and hitting other geese before falling down. After a few minutes, when the shooting stopped, there was no sound of goose voices anymore. A purplish-blue metallic smoke of burned gunpowder had enveloped atmosphere, and it was dissipating very slowly along with the thick smell of sulphur. In the air hung the quiet sadness of a finished battle, but without any aching sounds of wounded soldiers.

And then someone shouted out the festive slogan, *"Bala Sahib'a!"*—well done, my lord!—and a scene of tarnish turned into tribute. The *manganhar*[75] started beating their drums and playing victorious tunes on the *shernai*.[76] And there were standby *toba*[77] ready to dive in and snatch the kill and place it close to Sahib's feet. And probably amidst these festivities, a lonely blood-stained dead goose feather remained floating on the stagnant air, waiting to drop onto a soiled pink petal of a run-over lotus in those muddy waters of Lake Drigh.

And photographs were taken from a wooden box camera. Droves of villagers came out to look at this thing called a camera, this monstrous concoction of black leather straps and glass plating and knobs, all standing at chest height upon three wooden legs. The villagers kept staring that thing with their wide, glazed eyes and slightly open mouths. But all these people had to get out of the way before the photo shoot could happen.

Alam started taking photographs with an old banyan tree as a backdrop, as well as several huge Turkish Bergama rugs, which once used to be beautiful. They had once had a salmon-pink background and rich reds and cobalt hues, with liberal amounts of cool sky blue, pale golden yellow, and celadon green with ivory colours, and those medallions with crooked rectangular octagons and a series of small and large pairs of curling hooks, but nowadays all this could barely be seen because of years of dust and damage. But all of that is irrelevant because the photographs were black and white.

Flocks of dead geese with their webbed toes tied together were placed on ground in front of the Sahibs, who then seated themselves on worn-out carved mahogany armchairs that had been draped with velvet sheets. They sat with their

---

[75] *Manganhar:* local musicians.

[76] *Shernai:* a traditional wind instrument with a sound like an extra-pungent oboe.

[77] *Toba:* divers.

shoulders square to look more magisterial, their legs half-spread, one hand resting on the knee and the other elbow placed on the shotgun barrel, which gazed into lens. And before yelling 'ready,' somehow he figured out from that small upside-down image behind his camera that everybody's eyes were open and mouths were shut and that they were all looking at the camera.

He pushed a small brass gear protruding from the back meshes while holding a mechanical powder flash up high in his other hand, and the moment he said 'ready' there was a small explosion that created a yellowish sulphur cloud, and in that moment the scene was engraved in slow-light on the glass plate, with stoned-eyed grey imperials sitting in front of a stack of dead geese. A few indigenous Sindhis were allowed to stand on the peripheries of those group photographs, and somehow their complexion would always appear darker in those photos than in real life.

But today, Alam was going to the village not to take photographs but in the hope of finding his daughter and young son, who left home for school and disappeared. It was already dark, and to get to *Khahee* was a six-mile walk. A few days earlier a little girl had been strangled and thrown into a well, so he was feeling agitated by this and by thoughts of his student, Kanhaiyo Lal, who was kidnapped by two Pashtoons in broad daylight.

They had snatched him from street, dumped him in a jute grain sack and told him that if he made a beep they would cut his throat. They tied the sack at the top and placed it at a distance on the platform of the train stations, waiting for next train. Pashtoons like those two were notorious for kidnapping children and trafficking them into slave labour or selling them to a beggar master who would disfigure or blind them so that they could be effective beggars and unable to run away.

Terrified of such a fate, Kanhaiyo Lal was not making any noise. But out of anxiety he was constantly fidgeting. People standing at the station saw a grain sack that looked like it was filled with potatoes crawling around inside. So they gathered around it and ask if there was someone inside, but honest Kanhaiyo stayed quiet, following the instructions of his captors. And then one of those spectators yelled out, "who owns this sack?…Whose sack is this?"

No one replied, so they untied the knots, and the moment it opened someone else in the crowd yelled, *"Aaray hay ta Diwan'a joo putt'a!"*—*Hey, he is the son of the Diwan,* meaning the son of a local Hindu merchant. Since that day Kanhaiyo Lal was nicknamed sarcastically "Lalo Pathan."[78]

Alam took a shortcut through rice fields, and as he walked he was trying to focus on the happy ending of Kanhaiyo's horrific ordeal, which was injecting small bursts of hope into his troubled mind. He was wearing a vest and a dhoti, and on his feet were *hawai chappal*,[79] which were essentially flip-flops. He was moving fast on that thin strip of walkway between the two fields, holding the folds of his dhoti in one hand, when all of a sudden his one foot sank into the mud of the rice field, which snapped the string of his flip-flop. So he continued onwards barefoot.

After a short while, someone called to him, and Alam could make out a standing figure next to a huge pile of hay. It was pitch dark, but humans can see even in complete darkness by dilating their pupils, and somehow that damn perception kicked in for Alam. And he followed the voice and figured out that there was more than one person there. And by now he was sure that they were thieves.

"What do you have on you?" One of them asked.

"Nothing," he replied, and without pausing he said, said, "my kids are probably gone to Khaa-hee, to our relatives, so I'm going there to make sure they are safe. And who are you?"

And different voice said, "rebels."

And Alam said, "Fine. Could you spare a *beedi*?[80]"

The same voice asked, "What do you do?"

"I'm a school teacher. I teach children."

One of them offered him a beedi and a match. He lit the beedi and passed the burning stick towards one of them so that he could light his beedi too. As he did that, Alam peeked at his face. He had thick eyebrows, heavy smallpox scars on his face, and a handlebar moustache. He wore a loose white chikan-fabric shirt, and in one ear he had a *kavitee,* a kind of hoop earring made up of a brass needle whose thinner end was passed through the earlobe, spiralled around, and then attached to the thicker end in a solid ring so that it wouldn't come off—you would have to get it cut if you wanted to be rid of it.

---

[78] *Lalo Pathan:* 'Pathan' is an alternate name for Pashtoons, which is to say, native Afghan people who populate northern Pakistan as well as Afghanistan.

[79] *Hawai chappal:* this translates literally to 'air sandals'.

[80] *Beedi*: tobacco wrapped in a leaf.

Alam stood there among them, searching for the right words to beg permission to leave. He hadn't come up with anything when the man with the kaivtee said, *"Chango mastar'a, mashallahyoon."*—*So long then, teacher, and Godspeed*. And with that they simply let him go.

He continued on to Khaa-hee and was relieved to find there that his children were safe at their maternal grandmother's place. He waited there till daybreak and then brought them to Qamber. He probably said nothing to them, because he liked to spoil kids. Certainly he didn't punish them in any violent way; he was never violent toward children.

Most likely, he left the fun of disciplining to their mother. The first thing he did after reaching home was draw a rough sketch of the bandit he'd met, which he left at the police station, which was not far from their home.

After a few weeks, a police constable came to see him at school. "We caught a few suspects," the constable said. "One of them resembles your sketch. So the Inspector would like for you to come and identify him."

Alam nodded and said he'd come later in the day, though he was worried, entangled in "What ifs." But he did go to the police station that evening. When he met the Inspector, he said, "If you have someone who matches my sketch, then he is one of those bandits. But I don't want to be dragged into this."

But the Inspector replied, "He already confessed. But he also saw his sketch on the bulletin board, and wanted to see you."

So Alam was brought back to the lock-up, and someone called out, *"Wah Masta'ra wah!"*—*Well done, teacher*. And then he said, "don't be afraid, I'll not harm you. I just want to see you again. *too khay dat'te aa."*—*You are gifted*.

Later, the police inspector gave the sketch to a local newspaper reporter, who printed it with the story, and for a while Alam became a small town celebrity.

Chapter 8
Chinkoo Bhangi Doing Autopsies

Mohammad Alam had a keen and inquisitive mind. He wanted to know all, and he ended up knowing a whole lot, from Vedic hymns to the art of being a flamboyant young man in an early twentieth-century town which was really stuck somewhere in seventeenth century; from being a school art teacher to being a student of anatomy, someone who wanted to know all about human insides, and who watched Chinkoo Bhangi doing autopsies for the police surgeon, usually on murder victims, the unclaimed dead bodies of *karo-kari* honour killings or dacoits who were killed in police encounters.

And he was also a compassionate person, someone who fed a bare-naked and lost man named Kackoo with his own hands, placing a bolus of food on three fingers of his right hand and pushing it into the man's mouth with his thumb like a child. Kackoo was one of those many vagrant, selfless beings of Qamber, who were called *Mast malang mun moujis:* people who had only a first name and didn't need a last name, because they all shared the same last name, *'Mast'*.[81]

Probably, Kackoo belonged to that rare order of men who lived in the transcendental realm and didn't need any worldly possessions. So he would walk naked, his face always turned up toward the heavens, and he never spoke a single word, though he was not deaf. The hairs on his head were like complex arguments of logic and reasoning; they were like those riddles that had no right answer in the end.

That is to say, they were inseparably entangled in thick clumps. And he had the mannerisms of a blind person, though he was not blind, frequently nodding

---

[81] *Mast:* an ascetic mendicant of love, especially one who performs feats of magical forbearance, and a member of an order of friars who have foresworn all worldly possessions.

his head, rolling his eyes to the right, his hands shaking in small tremors. And he drank water from open sewers, and ate only so much as was needed to keep him alive. And sometimes he would sleep on doorsteps of the brothel, where the *kasabeyaniun*[82] would sometimes take care of him, giving him his only bath in years.

Sometimes he slept on the hard wooden table of police autopsy room, which was known as the 'dead-house'. Many people thought they had seen his limbs severed and chopped and scattered on that table in the autopsy room, but always on the next day they would see Kackoo running around the streets of Qamber, bare-naked as usual. That dead-house was a wretched place, too. It was a free-standing one-room building next to police station.

No one was willing to go near that place except for the police surgeon—who would try to make his visits quick, just taking a peek before signing his report—and Chinkoo Bhangi, who had to perform the actual autopsies. Chinkoo Bhangi had given his own name to that place, calling it *payt'a cheree* ('laparotomy-place'), and he actually spread some rumours intentionally to keep people away from it, mostly because he liked to work quietly and he had tremendous respect for the corpses. So people tended not to go there because of those countless horror stories that Chinkoo Bhangi had created, but Alam and Chinkoo got along well, and sometimes Chinkoo let Alam see him doing autopsies.

Chinkoo was an edgy, tense man of medium height, one of those people who look twenty-nine or thirty years old forever. He had dark skin and a lean strong body, but he had a hunch, and that was why he always had to lift his head up when replying and then drop his head down while listening. His day job was to sweep the streets of Qamber clean in the early morning with a *booharow,* which is a cocoyea broom. Those brooms had a long handle and a thick bunch of wooden needle shafts, and when used to stroke the ground in a right and left fashion it would leave behind a low-hanging and motionless cloud of fine dust behind for sunlight beam's to give a gleam of burnished glitters.

Chinkoo and his forefathers had been sweeping dirt for thousands of years, but at some point one of those rotating police surgeons, who would come there for few years before getting transferred somewhere else, happened to ask Chinkoo for help, and so Chinkoo learned how to perform autopsies.

---

[82] *Kasabeyaniun*: prostitutes.

Chinkoo had a tray-like wooden tool box littered with all those instruments: the scalpel blade and bone saw, the skull-breaker hammer along with the chisel, the manual sternal saw to cut open the chest, toothed forceps to hold the structure in place, a fine knife for the brain, which was a little less rusted than the others. He had given all those instruments his own names for them. There were also several specimen jars, rope, a speculum for rectal and vaginal examinations, aspiration tubes, and some cracked and chipped white and mustard yellow enamel-ware hospital pans, with navy-blue and algae-green rims, which all seemed quite worn too, in which he used to place bowels, guts, and intestines.

And over time, Chinkoo became very good at this. And Alam sometimes came to observe him in that autopsy room, which was a squarish hall with a high ceiling and open spaces where the windows and door should be. On one side of that hall there was a 55-gallon drum filled with water, and there was a well right outside the room, which was the only source of water. And there was a pale light bulb hanging above the table like an old cliché, a sad banality.

The wooden table on which the dead body lay was higher than a normal table, and there was a smell that could only be identified as death, that sly, kinky, unusual and cunning smell of soulless melting guts.

Alam always remembered one particular day when he was looking on, standing not far from that autopsy table. Within a few minutes, Chinkoo had ripped open the guts, and he showed Alam the quarter-size small patches on the liver of that corpse. He told him that this was *'karo-kamaun'*—liver cirrhosis, and he offered to let Alam feel the liver. Alam eagerly obliged and touched the liver to find that that part of it was hard like a baked brick.

Next to his art room in the school building there were living quarters of janitors, where they lived there with their families. In fact, the school didn't have any real place for an art room, so they gave Alam an empty quarter next to Chandagi and Raywo's living quarters. Chandagi and Raywo were two brothers who were both sweepers.

In the Asian subcontinent, that profession was not only a job but also a last name, a clan, a stigma, a whole class of people who were forced to wrap their shadows in their laps while passing close to a temple, because even their shadows were considered unholy and capable of contaminating the divinity of a place of worship. They were untouchables, whom Muslims called *khak-rob* and Hindus called *hari-jan*, but in the end no one called them by either of those fancy names.

Instead, they are called Bhangis, and Bhangis have been restricted to sweeping, scavenging dead bodies, and cleaning toilets for thousands of years. They would carry human defecated waste away in buckets on their heads, and because they cleansed the impurities of the whole society, they themselves were considered extremely polluted and outcast among the outcast. The privileged classes of the society considered themselves pure, and forced the Bhangis to live in malignant poverty for thousands of years.

According to legend this was all caused by two goddesses. The goddess Parvati, Shiva's wife, laid a cursed upon Kauri-bai,[83] a facet of the goddess Matangi whom the Bhangis worship. Kauri-bai was believed to be Shiva's sister, and obsessed with purity and cleanliness. She had complained to Parvati about Shiva's habits of consuming bhang,[84] mingling with ghosts and goblins, and cavorting in cremation grounds and dirtying her immaculate floors with the ashes of the dead.

But Parvati took the side of her husband, and the loser in this conflict was Kauri-bai, who had to bear Parvati's curse to be reborn and spend her eternal life as an untouchable. And since Kauri-bai was the one that the Bhangis followed and worshipped, they were then barred from entering the *mandir*,[85] forced instead to stand outside of every place of worship and clean everything over and over again, but still failing to clean away the ever-present stain of their goddess's curse.

But Alam did not feel bound by that ancient code, and he chose to stand with them outside places of worship, as if he were asking God to come out. Alam had a mind of his own when it came to the division of *varna*, which is the name of the fourfold categories into which Hinduism separated its people. The four varnas were part of their creation myth, and were said to have emanated from the Primeval Being.

The Creator's mouth became the Brahman priests, his two arms formed the Rajanya warriors and kings, his two thighs formed the Vaishya landowners and merchants, and from his feet were born the Shudra artisans and servants. Later, there developed a so-called 'fifth' varna: the Untouchables, who had been completely thrown out of Primeval Being's body. But it occurred to Alam that

---

[83] *Kauri-bai:* for more about this figure in Hindu mythology, see David R. Kinsley: *Tantric Visions of the Divine Feminine* (Motilal Banarsidass: 1998), page 214.

[84] *Bhang.* An intoxicating drink made from cannabis leaves.

[85] *Mandir*: temple (Hindu).

the system of varna did not explain the soul. So, according to Alam's own thinking, the Bhangis were the very core of that Primeval Being.

So Alam mixed freely with them, went to their homes whenever they invited him, held their kids in his lap, and ate food and drank water from their pots, which was not common then, or even now. Once, Alam's mother told Ali Gohar that Bhangis were unsacred, unsanctified, impure, and that if you touched them you would also become unholy.

One day, Alam took Ali Gohar to buy some *jalebiyun,* which are unbelievably sweet spirals of fried thick crusts dipped into cool melting sugar syrup, and which leaves a mysterious riddle of a juicy taste after you eat them—when eaten, it leave a mysterious, sweet riddley juicy taste. Alam loved them. So he took Ali Gohar with him to purchase some jalebiyoon, which the baker had wrapped in dry banana leaves and tied together with a thin cotton string.

While coming back, instead of renouncing his mother and telling his son that she was simply wrong—which he could have done!—he told Ali Gohar a tale that he had once learned at the ashram. He wanted to tell it exactly as he had heard it: "Time had seen it, it did happen in pour of history, in the bubble of time, there was a wise man. His name was Adi Shankarachrya. Once Adi was out walking and saw an old man of low caste coming his way, and he said 'get away from my path. Step aside now.'"

The old man replied to Adi by saying, "my lord, what is in your way? My body or my soul, which one does my lord want to get rid of?' But before the old man could finish his sentence, Adi Shankarachrya had realised what he had done, and he dropped to the ground and fall on to the feet of that *dalit*[86] and asked for his forgiveness. And the dalit placed his hand on the bowed head of Adi Shankarachrya,"—but instead of telling Ali Gohar all those details, Alam just said that Adi Shankarachrya was a great mystic, and that he had fallen at the feet of a low-caste person, after realising his own mistake of mistreating him based on his caste, and that Adi had renounced the caste system. And by the time Alam had finished saying this, Ali Gohar realised that Alam was heading to Raywo and Chandagi's home, in school backyard.

Alam asked one of his dearest students to teach his elder daughter how to read. This daughter never went to school as a child, instead, helping Dhayani to raise her younger siblings. Now she was too old to go to elementary school, so

---

[86] *Dalit*: an Untouchable.

Alam asked Maadho Ram to teach her how to read and write. Which Maadho did. He would come after school for an hour and sit with her in the backyard or under the shadow of the ber tree. She learned how to read very quickly.

Now, Maadho was a very studious and focused person, and he wanted to become a physician. He had achieved all the prerequisites to get into medical college, but he didn't have the money to enrol. He then became obsessed with the dictionary and memorised it in its entirety and became insane. He was the only child of his widowed mother, who had lost her husband at a young age and supported herself and Maadho by making pickles, homemade mango pickles. And man! what pickles she used to make, out of young green mangoes chopped into four pieces and then dipped in bitter mustard oil which she marinated in a long list of aromatic spices.

Many other people used to make and sell homemade pickles in Qamber with the same spices, but no one's recipe ever came close to hers. Everyone figured that she added some secret ingredient to make her pickles extremely tasty, but no one could guess what it might be, other than a few drops of her sweat, her tears, and a pinch of her shredded, dry, old, and unsatisfied lonely desires.

Later in his life, Maadho completed a doctorate in Greek medicine,[87] but no one cared about that, even though it sounded beautiful, with Olympian healers like Asclepius, the early god who specialised in mystic healing. But he did his doctorate in Greek medicine at Unani Tibbiya College, *Fakeer'a-jo-pir,* Hyderabad, Sindh. Maadho was a short, slim man with a face like Dustin Hoffman.

One evening in his school days, while Maadho was still tutoring Alam's elder daughter in reading and writing, Maadho came to Alam and asked, "How do people make gold?"

Alam looked at him and said, "sit."

Maadho sat on the edge of a kha-taa cot next to Alam. Alam said, "My friend Sirajuddin Morio is a treasure hunter and an alchemist."

Maadho kept looking at Alam's face with this dilemma unresolved; either making gold was possible or not. Alam went on, "He lives right across from the Larkano train station." That part of Larkano was known as *Daree Mohallo.*[88]

---

[87] *Greek medicine:* this refers to 'Unani' medicine, a form of South Asian and Middle Eastern medical practice that is based on ancient Greek sources.

[88] *Daree Mohallo*: this translates to 'neighbourhood of dunes' The word 'daree' refers to a small dune, and is feminine; larger dunes would be given a masculine noun.

Alam continued, "They say it used to be a posh locality somewhere back in time, God knows when. In that part of the town, there was a *pagalun jo shifakhano."* That is, a private psychiatric asylum. *Pagal* means insane, and that's the word that was always used for mentally disturbed people. The asylum was run by a holistic physician known as Hakim Maharaj-uddin Morio. He was a landlord and very wealthy, the heir of the *Gaadi* of Moriya Fakeer'a village.

This meant that he was next in line, the hereditary successor of clan Moriya's mystic descent, destined to become the spiritual hierarch. Simply put, the words *Hakim Maharaj-uddin Morio* ere a big deal. He held spiritual power, and at the same time was extremely rich.

As Alam told him these things, Maadho was still thinking, *what about making gold?* But patiently he kept listening to Alam, who was now telling him:

"The village of Moriya Fakeer'a is a place where once Qalandar Lal had sat in his mystic trance for forty days and forty nights, in front of a fire which represented his coveting, his desire to have, his greed, which he wanted to be rid of. That fire kept raging for forty day and thirty-nine nights, but on the fortieth night, before dawn broke, Qalandar was able to burn his coveting and his greed and reduce it to a smoky pile of ashes. And since that day, for the past hundreds and hundreds of years, there has been a person stationed at that spot, devoted to keeping the smoke alive. That devotee is called the smoke riser: *dohien du-kha-eendar*. That all is in Hakim's ancestral village."

"His holistic healing centre where he treated insane people, people who were out of their minds, was in the city of Larkano, across from station in Daree Mohallo, as I mentioned before."

Maadho was still looking at Alam, waiting for an answer on how to make gold. But Alam was saying:

"His holistic healing centre or private asylum was mainly to nurture the insane and bring them back, making them normal again like others. The 'others' meaning those who were not crazy, at least not enough out of their minds to be called anything other than normal. So, it was huge rectangular hall, like a gym, made up of solid baked red bricks with no real windows."

"Very high up on the walls, almost up against the ceiling, there were cylindrical horizontal windows called ventilators. Those ventilators would emit beams of brightness but wouldn't allow you to see the source of light. They let the air bring in shredded bits of intoxicating fragrance, but they didn't allow you to see the blooming flowers. They were the best example of complex reasoning to justify a God in whose existence you had to believe blindfolded. You might feel him if you are spiritually incline, but you can't see him."

Actually, that final philosophical interpretation of the ventilators was something that Alam just thought up in his mind, and didn't actually say aloud to Maadho. But nonetheless Maadho was getting tired and beginning to regret that he had ever asked Alam his question, but Alam continued.

"Beneath those ventilators on those high walls, the mentally disturbed people used to be shackled to the walls with chains. Hakim was known to fix violently disturbed patients in one month's time, but the quiet and passive ones always took longer, sometimes as much as a year. How he treated them therapeutically nobody knows."

"He used to grind some dry leaves, some chipped pieces of wood that might have been the outer bark of trees. And he would make them drink it, forcefully initially, and then they start drinking those concoctions on their own, and after that in a few weeks they usually got cured. What was in those concoctions no one knows. Hakim Maharaj-u-ddin Morio kept them in his heart and took them to his grave."

"Traditionally those holistic physicians used to pass on their trade secrets to their sons. But Hakim never did that. He did try to train his only son, Sirajuddin Morio, my friend." Alam took a pause here and then said, "and he wanted his son to become Hakim Sirajuddin Morio. But it didn't work. In the beginning, Siraj showed very keen interest in his father's trade of healing sick. But then he got caught into that intangible knowledge of alchemy."

"Sirajuddin Morio *Kimiyagar*," and when Alam used word 'Kimiyagar', which means 'alchemist', Maadho became alert. Alam went on, "Siraj was also an admirer of talented people, and he somehow got hold of me. Anyway, all of his alchemy friends were well off. One of them was a chief engineer and another one was a retired army colonel. Several others were big landlords and sons of merchants like Siraj himself."

"Alchemy is a very expensive hobby; you need lots of money and the ability to tolerate delays, trouble, and suffering without getting angry or upset. In other words, you need tons of patience. The main objective of gold-seeking alchemists is to kill the anxiety of the element mercury. To make it stable, to make it sit still and not move. They picked mercury because somehow the weight of mercury and gold seems the same to them."

"So, if they succeeded in killing the soul of mercury—and they say that literally, *paray jo pittoo maar,* to kill the esteem of mercury—then they could try to put the colour of gold onto mercury, and essentially they could make gold."

Then Alam got a little poetic and said, "Gold-seeking alchemy is a beautifully euphoric but also an elusive process. The alchemist, who wants to convert mercury into gold, goes to great lengths. They follow a long process to stabilise mercury, which could be from as little as thirteen steps to as many as ninety-seven steps."

Maadho was glued to Alam's speech by now and was absorbing every single word. "And this included cooling it or warming it, blending it with dry flakes of different herbs and spices called *'kakh'a'*. Sometimes, they boiled it in extreme heat by a medieval gold melting method, using a pit like a small campfire with rock charcoal burning at such a heat that they became embers of hell. They would achieve that by blowing air into the fiery pit through a bellows pump.

"Then they would place a small clay crucible called a *khothari* in the middle of the fire. Although that crucible is made up of clay, it looks like a cup carved out of hard rock. Inside the khothari would be the mercury and brimstone. And they would heat it. The trick would be that the brimstone should not convert into oily sulphur and mercury should not become ash.

"The romance of alchemy was so strong that no matter how many times they went through this process, after faithfully following thirteen or ninety-seven steps, when there was no gold in that khothari they didn't blame alchemy. Instead they blamed themselves, figuring that they must have missed a crucial step. And then they would do it all over again and again."

Then Alam said, "Alchemy was the reason why Hakim Maharaj-u-ddin Morio didn't pass on his secret healing remedies to cure the insane to his only son Sirajuddin Morio. Because to him, his son was insane too."

Alam then looked at straight at Maadho's face and said, "I was once in Larkano and went to see Siraj at his father's healing centre, which was also Siraj's alchemy lab. And when I walked in, I found several people there, Sirah's whole syndicate. I figured that they must be up to something. And sure enough, they were about to go through the whole the drill to make the mercury sit still and then colour it gold. The pit was burning.

"One of Siraj's fellow alchemists was blowing air onto the charcoal embers using a leather bellows. Siraj looked at me and said, 'Welcome, haven't seen you for long time. Come sit.' And he offered me a place to sit a four-legged wooden cot. I sat there and looked towards the back wall where two insane people were chained, far enough apart that they couldn't reach each other. One of them had cuddled himself all together, with his chin resting on his knees and his arms wrapped around his shins. And that person was staring at them unblinkingly.

"The other madman was also crunched down, but he was constantly reciting something by heart, and was counting some infinite number on four tips of his right hand fingers by just using his thumb. And every so often while reciting he would to look to the left and nod his head in approval, like he is agreeing with someone while praying. And there were other people in the room, too. There were a few teenage kids, and there was a barefooted jogi in a saffron robe. That jogi had a traditional colourful beaded necklace, with a cowbell hanging in the middle."

"I was curious to see what they were about to do, so I choose to stay a little longer. When the fire reached the ideal heat, one of them poured mercury into the khothari's mouth with some other additives. After a while, Sirajuddin said loudly, *'betho tha'wa'*, it had stabilised! He meant that the mercury was no longer moving.

"Then the jogi stood up from the cot where he had been sitting all along, and he cowbell in his necklace rang out with a strangulating sound, and he shovelled his hand into one of several pockets of his saffron robe. I was watching the jogi, but right behind him, on that back wall, those two insane patients came into view. They were still doing the same things, one of them gazing into emptiness and the other was murmuring quietly and tabulating his murmurs on his right hand fingers, but it felt to me that I was looking at them cuddled together."

"The jogi took out a small double drawstring pouch. Still staring at the khothari, the jogi kept relaxing the strings of his pouch and opening its mouth wider and wider. Then he came up to the khothari and unloaded the entire contents of his pouch in it with a snap, and stepped back with a jolt. At first, nothing happened—just the cowbell at his neck jingled, but then there was a sound of madly spinning firecracker, which exploded into a bluish white smoke cloud."

"Everyone close to fiery pit dropped on ground. That smoke smelled like fresh clean laundry. When the commotion stopped and everyone regained their footing, they saw that the khothari had broken in two, and its contents had fallen into the fire. Siraj and all his fellow alchemists rushed to the fiery pit and started grabbing red-hot embers with their bare hands. Some were using the long neck pliers that they usually used to hold the khothari by its neck."

"They were doing all that madding frenzy and they didn't want to pour water on it because it might change. Finally, the pit cooled down and extinguished the fire on her own. They gathered all the ashes into a pile on a wide metal tray and started blowing it gently. Slowly the ash was blowing away, leaving small round grey droplets, and apparently grey droplets means failure."

"But then, to their astonishment, slowly those droplets turned into gold pellets. Siraj and his friends were jubilant and laughing so much it seemed they were going to rip their lungs off. The teenage kids were running around the hall, celebrating their part of participation in making gold, which was no more than just looking at the process. The jogi was now sitting back on four-legged cot, and said, 'take it to the goldsmith,' with an unwavering confidence, like he already knew it was gold. The two insane men were unchanged, still doing what they had been doing all along."

"Later that day, I followed Siraj and the others to the goldsmith's shop. After carefully testing those pellets, the goldsmith announced, 'it's gold,' and he purchased it."

"Siraj rushed back to get the recipe of that mixture from the jogi so that he could make more. The whole procession, which now included the goldsmith and some others who happened to know the story were with us. We got back to the hall and found that the jogi was not there. All that was there were those two chained men at the back wall, the insane people. One of them was cuddled together and resting his chin on his knees, and staring without blinking, and other was crunched down, rocking back and forth, slowly murmuring and counting on the tips of his right hand fingers."

Then Alam told Maadho "That was my only experience of how people make gold. I won't suggest to you what to do. Go figure it out."

Maadho stood and then bowed down to touch Alam's feet. And he went on his way back home, talking to himself in small murmurs.

Once a year Alam would go to K. B. Sarkar to buy an entire year's worth of supplies for his elementary and intermediate drawing students. He always assumed that K. B. Sarkar was a Parsi stationery merchant, but perhaps it was owned by someone non-Parsi. In any case, that was his once-a-year ritual, and it was a lengthy process. He had to mail in his list of required supplies and then wait their acknowledgment, and again wait for confirmation of availability before planning his trip to Karachi. Alam never liked the city, so he would stay for a day or two at the most. He preferred to stay at the dharamsala of the Swaminarayan Mandir on Bandar Road, which was close to K.B. Sarkar and which catered food that was palatable to him.

Alam was a bold man. One could say he had bipolar attitudes towards life. He could be ultra-liberal at times and staunch conservative at other times. And he had no difficulty going against the grain of society. He never hesitated to become that first droplet of rain on sizzling desert sand, which simmers to steam in a billionth of a second. But that is what such a droplet is meant to do. When his daughter, his fifth child, passed elementary school, she hit a dead end.

No girl in Qamber went beyond fifth grade, because Qamber offered no higher grades for girls, and gender segregation was the social norm. The high school was only for boys, an all-male facility. But Alam went on and placed her in the all-boys' high school, which was unforeseen and unheard of. So his daughter was the only girl in a class of 63 boys, in a school of over 473 all male inhabitants, with the exception of Chandagi, the sweeper's wife, who would sweep the entire school every afternoon along with her husband Raywo.

It was just a short walk that Alam took, holding his little daughter's index finger, to the admission office of high school. But after that walk, everything changed.

Unofficially the name of that boy's high school became simply 'Municipal High School Qamber'. So Alam's daughter opened the door, or shall we say kicked open the door, to become the first girl to get her high school diploma from there. And countless talented girls followed her example, and they went on to become physicians and teachers and bankers and architects and playwrights.

The possibility of a change like this, of empowering young women, had probably first occurred to him though a small observation he made on one of his trips to Karachi. He was sitting on a small bench in K.B. Sarkar's graceless and small reception area, where if more than two people stand at a time, they would bump into the third person's knees.

As he was waiting, a beautiful woman walked in wearing a casual gown of light blue, but very, very light blue, what he could call 'king's blue light colour', and she walked on sophisticated white pumps with a contrasting trim highlighting the top line in grey with a low block heel. He just took a slight glance of her face, though he wanted to give her a deep gaze. She picked up her paints which, he heard from their conversation, were oil colours, and walked back to her roof-less off-white car, which was equally beautiful, with a small rear wheel arch covering almost half of the rear wheel.

He didn't care about the make or model of that car because he wouldn't have recognised it anyway. For him, cars were cars, be they big or small, old or new, ugly or gorgeous like the one he just saw, which was smooth and glossy like Cinderella's sandal. She drove off and disappeared behind an old coughing and perambulating tram-trolley that was suffering from parasomnia. And that noisy tram-trolley brought him back from that fantasy of beauty.

Later that day he hopped onto one of those same old coughing and perambulating tram-trolleys with its constant old fire engine bell noise to get back to the ashram. While sitting amidst that clamour of external and internal sounds, it probably occurred to him that women should be free and independent like that lady in the kings-blue gown.

Or maybe he started thinking about women's liberation as a result of his tireless reading habit, where he might have come across the story of Mehta Thakur Das, who converted and became Shaikh Abdullah. But that was not what made him great. He was great because he wanted to educate girls, and he opened the first girls' boarding school and created an awakening among the people regarding women's education.

Or he might have gotten the idea from somewhere else entirely. But in any case, Alam wanted his daughters to get higher education. He wanted them to be able to grasp life with their own hands, to have the feel of it directly without any intermediary.

The same daughter whom he got enrolled in the boys' high school came to Alam at one point and told him of her interest in learning how to ride a bicycle. If she had been the daughter of someone else in Qamber, those words would have felt like pouring melted iron in the parent's ears. But Alam closed his eyes gently, and he placed the curved index finger of his right hand on his upper lip and moustache and the right thumb under his chin, leaving the other three fingers curved rolled like a loose fist, and he said nothing to her. His pupils were moving under his eyelids like he was dreaming.

She took that quiet pause as a *no,* and slowly started to retreat, when Alam opened his eyes and told her, "Yes we can do that." And then he said, "I was thinking *how*. How, meaning, how could I teach you to ride a bike without having half of Qamber looking at us."

After this, a few times, very close to sunset, people might have seen Alam from a distance, in police ground, holding the back seat of a bicycle and running awkwardly and trying his best to teach bike riding to someone who suffered from bike learning disabilities. The moment when Alam would release his grip on the back seat, the little boy in a turban would drop like a dead bird, sometimes to his right and sometimes to his left.

Among Alam's many passions, palmistry was always high up on the list. He read palms without any material interest. He had probably had seen gurus from in his childhood days at the ashram reading palms, making peoples' horoscopes, and then reading them out for those people to give them a glimpse of their future and fortune. But it was Cheiro who taught him how to read palms.

Cheiro's self-educational booklets taught him how to read lines, how to palpate palms. Alam would look long and hard at those diagrams and learn them by heart. He learned how to look into people's eyes without blinking and feel their palms with both hands rubbing them gently with a soft touch. He would first take a good look at their palm lines, and he would close his big eyes but keep rolling his eyeballs under his eyelids. Then he would move his fingers over the fortune seeker's palm, trying to feel their texture and find any protruding mounds, bumps, soft spots, and calluses.

While taking those deep breaths, he probably had thought about the basic dynamic of inner dealing of principal elements, air, fire, water, earth and ether. Meanwhile the fortune seeker would keep looking at Alam's moving eyeballs under his vainly closed eyelids. This whole situation would mesmerise those seekers. Then Alam would peer through his black watchmaker's magnifying loupe—which looked like tequila glass, but a black plastic one—to see the shape of their thumbprints, which would reveal their personality and their element.

Those could be of any shape, like the swirling clouds of Van Gogh's 'Starry Night', which illustrates the element air; or one central line rising straight upwards like a flame conjoined with others lines engulfing it (fire); or several lines rising up and bending like 'The great wave off Kanagawa' (water); or horizontal flat lines being slowly pulled upward to make a dune, a hilly mount (earth); or circling maze-like lines complexly winding in on each other could be seen spirit (ether).

But who really knows whether he was really considering those details, or perhaps had simply made up a stock of basic profiles. That is to say, what good fortune could really have awaited the people of Qamber and its surrounding villages—there was nothing there at the time, and nothing had ever been there, other than suffocating poverty and their daily grinding of their hackneyed lives.

Everybody wanted to find some hope in their fortune, some good luck that might arrive in their future; after all, the future was tomorrow, which no one had seen, nor anyone ever will. But they still wanted someone like Alam to tell them that they were very lucky, their suffering part of life would soon be over.

That murky, gloomy Pluto had left them alone now, and seven years of prosperity ahead. And they would buy every single word he said and then send others to go and see him too.

But slowly his own fortune was slipping from his palms. He was trying his best to earn as much as he could from all viable sources, but his income was still not enough to support himself and his fourteen dependents. But this was not for lack of innovation.

Once he managed to capitalise on being suspended from his work for a year. He had landed that sentence along with four of his colleagues for beating a fellow teacher at a time when the undercurrent of racial-religious tension broke loose and overflowed into violence.

The town municipality hired his elder son Ali Gohar instead of him for that year. Being suspended allowed Alam to give birth to an ingenious idea. He used that time to go off on various photography tours to different shrines, covering their annual fairs with his minute camera. He would stay there for days on end taking photographs and reading palms.

Some of those annual fairs happened in the complete wilderness, places with no human civilisation for miles in all directions, but people would still show up there for three days and live there under blue skies in the day the full moon at night.

On his first trip, he planned to cover the annual fairs of two shrines in four weeks, where his trip started close to one full moon and ended on the next, with a visit to the city of Sukkur in between. It took its toll, but he did it, for four weeks in same clothes. In the city, he could use the barbers shop's paid bath, but around those shrines there was nothing. When he came back, his white clothes had turned a muddy tan, and all their seams were infested with the eggs of body lice.

The next year, using this new idea of earning extra money, he started taking all of his unused paid vacations from the past several years. He placed his son as substitute art teacher and went on sprees of four or five weeks, covering a couple fairs at shrines and spending the rest of his time in some town.

He was an optimistic man without any optimism around him—probably because of those raw aesthetics, that will to appreciate un-tappable beauty. He would ask his young children to quickly find a shape in a slow moving cloud, and when they did he would reward them with a penny.

But all of his extremely tiring efforts were still falling short; he wasn't able to make ends meet. This was making him irritable about weird things. He started to ask his wife Dhayani things like, *why did you go to the door?* Or, *why did a strange man walk outside our home on the street?* Or he would ask his grownup young daughters not to give grain offerings or other left over food to street beggars, because years back, he himself used to dress as a bagger to carry out his romantic affairs.

But he was not aware of his bizarre behaviour; in his mind he was protecting them from some invisible harm. By now, Alam was in early fifties, and exertion and grumpiness circled his head like a halo. They say that irritability in males of Alam's age is a symptom of hormonal imbalance—a fact of life, but most males deny it, thinking it unmanly. His hair had turned grey now, but his moustache was not only grey but also pale yellowish under his nostrils because of his excessive smoking of bidis, tobacco wrapped in leaves like thin primitive cigars. Quite often he would roll his fingers on his forehead with closed eyes and then bring all his fingers down to his chin, leaving only his index finger on his upper lip, like he was thinking of something.

In the early 60s, Ali Gohar got a job in Hyderabad. Sometimes, Alam's bizarre behaviour of involving himself in unnecessary matters would lead to Dhayani sending telegrams to Ali Gohar, asking him to come and rescue the situation. And on one of those trips back and forth, Ali Gohar asked his mother and siblings to come with him and move to Hyderabad. Alam didn't object; he just kept himself at a distance. In the first phase, Ali Gohar was able to move his mother and half of his brothers and sisters to Hyderabad. After a few trips, all but three of Alam's twelve children had moved to Hyderabad with Ali Gohar.

This gave Alam a little freedom from the financial stresses that had been tearing at his senses for years. Now he didn't have to provide for twelve souls. After a few months, Alam realised that after paying all the bills he actually had some money left over, which had never happened before ever. And at retiring age, Alam started dreaming of saving money.

Those were the times when all of a sudden government introduced a law that every citizen should have a picture identity card, and they established a whole new department to make those picture IDs. A year or so after the law was passed, someone in government claimed that the word 'mandatory' was mentioned in the law, and the police were instructed to check for the IDs, and people who didn't have them started getting fined.

He was still the only photographer in Qamber and the surrounding area, which comprised hundreds of small villages and thousands and thousands of people. And all the adults needed three passport-sized photographs to get their ID cards. So it started. In the beginning, he got ten or twenty people who wanted their photograph taken for a picture ID, and then that number increased manyfold and he was taking scores of passport photos daily. That influx of business lasted for quite some time and brought him sizeable wealth, and he was overjoyed at his new monetary possession.

Chapter 9
Throwing Flowers Like Cupid's Arrows

Alam was alone in Qamber now in his huge house; only his mother Sharma Khatoon still lived there, but she had her own big portion of the house, with Fakeer's livery stable. Even though Fakeer had died long time ago, the stable was still there and she was still running it. But all of Alam's children had gone to Hyderabad with Ali Gohar almost ten years ago.

In those ten years, they had evolved. Ali Gohar had become a junior faculty member of the University, and couple of Alam's five other sons had also gotten university jobs. In fact, all of them got some sort of job initially. Two of them stuck with their jobs and the other three quit.

After working for a while, one chose to become a playwright and never went back. He used to make dreams, real dreams, the kind that could breathe and have faces and shapes that one could see, feel and touch, so much that many people started believing that his dreams were real. And more than anybody else, he himself lived inside those dreams.

So that was the Dreamer, who was Alam's second son, after Ali Gohar. While staying in Hyderabad, the Dreamer somehow got the hang of the radio business. In the mid-sixties, radio was a big deal, and broadcasters were real celebrities. Since they couldn't see them, listeners would weave whatever face they wanted around their favourite broadcaster's voice. Programmes were segregated by language, and all the prime time shows were in Urdu. But this radio station in Hyderabad was accommodating little bit of native programming.

So a space was created for a new breed of Sindhi drama writers for radio, and a few Sindhi writers who had been assisting in writing prime time Urdu shows got a chance to write independently for Sindhi programmes. One of these new radio dramatists was a supervisor in the University, and he became known by his pen name, *'Prince Rosé-face'*.

This Prince Rosé-face looked like an Ogre, but he said he was Prince Rosé-face, so he was Prince Rosé-face. The Dreamer got close to him; start reading his scripts back and forth, and through Prince Rosé-face the Dreamer met Ali Baba, another titan of modern Sindhi short story and drama writing.

While everyone else pursued different occupations, it was Ali Baba who likely inspired the Dreamer to quit his job and become a full-time writer. This decision was daunting in a society where art lacked patronage, and being a full-time writer felt akin to blending oneself into the tumultuous whirl of life. But Ali Baba did it, and so did the Dreamer.

Another one of Alam's sons was a telephone operator and used to connect calls through a mini telephone exchange, literally by pushing male-female jacks in a switchboard in a small room somewhere in the basement of the university gym. While doing that, he would listen in on the intimate conversations of couples. At times, those intimate conversations would spill into another territory, where the conversing pairs would stop talking altogether and start listening to each other's heavy breathing and steamy sighs.

In that listening process, he sometimes got carried away and pulled the plug of the boy's phone line from switchboard and kept listening to the heavy breathing and steamy sighs of the girl. He was not aware that he was unknowingly drifting into voyeurism. He wasn't actually watching those girls, but their steamy voices were doing that trick for him, and he started to imagine that he himself was the boyfriend of one of these girls. And he showed up at the waiting room of the girls' hostel to call upon her. That girls' hostel was the only female hostel of Sindh University, and had two waiting rooms, one on either side of its huge jailhouse-sized gate.

Usually, male students would wait in one of those waiting rooms after calling for the girl that they wanted to see, and an attendant would deliver their message, and after some time the girl would come out. Then supposedly the couple would sit there alone, engaging in meaningful talk about their platonic relationship—at least, that was the social understanding that enabled the couples to meet one another in those rooms alone.

But the operator son of Alam had no idea of a platonic relationship. He would skip that and define for those girls the playful meaning of love that he had in his heart for them, with full disclosure and a graphic interpretation of Freudian term 'libido'. So that was the reason why he got fired from his job as a telephone operator.

Despite his paraphiliac tendencies, he turned out to be an excellent stage actor and would deliver long monologues flawlessly, and the audience, who mainly used to come to watch provocative dances that girls would perform in those stage plays, were usually quite affected by his performances, and they applaud him at length and again give him their standing ovation at the end when he appeared with other cast members to bow. This would happen in that one and only open-air theatre in Hyderabad, which ironically was also in the middle of the Hyderabad Zoo.

A third one of these brothers was also laid off, or one could say he sacked his boss from being his boss and relieved himself from performing duties. His name was Punnu and he was Alam's youngest son. After getting his high school diploma, he started working as a librarian in one of the teaching departments. He was a person whom Cupid bothered a lot, always stabbing the tip of that sweet arrow in his heart. This bugging of Cupid's made him throw flowers in air, and some of those flowers found their way and fell upon the chests of pretty girls.

Punnu was also writing short stories, and his second story, 'Yellow fog', which by its name seems radioactive, was praised and published in a literary magazine. But that was all, apart from his clerical work of lending textbooks to students and faculty members and then logging them, placing returned books back by author or category in alphabetical order.

At work, someone filed a complaint of recalcitrance against him. Nobody knew who did that, but Punnu didn't give a damn anyway. It could have been one of the girls, or a faculty member, or anybody else, but being a poetic writer, Punnu would have preferred if that complaint had been filed by that silly Cupid himself, or by one of those flowers.

Regardless of who had complained, now he had to show up at the university Vice President's office to answer for his conduct. In that official hearing, he was asked by the Vice President, "did you throw flowers onto girls?"

And Punnu replied, "yes, I did," while standing in front of this Vice President of the university. He answered as a young highbrow writer would, casually, with both hands in his jeans pockets. And his hands in his jeans pockets were bothering that Vice President more than his throwing of flowers that landed on the firm virgin bosoms of those perky girls. And Punnu's uptight, headlong, and headstrong Vice President, whose ego was shattered by Punnu's relaxed demeanour, got more concerned about his own ego's damage control and became flabbergasted.

They say, that Vice President, who himself was not very old, had married a Persian woman. For Sindhi men, all non-Sindhi women were pretty, and Persian women were considered especially charming. So to Punnu's boss, who came from a feudal Sindhi background, and in whose mind every night of making out with his Persian wife was as good as banging and screwing Omar Khayyam himself, to him a Sindhi short story writer, especially one of dark skin, was almost a non-entity. So he suddenly yelled in anger, "Get your hands out of your pockets and then answer my question!"

Then Punnu answered something equally harsh. He would have been suspended anyway, but because of his outrageous reply that Vice President terminated him on the spot, and Punnu might has well have been twerking as he sauntered out of there.

Those were a few of Alam's children, who were all now grown-up young men and women. Some of them still came to see him every now and then. He himself had been to Jamshoro, where the University is, a couple of times in last ten years just to see Ali Gohar's children, his grandchildren.

But in general he lived in Qamber alone. He took photographs and ran his studio for a couple of hours in the morning and also a couple of hours in the evening, but still he was left with a whole lot of time to kill. He would develop and process prints in the afternoon, but that only took half an hour.

Then he started reading the entire newspaper every day, then books of all different sorts, everything he could get a hold of from that dilapidated town library. His progressing deafness kept worsening with time, so people would have to yell into his right ear as he became completely deaf in his left ear, and after a while they pretty much didn't talk to him at all.

He started spending the middle of the day sitting in the thin shadows of the barr tree, that lonely tree that one of his students had grown against all odds, many, many years ago in his huge backyard. Alam knew that this tree was older than a number of his children, and the tree was eccentric in her own right: short, tilted awkwardly to one of her sides, making way for one of its long branches to grow on that same tilted side.

She had survived many wind and dust storms in her lifetime and kept bearing that disproportionate weight on her tilted side. He would sit or lie down on a cot under her for hours and hours on end, covering his face with some thin veil because her shadows were porous. But Alam still loved that barr tree because of her sheer resilience and will to grow in such a harsh environment of salt-drenched and almost rock-solid soil.

There on that small four-legged cot he would sit and think about something, god knows what! Then a squirrel started showing up, and he would come very close to his cot but then run away. And Alam thought, "*I wonder if I could somehow make that squirrel believe that I'm not going to hurt him.*" He started buying and peeling peanuts for the squirrel and offering them to him, placing them at a safe distance from the four-legged cot.

In the beginning, the squirrel wouldn't come close to those peanuts, even at that safe distance away from that cot on which Alam sat, and he would only take those peanuts when Alam was not there. Then one day the squirrel grabbed a peanut, from that safe distance, in Alma's presence. After that, the squirrel loosened up a little and started scampering and leaping around Alam's shoes.

When Alam lay down on the cot in the thin shadows of the barr tree leaves, the squirrel would climb up onto the cot and then jump back to the ground, but Alam kept lying there motionless, and probably talking to that squirrel in the realm of his mind. That was the closest relationship that the squirrel and Alam could develop.

One day, Alam was sitting with his mother in her livery stable, when she said, "I want to see Shamshad one more time." Shamshad was Alam's third child, and she was very close to Sharma Khatoon. Alam sent out the message, and in a few days Dhayani, Nisa, Punnu, and Shamshad came rushing in, thinking that Sharma Khatoon was about to sign off—that she was about to get called.

But they all found her fine and in high spirits. She just wanted to see them, especially Shamshad whom she used to tell the things of her heart. After a few days, she asked them all to take her, to Bhattiyain-jo-Shehar, the place where she was born and where she got married a lifetime ago to Fakeer on a rainy night, where her wicked uncle had lied about her age and sold her for 123 rupees. She wanted to go back there, so they took her. She was fine, chatting with everyone, walking on her own. Every night before sleeping she would hug everyone and say her goodbyes, but then she would wake up the next morning and laugh at her own gesture of the previous night. But on one of those nights she hugged everyone and went to sleep and never woke up and never laughed at herself again.

According to her wish she was buried in the graveyard of Bhattiyain-jo-Shehar, where her forefathers had been laid to rest. The next day the whole house filled with relatives, and all of Alam's other children came. Ali Gohar came with his wife and two little kids, and the house was buzzing again with life upon Sharma's death.

After a few days that buzzing life gradually went back to where it had come from. Alam was left alone once again, but this time there was not even Sharma, his mother, with whom he used to talk at least a couple of times a day. But then, the whole of Qamber was still alive, who knows, Alam's hundreds and hundreds of students and their children and lots of Alam's friends were still around. By now, there was another photo studio in town, but Alam's patrons were like carvings on cave walls—they were not going anywhere. Whenever they needed a photo taken promptly, they would come to Alam's modest studio.

Winters in Qamber were really frigid. They called those winters *'jawoo paroo'* in Sindhi, which means frozen mercury. So in winters Alam would sleep in his studio to keep himself warm. One of those nights as he was sleeping—the first part of the night had probably passed—he awoke feeling as if someone was breathing on his forehead. He kept pretending that he was asleep.

It was dark, but from the cracked planks of studio door a frail light of street lamps was creeping in, allowing him to see bits of movements of two figures. Sometimes, as they were moving they were intersecting with those dull light beams, and Alam could see cold breaths exhaling from their nostrils and emitting a steam. Alam lay there motionless.

The thieves had probably come to find Alam's money, which was not there because he kept it in a kind of bank or credit union that the post office ran on the side, and it was called national savings account. So thieves found no money, but they made out with some solid, heavy brass bowls and other small things.

The next morning Alam filed a police report, and the police inspector called for a traditional foot tracker. Foot tracking is an art and has to do nothing with forensic medicine or investigative science, but it seemed to have worked for thousands of years. These foot trackers were extraordinary people who memorised foot indentations in the ground of individuals of their area, and by just looking at foot impression on soft surface, they could pinpoint a particular person or a person belonging a specific clan or tribe. Or sometimes they would report that an impression was not from this area, meaning that the thief or thieves had come in from somewhere outside.

In a few hours, the *payree* arrived—that's what foot trackers were called. He was an old worn-out man with a white scattered beard that left some wrinkled thin skin on his cheeks, and a flood of those same fine wrinkles covered his forehead. Every rolled wrinkle of his forehead was like a Dead Sea scroll in its own right, holding oceans of stories in it. But his extinguishing grey halo eyes were hiding a laser sharp gaze in them.

Alam removed the domed pans and a few oval rattan baskets. These baskets were commonly used to cover free-roaming chickens at night, with a heavy weight placed over them to secure the birds and protect them from wild foxes and dogs. But Alam had placed them that morning over the footprints to save them from getting disturbed. The payree examined the foot impression several times, looking back and forth like he was dissecting and slicing in his mind, and then he stood up and said with his eyebrows stretched, *'Gopang haa'*—they were Gopang's. That concluded the entire investigation, and it was presumed that two of the Gopang family did it.

But no one got caught, that complaint from Alam went into files of police station, and probably into one of those forehead wrinkles of the payree's memory scrolls.

Alam stayed in Qamber, but his photography business was all but gone. He started forgetting things, placing wrong photos in envelopes, processing ordinary orders as urgent and leaving urgent orders unprocessed all together. He was still opening his studio every day, but on those rare occasions when a customer showed up, he would send them to the other photo studio, apologising and saying, "Thank you for coming, but I no longer take photographs."

Chapter 10
A Heart That Stopped Beating, but Was Still Saying, 'I'm Fine'

One day, he woke up and went to the barbershop to get his hair cut and beard trimmed, and then took a shower there. Small-town barbers also offered baths, but nothing fancy like Turkish baths; these were cramped, the size of a vintage phone booth, in which one could barely stand and bathe. But he took a bath there, went to the launderer to pick up his white salwar kameez that he occasionally wore. Then he returned home, collected a few more items, and placed them in a chunky braided cylindrical basket made of rusty dried date leaves. The basket had a pair of sturdy handles that felt soft to the touch while being strong enough to support its weight.

He put on that freshly washed and pressed salwar kameez and then locked all the doors, which was an effort, because some of the doors had not been locked or even shut together for decades. He pulled both door-planks together and then guided that rusted chain head into the catch. Then he fastened those shackled old padlocks, holding the shackles end in the lock's mouth and twisting the key two and a half times. He also went and locked Fakeer and Sharma Khatoon's livery stable, which had turned into a shack since Sharma's death because Alam had shut down the stable business.

But today, he just walked in and shut its door and walked out. He didn't look at anything, and here was nothing to look at anyway, other than those big cracked and dry round baked red-clay water dispensing tanks for the horses and bulls, which had now turned cement grey couldn't hold water in them anymore. Once they used to be filled with cool water, and Sharma used to look at her reflection every now and then in its languidly calm surface.

But Alam never got a chance to look at those water dispensers. He even didn't give a good look to the barr tree. He just locked the house, picked up his basket and left for Larkano. He went straight to the train station, bought a ticket, and boarded the train. After a while in the journey, someone sitting next to him asked, "where are you going?"

He didn't hear that person because of his deafness. But he guessed the question and answered, "To see my children."

He lived another seventeen years and never once came back to Qamber. In those years, he kept forgetting things. After moving to Jamshoro, he would roam around freely, and to people there he was a benign old man who very carefully placed his feet on pebbly paths of that university town, walking all throughout that colony and its outskirts. Sometimes, go and sit on a bench at the university train station platform and watch people getting off trains and boarding them. The stationmaster there was from Qamber, of all the places in the world, and to defy the idiom that lightning doesn't strike twice, that stationmaster was his student, too.

On other times, he would go to the university museum, though at that time there wasn't much to see there other than 10 or 12 paintings. One painting out of that tiny collection was a figure study of a young man sitting on a stool, which was the thesis assignment of one of the teachers from the university's fine arts departments. The painting was from his school days, when he was studying somewhere else, and somehow by a long shot that managed to qualify as Sindhi heritage too.

Other than those paintings there were a couple hundred photographs also on display there, one of them an unbelievably sad picture in black and white, showing a lonely deserted stone paved alley of the desert town of Mithi, in Tharparkar, Sindh. And there was also a gallery of prominent personalities, which at that time displayed hardly 8 or 10 prominent people from all of Sindh and her five thousand year history. Probably, people who curated that gallery had extremely stringent criteria and didn't want to place anybody in there.

There was also a rich music library with some of the rarest 78 RPM vinyl gramophone records of Sindhi music in there too, but Alam didn't care for anything that involved hearing because he wouldn't be able to listen. But then, much of that music has never been heard by anyone else in that library either, other than the music library's angel-faced innocent looking director. He and only he collected all those musical gems, preserving and protecting that timeless treasure.

Occasionally that angel-faced innocent-looking director used to listen to those records, picking ones that he thought people were going to like. He would take them home with him and make copies of them, which then his children and other family members converted from 78 RPM to analogue cassette tapes and then mass-produced them into cassette albums. Later he sold them commercially through his own private limited. Copyright infringement was nothing then; everything was in the public domain. It was the law of the jungle: if you have power, grab it; if you are wicked, trap it; if you are dumb, hell with you.

Alam didn't care about that. And he didn't pay attention to that oddly placed painting which in reality had nothing to do with the culture or heritage of Sindh, nor did he care that there were fewer than 10 noteworthy Sindhis in the museum's gallery of prominent people. But somehow he just loved all that. He couldn't explain that there was so much more heritage was in his mind, but others couldn't see what was in his mind. But over there in that museum, anybody could walk in and see priceless treasures of Sindhi heritage. And with all those faults it was still a beautiful place.

After some time, he stopped roaming around that university campus and confined himself to the government quarters. And he kept moving between the walls, like an intelligent robot vacuum that bangs into a wall, reverses, and starts heading towards another wall. Then he stopped doing even, that and chose to become unbudgingly stationary, parking himself on a four-legged cot in one of the hallway corner of that house.

Lying there on the cot, he started addressing everyone formally and thanking his own children and grandchildren as if they were strangers, and all of his recent memory ran empty. One day, he broke his hip and never recovered his ability to walk after the surgery, so his elder daughter Nisa and Dhayani would carry him every morning into the tiny backyard garden of their government quarters so that he could enjoy fresh air and winter morning sun.

On one of those cool winter mornings, while Dhayani sat on the cot in a crouched posture, allowing Alam to lean and rest his head on her frail, fragile chest resembling a sparrow's nest, he coughed, and something lodged in his throat.

Dhayani brought one of her hands close to his mouth and asked him to spit in her hand. He coughed again and spat a glob of his blood onto her palm, and then he looked up towards Dhayani's face and said in a gravelly voice, *"Dhanull, ma theek aahiyan."*—*Dhanull, I'm fine.* 'Dhanull' was a name that he used for

Dhayani. In that moment, he was telling her he was okay, and probably he was. She looked at him and he repositioned his head on her bony chest like young people usually do in their sweet and deaf youthful sleep, somewhere under the open heavens.

But shortly after that he stopped moving there, in her lap, on her chest, but she kept holding him there, and didn't cry or yell or make any other noise. But her old heart couldn't keep quiet; it kept on beating crazily behind her little rib cage, which was barely holding itself together.

Story III: Ali Gohar

Chapter 1
So It Begins

His eyes were glued on that cut-loose kite that was rising and falling and drifting on the gentle wind. He knew that the other boys were also in pursuit, so with lightning speed he climbed to the roof of the meat market where the kite's string was touching the roof's surface. He scraped his shin against a rusted iron bar on the way, but he kept going to grab the kite, unaware that this small cut on his shin would end up becoming a *nasoor*—a sore wound infested with maggots.

He had to get that wound treated at the dispensary, and he was supposed to return daily to have it inspected. Each morning his mother gave him twelve paisa for getting his bandage changed, but he used the money instead to buy candy. After several days, while he was sleeping, his mother noticed a distinct and foul smell and realised that it was coming from his wound. When she opened the bandage, she found that the wound was filled with maggots. First thing in the morning he went to the dispensary with his father, and after examining the wound the doctor suggested amputation from right above the knee.

He ran away from dispensary and came home crying and yelling. Luckily, Maasurar Kando,[89] the husband of his maternal aunt, was visiting at this time, having come to town to sell his grain crop. His real name was Ghulam Qadir Shaikh, but everyone called him *Kandayro*—'thorny shrub'—because his mother had had multiple miscarriages before him, and she had solemnly sworn that, if her child survived, she would call him a useless thorny shrub. And it was Maasurar Kando who suggested a witch doctor's therapy for him—a recipe that required the bone shell of dead turtle, which had been burned to ashes and then

---

[89] *Maasurar Kando*: 'Maasurar' means 'uncle', but specifically an uncle who is the husband of a maternal aunt.

ground to fine dust and then blended with fresh sweet butter to make a salve, to be applied to the wound.

His mother, who was weeping and was already in distress, turned her anger onto her brother-in-law. "So are you going to get the turtle shell, or just sit there?" And she started cursing at him: "*Moaa!*"—'you dead man'—and demanding that he go and get a dead turtle's shell right away. So poor Maasurar Kando went and got all the ingredients, and the salve was made. No one expected that the wound actually be healed! But it was. How did it heal? It was a deathless riddle.

He had been born prematurely, because his mother had gotten scared of a shadow and gone in to labour early. His grandmother helped her to deliver him in a small stagnant dark dungeon-like storeroom with no light. They laid the frail, tiny infant in a bucket of hay covered with soft linen. He could not move his jaw to suck, so they had to pour milk into his mouth through a tiny seashell. His father went to the local grocer, who said there was a new dry formula for newborn babies that came from England, and would he like to give it to his child?

So his father purchased it, and for a few months that infant formula was working like a charm. But then it happened one of those packages of formula had expired. It did not occur to poor Alam and his wife that, packed in this beautiful coloured tin-can with a smiling baby, there could be expired and toxic milk which would nearly kill their son.

They assumed that the milk was good, and that he was throwing up because of some other illness. They kept giving him the milk, and his condition kept getting worse. In the span of a few days, they took him to every health practitioner they could find, including the quack and the holistic medicine man, but his condition only got worse.

Their last resort was a Marathi lady doctor in Qamber. She had a thorny disposition and was rumoured to curse women and their children, so no one liked to go to her, but she was also known to be very good at curing the sick. So Alam's mother urged him to seek this woman's help. Alam agreed and set off with his mother Sharma and tiny son Ali Gohar right away.

It was mid-afternoon. The doctor's watchman, who was sitting outside of her practice, said that she rested in the afternoons and wouldn't see any patients. But Alam was desperate, so, holding his ailing son in his arms, he started climbing the stairs up to her residence above the dispensary.

Knowing that she was Marathi, he called out to her in his own feeble and broken Marathi: "God has given you this blessing to treat the vulnerable and sick. I have come here to your doorstep holding my only son, who is gravely ill, so please have mercy."

But the watchman dragged Alam back and barred him from going up any further, telling him again that she would not see any patients at this time of day, and did he want him to lose his job? And suddenly her apartment door opened, and she pushed aside the straw *chick'a* blinds and stepped into partial view. And her watchman in desperation was trying to push Alam and his mother back down, apologising profusely to the lady doctor. "I told them that Doctor Sahiba doesn't see patients at this hour, but they wouldn't listen."

But she was not alarmed. She told the watchman to go and open the dispensary and seat Alam and his mother inside, and she said that she would be down to see them soon.

And indeed, after a few minutes she came down and examined Ali Gohar, who was barely responsive. She listened to his chest sounds and asked Alam what had happened. He told her that all of the sudden his son had started throwing up and becoming weaker and weaker. And she asked what they had been feeding him and quickly deduced that surely that infant formula was bad, and she ordered them to stop that at once.

She gave them some powdered medicine and instructed Alam to administer it along with a drop of brandy every few hours. She told them that if the baby survived for next forty-eight hours, there was a great chance that he would live.

And right as they were leaving, she turned to Alam and said, "By the way you speak very bad Marathi, but I had not heard even bad Marathi for a very long time. Half of what you said was not even really Marathi, but still—it was moving."

Alam thanked her and said, "*aamhi tumche mana pasna aabhari aahoth.*"—We thank you from bottoms of our heart.

She smiled, and they went on their way back home. Alam dropped off his mother and child and went to the *ghutto*[90] to get the brandy. And they started Ali Gohar's course of medicine and drops of brandy, and in few hours he started moving his limbs slowly. His grandmother took a solemn vow to Shams Tabrez,

---

[90] *Ghutto*: a state-run liquor store.

saying to herself, *"If Ali Gohar my grandson survives, I will carry him and walk to your shrine."*

And in a few days he recovered completely.

Alam wanted to go and thank the Marathi lady doctor, and he felt they ought to give her something out of gratitude. And his father, Fakeer Sher Mohammad, cast his gaze toward his dearest lamb, which liked to sleep curled up like a shrimp on the bed next to Fakeer's feet. And Fakeer said, "take her."

The doctor was busy with patients when they reached her practice, so they waited outside, holding Ali Gohar and the lamb, who were both making noises. Eventually, the lady doctor called them in and saw Ali Gohar giggling in his grandmother's arms.

"He recovered because of your treatment and medicine," said Alam. "So we came here to thank you. And my father has sent this lamb, who is very dear to him, for you."

And the lady doctor smiled and stroked Ali Gohar's head. "I didn't want to break your heart when you came to me," she said. "Your son had very few breaths left in him at that time, so I just gave you some glucose powder and prescribed the brandy to comfort him. He must have survived because he was supposed to live."

And then she said, "I will accept this lamb, and give it back to your son. It looks like your father really loves his grandson."

Alam thanked her again by saying, *"Dev tumcha bhala karo!"*—God bless you.

Now that Ali Gohar had recovered from that dangerous situation, Alam's mother Sharma Khatoon bore a moral burden to walk to the shrine of Shams Tabrez to fulfil her solemn vow. In a few months, there was a caravan leaving for Multan, and several devotees from Qamber were going to pay their respects, so Sharma Khatoon joined them, carrying Ali Gohar with her. That caravan was not walking to Multan, though—instead they were using benefit of technology and travelling by train. She did not like that but she had no other choice. So she stood on both feet all the way carrying Ali Gohar in her arms. When they reached Multan, her feet were swollen and she could barely walk.

They stayed in a nearby *serai*[91] that night, and the next morning they headed to the shrine of great Shams Tabrez. She was thinking about all those myths and

---

[91] *Serai*: a roadside bed rental.

mysteries, especially the one in which Shams Tabrez—and 'Shams' is Arabic for 'sun'—got angry at the townspeople who had refused to lend him fire to cook a dead fish, and who had pushed him away, showing their distaste because of his appearance. Shams then had looked up to sun and said, *"I am the sun just as you are, and I command you to come to me."* And the great sun came down to within arm's length of Shams, according to legend, and the whole atmosphere started simmering.

And as she was walking towards the shrine, she was talking to Shah Shams Tabrez in her heart, explaining to him, *"Budheen tho, o pak piyara pir muhanja"*—are you listening, you my loving, holy saint?—"I had every intention to walk, but the caravan people choose to come here by train." And then she added, "I did not sit; rather I stood on both feet all the way, so please forgive me, my loving saint."

She kept walking, breathing heavily because she was climbing stairs and carrying her grandson in her arms. And she was not paying any attention to that squeaky clean blue sky which was glowing, or to that faded emerald green mausoleum dome of the shrine, with its inward-tilting hexagonal walls, sitting on a squarish platform of red bricks that were no longer red but rather a muddy pink. She saw that the lower square platform had four minarets, and each hexagonal angle also had a small minaret right under dome.

She did lean against that wild ber tree[92] to catch her breath before approaching the first staircase leading up to the square platform. She looked at the branches of the wild ber tree, which were covered with thin multi-coloured strips of used fabric, and she knew that each narrow coloured strand was carrying the heavy weight of a devotee's unfulfilled desire. But she did not entangle her thoughts in that. She pressed onward, and after climbing several steps up onto the large pedestal-like platform, she could see a panoramic view of Multan.

But she paid no attention even to that, because she was trying to find the door that would lead her to the final resting place of Shah Shams Tabrez. She finally found it and stepped into a room where sunlight streaked the floor with angular beams, coming from small openings at the top. And dust particles were doing their space walk in those beams, and pigeons were continuously making their unexplainable rhythmic noise, *guoo-tar, goo; guoo-tar, goo*. She sat close to his grave and started talking to this saint, without knowing that this was *the* Shah

---

[92] Ber tree: *jujube* tree, not to be confused with jojoba.

Shams Tabrez, who was the reason for Jalaluddin Rumi's poetry; he was the one who was the ocean of love for a thirsty Rumi. She was sitting in front of him, and at first she had nothing to say, and was simply that she had fulfilled her vow. But then desire sparked in her greedy heart, and after rearranging her composure she held the lower end of her cheesecloth veil over both her hands and started to speak to Shams Tabrez.

"With your blessing and your ocean of mercy, my Ali Gohar, my grandson, survived. I can't thank you enough for that, and Allah-saeen gave me strength so that I could come to your *deedar*.[93]"

And then abruptly she became a little more personal with Shah Shams Tabrez, and went on, "You have nothing to lose—you are already a saint—so what would it cost you if you could give Mohammad Alam another son. And make it a pair."

While making her plea, she pushed herself forward, close to his grave, placing her right palm on ground. And in that moment, her hand got all wet, and she snapped her head down to her right with a lightning speed, and there was little Ali Gohar who had just soiled himself. And without losing a beat she snatched her cheesecloth veil from her head and started wiping the floor bare-headed, and endless tears were rolling from her eyes.

She ran out of the mausoleum, still carrying her grandson, to the outer courtyard, where she found a clay pot filled with water. She soaked her veil in the fresh water and then went back in to wipe the floor some more. And she kept saying, "please forgive him, he is just an innocent toddler, and you merciful ocean of love, for the sake of you loved ones, please forgive him." And she kept crying, without knowing that, to Shah Shams Tabrez, her toddler grandson was like one of the pigeons on his rooftop that kept spitting their droppings on his dome, and he never minded.

She carried Ali Gohar back outside and sat under the ber tree for that entire evening. And probably she was weeping all that time. She softly patted Ali Gohar's chest to comfort him as he slept. Her teardrops dried on her cheeks, leaving behind a white streak of salt. And soon she was also sinking into and coming out of a trance, meanwhile looking down at carefree Ali Gohar in his deep sleep.

---

[93] *Deedar*: literally 'sight' or 'vision', but not in a mundane sense. 'Deedar' implies that the viewer is filled with love and reverence for the object of the gaze.

Then she would think about how to reverse what had happened that day, as guilt was clutching her tightly. Then something that was probably her subconscious in the form of a bright light falling on her forehead kicked in to rescue her and assure her that it was just a naïve occurrence. And a peaceful force pushed her and seemed to ask her to wake up. She opened her eyes and came out of that anxious trance. She noticed she had been perspiring. Dawn had just broken; the skies were turning an inviting fresh pink at the horizon.

But then those pinkish tones started turning into fresh light blues, and darkness was melting into the brightness of a great sun—or Shams, shall we say! And she saw five bright orange ripe berries on the tree, although it was not ber season. She grabbed them and shut them in her closed palms, and a beam of happiness radiated in her being. She opened her palms, kissed the berries, and tied them in the corner of her cheesecloth veil. Her stress was gone and she was feather-light.

On her return, she gave those five ber berries to Dhayani. And, though not right away, Dhayani did indeed give birth to six sons in succession after that, and five of her sons survived and lived their life to fullest.

Chapter 2
Two Sugar Dolls

Fakeer loved Ali Gohar.
One day, he glanced up through the half-open doors of his stables and saw Ali Gohar weeping as he walked off to school. So he went over to Alam's living quarters and asked Dhayani, *"Amma, Abbo saeen rooiendo wanain payoo?"* The question translates simply enough—Fakeer was asking why Ali Gohar was crying—but the Sindhi words bear more meaning than just this. Because Fakeer addressed Dhayani, his daughter-in-law, as if she was his own mother (*'Amma'*), and he referred to Ali Gohar as *Abbo Saeen*, which is an honorific address for a father.

Such is the nature of familial affection among Sindhi people that younger people are often addressed with this kind of elevated language out of sheer love.

And Dhayani replied, "He was asking for pocket money, and I don't have it today, so I didn't gave him any. That's why he was crying."

So Fakeer walked to elementary school ground and sat under shadow of a tali tree* and waited for couple of hours until the midday break. He could have walked into Ali Gohar's class, but he chose to sit crunched down in the cool shadow of the tali tree, watching the fat-headed black garden ants with their open clamp jaws as they ran up and down the tree trunk, doing something very important.

While Fakeer was observing the garden ants' rushing commute, he was absent-mindedly holding a lone tali leaf between his fingers, rolling his thumb over the waxy surface of tali leaf, which were a fancy curly bracket shape like the parentheses in algebra. And instinctively he started tearing them and then mashing and ripping them around, until finally he tossed that badly smushed lone tali leaf to the ground.

And there was a sound of the bell, that constant bell, but after its third of forth clang that bell sound faded into a jazzy enchantment of happy children coming out of all the classrooms like someone had poured water on the black garden ants' nest. Fakeer was trying to find Ali Gohar among hundreds of kids of the same size, and while he was doing that, a smiling Ali Gohar was already standing right in front of him. Fakeer knelt down so that he could see Ali Gohar's face, and when he took a good look at him, happiness illuminated Fakeer's own face, which looked like a slot machine when it hits its jackpot and starts making happy noises.

He looked at Ali Gohar and said, "You silly boy, don't cry for money ever again." And while saying that he pressed a coin with an image of King George VI into Ali Gohar's palm. It looked like a disc-shaped safety washer made of copper, with a big fat hole in the middle.

It was only 1/63 of a rupee, but it could buy Ali Gohar three small treats, a handful of roasted chickpeas, a pinkie-finger sized sugar candy doll that had lost all its sculpture detail and didn't look a bit like a doll, rather it looked like a pinkie-sized wrapped Egyptian mummy, and five small pieces of sweet sap sugarcane core. But Ali Gohar didn't like sweet sap pieces of sugarcane core. So instead he would take two sugar dolls and a handful of roasted chickpeas.

It was a midsummer day in Qamber, in that part of the day when everything looks bright grey, from the dirt on ground to the walls to the skies, and only shade looks appealing. Perspiration bubbles up on the forehead and every irritatingly acrid smell of the body is amplified. Ali Gohar was walking through the grain market, his head and face all covered in dirt, which made his dry tear streaks even more prominent, starting from the corners of both eyes and fanning out towards his temples.

Fakeer was passing through same street for some reason that became completely irrelevant the moment he saw Ali Gohar in tears. He hugged him and brushed his hair with all ten fingers, trying to get that dirt out. He wiped Ali Gohar's face with long front fall of his shirt. "What happened?" Fakeer asked.

Ali Gohar replied, "I was playing in the library garden with Roopu, and he started pouring dirt on my head, and then he hit me."

Fakeer shook his head in dismay and uttered a curse word that involved the genitals of Roopu's female caregiver. And he confirmed, "This is the same Roopu Chand who is Bharumal the grocer's grandson?"

Ali Gohar nodded his head yes. Fakeer grabbed his hand and started leading them towards Bharumal's shop. And when Ali Gohar saw Roopu there, instead of running away somewhere else, Roopu made the colossal mistake of taking refuge inside his grandfather's shop. The interior was an old hallway-shaped room filled with sacks of grain, lentils, sugar, and dry sugarcane chunks, with their rolled back sleeves, and canisters of all sort of oils, from cooking oil to coconut oil to kerosene oil.

Bharumal was a typical merchant, a semi-sophisticated man, who wore a snow-white *pahiryan*[94] over his dhoti. So Roopu ran into his shop and hid behind Bharumal, and shortly after that Fakeer arrived holding Ali Gohar's hand. And Fakeer cut straight to the chase and told Bharumal, "Your grandson put dirt on my grandson's head. Now either you send your grandson out so that my grandson can put dirt on his head, or forget about our grandsons and instead *you* come out, and we can settle it between us."

Apparently, Bharumal understood Fakeer's statement very clearly. Without saying a single word in contest, Bharumal grabbed the arm of Roopu, who was still hiding behind him, and pushed him out onto street. Roopu hit the ground and crumpled. But Fakeer told Ali Gohar out loud, "*Chaday deens*"—Let him go.

Ali Gohar looked up at Fakeer's face like he wanted to put dirt on Roopu's head, but was now going to bear the pain of tolerance. Ali Gohar didn't want to let that *bhenchod*[95] Roopu go free, but Fakeer grabbed Ali Gohar's arm and said, "Let's go."

And as they walked away, Ali Gohar's first steps were heavy like his feet were glued to the ground. On his way back, he grumbled, "Why didn't you let me put dirt on his head?"

Fakeer kept walking quietly, periodically looking down at Ali Gohar, wanting to kiss his forehead. And Fakeer wanted to tell Ali Gohar a story, but he didn't know where to start from. So he started it abruptly. "There was a lion, a lion among lions. He was so brave that they call him the lion of God. He used to fight for his people, for their cause—"

And Ali Gohar interrupted and said, "How could a lion fight for people? Lions eat people!"

---

[94] *Pahiryarn*: a long loose shirt that falls below the knees.
[95] *Bhenchod*: obscene abuse word (literally, sister-fucker).

Fakeer listened to Ali Gohar and made a humming yes. And after a few seconds he said, "But he was a man, a man made up of *noor*.[96] They call him a lion because of his valiance. He fought for their cause, but deep inside his soul he was a peace-loving man. He didn't believe in hurting his fellow living breathing creatures."

And Ali Gohar was listening to Fakeer's every word, and was rolling his head back every now and then to look at Fakeer's face while walking. And he forgot all about that sadness that he'd had a little while ago, when he lost the chance to pour dirt on Roopu's head. And Fakeer continued telling him that story with all its beauty and glory and lessons of how to tame the ego.

It was unusual, but his father sometimes took him and his elder sister Zaybull to the library in the evenings, way after dark. There were mostly old people there, some community elders, and there was a big radio mounted on a table in the middle of the lawn. He had seen this radio several times before. His father used to bring him and his sister there every now and then to listen to the news bulletin, or, very rarely, if the radio operator was in a good mood, they could listen to a radio drama on this machine.

It was a rectangular box made of fine polished red wood, standing upright, and it had a big glowing glass circle in the centre, with numerous numbers and a needle that spun in a circular motion. It had a brass trim and four little knobs, one on the top and the three others in formation.

But the radio operator only used one of them to turn it on and off, and when he turned it on, it took several minutes to warm up, and right before it worked it would emit a fine, high beeping sound. At first, he thought that he was the only one who could hear that beep, but after a while he shared his discovery with his father and sister, and was heartbroken to learn that they also could hear that fine beeping signal.

On this particular evening, people were discussing something important and whispering in each other's ears. Alam told Ali Gohar and his sister to stay quiet, and the children expected some song to begin soon on the radio. But everyone became attentive when they heard a scratchy voice, which was saying:

"I am glad that I am afforded an opportunity to speak to you directly through this radio from Delhi. It is the first time, I believe, that a non-official has been

---

[96] *Noor*: divine light.

afforded an opportunity to address the people through the medium of this powerful instrument direct to the people on a political matter. It augurs well and I hope that in the future I shall have greater facilities to enable me to voice my views and opinions which will reach you directly."

He had serious doubts that the radio was just a machine. He believed instead that there must be some small people living in that piece of furniture. And he was not at all enthusiastic today about this constant voice coming out of the radio without music.

In the past, whenever he had come to the library to listen to the radio, there was always some music or some story shared between male and female voices. He and his sister were pulling at their father's sleeve to go home, but Alam placed his index finger on his lips and whispered, "*Listen to this! It's history in the making."*

And then the scratchy voice went on:

"The statement of His Majesty's Government embodying the plan for the transfer of power to the peoples of India has already been broadcast and will be released to the press to be published in India and abroad tomorrow morning. It gives the outlines of the plan for us to give it our most earnest consideration. We must remember that we have to take momentous decisions and handle grave issues facing us in the solution of the complex political problem of this great subcontinent inhabited by 300 million people. The world has no parallel for the most onerous and difficult task which we have to perform.

"Grave responsibility lies particularly on the shoulders of Indian leaders. Therefore, we must galvanise and concentrate all our energy to see that the transfer of power is effected in a peaceful and orderly manner. I most earnestly appeal to every community and particularly to Muslim India to maintain peace and order. We must examine the plan, in its letter and in its spirit and come to our conclusions and take our decisions. I pray to God that, at this critical moment, He may guide us and enable us to discharge our responsibilities in a wise and statesmanlike manner."

His father pulled a beedi out of a small bundle and kept squeezing it between the thumb and index finger of his right hand while listening to the scratchy voice. Then he bit down to hold the thin flat part of the beedi in place, and he pulled a stick out of a matchbox and struck it on the igniting surface. A glow of flame appeared, which he quickly grabbed between his both palms and lit the beedi. He inhaled a deep puff while listening to the scratchy voice, and then released it.

It is clear that the plan does not meet in some important respects our point of view and we cannot say or feel that we are satisfied or that we agree with some of the matters dealt with by the plan. It is for us now to consider whether the plan as presented to us by His Majesty's Government should be accepted by us as a compromise or a settlement. On this point, I do not wish to prejudge the decision of the Council of the All-India Muslim League, which has been summoned to meet on Monday, June 9; and the final decision can only be taken by the Council according to our constitution, precedents and practice. But so far as I have been able to gather on the whole, reaction in the Muslim League circles in Delhi has been hopeful. Of course the plan has got to be very carefully examined in its pros and cons before the final decision can be taken.

I must say that I feel that the Viceroy has battled against various forces very bravely and the impression that he has left on my mind is that he was actuated by a high sense of fairness and impartiality, and it is up to us now to make his task less difficult and help him as far as it lies in our power in order that he may fulfil his mission of transfer of power to the people of India, in a peaceful and orderly manner.

Now the plan that has been broadcast already makes it clear in paragraph II that a referendum will be made to the electorates of the present Legislative Assembly in the North West Frontier Province who will choose which of the two alternatives in paragraph four they wish to adopt; and the referendum will be held under the aegis of the Governor-general in consultation with the provincial government. Hence it is clear that the verdict and the mandate of the people of the Frontier Province will be obtained as to whether they want to join Pakistan Constituent Assembly or the Hindustan Constituent Assembly.

In these circumstances, I request the Provincial Muslim League of the Frontier Province to withdraw the movement of peaceful civil disobedience which they had perforce to resort to; and I call upon all the leaders of the Muslim League and Mussalmans generally to organise our people to face this referendum with hope and courage, and I feel confident that the people of the Frontier will give their verdict by a solid vote to join the Pakistan Constituent Assembly.

I cannot but express my appreciation of the sufferings and sacrifices made by all the classes of Mussalmans and particularly the great part the women of the Frontier played in the fight for our civil liberties. Without apportioning blame, and this is hardly the moment to do so, I deeply sympathise with all those who have suffered and those who died or whose properties were subjected to destruction and I fervently hope that Frontier will go through this referendum in a peaceful manner and it should be the anxiety of everyone to obtain a fair, free and true verdict of the people of the Frontier. Once more I most earnestly appeal to all to maintain peace and order.

Pakistan Zindabad.

And his father murmured, like he was talking to himself, saying, *"kardan dar guftan; basyar farqast.*[97]*"* He did not understand what his father had murmured, but he was glad that it was over and that scratchy voice was quiet now, because he did not understand a single word in that speech other than *Hindustan, Mussalmans, Pakistan* and *Zindabad*.

He was not alone in that; there were millions and millions who had no idea what was happening. Fifteen million people were going to be mobilised and displaced, more than one million were going to be killed, an undisclosed number of girls and women were going to be raped, an unknown number of children would become orphans. And years after this day, an elderly rugged Sikh man would lose his voice and dive into deep pauses, swinging his head like a restless horse to hide his emotions from the camera, before describing a half a century old memory from his childhood, when his father had called his eighteen-year-old sister into the courtyard of their home, kissed her forehead, and asked her to kneel down and bow her head gently and move her veil and braided hair to expose the back of her neck, and then with a single blow decapitated her, because their house was besieged by a Muslim mob, and they were outnumbered, and he feared that the women would be forcefully converted or raped.

It was an ordinary hot dusty summer day, the kind of day that you never remember. He was walking home barefoot from school, in the scorching sun. The worst thing was that in summer the salt-drenched soil turned into a hot frying pan, and those crystallised salt fragments penetrated into the soles of your feet

---

[97] *Kardan...farqast*: Persian: "There's a difference between saying and doing."

like hot amber going through a butter cube. So he had to run in a zigzag manner, pausing every ten or fifteen yards in shadows to rest his soles.

And in one of those stops, under a long straw canopy, he heard people at the barbershop saying that there was going to be a new country, and that Qamber was going to be a part of it. And he was so happy, because everything was going to be new: roads, homes, streets, skies, trees, walls and everything!

And since that day he had been eagerly waiting for this new country to be formed. After a few months, he asked his father, "When is Qamber going to become part of this new country?"

And his father replied, "It already did!"

But it never really did happen for him, or for anyone, for that matter. He had very serious doubts about his father's claim that this new country was already formed, because nothing was new. Everything was as old as it could be.

But things did become different in some ways. After a few days, he saw that the entire ground in front of the police station had been converted into a campsite. He had no idea what it was for, but curiosity drew him towards it. When he went closer, he found rows of empty camps for the *Muhajirs*.[98] And they had also converted the primary school and English school buildings ('English' was the nickname for the high school, because beginning in eighth grade the students had to study English) into Muhajirs' camps.

His father said that on such and such a day trains of immigrants were going to arrive at the town train station. And finally that fateful day arrived. Local political leaders, who were the landlords too, had arranged a welcoming gala. There were coloured banners showing two cartoonish human figures dressed in traditional Sindhi and north Indian clothes hugging each other, and at the top of that banner was printed in Sindhi, *"Bhali Karay Aai Muhanja Bhaa"*—Welcome, my brother.

Bull carts were decorated in peacock blue, and red scarves were tied around all the bulls' horns, and heavy *taviz*[99] pendants were draped around their necks. These silver necklaces had triangular spacers called *tekka* at the top and bottom, connected to silver chains which bore the large taviz container at the centre, surrounded with coloured glass beads and *ghungroos*.[100] And those bulls were

---

[98] *Muhajirs*: literally 'pilgrims', this is the word used to describe the millions of Muslim Indians who moved to the new state of Pakistan at the time of the Partition.
[99] *Taviz*: an amulet prayer box made of sterling silver.
[100] *Ghungroos*: small bells strung on a strand, often to be worn around a dancer's ankles.

also tattooed with a stain of yellow or orange or red-brown *mehndi*,[101] and the carts were filled with a thin layer of loose hay covered with *tuuka jee ralliyoon*[102] of shockingly vibrant colours to honour the new arrivals.

He was waiting with his father at the platform, where there was no shade. The platform was paved with faded red bricks in a block-texture pattern. More than half of those bricks were cracked.

Droves of other people had also come to greet the Muhajirs. There were women sitting in the triangular shadow of the one-room ticket office. They had to keep adjusting because that shadow was constantly shrinking, but they were singing *shara,* wedding songs. No one was getting married there, but in Sindh these wedding songs could be sung on any happy occasion. They were normally custom-fitted with the proper names of the bridal couple, but today, they were using only a general noun: *"Muhanja Musalmeen bha-air bhalee Aaya; Muhanja Panhageer bha-air bhalee Aaya."*—*Welcome to my Muslim brothers; welcome to my refugee brothers.*

In the midst of all this, he thought about how he had brushed up his Urdu a little bit by watching the bioscope—that was the name used at the time for the movies. And then someone said *here she comes*, and everybody leaned toward the tracks to see the train. And, sure enough, he could see a small black dot urging violently left and right, exhaling thick blackish-grey smoke, and getting bigger and bigger.

Finally, the train arrived at the platform and came to a stop. A tremendous amount of steam was released from every pore of the locomotive, as if she were heaving a sigh of relief after crossing the finish line. Lots of people were hanging around near the doors, and already a few of the doors started opening. He was expecting to see the kind of people he'd seen in the bioscope: beautiful women like Suraiya or Nargis, men like Pradeep Kumar or Balraj Sahni. Little did he know that this train had come from Mehrauli-Gurgaon carrying a load of Rangur villagers. So this was the second disappointment for him.

First there had been a new country that had literally nothing new, and now this trainload of people was no different from the ones who were already there, except that they were speaking Rungri.

And these immigrants were not greeted—not because no one wanted to greet them, but because the moment train stopped there was mayhem. Some people

---

[101] *Mehndi*: henna.

[102] *Tuuka jee ralliyoon*: traditional hand-stitched patchwork Sindhi quilts.

were jumping out of windows, kids were crying. Most of them couldn't understand a word that was said to them, and the Sindhis couldn't understand them, and it seemed like the whole train fell apart. Finally, someone who could speak Urdu communicated with local elders, and people were gathered into bull carts to be brought to the camps in a procession.

For a few weeks or a month they stayed in those camps, but then gradually they started moving into the properties that Hindus had abandoned. Some got hold of them with claims, while others broke locks to get in and later got the properties transferred to their names by offering some gratuity to employees of the settlement commission.

Ali Gohar was so young that he had to stand up to take his elementary drawing exam, because if he sat on the low bench the desktop would be too high for him. His father took him to all the way to Larkano high school, some 22 miles away from Qamber, to take that exam. He could have taken it in Qamber, but then Alam would have had to be the exam proctor, and he didn't want any shred of suspicion that he might have helped his own son to pass or get a higher score in the exam. So he deliberately asked the examining board to send his son to another centre with a different proctor, and this took them to Larkano.

And Ali Gohar successfully passed that exam and made first class, which was like getting an A. In the British system, there always used to be three classes, first class, second class, and third class, in everything from railway compartments to exams to bureaucracy. Ironically, in railway compartments they even had a fourth class, called 'inter'. Local indigenous Indians were only allowed to travel in the third and inter classes.

Even those local people who had money to buy a first or second class ticket were still required to sit in third or inter class, which, by the way, were not equipped with passenger toilets, because the British thought Indians were such spiritually motivated and enlightened souls that they didn't need to urinate or defecate; after all Buddha was one of them.

So Ali Gohar heard in school that he had passed the exam and gotten first class marks. He came home that afternoon and told his mother the good news. But when Dhayani heard the words 'first class', she hit her right palm against her forehead in distress, making a slapping noise. And she said ruefully to Ali Gohar, "What have you done? Your father is going to be terribly mad. He was saying all along that he'd be glad if you could pass that exam even in second class, but what will he think when he hears that you only got first class!"

And Ali Gohar dropped to the ground rolling in laughter. He told his mother, "first class is *better*, and higher than second class, *charee!*[103]"

It was a scorcher even at quarter past seven in the morning. The piercing rays of the sun were stinging like wasps. He was standing in assembly, where all the students and teachers were gathered. An elder teacher would speak some words of wisdom, and then there would be some recitation from the Holy Scriptures, and at the end everybody would disperse to their allocated classroom. But this day was different, and it would change the lives of many people, including his.

The Assistant Headmaster was interrupting the procedure, as was his normal habit, to ask kids to stay in line or to make a straight formation between the holy recital. And this Assistant Headmaster happened to be a Hindu. Several of his Muslim colleagues had asked him not to do that, but probably he was a creature of habit. So some of the Muslim teachers cooked up a plan, where they decided that if he interrupted again, the reciting teacher would stop him, saying, "Quiet, you Devil!"—and that would be a cue for the other four to rip him apart. Indeed, it did happen on that day that he interrupted, out of his usual habit, during the holy recital.

The person reciting the Holy Scripture was focusing more eagerly on his likely interruption than on the Arabic text, which most probably suggested love and tolerance, but which was given a very different meaning on that day. And the reciting teacher yelled at the Assistant Headmaster, "Shut up, you Lucifer!" And the other four who were lying in wait, including Ali Gohar's father, unleashed their venomous hatred on him, slapping him and kicking, tearing his clothes, pulling his hair, and finally ripping his pants off and leaving him stark naked.

While they were beating, him he kept saying, "Listen to me, *na-Na-O-na-O-na-na*, for heaven's sake! Listen to me, *Ba-ba-O-aba-O-aba*, what are you—? How could you? Listen please, no! No…What are!…you doing!"

But they kept beating him in front of the entire school, and Ali Gohar kept looking at their raging faces like burning hot copper, circling and hunching over him and taking turns. The edges of their grimacing mouths extended to their earlobes, and their noses crawled up all the way between their eyebrows, which caused their eyes to squeeze into thin lines, and saliva drops were flying out of their wide-open mouths that revealed their tobacco-stained teeth. And they kept

---

[103] *Char*ee "You silly!"

beating him for what felt like a long time before some of the other teachers could intervene and bring the commotion to an end.

By now, the Assistant Headmaster's left foot and both hands were shaking involuntarily, and he was trying to hide his genitals with his black velvet cap, that was all covered in dirt. And it felt to Ali Gohar that his Assistant Headmaster was looking right at him with his flushed red face, which was covered with bruises, and he pretended to smile, but his one cheek was twitching like crazy.

Obviously, there were consequences to this. All five schoolteachers, including Ali Gohar's father Mohammad Alam, were reprimanded. The chairman of the municipal committee formed a team of officials to investigate and dig up the truth, and he suspended all of them until further notice. The Assistant Headmaster never came back to the school, and shortly after that incident he moved to India for good.

And the fact-finding team of officials came up with their report, resulting in a one-year suspension from work without pay for all five of the teachers who had violated the code of conduct and fallen below all criteria of common decency, and had abused their fellow teacher, who was their superior, too.

Ali Gohar was hired to fill the vacancy left by his father for that year until the suspension had ended. And so, at the age of fourteen, he became the teacher of the same students with whom he had been studying in eighth grade until yesterday. After a year, his father came back and resumed his duties as the art teacher, but Ali Gohar never went back to school as regular student again. Instead, he became an 'external candidate', something like a home-school student.

He worked as a mechanic at the powerhouse. It's hard to believe that there could even have been a powerhouse there, a private electric powerhouse in Qamber, a town which had been indecorously wrapped and tossed by time into the warehouse of history so carelessly that time himself had no idea where Qamber was in there. But the powerhouse was there, and a young man named Anwar kept switching those two generators, making sure they kept running. The powerhouse was owned by Seth Tarachand's widow.

Nobody had ever seen her in Qamber, but it felt like she lived there, among them, probably because she sold them a little light every night, and brightened a few streets of Qamber after dark. The powerhouse was a huge shed that housed two giant generators. The local people called them *'enjin'a'*, the Sindhi version of word 'engine'. And they kept running all the time. Anwar was their technician, operator, and mechanic, tending to them in all they needed, and he was very good at doing that. His full name was *Anwar Sonaarow*, and incidentally the word 'sonaarow' literally means 'goldsmith' in Sindhi.

But apart from that he couldn't read or write a single word up till the age of twenty, when all of the sudden, one evening, he was sitting outside power house and saw some young high school boys playing something, probably soccer. But what he noticed was their freedom. And that inspired him to learn, and in three short years he went from being illiterate to becoming a high school graduate, and he also passed the inter-drawing exam, under watchful eye of Alam. And there he became a friend of Ali Gohar. Four more years after that, he got his bachelor's degree.

Anwar discovered how to use people like ladders: one moment he would be looking at a rung at eye level, and the next moment that same rung was under his feet. The psyche of climbing is that you have to keep stepping up. But Ali Gohar never cared much for Anwar.

His father ran a successful art class at Qamber high school, in that his students generally passed elementary and inter-drawing. Over time this gave him a strong reputation, so hopeful drawing exam candidates started coming from areas as far-flung as Quetta and staying as boarders in the dormitory, which also brought revenue to the municipality that owned the school.

Those students would bring gifts as a token of their appreciation for their teacher, like big bunch of lotus roots, or a quart of wild honey, or a box of *mao*,[104] or s*hirkarpuri-aachara*.[105] Some of the poorer students, who couldn't afford those novelties but still wanted to show their gratitude and respect, would cut fresh grass and bundle it into a bale-load, which they would carry on their head to present it to him.

Alam always refused to accept the gifts, saying that they were really bribes, and that the municipality paid his salary. But Dhayani would always accept the gifts anyway, disregarding Alam's rhetoric, probably because she was the one who actually worked the stone grain mill, placing a handful of wheat or rice in it and grinding it to fine flour, and it was she who ground thousands of her own desires into dust between those same two circular stone bed rocks.

She tried to plant several young trees in that huge open courtyard of her home, but unfortunately nothing survived in that salt-drenched bitter hard rock-

---

[104] *Mao*: milk cakes.

[105] *Shikarpuri-aachara*: famous pickles made in Shikarpur.

like dark grey soil. And one day a student of Alam, a boy named Qabill, brought a bale of grass as a gift, probably because that's what he could afford. He said to Dhayani, "Amma, here is a bale of grass for your cows." Alam's students always called Dhayani 'amma', meaning 'mother'.

And Dhayani, who was probably frustrated about her unsuccessful attempts in planting trees, was uncharacteristically harsh toward the poor fellow who probably couldn't afford anything other than this bale of grass, which was useless to her, and said, "What I'm going to do with all this grass?" She asked him instead to help her to plant some young trees in their yard. He looked at that hard, salt-drenched soil, and after a small pause he replied, "I'll do it for you, Amma."

He was the son of a peasant farmer, so in that small pause he recognised the difficulty of that task. But over the next few days, Qabill devoted many hours to digging a waist-deep trench, a couple of yards wide and long. To fill the trench, he brought a few bull-cart loads of a sweet clay-sand all the way from his father's fertile land. He planted several young trees there, but only the ber tree survived. And it was more precious than all those charming quarts of pure honey, those bunches of lotus roots, those Shikarpuri-aachara and milk-cakes. The ber tree was always remembered as *'Qabill'a jee ber'*—Qabill's ber tree.

Chapter 3
People of the Unseen

Ali Gohar was very close to both of his parents. His mother showered love upon him like the self-enslaved devotees who would keep filling the *lotiyoon*[106] outside a saint's shrine, by their own free will, and never tiring of doing that. And his father taught him everything he knew, including how to restrain yourself and not judge people, because Alam believed that only One could judge, and you are not him! And Alam loved him too, and used to take him almost everywhere, and he would tell him and his sisters all about his experiences, mostly in winter nights.

Winters are wearying everywhere, and so they were also in Qamber, lingering on as if summer would never come. They called the dipping temperatures *jahoo paroo*, 'frigid mercury'. He remembered that all of them used to cuddle together and sleep on a bed called a pathari, which was made up of loose hay, held in place by a structure of bricks and then covered by layers of quilts. And their father would pick a topic and tell them all about it. And those topics could be poles apart.

For example, he might explain how a foetus initially is of a peanut's size in its mother's womb. Or he would talk about the mystic order of Rijal-ul-Ghaib, 'People of the Unseen', a mysterious order of human beings in Islam to whom God had given a special power, but whose secret was kept into the spiritual realm and never brought into the open, in the world of acquisition. Or he might talk about the electric trams of Chandni Chowk,[107] or explain that a real human eyeball is the same size as a red plum.

---

[106] *Lotiyoon*: red-clay water pots.

[107] *Chandni Chowk*: 'Moonlight Square', a famous market square in Delhi.

Those stories were unbelievably fascinating to Ali Gohar. He would get lost in the back alleys of those stories. One evening his father described how Chinkoo had cut open an eyeball during an autopsy, and that it was filled with water, and he kept wondering, how come the eye is filled with water yet still we see clearly, but whenever he went swimming he couldn't see anything underwater at all.

But he figured that because Baba—that's what he called his father—had said that the eye is filled with water, then surely one day he'd be able to see clearly underwater. And he kept pondering how it could be that the eye, which looks to be like an almond, could really be more like a red plum. That left an ugly impression of an otherwise beautiful eye in his mind. On other sometimes that Chandni Chowk would appear in his mind, and instead of tram trolleys he would think about some beautiful princess, whose name Ali Gohar couldn't remember but his father knew the name, who made this garden with a pond full of jasmine petals, though it was now a market, where you could find *halwai*[1] selling *uprath'a*,[2] and his father had ridden in electric tram trolleys there.

He keep drifting off to sleep, and he kept thinking in a loop, about gardens with ponds filled with jasmines and swans, and then halwai frying Indian flat bread and trams crisscrossing and ringing fire engines and balls and princes, and his mother would be singing:

Lullaby to you my precious Lullaby; may sorrow not touch you ever,
Lullaby to you my precious Lullaby, may you grow untouched like bitter shrubs,
Lullaby to you my precious Lullaby, may joy keep filling your bowl;
Lullaby to you my precious Lullaby, Lullaby to you my precious Lullaby…

And he would listen to her, looking at smoke rising from the dying fire, which would first rise quickly upward in a straight line, but then get entangled between joists in the ceiling, unable to find way out, then decide to stay there, turning that part of the ceiling a velvety black.

In Qamber, there was a used clothes shop called Landa Bazaar. They called it a 'bazaar' even though it was actually only one shop. It was run by Zardar Khan, a Pushtoon. He would bring big bundles of used western clothes from the city, things that had been thrown away by rich people but still worked as sweet dreams for the poor.

Zardar Khan's shop was partly hidden in an alley behind the main bazaar, but that was irrelevant, because whoever wanted a bargain would find him, even in that back alley. His shop was a mud hut with only one front wooden door made up of two sections of four thin strips folded into each other, a kind of a four-panel colonist bi-fold door. But his humble door didn't have any of that colonial finish, that consistent beauty of a real colonist door.

Inside he used to have two or sometimes three huge piles of used clothes, with a distinct smell which combined the perspiration of thousands of former wearers along with insecticide-treatment and some residue of salty damp ocean air, but no one minded that; rather people liked it, because it assured them that these clothes were *velayatee*—'foreign'. They were used, perhaps, but still velayatee.

There was a small porch right in front next to a big neem tree, and Zardar would hang a few of the better clothes from the rusted wire hangers on that porch and neem trunk. One day, in that fateful winter, Ali Gohar saw a used grey tweed sports jacket hanging outside Zardar Khan's Landa Bazaar, and his heart fixed onto it.

It was a beautiful grey houndstooth tweed, but he didn't know what a houndstooth pattern was; for him it was a beautiful coat (that's what they called a sports jacket there: a coat), with a pattern of small and large broken checks, with a hint of very small burgundy dots inside each triangular check, and another set of thin light blue and lemon yellow lines running vertically, and another thin orange line going perpendicularly to make barely visible bigger squares.

So he asked Zardar to pull that jacket down so that he could try it on. Zardar did that and brushed both shoulders of that coat with his bare hand before handing it over to him. Ali Gohar took it and held it in his hands and checked it from all sides, pretending he had a great knowledge of sport jackets. He slowly slid his arm into one of the sleeves and felt coolness of its inner lining before sliding in the other.

It fit him like a glove. He looked at himself in that foggy mirror, which had crawling stains like the scrolled edges of partly burned paper, but still one could see in it, and he exactly did that, craning his head up to pull his neck a few inches longer. He tilted his head and looked into the mirror with one eyebrow raised, and he erected both tips of his shirt collar. And he said to himself, *I look so beautiful in this coat*. And while thinking that, he asked Zardar Khan, "How much is it?"

Zardar, who had just pulled his lower lip open with his left hand to plug it with a moist *naswar*[108] snuff chunk, completed that movement swiftly and then replied in a mumbling voice, "sixteen rupees," and he dusted his hands clean in a clapping manner, packing the naswar chunk with his tongue between his gum and lip at the same time.

When he heard the price, his shoulders shrugged down on their own. He thought, *It's almost half of my father's monthly salary, on which fourteen people survive*. He pulled his arms out of its sleeves and gave it back to Zardar.

And was about to leave when Zardar said, "Listen, how much you want to pay, tell me."

That gave him a frail hope, and out of nowhere he said, "ten rupees," though he didn't even that.

And Zardar replied, "twelve rupees and it's yours, take it."

"I'll come back for it," he said and left Zardar's Landa Bazaar wondering how to get twelve rupees.

He thought of Fakeer Sher Mohammed, his grandfather, who used to spare silver coins on a half folded linen and ask him to take as much as his palms could hold, and he would join his palms along with wrist together up to the elbows and take much more than two palms could hold. And Fakeer would to smile and laugh out of sheer joy on his ingenious act.

But Fakeer was dead; otherwise he could have given him all sixteen rupees to buy that coat.

Then his grandmother came into his mind, and she was still alive and kicking, but she was not going to give him money either. And slowly his desire to buy that tweed, that used tweed, died down and he convinced his heart that it would be impossible to raise twelve rupees. Walking through the snaking alleys of town led him to a wider street, and he could see distant trees whose shadows were being lengthened by the winter sun, who himself was about to go, leaving everything behind to dusk.

White smoke was rising from the houses, travelling straight up at first but then taking a sharp horizontal turn in winter evening and then hanging there lazily, like trees in traditional Chinese paintings. He was looking at the long

---

[108] *Naswar*: crushed green tobacco leaves with slaked lime.

shadows and horizontal smoke to try to distract his mind from that grey houndstooth used tweed, but it was still there.

He came home and did nothing, sitting on the veranda for a while and then lying down. He saw his old rubber eraser, which still had faded green letters, and he thought, *what if I could shave rubber around those letters.* So he got up and went to the garbage where his father threw blades every morning after shaving, those old single-edged barber's blades. He picked one out and broke it in half and then started carving into the eraser around those green letters, and after a few fatal mistakes he learned how to carve the structure of the letter.

Anyway, that eraser was ruined. The next day after school he came home and got hold of his father's few used rubber erasers and started practicing on those. Within a few hours, he succeeded in etching his own name on the eraser, and was happy to have created a rubber stamp bearing his name, like one his school headmaster had. He wanted to try it out to see its impression. He knew they didn't have any stamping pad, so he rubbed a few drops of ink directly onto it and pressed it against some paper just to see the result.

He was shocked to see that his name was reversed—it was reading the other way around. But he was still happy that he had succeeded, apart from the apparent need to figure out how to etch words backwards. After spoiling a few more erasers, he was able to carve his name backwards and leave a perfect impression of his name on the paper.

He couldn't wait to show this new thing to his friends at school. The next morning, the first thing that he did at school was to take out that eraser stamp and make an impression on his notebook, stamping his fist on it with a bang and then lifting rubber up carefully to leave a neat impression of his name on the notebook. That caused a ripple of wow! which resonated for a long while, and one of his friends said, "Could you make me one?"

And he was about to say yes to him, but then a goldsmith's son said, "I'll give three quarters if you make me one." So he started making rubber stamps for the rich kids of Sheikhs and Mahajans, and in a few days he started getting requests from other classes, and for a while it was very lucrative for him. Before long, he had collected five rupees and three quarters, and the thought of that used grey houndstooth tweed started to breathe again.

So he swung by outside Zardar Khan's shop, and sure enough that coat was still hanging on the neem trunk. He approached and touched that coat again and felt that rough texture and that beautiful breaking check pattern with burgundy dots, and maroon inner lining which smooth like silk and he said to Zardar Khan, "could you hold this for a few day, I have collected almost six rupees and I will arrange six more very soon."

Zardar Khan replied, "Yes, this coat is yours, you have my word."

That gave him assurance, because Pashtoons are known to keep their word. But he still had to come up with six more rupees. In fact, six rupees and quarter more, to make it twelve.

In a few days, his father offered him some more work. Alam had been working a part-time job painting banners in the evenings for Murli Talkies, a local theatre. But now he asked Ali Gohar to take over that job, because his photo studio was struggling and he wanted to focus more on that. And he said to himself, *bingo*, because the theatre would pay one rupee every three or four nights, whenever they showed a new movie. So now, he had to paint new signs with the movie's cast, and a few words of introduction, which could be completely false as long as it attracted crowds. He said, "yes" to father with a great big smile, knowing that in three or four more weeks he'd be able to gather all twelve rupees.

And this new job gave him an opportunity to watch a movie every night, though obviously it was the same movie for three or four nights in a row before they would change. That theatre had no roof or ceiling, so they could only run one show after dark, but for him that was the best part, because he could watch movies and at the same time look at the star-littered night skies, with their sometimes fast and sometimes slow rolling clouds.

On one occasion, there was a full moon, and the moonlight was so bright that it dulled the screen image, and some members of the audience got mad at the moon, probably because they knew that theatre had no roof and they couldn't get mad at the management.

One evening he saw Shadee there in the theatre. Shadee was his class fellow from grade two, an innocent-looking girl who wanted to become a doctor later in her life. No one including Ali Gohar himself mingled with her, even in grade two, even at that young age, because Shadee was a *kasbeeyani*, the daughter of a prostitute, and lived in Qamber's brothel.

It was a segregated theatre, meaning that it had a family balcony all the way in the end where women with their children could sit behind a thin curtain and watch movies. But prostitutes were not allowed to sit in that balcony—instead they would sit in main hall with male crowd.

So Ali Gohar keep looking at Shadee with mixed thoughts, believing that she could never become anything other than a prostitute, but at the same time he wanted her to become a doctor. In any case, she appeared to be enjoying herself that evening.

In four weeks, he gathered six more rupees and finally had his full twelve to buy that used grey houndstooth tweed jacket. He was glad that he could buy it in time for the winter season, and wear it for the rest of this winter and then get it dry cleaned for next year. He was telling himself that these foreign warm clothes were very durable, they last for years, and with this giggling tickle of joy he made his last turn that leads to Zardar Khan's Landa Bazaar, and after few steps felt a jolt in his heart, with little awe, because he did not see the coat hanging on the neem tree.

But the joy held in Zardar's promise kept that dreadful feeling at bay, until he stepped into the shop and saw Zardar's face and knew that the coat was gone. And before he could say something Zardar Khan said, "I'll get a better coat for you, even nicer then that grey one, when I go to city next time."

Without saying a word in response, he turned around and walked away, telling himself winter was already gone, what good that used coat be any way, that used grey tweed with small and large broken checks, with a hint of very small burgundy dots inside each triangular check.

He emerged from the alley and turned onto Main Street, where there was a political rally of ten to fifteen *haarees*[109] who were yelling slogans like, *"Bachay bookh na marnay daay ga—Haider Bux Jatoi, ra-baba, Haider Bux Jatoi."*—*He'll not let your kid starve in vain! Who? Haider Bux Jatoi, folks. Haider Bux Jatoi.* And there was no echo of their voices, which were instead absorbed by the red-hot amber skies of twilight.

Those landless farmers belonged to the Sindh Haari Committee, and Haider Bux Jatoi was the one-man show of that political communist party of landless peasants. He wanted to do the unthinkable by putting voice in a deaf-mute's mouth. These people had been marginalised for thousands of years, and society had shoved them under its carpet, but Haider Bux Jatoi made their voice heard for a while. Then came dictatorship, and the only voice that could be heard after that was of someone making gulping noises during water-boarding. Ali Gohar listened to them and their fiery slogans, so loud it seemed they were going to flip

---

[109] *Haarees*: landless peasant farmers.

the earth inside out, but in just a few minutes the slogans disappeared, along with the voices.

Ali Gohar earned his high school diploma and left Qamber at the tender age of eighteen. He had always dreamed of going somewhere else, to some bigger city with more opportunities, and he left Qamber with no plan of coming back. That very same Qamber where he had chiselled his name on school desks, where he had been overjoyed by pedalling and balancing on a bicycle for the very first time, where he had known everyone and every alley, street, tree, probably even every mad alley dog too.

He was leaving that very same Qamber where girls who played with him as child now pulled their veils over their faces in front of him, sometimes holding those veils in one corner between their teeth out of shyness. And he was leaving that very same Qamber where, for quite some time, he had felt someone looking at him from the corner of her eye, from a shaded elevated balcony when he walked past her home.

Once he had passed out of sight this last time, she probably closed her eyes slowly and rested her head back against the wall, then gently banged against on it by pulling her chin upward, and a warm teardrop rolled down her cheek, and her heart was probably jumping in her bosom like a poorly slaughtered bird who was not yet completely decapitated.

He didn't fully know why he was leaving that same Qamber where he had failed to gather sixteen rupees to buy a used tweed jacket from the Landa Bazaar. And he didn't even realise that he was leaving that same Qamber that his grandfather, Fakeer Sher Mohammad had once found astonishing some seventy years earlier, where along with Kalb Ali Fakeer and Lal Fakeer he had wandered singing mystic hymns.

But in the end he simply wanted to go. And for a while it seemed that Qamber honoured his desire too, and cut him loose. His friend Mirral'o had helped him to rent a room in Larkano, but nonetheless Ali Gohar still tended to go back to Qamber every evening. He found it wasn't so easy to get out of Qamber, or to kick Qamber out of him.

He got his first job as a clerk in settlement commission. The lucrative charms of this position, he soon found out, were several times more attractive than the forty rupees per month salary. His childhood friend Panaah Totani got him this job, and a job for himself as well, by buttering some palms. Panaah was a chubby guy, but made up of solid meat like a fat marble sculpture, with a round face and dark olive complexion, and an oil-drenched Caesar haircut, and a fine thin moustache that you'd have to be paying attention to locate in the margin between his nose and his upper lip.

But he was a man with golden heart, who would live to tie the turban on his son's and then his grandson's heads on their respective wedding days.

So along with Panaah he started this new job, where his responsibilities were to identify abandoned property and arrange for it to be sold at public auctions. He would place notices in local newspapers, make complete files of the auction proceedings, for his superiors, and then he would collect earnest money from the bid winners and deposit it into the treasury. Mostly these were properties that had been left by Hindus who migrated to India and not claimed by anyone since.

The fun part was that people would try to get a deal of five cents on the dollar for those properties, and so they would bribe him and his friend and others to not to run advertisements on the properties they wanted, or to run ambiguous adds so only they could bid and win the auction. Ali Gohar was going with flow, and things were rosy. He was making so much money that sometimes he forgot to pick up his salary.

But everything has a beginning and an end, and the end of this lucrative job came swiftly. He was few months in, and things were rolling smoothly like an ivory ball gliding on a marble surface. And another lucrative deal came lurking towards him when a prospective bidder came to him and identified a commercial location that had been owned by a Hindu who left eleven years ago, and this person wanted to win this property in bidding. It was as straightforward a deal as any—an abandoned commercial property, and someone wanted it, someone who was going to butter his palm, and the rest was just paperwork.

So next day he went to see the site of the property in question, but there was a twist, which the prospective buyer had not revealed. By the way, this buyer was of Indian descent and had migrated few years earlier to Larkano, where his elder brother and extended family had been living since 1937. And the twist was that this property was documented under the name of one Ghansham Das Motwani, who himself had left for India, but his younger brother, Arjun Das Motwani (who was called Arjan'o), who had not wanted to go to India, was still running his hardware business at that location.

That was his only livelihood and source of income. But somehow that prospective buyer got proof that the current occupier's brother had already filed and settled his claim in India against this property, so legally this property was up for grabs, and the prospective buyer's family had already laid a claim to the entire mansion that had once been owned by Ghansham Das Motwani. Ghansham himself had long not lived there, having converted that space to a stable for his horses even before leaving for India, and more recently Arjan'o had converted it into his hardware business. But now this immigrant from India just wanted to have the entire property to himself. And who could blame him, really? It's a basic human instinct to grab whatever you can get.

So Ali Gohar went with this assignment for a while, with Yamin Khan Ghori—that was the name of this immigrant from India, who was a very ordinary man, with few distinguishing features other than that he was always persistently chewing some betelnut-paan and always had few drops of perspiration on his forehead, which he kept wiping and then wiping his nose with the same hand.

Ali Gohar had few meetings with Arjan'o, who was hostile, but Ali Gohar told him to calm down and listen to him or else be evicted. And in their third meeting, Arjan'o, who was a middle-aged man of extremely fair skin with a receding hairline and the heavy husky voice of a chain smoker, broke into tears and wept like a kindergartner. He revealed that the horse stables had been his share of his family property, which he had since converted into the hardware shop.

He had managed to get that piece of the lot transferred into his own name and registered, and that was why Yamin Khan's family couldn't get hold of this small piece even though they had the whole mansion. Now they had managed to switch the registration records, and that this is his only source of income. His elder brother had asked him to move to Bombay, where he had established a pretty good wholesale grain business, but he didn't want to go, because his elder daughter would soon be getting married here.

Then he blew his nose into the long fall corner of his shirt, and said that the ashes of his elders were floating in Sindhu, and this was his home, why should he leave, and why should he give up his business, which was legally his, and he had the documents, though they had unfortunately been manipulated. And he finished his sentence with a sombre voice and a straight look of resolve from his bloodshot eyes into Ali Gohar's.

The next day in the mid-morning, Ali Gohar was working on some files at his desk when Yamin Khan came to see him and ask about his progress. He raised his head and looked at Yamin Khan, who was smiling with his signature betelnut-paan stained burgundy lips, whose margins were a dry brownish maroon. He pulled his chin up and made a cup out of his lower lip and started speaking in a gargling kind of voice while still looking at ceiling, just to hold his betelnut-paan and saliva in his mouth. And he asked brusquely, "What happened?" And then he brought his head down to hear Ali Gohar's response.

"I met Arjan'o Das a couple of times. He owns that property and has the registry in his name. How could we auction out someone's legitimate property?"

Yamin Khan wanted to reply but scrambled and looked to his right and then left to find a place to unload his mouth full of paan-spit, ultimately spitting it into the corner of the wall, staining it a splashing red. And he started talking while still wiping his mouth. "Don't worry about his registry of deed," he said, and then suddenly lowered his voice to add: "we already took care of it, you just move the file."

Ali Gohar looked at Yamin Khan, who was now glaring back at him open-mouthed, his teeth and tongue all bright red like he had just finished drinking blood. Ali Gohar said, "This is his only livelihood. Why you want to destroy someone? Arjan'o can't even outbid you in the auction. He has no money. And the city of Larkano is littered with abandoned commercial properties—you could buy any of them."

Yamin Khan replied with some resentment, "But we are paying you money for this, and remember, whoever is responsible for driving away these kafirs[110] should be proud of it. We are all collectively responsible for cleansing this land and should be claiming credit for it, not shying away from it. Pakistan was created for preservation and propagation of Islam, and anyone pretending otherwise is a kafir too!"

Ali Gohar looked at him and said, "Yamin Khan, you know what my heart is asking me to do?"

Yamin Khan answered reluctantly, "What?"

"My heart is asking me to push my pointer finger forcefully into my throat so that I could throw up on your face whatever residue of that leftover food which might still be inside me, which you paid me a few nights ago as a gesture of your goodwill."

Yamin Khan's jaw dropped. In a consolatory tone, he said, "But Ali Gohar, aren't we friends?"

Ali Gohar did not reply, and stepped out for a walk.

---

[110] Kafirs: 'infidels'. When Yamin Khan speaks of 'cleansing' the country, he indirectly refers to the new nation's name, since 'Pak' means 'pure' (Arabic).

After a few days, the office superintendent, his superior, called him to his desk. "We have to go with these auctions," he said, handing him a few files. Arjun Das's file was in there.

The next morning, he went back to the office superintendent and told him all about Arjun Das. After listening to him very carefully, his superior said, "As Arjun Das doesn't have registry documents, my hands are tied. We have to proceed with the auction."

"Very well sir," Ali Gohar said to his boss. He went on to finalise the auction process, and in the meantime he paid a visit to Arjan'o and told him to participate in the bidding.

And Arjan'o kept looking at him and said, "I wept and cried and stripped my soul bare naked in front of you to explain that I have nothing in the world except this business, and you are asking me to bid? Either I'm crazy or you are stupid." In anxiety, he started scratching his right shoulder with his left hand. Ali Gohar left, while Arjan'o was lost in thought and still scratching his shoulder indiscriminately.

The auction day was an ordinary day, one of those Mondays that comes and goes. It was ten in the morning, and there were a few bidders, including Yamin Khan Ghori and a drained Arjun Das Motwani. Right before the bidding started, his friend Panaah Totani went and whispered something in Arjan'o's ear, which injected some glow in his face and elevated his sprits. And when the auction started, Arjan'o kept outbidding Yamin Khan and finally reached a winning bid of a whopping thirty-three hundred rupees, a price inflated far beyond the going market value.

When everything was set and done and pretty much everybody was gone, Arjan'o came to Ali Gohar, who was sorting out papers with Panaah Totani, and quietly gave him a long hug. And then he squeezed Ali Gohar's right hand with both his hands and kept looking at him, and Arjan'o's facial muscles were twitching like they didn't know whether to spread into a smile or burst into tears, but then he settled on a mournful smile, leaving his chin shaking.

And Panaah said, "As I told you before auction you keep outbidding all and don't worry about money. Because it's Ali Gohar's file, and he's going to destroy it, and then it's going to take them five or six years to deal with it, because of the backlog. So you are good for five to six years. That's the best we could do—now go."

That evening Ali Gohar crossed the bridge over the Raees canal like he did every day before hopping the day's last bus to Qamber. But today, he stopped in the middle of the bridge, leaned over the short wall and threw something into the fast moving water currents of the canal and went on his way.

He quit his job, probably because he couldn't poke his pointer finger into his throat again and again and keep throwing up on everyone. Or who knows, it might be an echo of Fakeer Sher Mohammad's cry reiterating divine promise: *aahay ko Allah?*—Is there a God?—that was quietly bugging him.

There was an opening for an art teacher and he accepted it, at the high school in Tangwani—a place either at the end of the world or at the beginning of the time. Either way it was lonely, so lonely that it got even uglier, but that was life and he jumped on it, because he wanted to go somewhere even if it meant going back in time.

It was a building with no doors or windows, just walls and ceiling and open spaces where doors and windows should have been. There were only two rooms that did have doors, and those were the office of the headmaster and the storage room. So he had to settle in that storage space, which was a hushed ruin, filled with shattered benches, snapped chairs and old cupboards with broken doors, missing either their upper or lower hinges, which forced those doors to tilt on their sides, giving a lost look.

Those cupboards had been relieved from their duties because they weren't able to guard things anymore, and were useless and retired now. That storage room looked like a dump where memories quietly gathered dirt. But Ali Gohar had to somehow make himself comfortable there, and he did it. Because other than that school, a nearby police station, and a railway station some three miles away, there was not a living soul or a decent animal for miles.

There were several different species of deadly snakes, some real and some legends, like the one who jumped and bit a horseman sitting in the saddle. They called that phantom snake '*ghorail'o*', which literally translates to 'one who bites the horse'. That one was kind of a stretch, but they also had real deadly ones, like the *khapur'o, hanu-khanu*, and of course the *karihar'o*.[111] He never saw any of them, but did find snake tracks every few mornings on the dirt floor right under his bed.

---

[111] *Karihar'o*: cobra.

Apart from Ali Gohar, everyone else would come to the school from different villages and small hamlets, most of them simply walking or riding their horses or donkeys, though some would hop an early morning local train and then walk four miles from the train station. After a few days, he found a companion, Ali Akbar Jakhrani, the teacher of mathematics who also had no other place to go home to.

So that made life a little easier. Every evening, they would go on a long walk to the train station, and sometimes they would wait for that 6:30 local train, just to watch the people there in the train and at the station. Quite often the train arrived late or stayed at station for longer than it should. And they would watch the train finally leave the station and get constantly smaller and smaller and turn into a speck and finally disappear.

Or sometimes they would miss the train and walk farther down along the tracks for another couple of miles, telling each other their life stories. One evening they were walking along the tracks and Ali Gohar said something about excruciating pain, and Akbar Jakhrani interrupted suddenly to say, "You don't know what physical pain is?"

Then he stopped and grabbed Ali Gohar's shoulder and turned his face towards him before continuing. "I'm from the *Jakhrani* clan. Tribal skirmishes are very normal for us, and people get killed in those conflicts, and that's normal too. My father was murdered in them, and that was unfortunate, but worst part is that I saw all that. My father and I went to town from our village where he had to buy some seed for his crop. That was boring for me, so afterwards he took me to get some *kulfi*,[112] and that was my delight. I was licking sweet kulfi on a stick and it was dripping all over me."

"My hand was covered with kulfi, and some streaks of it went all the way to my elbow. And then four men appeared with axes and long draggers. My father look at them and pushed me forcefully aside towards the corner, and while he was gripping his own axe, they swung several blows, which cut open his belly, and I saw shiny and liquid round things covered in blood, which were his intestines, falling to the ground, and then he dropped to the ground face-down. And then those assassins looked at me and I thought they were going to kill me too, but they let me live, saying to each other, "He is too young, let him grow."

---

[112] *Kulfi*: Indian ice cream.

"And so they sowed the seed in me, and then ran away assuming that my father was dead, though he wasn't yet. He lived for a few more moments, and those were the moments of someone enduring pain of unbearable proportions. When my father flipped over to bring his face up, then grabbed his turban and loosened it. He tried to sit, rising on his elbows, and in a half sitting position he tried to lift himself up. He cut open the skin and muscles of his stomach with his one hand and shovelled his dirt-covered intestines back into his body with his other hand. Then he wrapped his turban around it all and sat there for few moments, looking at me quietly blinking, and then died."

"I was crying out of despair and tears were rolling and my nose got all stuffed, and somehow I wiped my nose and my fingers touched my mouth and I felt sweet taste of kulfi in my mouth again. No one came to help him, and now I don't like sweets, ever since that day. So that is physical pain, Ali Gohar. That's what I call 'pain', and I've been reliving that pain since my childhood."

Neither of them spoke any other word as they walked back that evening.

Chapter 4
Showering Moonshine

Ali Gohar found an over-aged Brohi student who had been failing a certain grade consecutively for years. He must have had some learning disability, but he had a great talent for playing the *chang'u*.[113] And he would play his chang'u pretty much every evening. On one night, there was a harvest moon, which did not wait for the sun to set, and came out on its own before sunset.

Probably, the moon wanted to listen to the chang'u, and it was moving slower than a snail on that autumn sky. And that resonating chang'u was weaving an euphoric trance. The young Brohi was holding the instrument's arm-jaws between his lips and plucking it, or rather beating its triggering loop repeatedly with his forefingers, and his tongue dangled from his mouth like a fish out of water to make that melody sound. And it seemed like the moon stopped and waited for this young man to finish his gig, and then it applauded by showering tons of moonlight on everything, as intoxicating as moonshine.

And like that moon, Ali Gohar took a shine to that talented folk musician. He started teaching him from scratch, right from alphabetical characters and their phonics. This student felt embarrassed in class, so Ali Gohar would teach him after hours. Anyway, Ali Gohar was not a language teacher to begin with—he was an art teacher. But he took on this struggling student as a project.

Initially, it was a bumpy ride, but slowly he started pronouncing two-letter words, then three-letter words, and the rest was history. Soon, he started reading the newspaper, haltingly, like a new driver who sometimes puts the car into the wrong gear, but he kept learning and improving.

Meanwhile life was becoming stagnant for Ali Gohar. It was so slow that keeping track of time was useless. His mother would make him a canister full of

---

[113] *Chang'u*: Jew's harp.

fat cookies which would last him for two months, and he used to eat one cookie at breakfast every day, and when that canister started showing only five or six cookies at the bottom, that would give him a sense of the time elapsed, and he would realise that almost two months had past.

He became interested in joining words together into short lines that should rhyme. He thought poetry must be too difficult for him, so that's why he never called his couplets poetry. But they were his poems, which he used to compose while lying on his portable bed, which his faithful student would prepare for him every evening out in the open on a wooden four-legged khataa. He wrote poetry while looking into that same night sky, with that same Big Dipper, and Orion the hunter, and those same seven sisters.

And the Brohi student would play his chang'u, and his heart wanted to open those hidden scrolls again, in which she would be looking at him from corner of her eyes from her wooden upstairs balcony. And he kept trying to tame his eager heart, telling him, *easy boy...easy!*

One evening his father showed up. He was now known as Mastaar MohandAlam, which was a combination of a wrong pronunciation of the word 'master' and a quick throwing together of the two words Mohammad and Alam into one. So he arrived and told Ali Gohar, "You've been transferred to the Government High School Larkano"—and though Larkano was actually 22 miles from Qamber, it sure seemed like a call home after this time in Tangwani.

"We got a telegram at home from the Department of Education announcing your transfer. So I came all this way to tell you myself, and it almost took me day and a half to reach to this dreadful place. How the hell have you lived here for so long?"

That 'so long' was just two years, but they were eternal ones. But suddenly they came to an end. The very next day, after getting his relieving paperwork done, he and his father went back to Qamber.

He was back again in Qamber, probably for one last time, the town that he had already let go. It was like a small-town broken relationship, where you see your erstwhile partner coming out of a post office or going into a deli and you both ignore each other. Actually, he was not ignoring Qamber, and Qamber was loving him more than ever, but still he just wanted to get out of there.

He needed to get out of that place where he had once walked on the banks of the Norang, where he had learned how to swim as a child, and where he had once almost drowned when playing with his childhood friends.

And he wept quietly, sitting in the window-side seat of the commuter bus from Larkano to Qamber. It was evening, and like a procrastinator he always took this last bus, which was always overloaded with more procrastinators. And no one noticed that he was weeping because the window next to him was broken, and cool wind was blowing on his face while he was remembering his childhood friend Mirral'o, who died a few days ago, maybe of *karo-kamarn*.[114]

When he saw him for the last time, a few days earlier, he couldn't even recognise him. It was at that same bus stand from where he had gotten on today. He heard someone call his name in a weak voice from that part of bus stop that was known as the beggars' and lepers' corner. He tried to avoid him, pretending he hadn't heard, though he had heard it clearly. After he took a few steps away, that weak voice made another attempt, stating his name with all the energy and force that it could afford, and then it collapsed like a gunshot victim crawling on his elbows a few last inches before dropping.

Ali Gohar turned around reluctantly to follow the voice. He saw a beggar covered in a dirty quilt, with a completely wasted face, breathing heavily, probably because of the exertion of yelling his name. But when he looked at Ali Gohar, the skin around his eyes relaxed, like dying sprouts being given an extra splash of life when someone sprinkles water on them. And Ali Gohar looked at him, in the mealy crumbling light of the setting sun, and his name came out of Ali Gohar's lips: 'Mirral'a'.

He sat down in front of him on the ground. Mirral'o was sniffing the air in rapid successions, like he didn't have time left to breathe, or the air was running away somewhere else. Ali Gohar said, "What happened to you," because he had nothing else to say. And Mirral'o didn't answer, rather kept looking at him and kept sniffing air. And after a long pause, Ali Gohar remembered that he started conversation with this stupid question, and nonetheless attempted it again: "What happened?"

And again Mirral'o did not reply, but just kept looking at him, and his eyes were absorbing the image of Ali Gohar's face, out of that reminiscence of love and romantic attraction that he'd had for Ali Gohar years back when they were teenagers, and probably still had. Ali Gohar asked him to come along and offered to take him home, but Mirral'o was a stubborn and egocentric son of a bitch, always doggedly loyal to his ego. He never went back home, and died on a street

---

[114] *Karo-kamarn*: cirrhosis of the liver.

corner, all because he had fallen out with his father since his father got remarried, and had started beating him for no reason. Ali Gohar remembered that he stayed talking with him that evening for while, where he was doing almost all the talking, and Mirral'o was mostly looking at him and sometimes interrupting by saying, "Humm…haaa," meaning, *yes*…and again, *yes*…At some point Mirral'o realised that it was getting close to the departure time of the last bus, and he asked Ali Gohar to leave and assured him that he'd be fine. Knowing that he actually would not be fine, Ali Gohar left Mirral'o, and that was that.

Ali Gohar had been on a quest to move forward, but now he was back at Larkano Govt: High School, where he had been two years ago. His quest to move forward was seeming more like a circle. But he was utterly optimistic, and Larkano was poles apart from that snake infested dreadful place. Plus, he was coming back home every night, where he could see his mother, his sisters, and younger brothers.

After a year or so teaching at Larkano, he applied for a one-year drawing teacher's training in Hyderabad, and he got accepted, which was a kind of a big deal because there were fewer than fifteen openings every year for hundreds of applicants. Every candidate had to send an application along with specimens of work in each of three disciplines, that is, still life, nature study, and graphic design, which they called 'free-hand art'.

The selection board then chose the top thirty applicants and invited them to come to Hyderabad and participate in an in-house competition on a subject which could come from any of those three disciplines. Each artist was given the subject on the spot and told to draw it, and then fifteen were chosen from that batch.

So it wasn't an easy task, and that year the competition was particularly intense because a renowned art teacher had just came back from a year of design training in Bristol, England. He had given up his career as a physician years ago for art, and was an artist to his core, kind of a tough guy to please, intimidating for the applicants.

Ali Gohar arrived at Hyderabad for a year long training, but little did he know that he would be staying there for a very long time, and he would make friends there, pick fights, endure difficult times going days on end without eating food, explore the Bombay bakery by accident, switch jobs, hang around every evening with his friends at the Persian café Meharban, and later wear custom-made oxford perforated cap-toe shoes later, and commit the taboo act of falling in love against all odds with a girl from another ethnic group.

He arrived in Hyderabad in the spring of 1961, at the age of twenty-one. He was a dark-skinned young man of *Saamart*[115] origin, with thick hair that was nonetheless receding toward baldness in the front. He was of moderate height and skinny build, but was always buzzing with energy, and ambition sprouted from him in high jets like a musical fountain.

He arrived in Kotri in the evening. This was supposed to be Hyderabad's twin-city, but somehow Kotri had never grown big. It always remained nothing more than a train station and a bridge. Ali Gohar stepped down onto the platform in at that train station. If it had been a movie, there would have been grand theme music at that moment when his foot touched the ground, with big brass sounds of trumpets, horns, and tubas going crazy, and cymbals making bright, glitzy, attention grabbing multiple bangs to announce his arrival.

It would be the sound of something new coming into being, with all its magical adventures and mysterious passion, like effervescent bubbles about to spill over the brim. But it was not a movie, so none of this happened at his arrival. Rather, like anybody else, Ali Gohar stepped onto the platform, a little nervous, and walked away with the diffusing crowd into the flickering, almost dying lights of the kerosene oil street lamps.

The first day of training was a kind of introduction and orientation. There were fifteen students: thirteen boys, all from different dusty small towns of Sindh. Most of them wanted to do this training to get accreditation for their jobs, though there were two city girls from affluent and noble families, who had both attended convents before this, and were just doing this course to kill time.

Most of these students had no idea what painting really was! No they didn't. Not from a professional perspective, anyway. All of them had explored it on their own. Some thought painting was to draw an apple sitting on a stool like a model, maybe next to some knives or in front of a jar, and then just fill it in with paint. Others believed art was the combination if simple geometrical forms such as circles triangles and squares into a design, which it is, in a way.

Some of them also knew the origin of the word 'geometry', meaning measuring the earth. But little did they know that it isn't just the geometry at play but also algebraic arguments that geometry facilitates, and that modern algebraic geometry is based on certain very abstract concepts from fields such as commutative algebra. But that was far from their grasp in what they understood

---

[115] *Saamart*: ethnically native to Sindh.

as geometry. And they were not required to know all that in order to pass their geometry courses. For that, understanding lengths and areas and volumes was enough.

Their classroom was a long series of three large halls with high ceilings, with a distinct smell of freshly wet clay, which he kind of liked. The walls were covered from top to bottom with all different pieces of art. They were all masterpieces, though critics might dispute that, made by students of past years, and there were several baked clay pots with different floral plants scattered around, and in the end of those halls there was a small oval office, which was the teacher's office. He emerged from that office and walked into classroom slowly, and there was roaring echo of chairs being pushed back because everybody stood, a traditional sign of respect from the students.

"No-no-no-no!" He said emphatically. "None of you needs to stand when I enter the classroom."

He gestured with open hands pushing downward slowly in the air and said, "Sit. We all are going to work together for next twelve months, and believe me I'm going to learn a lot from you too." Those were the first words of A.K.B. Shaikh, which calmly defused the tension in the room. A.K.B. Shaikh introduced himself and then asked everyone else to do the same. As the conversation continued, Ali Gohar kept watching this amazing man who was going to open the floodgates of knowledge for him.

After introductions, Mr Shaikh said, "I want all of you to get a sketchbook and carry it with you all the time, and draw whatever inspires you, and it should not be perfect." Then he paused and said, "Listen carefully."

Everyone was already listening to him carefully, but some still pulled their necks up a little further in anxiety. He went on, "There is nothing perfect or flawless, so do the best you can. And that is going to be your assignment every day for the next twelve months."

Ali Gohar had not heard that kind of language before. They were made up of honey, pure honey, those words he had just heard from A.K.B. Shaikh. And he said to himself, *what a man! It doesn't look like he has an ill bone in his body.* A.K.B. Shaikh might have had his own demons, but on surface he seemed flawless, with a single jasmine flower on left lapel of his double-breasted suit. And no one called him A.K.B. Shaikh; everybody called him Shaikh Sahib, where *sahib* is an honorific title like 'sir'.

And Shaikh Sahib concluded that orientation class by advising them not to buy sketchbooks from the stationery store, because that might be very expensive for some. Clearly he understood that most of the students were dirt poor. He suggested that they instead buy loose art paper and give it to Gulloo, the gardener of college, and he would sew it together. In few days, they had all managed to get their sketchbooks.

This Gulloo was an ordinary man, a gardener *cum* orderly *cum* model for figure study class, but he was also a practical proof of Shaikh Sahib's belief in the equal value of all humanity. Everyone always agrees to that in principle, but Shaikh Sahib was actually practicing it, by elevating Gulloo's status to his own, or bringing his status to Gulloo's. He would make two cups of tea around mid-morning every day, and they use to sip it together, in his office, while exchanging thoughts on first name basis with one another. That was unheard of at the time, and even today it is rare in the decaying remains of Sindh's imperial bureaucracy.

Ali Gohar soon found himself doing sketches, making paintings, drawing designs and enjoying every single moment of it. And he made some friends, including Ali Akber Mangi, who was a thin young man with a black-olive complexion and a round face. Because he was lean, the outline of his round face looked more like a heptagon. Ali Akber always wore a white shirt tucked into white drainpipe trousers with a thin black leather belt. In general, he was a man of few words, but whenever he spoke he would dump out whatever was in his mind in a roaring voice, as if he were unloading a recycling receptacle full of empty cans.

He was Ali Gohar's senior and was already an instructor at the college, but they got along well. They started making watercolour landscapes of Hyderabad together, and for an epoch in time, there were really amateur artists who were physically seen on streets of Hyderabad. Ali Gohar prepared a couple of drawing boards, using an old technique of stretching wet art paper on the boards, fixing them with paper glue tape, then letting it dry. Multiple washes would stretch the art paper and prevent wrinkling.

Ali Gohar and Ali Akber chose to work on their landscape during midmornings. Ali Gohar wanted to capture the entire mood of the main street of downtown Hyderabad, *Thandi Sadak*,[116] which was overlooked by the majestic

---

[116] *Thandi Sarak*: 'Breezy Way'. The crosstown avenue got its name after tall shaded trees alongside the way. Legend has it that once Rabindranath Tagore spent his summer

clock tower of Sindh University's old campus. The first time Ali Gohar saw it, the clock tower with its iron dial and roman numerals reminded him of the face of a gold pocket-watch that belonged to an old man from Qamber, Mohammad Sumar Khan Rajper.

The tower was maybe six stories tall, but it always looked taller than that to Ali Gohar. Those black roman numerals were fitted between two cast-iron circles, and there was a six-petal floral geometry beneath the hands of the clock, and sixty picket notches at the rim of the outermost circle, outside the roman numerals, and all that was on top of an ivory-white background. But all those details were not as important to Ali Gohar as its resemblance to Mohammad Sumar Khan Rajper's pocket watch.

So all this was in his mind as he started painting—or rather sculpting—a watercolour of this completely outlandish and non-indigenous quasi-medieval cathedral-like structure, depicting the elaborate bright yellow lime stone walls of the rising tower, and next to the tower there was a row of five paired narrow lancet windows, each with pointed arches and spandrels and decorative mouldings of limestone.

At the top of the tower, there were four raised merlons with three crenels in between, and the rest of the building had several more merlons and crenels mingled into each other. At the end of each corner, there were small and humble pinnacles with decorative lotus finials that rose up from them. At the base of the tower, there was a grand archivolt entrance, with five carved store doorjambs with arched voussoirs. There were several rainspout gargoyles with protruding tongues perched along the rooftop.

That was all in the background. In front, there was a great aa-sirheen spreading his ubiquitous presence around that peacockish Thandi Sadak of Hyderabad. The street was teeming with life, from pedestrians, to jet-black water buffaloes with bells on their necks that chimed as sweetly as someone ringing god's doorbell, to ox-drawn carts, to a half-naked *pehlwan*[117] selling *gol-gappa*[118] on his cart.

---

in Hyderabad where he used to go to the river bank for a walk every evening talking this three quarters of mile avenue there. Thus gave it the nickname Thandi Sarak.

[117] *Pehlwan*: a wrestler, or, more generally, a large or strong man.

[118] *Gol-gappa*: a snack made of several tiny deep fried popped breads, thumb pinched from one side to be stuffed with boiled garbanzo beans and potatoes, and dipped in a sweet and sour water mixed with tamarind, mint and many spices.

He and Ali Akber were painting their landscapes, and the day was all gone and it was late afternoon, knocking on evening's door, when a tall and graceful middle-aged man came and stood right behind them. He was clean-shaven with a grey military haircut, and he was wearing a light-blue cotton bush-shirt with a pattern of yellow heart shapes and small leaves within a wide squarish pattern and casual trousers. He looked at their landscapes for some time, and then he crunched down and sat with them, without seeming intrusive or gauche.

Ali Gohar noticed that this man was wearing white cotton tennis shoes, and his ears were a little large, and cupping out. Ali Akber recognised him, but before he could tell Ali Gohar anything about, the man said to Ali Akber, "Your washing brushstrokes are sedate in tone, there is calmness in your skies, but on the clock tower you did careful brushwork, with much more controlled washes on those tight, structural details." And to Ali Gohar he just said, "Your landscape is nice too, but your colours are hard—there is fire in your colours."

Then the man stood up and said, "Let me know if I can do anything for you two, and keep up the good work." Then he walked briskly away.

Ali Akber whispered in Ali Gohar's ear that this man was the current Commissioner of Hyderabad division and a philatelist too. In the overseas possessions of the British Commonwealth, especially during the years of colonialism, the title of Commissioner held immense administrative power. Even after the British left south Asia, that immense power was still there. So in simple words, that guy who crunched down and was sitting on the gravel with them was administrative head of over 8 million people and the overseer of a territory of 53000 square miles.

And Ali Gohar out his astonishment said to Ali Akber, "He may be the Commissioner, but how come he knows so much about painting?"

"He is an admirer of the fine arts," Ali Akber replied. "He's one of the people who started an annual painting exhibition at Bhit Shah."

When they had finished painting the Thandi Sadak, they moved on to a new site: the tomb of the emperor Mir Ghulam Shah Kalhoro. Hyderabad had been born first in his mind, and then he built his city in brick and mortar. And after building it, that emperor had fallen in love with his city—who knows why!

They had to walk there, carrying their drawing boards and all their gear. As they crossed through Hirabad, Ali Akber felt inspired to narrate. "This is one of the oldest and poshest neighbourhoods of Hyderabad…with its exotic mansions, which you could call palaces..." They were like the Upper West Side brownstones of Hyderabad.

"But nobody lives there it seems?" Ali Gohar said, with astonishment, looking up like a child at those deserted but beautiful observatories visible behind balconies, long balconies that covered the whole façade of those mansions. They were shared balconies, which were common then; the concept of a separate balcony for every room was not quite evolved yet.

Ali Gohar was wondering, *"why are they all closed shut?"* And quiet, like no one is living behind these deep-blue, bottle-green and ink-red stained glass windows, which by the way were moulded in exquisite Burmese teak woodwork, and right under those windows there were cast-iron intricate-knotty floral railings which seemed plain and simple in first glance but could then draw you in like a riddle.

This neighbourhood had three avenues slicing multiple streets, and they strolled along one of these, without taking any notice of the huge pipal tree providing a canopy overhead and a carpet of perfect heart-shaped dead leaves underfoot. That was the notorious lone pipal tree of Hirabad, who refused to die and had entrenched her roots deep inside the heart of a rock. That's where Hirabad was built, on top of the wide chest of a cliff.

Right outside of Hirabad, they walked beside a jail, an old jail of Hyderabad that now appeared mute. But that place that now seemed at a loss for words actually carried inside it nothing short of legends, beautiful and far-fetched tales that were no longer told. One of those was about the outlaw Rahim Hingoro, who was a resistance fighter for some, a merciless dacoit for others—but that's not why he was remembered.

The legend was that he sent a message from this jail to his wife to help him escape, and she did came and break him free from confinement. But he was shot in the very end just before getting over the exterior wall and died during the escape, and they say she took his body with her, jumping from the west wall onto a horse. That west wall was built on the cliff edge, and no one saw them ever again. But then, god knows how people knew, that he died? If no one saw them ever again!

So maybe like those miscellaneous cash shortages or general ledger account overages that are attributed to 'creative accounting', blankets of legends have always appeared to cover up the logical imperfections in otherwise epic sagas.

Thus Rahim Hingoro's wife, after jumping of off a cliff edge, took his lifeless body and walked into foggy insensibility of heroic history.

Ali Gohar was not thinking about Rahim Hingoro's elusive get-away; rather he was thinking about his grandfather, Fakeer Sher Mohammad's humble prison time. He had been imprisoned here too, while he was fighting and losing his lawsuit against the monastery. But there was no daring escape attempt associated with Fakeer; instead he used to ask permission from the jail superintendent to allow him to go to the neighbouring villagers and ask them for a *doodh-lassi*.[119]

Fakeer was so benign that after a while the jail superintendent would simply unchain him and let him roam around the neighbouring villages in his prison clothes asking for a doodh-lassi. He would wander about the fields and sometime around the wells. Sometimes, women would drop their filled water pots on the ground and run away yelling and crying, thinking that Fakeer was a dangerous fugitive. And he would call out to them, "No, no! My child, don't be afraid. I'm harmless Fakeer."

Ali Gohar was still thinking about all that when Ali Akber said, "there they are," pointing towards a series of humble and impecunious-looking muddy greyish-white rotundas covered in downward streaks of dead algae. Slowly they reached the main entrance in the mud castle wall. It looked like time had licked and licked that wall had not yet managed to melt it completely. What a lost tomb complex it was, in the middle of nowhere on the extreme north-western edge of Hyderabad.

At the entrance of the burial site, there were three scattered tombs: a big one, a small one, and an elongated one like a tilted boat. But they all gave a lost look, like the few survivors of a lost desert caravan, with dehydrated and wasted bodies. But as Ali Gohar got closer to them, he found beauty in those sad ruins. The entrance gate of the tomb complex was much smaller than the one in the outer façade, which was a big Tudor arch with another smaller Tudor arch in it. That larger entrance led to the smaller doorway inside like an old doorman who touches his hat with a smile, communicating without saying a word.

They crossed over to the main arcade, where there was a five-floor high square mausoleum with four small hexagonal towers. Each tower had a cupola with six arch-shaped openings, and each one of those towers seemed to be

---

[119] *Doodh-lassi*: a drink made from thin, watery buttermilk.

looking at the others. But the king's mausoleum had no tomb! It seemed to have undergone a mastectomy, and there was a noticeable emptiness left there.

The two artists walked around the site, trying to find a view. Ali Gohar picked the west end, looking at the crumbling wall of Ghulam Shah Kalhoro's tomb. It had thirty-three arches on it like someone had wanted to make thirty-three windows, but had then changed his mind and concealed them. They were in three sets of eleven arches, one on the top of the other. A porcelain mosaic made of eroded Kashi tiles[120] decorated each arch of that wall.

Most of it had been chipped away, but it was of high quality, brilliantly enamelled, with navy blue and turquoise encaustic tiles and frescoes of exquisite beauty. Its motifs seemed to be mostly Ottoman Turkish designs gone berserk with the influence of Sindhi styles, with turquoise and navy blue lines taking jasmine floral shapes on both ends of something that looked like a vertical dog bone, with star and cross, and square base variations involving diagonal trellises originally. But the traces that were left in those arches were unbelievably fresh, like a pure peppermint fragrance: glazed mosaics of all blues from navy blue to turquoise and everything in between.

So Ali Gohar painted this landscape showing this sad side of the tomb, with thirty-three arches leading nowhere, rather all hitting the wall with crumbled chipped away tiles, leaving big voids of vanishing plaster. He finished his landscape with a bright cobalt blue summer sky, littered with ill-shaped fluffy cotton ball clouds, giving a stubbornly motionless impression.

Its landmarks, like shrines, and its muddy puddle streets and foul stagnant ditches with swimming black water buffalo who moved their heads with great arrogance, like they were proud of their perfect curly horns.

Ali Gohar would watch with hushed admiration as Ali Akber painted. The way he applied the paint made it seem like it projected upward, giving the impression of a third dimension. And this even though it was watercolour, which is difficult to hold on to in the first place. That day, after a thin outline pencil sketch, Ali Gohar saw him blend a valour blue with cobalt for the skies, which he started mopping in one direction, and when he came to the horizon he threw in a hint of crimson with navy-blue to express the blurring purple depth of that hot day.

---

[120] Kashi tiles: exotic earthenware tiles of blue or green enamel, hand-made and painted and then baked in a clay oven by village potters called *Kumbhara*.

Shaikh Sahib would discuss every student's sketch of prior day, mesmerising the students with the new influx of knowledge about technique and art history. Even though it was just a one-year elementary training course, Shaikh Sahib would dump loads of whatever he had on them. During a simple still life class, he got involved in explaining how a solid white stroke can enhance the glare of reflecting light on an apple.

He talked about impressionism, and his words were like a stampede, bumping and jabbing sharp elbows into each other just to come out of his lips first because they were so eager to be heard. But Shaikh Sahib kept on sailing, saying, "Impressionism is an optical illusion: it's just a perception of colours. Optical colour mixing is created through our perception of colour." Then he looked at them and asked, "Are you following me?" And everybody nodded their heads in in consent, but Ali Gohar doubted that anyone understood a single word.

But Shaikh Sahib kept on. "When one looks at two amounts of different colours laid down side by side, the two appear to create a different colour. This colour is usually something similar to the result when the two are mixed in pigment. The only difference is that when two colours are mixed in pigment, they lose some of their intensity. When two colours mix optically, they retain their intensity and they sometime appear brighter."

It was a deafening experience. Ali Gohar had never heard someone who could talk that much on a white speck of paint on an apple in a still life. Soon, the lecture was over, and Ali Gohar noticed that while Shaikh Sahib was leaving the classroom, he paused to caress a petal of a bloom in a clay pot.

Ali Gohar followed him to his office. The office door was open, so Ali Gohar peeked in, and Shaikh Sahib asked him to come in. "Is everything okay?" he asked.

"Yes!" Ali Gohar replied. "Your lecture was very informative. But I missed so many things that you said."

Shaikh Sahib asked Ali Gohar to grab a thick book sitting on his old wooden bookshelf and then another couple of books as well. Ali Gohar did so, and Shaikh Sahib motioned for him to come stand next to him as he opened the first volume, as if saying, "open sesame." It was a book on French impressionism. He kept flipping the pages, as if trying to find a particular picture, and kept talking while holding a burning cigarette between his lips, which was bobbing up and down and its rising smoke was bothering one of his eyes, which he squeezed almost shut while words were still coming out of his mouth.

"Impressionism is a movement in French painting, sometimes called optical realism because its actual deceiving illusion creates the experience of movement of light, and it takes an almost scientific interest in the actual visual experience and effect of brightness and movement on the appearance of a still object."

Then he paused briefly to hold his cigarette between two fingers of his right hand, and placed his thumb on his tilted right temple, and extended the fingers that were holding the cigarette up, making it look like his whole tilted head was resting upon his thumb. And he opened the second book, which was entirely about Claude Monet, to a painting of a woman with a parasol.

"This is a perfect example of the brightness of light and the intensity of shadow at the same time, where subject is covered by the shadow of her umbrella. And Monet had used only calming colours, see those blues, greens, browns and other natural colours, to give a comforting and quiet feeling. See that beautiful blue sky with white clouds and sparkling green shades of morning grass, and how he emphasised the entire atmosphere, but keep looking for his subject in the shadow."

"That's the optical effect: you want to see her, but he instead forces you to see the skies and bright grass. That's what I was talking earlier in class. When you look at two amounts of different colours laid down side by side, the two appear to create a different colour. Of course, some painters would achieve this by actually mixing the pigment. But you see, when the two colours are mixed in pigment, they lose some of their intensity. When the two colours mix in the eye instead of in the paint, they retain their intensity—and they can even appear brighter."

But Ali Gohar sighed hopelessly. "It's too much for me to grasp."

Shaikh Sahib interrupted that mood, saying, "Don't get discouraged. Just keep these things in mind, and keep pushing forward."

So he kept pushing forward. He came out of a colossal Dickensian pit of despair. The only thing that he was holding close to his chest was desire to be somewhere in that ambitious domain, which is always somewhere further down the path.

And in that everything-is-fine situation, where his school was going great and he was getting close to lots of people; he had his first experience of a group painting exhibition. And yet his damn heart started to dupe him again, bringing that along that lousy restlessness, that anathematic feeling called love. And it brought with it all the essential agonies of a generic romance, where you don't know what's in the mind of the person you've fallen in love with.

And he was very much immersed in that pushing forward when he got a telegram from home which read, "u r g e n t - m o t h e r - s e r I o u s l y - i l l." He forgot everything about painting and rushed back to Qamber, only to find that his mother was physically completely fine, though his father's baseless allegation had made her emotionally drained.

He wanted to stay in Hyderabad, believing that whatever good is going to come in his future would happen there in the city. But after his training was completed he was again thrown back to a place that, it seemed to him, time had not yet discovered. This time it was Kandhkot. But he was making regular trips to Qamber from Kandhkot because the frequency of urgent telegrams from home increased, and he had to be the mediator between his father's irresponsible behaviour and his mother's annoyance.

Around this time, Ali Gohar met an unusual, fruitcake like person, a friend of his younger brother, who was full of surprises. He was hip and groovy and intelligent all at once. Ali Gohar had not seen this groovy person since childhood in Qamber, but now he found him to have become an extremely good-looking young man, clean-shaven with a complexion as fair as a Caucasian. He had muttonchops, a hairstyle that would be best described as not a style at all, just overgrown hairs. He was near-sighted and wore glasses so big that they covered a third of his face.

They met accidentally. The groovy person was selling term and full life insurance policies. After a few meetings, Ali Gohar told him that he was too intelligent and skilled to be doing under-appreciated work in this business. Groovy Person replied, "This is just for the time being. Once I finish my masters, I'm going to go abroad, to America. I'll do a PhD there. There's nothing here— it's all just dirt here. I want to take my chances where my talent will be appreciated."

Groovy's thought tickled Ali Gohar's mind. He wandered back along his own memory lane and dusted off some thoughts, to remember those other few people from Qamber who had gone abroad too, for getting their fellowships in medicine.

And Groovy Person took Ali Gohar to the library of the Pakistani-American Cultural Centre, in the neighbourhood called Tilak-incline. Tilak-incline was still beautiful in early seventies, there were still some huge limestone carving mansions there, patiently waiting for someone to look at them, knowing that they would inevitably step aside in favour of some multi-story box building.

The American Centre had also rented one of those palaces-like buildings, a double story grand mansion, where students could enrol in English language classes. They would enter the mansion through a huge arch entrance with a cast-iron gate, which was made of spiral rods knotted together in a delicate fashion so that they appeared soft, like they were made of silk ropes instead of cast-iron bars. The gate led only upwards to a staircase, which then opened into an airy courtyard, which was surrounded by high-ceilinged rooms, with windmill patterned Victorian floor tiles.

And those were the classrooms, which were filled with mostly middle class young people quietly listening to the echoing voices of their tutors teaching them how to articulate each word in American style, which involved how you shaped your mouth, where you placed your tongue, and how you aspirated on various parts of the word, like 'schedule' and 'lieutenant'.

They shared certain rather dubious information as well, such as how, in an American accent letter 'J' is pronounced like an 'H' instead of a soft 'G', because of the influence of Spanish, but they didn't bother to tell them it was only true for Spanish words. And those tutors would teach a bit of slang too! Words like bullshit, and the myth behind word asshole, or the mammoth difference between the words guy and gay.

Everyone who attends those classes wanted to go to the country they were used to pronouncing as 'Amreeka'.

And Groovy also told him about Athah Ameeq Sufi, his childhood acquaintance, who had become a research scientist at Rockefeller University in New York. Athah Ameeq Sufi was from a place that wasn't even a hamlet: it was a small group of mud-huts hugging together, circling a gigantic banyan tree. That tiny townlet was called *Aali-Khabaruu*, which literally translates to 'wet banyan'.

Legend had it that a saint had once come there chewing a piece of banyan branch, and then he threw that piece of banyan into the wet soil. And then that small piece turned into a giant banyan tree, probably right then and there, out of thin air. Aali-Khabaruu was like an impressionistic landscape, with its stunningly vibrant, soft but inquiring skies, which kept flirting with cobalt but were constantly morphing, blending greys into whites, which then turned into turquoises and finally lost everything into light blues. Sometimes, in late winter mornings Aali-Khabaruu skies hosted a full moon sunrise, where a drunken full moon with heavy eyelids waits and waits and waits, so that before leaving he could see the sunrise himself.

Those were the skies of Aali-Khabaruu. It also had everything else a tiny village should have, starting with a dusty street that knew every doorstep of Aali-Khabaruu by heart. That dusty street hesitantly led its way to the bank of a watercourse, but that was the farthest it went before quickly returning back to Aali-Khabaruu, out of fear of getting lost.

There were lush green fields of crops of all sorts, and a pond that was bigger than the combined area of all of its mud huts, and strewn with lotus leaves. Some of those big green leaves were the size of drum lids, and morning dew and pond water would congregate freely in them and roll like liquid mercury on their velvety surfaces.

And there was an orchard, too, of six or seven Chinee apple ber trees. Four of them stood bunched together in a crescent arch formation, and their branches grew entangled in each other, making an incomplete dome, which from the inside looked like three quarters of an obscure shrine's unfinished rotunda, made up of fat and thin branches all snaked into each other. There was only handful of trees, but they still called it an orchard.

Those Chinee apple ber trees bore big juicy seedless ber-berries, almost as big as small apples. The owner of the orchard was Sufi's elder brother, who was his brother-in-law too, and who looked like Victor Hugo's hunchback of Notre Dame. He lived in that orchard alone, under the shadows of his trees.

As to why his brother was also his brother-in-law—that's because when Sufi's mother died, he was her only child. His father remarried to a widow who had four children of her own from her prior marriage. And when Sufi turn fifteen his father force him to marry one of his stepmother's daughters. Thus his stepbrothers become his brothers-in-law.

Sufi was a brilliant student, though he was quiet like a mute. He was also Hafez, which means he had learned and memorised the entire Qur'an by heart before the age of seven. His father was a poor man who couldn't even afford to send Sufi to high school at Qamber. So Sufi earned and learned his way up by giving Qur'an lessons at a mosque in Qamber, and he would also recite the entire Qur'an by heart over several hours at funerals of wealthy people, which earned him enough money to pay his tuition fees.

He kept winning scholarships and grasping opportunities and eventually found himself with a PhD in New York City, driving around during the snowstorm of February 1963, in a beat-up orange Beetle bug. Incidentally, the Beatles were in New York too on their very first American tour, but Athah Ameeq Sufi didn't care for the Beatles.

Ali Gohar met Sufi after a long time through Groovy Person, while Sufi was visiting his family during one of those summers in early 70s. Sufi's wife along with their five children was living in the upscale suburbs of Hyderabad, not very far from that Kala Board Mustafa Masjid community where Ali Gohar with his wife and kids recently had moved from Jamshoro.

These urban build-ups were mind-boggling amalgamations of high-class chic neighbourhoods with struggling blue-collar localities. On a single street, you could move from a slum to a posh district just by crossing a simple tarmac paved road. A simple line could demarcate a blue-blood old-money haven from a rat-hole slum, which eagerly wanted to become at least a blue-collar working class area—but that kind of transformation took generations.

Millions and millions of struggling lower-middle-class members of society worked their shirts off to try to cross those simple lines in their lifetimes. But it would take a lifetime and a half, and if they finally managed to do it, they would find themselves in short change for whatever time they had left.

But Ali Gohar wanted to accomplish all that within his own lifetime. He wanted to become the perpendicular fret and was willing to get pressed hard against the tight strings of life, because he wanted to be heard.

But in the midst of all this, Sufi seemed to be seasoned, seemed to have seen all. And Ali Gohar was feeling an urge to follow in his footsteps, thinking, *you could go abroad too!* But he would quickly pushed that thought aside, the way a staunch believer might briefly think *"there is no god,"* but then rapidly push that out of his mind, shaking his head and clicking his tongue out of distaste for that thought, mercilessly blaming everything on the devil's account and asking for divine forgiveness.

But unlike a believer, Ali Gohar started to entertain that thought, that desire, that mere possibility. He started brushing up his English at the Pakistan-American cultural centre, and he got admission at New York University. Even though he was just barely making ends meet and had no savings at all, Ali Gohar kept flirting with this dream of going abroad.

He applied for a scholarship, fulfilled all of its requirements. And he waited, and waited, and nothing happened. He got no reply from federal ministry of education. This frustrated him, because he was after all an employee of the university, but then all universities fell under the control of the federal ministry, which was some fourteen hundred miles away in the capital city of Islamabad.

The impossibility of it all was causing his dream to fade, but then he got the idea to borrow money from his father. And once again those thoughts were rekindled: "*I could still go.*"

So one day he went back to Qamber, finding everything the same there as it always had been. When he arrived home, he met Alam who was busy taking pictures, three passport-size photographs of each person. And there were droves of people waiting because they all needed these photos for their picture IDs, and almost all of them were complaining and hating the government, which was forcing them to do it.

So Ali Gohar didn't have a chance to talk to Alam. He left his small bag there and stepped out to see if any of his friends were still there. Sure enough, a few were still there, and they spent the day walking along the dusty alleys and tasting Saful's infamous handmade ice cream.

And Ali Gohar's friends were cracking funny vulgar jokes to please him, but at the same time they were slipping their personal tragedies very casually in between those jokes, because they didn't want to burden Ali Gohar, but they did want to tell him what had happened in their lives since he had left. So they kept cushioning their sorrows in funny stories, but Ali Gohar was not really paying attention because the thought of how he was going to ask his father for money kept nagging at the back of his mind.

When evening fell and it start getting late, he said goodbye to his friends with hugs and walked alone back home. On his way, he passed under that balcony where, in his youth, he used to hear the sad snuffles of someone's calling, but today, it felt quiet, almost hollow. He turned his head and looked up, which he had never done before, and there was nothing there other than old pillars with wood carvings holding on to a sagging canopy. The whole balcony was blanketed in darkness. He passed the grain market, which was deserted at that late hour, and there were only a few alley dogs sleeping there carelessly. Hay and dust were creeping from both edges of the road, and little heaps of cow's dung were dropped about sporadically.

When Ali Gohar reached home, he found that Alam had left the door unhooked. He pushed the door open, came in, and then put latch chain back in the hook. It was June and even that late in the evening it was steamy. Alam had already spread a new rallee quilt on a cot for him. There was a dull light bulb outside veranda, which Alam had not turned off. Ali Gohar lay down on that quilted cot, not wanting to disturb his father who must already be asleep, thinking that he would instead talk to him the next morning. Or so! That is what he said to himself. May be he didn't want to ask his father for money at all.

It was stiflingly warm and there was barely any wind, but still whatever little wind was moving was causing the ber tree leaves of their backyard to make a slow humming noise. As if that ber also wanted to tell Ali Gohar funny jokes, and was trying to slip her own years of despair in between them. But he didn't want to listen to all those pathetic stories. He wanted to think big, to go away to a land that these poor Qamber dwellers couldn't even imagine.

Then, like a wise old woman, that ber tree picked up on his mood and completely understood his thinking, and on her own she turned those humming sounds of her leaves into soothing lullabies, and she kept rolling those sounds on his forehead like mother's gentle touch. At least, that's what he thought before falling asleep.

The next morning they both woke up early. Alam got tea and two cookies like elephant ears, which were a kind of French cookies, also called Palmiers. Their buttery insides were wrapped in a thin, crispy layer, sprinkled with sugar crystals. The trick was to make sure the sugar crystals didn't melt completely while baking, so they would form an icy texture. And this French recipe had somehow found its way here to Qamber.

There, sitting in front of his father, Ali Gohar was scrambling for words. Since he took his mother and his siblings to Hyderabad with him some ten years ago, he and his father had become estranged. At that time, Ali Gohar had only wanted peace of mind for everyone who was being grinded at that juncture of their lives, especially Alam and Dhayani and his elder sister Nisa and he himself were being directly affected by Alam's war of roses, in which Alam obnoxiously placed all blame upon Dhayani. And at the height of that craziness, there had been no other solution left but to take everyone away from Alam.

And in doing so, Ali Gohar said very few words to his father: "If you don't want to keep them, fine. I'll take them with me. But for heaven's sake, don't say these awful things about her, she is our mother." And then Ali Gohar looked into Alam's eyes, who just said in a mild voice, "What are you doing, Baba?"

"I just want to tell you that I'm taking them with me to Hyderabad." And with those words he had effectively, if unintentionally, overthrown his father. So he had good reason to hesitate before asking Alam for money.

"You remember?" Ali Gohar said after breakfast that morning. "Athah Ameeq Sufi used to be your student."

But Alam wasn't paying attention; rather he moved and sat beside Ali Gohar on the cot and started looking at Ali Gohar's left palm, while Ali Gohar ploughed on. "Sufi lives in America and works there in a university in New York."

Alam keep looking at Ali Gohar's palm, stretching it, and then joining his four fingers together and pushing them down to extend his palm so that he could see the lines, and then rotating Ali Gohar's thumb gently with his other free hand, like doctors do while examining, still holding the four fingers together.

Ali Gohar went on, "I met him in Hyderabad through." And then he mentioned Groovy Person's name, because Alam knew Groovy well, too. "Sufi's family lives in Hyderabad, he comes ever so often to see them there."

Ali Gohar still couldn't find the strength in his heart to ask for money. So he went on, and told Alam everything about Sufi and his achievements, as if he had come here all the way from Hyderabad just to tell Alam what Sufi have had accomplished in his life thus far. He told how "Sufi is a research scientist at Rockefeller University," and also that, "Sufi got gold medals for his academic achievements form Sindh University before going to the United States…" But still he hadn't asked Alam to lend him money so that he could go abroad.

By now, Alam had stopped looking at his palm and was deep in thought about something, but dropping his head down and placing his right thumb and middle finger on his two eyes and leaving his index finger between them on his forehead and squeezing his eyes hard, like people do when they get headaches. Then Alam lifted his head and opened his eyes and said, "There is a long journey in your fate! Soon, you will embark on it."

And somehow Ali Gohar just went on and said in one long sentence, "Sufi got me admission in one of the universities there, so I came here to ask you if you could lend me money, just for the passage and first six months there, and I'll pay you back once I go there and get some work—believe me I will pay you back every single penny."

Then he stopped and just looked at Alam's face. After few moments, Alam said, *"vilayat wannay tho chha?"*—*are you looking to go to an affluent foreign land?* And then he said, "You will go, it's written."

Alam hadn't replied to Ali Gohar's direct question, and now Ali Gohar ducked it as if nothing had happened and he hadn't ever asked for money at all. They both sat there for a little longer and finished their tea. Later that morning he left again for Hyderabad.

Chapter 5
The Sweet, Biting Smell of Wild Cannabis

Like Cinderella's fairy godmother had saved the day for her, by a sheer stroke of luck, Ali Gohar received an invitation. He was asked to participate in a week-long workshop meeting to incorporate art and craft in elementary education, organised by some board of curriculum. Which was just as boring as it sounds, but out of all possible places, the meeting venue was in Islamabad, where his scholarship application to the US was still hanging in limbo.

Normally, he wouldn't have had the means to travel that far, but now he had a chance. So he packed his bags and hopped a train to Islamabad. His long time friend Ali Akber Mangi and a few other colleagues were also attending the meeting, so they all travelled together and arrived after a day and a half of train ride.

This was his first time seeing the capital city. It was a beautiful place with lush green hills covered with pine trees and wild cannabis everywhere else like dandelion weeds. It was raining pretty much every day. They spent their entire days in meetings and saved sightseeing for the evenings, and the week went by in a flash.

On Friday evening, they boarded train heading back south. After seven hours, as the train was arriving in Lahore, Ali Gohar turned to Ali Akber and said suddenly, "I'm going back to Islamabad to check the status of my scholarship application."

"Are you out of—!" Ali Akbar caught himself and rephrased. "But we were there for a week!"

"Yes, you are right, we were there, and I was contemplating this all along and coming up with stupid answers and excuses. But now I'm clear. I should have checked what happened to my application."

Though they were surprised, his companions had no reason to object. So he switched trains in Lahore and by next morning he was back in Islamabad, that lush green place with the sweet biting smell of wild cannabis in the air.

The next morning he took a bus from his hotel to the federal secretariat. This was a series of four-story ivory white L-shaped buildings, like several giant carpenters' squares arranged diagonally to each other. He knew that one of those buildings was federal secretariat of education, and after asking directions from few passers-by he found it.

But then he was confronted a problem even bigger than finding the building, which was how to find the status of his application. It took an entire day to track down the appropriate section in which to inquire and then locate the actual person who processed those applications.

That person turned out to be a section officer. Section officers were usually rookie civil servants who had just passed the very arduous Central Superior Services exam. Passing that exam gave them permanent membership in the elite bureaucratic authority, making them each a key wheel on which the entire operation of the state would run.

Chaudhry Muzaffar was the particular wheel who was supposed to move Ali Gohar's scholarship application forward. But Chaudhry Muzaffar had gotten stuck. He was a chronically impolite person who seemed not yet to have emerged from the euphoric trance of having successfully become a civil servant.

Ali Gohar had finally uncovered Chaudhry Muzaffar's name when he approached a clerk in a huge room where several other clerks were scratching their pens against files. A few of them were smoking unfiltered cheap cigarettes. And that clerk was able to tell Ali Gohar that his application was at Mr Chaudhry's desk.

That clerk was a nice man, and he definitely had a name too. He looked like someone with protruding cheekbones, sunken cheeks, unusually dark skin, thick oil-soaked hair that was parked on left side of his face, and a broad forehead. His was a cadaver's face, but he was alive.

Clerks are clerks. They have their families, their problems, their backs pushed to the wall of life. They probably do fall in love too, and breathe in, and adore the smell coming from the drenched soil, or maybe from the dirty veils of their precious beloveds, their darlings. Like everyone else, they probably don't notice the tinkling sounds of the red and green glass bangles on their lovers' wrists while making love to them.

They probably write poetry and have tons of unfulfilled physical desires. They probably carry credits and loans that are unbelievably difficult to pay back, so much that they can't even pay the interest on those loans, and get insulted instead, and maybe they hate the guts of their being. But at the end of the day they are all like peasant workers, only they are tending offices instead of fields, and they are called clerks. They are like a shovelful of coal thrown in a locomotive's firebox, which then burns quietly and turns to ash, but before turning to ash it does propel the machine forward.

It was already the end of the day when Ali Gohar met that clerk who gave him Chaudhry Muzaffar's name. So he came back the next morning to meet with Chaudhry Muzaffar himself.

Chaudhry was fine in the initial introduction phase of their conversation, but hardened when Ali Gohar started to explain himself.

"I'm from University of Sindh, and I had applied for a scholarship. Every year there are five scholarships are awarded to our university. But this year there were not many applicants—only three, including me. The two others got their approvals, but I'm still waiting of my answer."

Chaudhry replied, "I'm not supposed to answer questions like yours, Mr Gohar, and off the top of my head I don't remember each and every application. Please follow up later or wait for your answer."

Ali Gohar left no pause at the end of Chaudry's sentence. "Mr Chaudhry, it's already the end of July, and my semester starts there in less than 30 days."

Without looking at Ali Gohar, Chaudhry said, "What you want me to do! Go back and wait?"

So that was it. Ali Gohar left Chaudhry's desk, probably to find some comfort in that other huge room, where there were several other people like him, including that good-hearted clerk who had helped him before.

And he told him what had happened. The clerk replied very casually, "No worries. Go and see *baray sahib.*"

Ali Gohar thought to himself, if a mere section officer could be so rude, then how much more inconsiderate might this baray sahib—meaning the Federal Secretary of Education—be to him. And then there was a commotion of noise as all the chairs in the room were pushed back and all the clerks rose to their feet, and all those in the room who were not clerks, the people who were present to see the clerks, also did the same instinctively. And a tall man with crew cut hair and a silver-grey safari suit came and went. The only correct place to wear safari suits should be the jungle, but it was the 70s and James Bond had started the trend.

In a fraction of a second Ali Gohar recognised him: he was the same man who sometimes uses to sit behind him and Ali Akbar while they painted landscapes of Hyderabad. Before Ali Gohar could ask, clerk said, "He is the Federal Secretary of Education now," and the flame of hope that had just been extinguished ignited once again on its own.

But you can't just saunter in to a federal secretary's office, like people use to drop in to President Lincoln's office, just to say hi to him, and then walk out of White House and continue on their merry ways. In this modern world, Ali Gohar first had to see the personal secretary of this federal secretary, and then there was the doorman of the federal secretary, and without the doorman's approval no one could enter federal secretary's office.

The personal secretary told Ali Gohar that he would have to make an appointment, for which he would have to wait two weeks. Ali Gohar tried to explain that for one thing his leave from work was already ending, and for another that he didn't have money to stay there for that long, and implored to be squeezed in between appointments or before or after the Secretary's lunch or tea break. But the personal secretary was not swayed. And when Ali Gohar approached the doorman directly, the latter simply said, "I can't let you in. You don't have an appointment."

Still determined to meet him, Ali Gohar stood outside the federal secretary's office door that whole day, and when that day had passed, he came back the next morning and did the same. After a few wasted hours of standing there on that second day, an idea came into his mind, and he picked an angle in the hallway from which he could actually see into the federal secretary's office and get a glimpse of the man himself each time the door was opened.

This meant that the federal secretary looked at him in return whenever he looked at the person who was entering his office. This kept happening for two more days, and on those two days the federal secretary noticed Ali Gohar's presence in the morning coming in and in the evening while leaving his office as well.

On the third day the federal secretary asked his doorman, "Who is this person standing outside my office all day long?" And asked his doorman to call him in.

Ali Gohar had been preparing himself for that one minute. He regurgitated everything, the whole situation, from his making landscapes alongside Ali Akber years back in Hyderabad, to the fulfilling of each and every requirement for this scholarship which was a near impossibility for him, to the inconsiderate behaviour of the section officer, and he managed to say all these things with a few seconds out of his one minute to spare.

The federal secretary offered him tea. By now, he remembered him clearly as that painter who used to make landscapes of Hyderabad. And he called for Chaudhry Muzaffar, who came in sat beside him in front of the federal secretary without looking at Ali Gohar.

"Muzaffar, this is Mr Gohar," said the federal secretary. "I heard that you've already met him. Now, he has applied for scholarship. I remember his file, and I also remember that I put a note on it to check all requirements. So, is Mr Gohar missing any prerequisites for his scholarship approval?"

Chaudhry replied, "Sir we had already awarded three out of five scholarship of university of Sindh to other universities, this year."

The federal secretary said, "All right, that's fine. So I presume that Mr Gohar failed to fulfil the requirements for his scholarship."

And there was silence. Chaudhry Muzaffar said nothing.

"Muzaffar?" The federal secretary prompted him.

And Chaudhry said, "No sir, there is nothing missing in Mr Gohar's application."

The federal secretary's military face became rigid. And he said to Chaudhry Muzaffar, "Go and find a scholarship for Mr Gohar before the end of today. And if you don't find one, then I'll send him on my expense, but believe me, you'll pay for it."

Chaudhry Muzaffar grabbed the file and hurried out of the Secretary's office. And to Ali Gohar the Secretary said, "You keep coming here every day and see me until this matter is resolved."

Two more days passed and there was still no solution. On both of those two days, to avoid hurdles, Ali Gohar went in very early and waited for the federal secretary in the parking lot of the secretariat building and then walked with him almost to his office, just to remind him of his presence. And then he waited all day long in that huge room with that good-hearted clerk, who brought tea all throughout the day for Ali Gohar.

On the third day, Ali Gohar waited and waited and waited in that parking lot, but the federal secretary didn't arrive. Later that morning he went to the good-hearted clerk and came to know that the federal secretary had gone to Karachi on an urgent official trip, and that poor man's friend, bad luck, started whistling into Ali Gohar's ear.

But then the good-hearted clerk added, "But the federal secretary left clear instructions for his personal secretary to call a meeting at 2pm, over which the Deputy Secretary will preside. The federal secretary will join them on phone, and they will review what needs to be done, including make their decision about your scholarship matter. The Deputy Secretary had called me earlier this morning and told me all of this and asked for the relevant files."

Then that good-hearted clerk asked Ali Gohar to go back to his hotel and wait there, promising to call him with an update about the meeting. Ali Gohar gave him the hotel phone number and left. And later that day he received that call. Because it was a cheap hotel, Ali Gohar had to wait for the room services boy to come and tell him there was a call for him, at which point he scurried down to the reception desk to take it.

Chaudhry Muzaffar was on line, and said a few words so clearly that Ali Gohar could even hear the punctuations in Chaudhry Muzaffar's voice. "Mr Gohar, we have arranged and awarded a scholarship for you. You should now head back to Hyderabad. Our office has already sent a telegram to your home address and to your university. Follow the further steps according to that telegram for good luck."

Ali Gohar formally said a long thanks and that was it. But this thought did come into his mind, that now Mr Chaudhry had probably snatched someone else's scholarship and given it to him. But he didn't puzzle over it any more than that, on the eighteenth day from that fateful afternoon.

Chapter 6
A Rotten Breeze Blew By

He was in New York City with Sufi, sitting with him in his ultra-compact East Side apartment, which was on 63th, between 1st and York. His first experience of this place, apart from simply looking at this unending city was, in the airport bathroom. When he turned on the sink faucet, it felt to him like liquid glass started pouring out of it. He had never seen such clean water in his life before.

It was a late summer day, and Sufi took him out on that very first evening to see Manhattan. They walked across several avenues on 63th street, past many cosy restaurants on the corner of Lexington Ave. He noticed that one of those restaurants had a series of dull light bulbs twined together in a long vine covering its entire canopy. The illumination of those bulbs was so weak that you could gaze them for as long as you wanted and their light won't hurt your eyes.

Then they passed an avenue that had a grassy lawn with small trees in the middle of it, and traffic was running on both sides of the lawn. There were stairs going down inside the ground, and Sufi said, "Let's go—we'll take the subway to Broadway."

So he followed Sufi into the ground. Once in there, Sufi gave Ali Gohar a copper coin with hole in it, and said, "It's a subway token." Sufi himself dropped one into a slot and pushed against a revolving iron cage, which spun around and suddenly Sufi was on the other side. Ali Gohar did the same.

Sufi was telling him something else about the subway, when a completely unintelligible blared from a speaker, followed by some screeching metallic noise. A gentle but foul-smelling rotten breeze blew by, and then the train barged right in, a whole stainless steel darn train beneath the ground. They boarded that train and got off wherever Sufi said to get off.

He walked up the stairs and emerged at the bottom of a plunging basin of lights falling from a great height, a Niagara Falls of neon lights. "This is Times Square," said Sufi.

He walked around mesmerised, staring at those buildings covered with colourful signs, and real steam exhaling from a giant coffee mug. It looked expensive. Those entire buildings seemed to be made up of—! Ali Gohar struggled for the right word, until 'money-garlands' came into his mind. In wedding ceremonies back home, new grooms would be draped with garlands of cash and flowers, which they wore on their peacock-erected necks and looked precious. And he said to himself, *"yes, these buildings are wearing money-garlands."*

The lights were shrinking and expanding on huge boards in Times Square, like someone was constantly tickling them and they were bursting into laughter. Humans have this tendency to hide their astonishment, and that's what he was doing as he walked along with Sufi, pretending it was all ordinary, though his heart was telling him otherwise.

It was summer of 1975, and although Ali Gohar had no interest in songs, he still couldn't avoid hearing Billy Joel's 'Piano man' playing all day long on the radio. And thus starts the life of a man from the countryside, who had only barely gotten acclimated to urban Hyderabad, who suddenly ended up in a great metropolis.

This was a place where one needed cardinal directions just to orient oneself enough to move around. Ali Gohar had no idea of East Side and West Side or uptown and downtown Manhattan. He was living in the East Side, and NYU was in Greenwich Village downtown. Sufi told Ali Gohar to get himself familiarised with the subway and to check out the nearest subway station, so he went out and found the station at Lexington and 53rd Street. He descended several flights into the ground, not differentiating east from west.

But he could see that this station had four levels, a G and a B1 and a B2 and a B3. B1 alone had black boards with white written words saying *Northbound local*, followed by a green circle with the number 6, and a green diamond shape also with the number 6, toward Pelham Bay Park or Parkchester. On the other side of the platform, it said *Southbound local*, and again that green circle and diamond number 6, toward Brooklyn Bridge—City Hall, and those routes were all for only one train. There were also blue signs for an E train and an orange sign for an M train, all with their own long names of routes written on separate black and white boards on the B2 and B3 levels.

He quickly felt that he needed to get out of there, but the revolving iron door he had taken to get in was only allowing people to get in. But he had just come here to check—he wasn't going anywhere. Now he wanted to go out, but there was only the way in, and he felt like he had lost the magic trick, forgotten how to say open sesame again. He stood there helplessly, occasionally trying and failing to exit from an entrance. Then he gave up and watched the people coming in.

After a while, a synthetic microphone voice came from the dirty smoke-littered horn-shaped mini loudspeakers, the same voice that had been methodically announcing arrivals and departures of trains all along. But now that voice was saying, "Sir you want to go out, sir you want to go out?" And on the third announcement, Ali Gohar realised that the voice was talking to him, so he confoundedly looked around, and he saw someone waving to him from behind the bluish-grey glass of the ticket booth, and sure enough that was the someone who was talking to him.

The voice said, "I'm going to open the locked door. Please step back." He stepped back, and after a weird electrocuting noise that door opened automatically, like that man sitting behind the bluish-grey glass window had just whispered into the door's ear, *open sesame*, just like that.

Several months after that day he was still taking wrong trains, often taking the downtown train when he should have taken the uptown, and missing stations, assuming each train would stop at all the stations, like it used to happened back home, where for over hundred years all trains passed the same stations every time because there was only one track. So, if you boarded any train for Kotri from Karachi, Jhampir was going to come in your way to Kotri no matter what. But here the trains came in three colours, chocolate brown, fatigue green, or stainless steel, with a small roll sign on each car, but all had their own tracks and stations.

Only yellow N, Q and R trains were going to pass through the 8th street NYU station, but he used to assume that the green 3, 5 and 6 trains could take him there also. And sometimes, riding a number 3 train, he would end up all the way at Utica Ave, Brooklyn.

But he did learn how to diagnose these problems by using all of his available senses, including the popping of his ears, which told him that train was now crossing under the river and heading towards Brooklyn, meaning that again he had missed his downtown Manhattan station. And he acquainted himself with his physical position on the city grid, with its four cardinal directions and its up and downtown. But he couldn't pay attention to those subway train announcements because they were still Greek to him.

One of his seniors from the University of Sindh who had been there in New York for the past few years told him that he himself still didn't understand those subway train announcements, and he would ask his young son whenever he was travelling with him to tell him what the announcement had said. And his son would tell him in Sindhi, *"Chawan tha ta, aasanjee station bi aachanwaree aa"*—they are saying that our destination is the next stop.

That senior colleague of Ali Gohar was one T.M. Halepoto, who was now doing his PhD at Columbia, having already completed two Master's Degrees, one from NYU and another one from Columbia. He had gotten divorced during this whole education process here in New York and was now living in the city with his only child, an eight-year-old boy.

Legend has it that he never visited his family in years, and his young wife had started to stray and gotten caught with a hand in the cookie jar—and obviously that hand belonged to someone else. She had begged for his forgiveness, but he was a true alpha male who had probably never heard these words: *"Mary, Mother of Forgiveness, may I forgive others as you forgave me in imitation of your Son. Mary, take my hand and lead me as I decide to accept God's grace to forgive (name the person) for (name the sin)."*

T.M. Halepoto burned her to toast, and so she ditched him after her unsuccessful pleas of forgiveness. She ran away with the same guy who'd had his hand in the cookie jar.

T.M. Halepoto was an average-looking man, like some unimportant peacetime secretary of defence. He had a combination of David Frost's facial features and the clumsiness of Lt. Colombo. His son, Alamgir, had been living with a distant relative until T.M. Halepoto made arrangements to get him here. The arrangement was that Alamgir would accompany Sufi all the way from Goth Tayyab Thaheem, close to Tando Allahyar, when Sufi was returning from one of his visits to his family.

Sufi remembered that when he went to pick up Alamgir, a simple-hearted village relative handed the boy over to him. Alamgir had just been bathed and had bitter mustard seed oil in his hair and on his face, and he was wearing a light blue salwar kameez, rough leather shoes on his feet, and around his head an old faded Ajrak had been wrapped in a *boekee*.

A boekee in Sindhi is a style of wearing a scarf in cold weather, where middle of the scarf is placed on the top of the head, leaving both ends to fall onto the person's chest; those ends are then rolled back and front twice to cover the mouth and nose and then knotted at the back of the neck, so that the whole face is covered, leaving just enough space to see and breathe.

So that was how Sufi found him at Goth Tayyab Thaheem and brought him to New York City.

Alamgir was a smart boy, and in a very short time he became a New Yorker. He was like a seeing-eye dog to T.M. Halepoto, who used his help to buy groceries, navigate the streets of New York City, remember and interpret the subway transfer announcements, drop off and pick up laundry from the Laundromat next-door to their building, and without his own knowledge Alamgir became a New Yorker and blended into that city's perpetuity.

Ali Gohar knew that he had to pace himself vigorously here. He had to do so much in a short time. Had to successfully finish his degree. Had to do odd jobs so that he could make extra money, which might help him to improve his and his family's quality of life back home. And had to overcome this anxiety of separation which was dragging him into depression.

Six weeks into his first semester, one of his art history professors assigned a paper and gave him a list of some sixteen reference books to consult. He went to university and library picked all sixteen reference books, gathered them on a table, and sat there and wept. He hadn't been a regular student since eighth grade. Way back then, when his father was suspended, he had quit studies and became a drawing teacher after a year.

And when Alam was reinstated, he didn't go back to school, because they all felt that it made no sense for him to be a student again alongside those same students that he had taught. So he quit school and took all of his high school exams as an external candidate. After that, he started working, and did his undergraduate and post-graduate exams also as an external candidate, and so he had managed to get a Master's in literature without ever placing a foot in a classroom as a student.

When he was done weeping, he opened the books and pressed on.

Sufi told him that he'd seen a help-wanted ad in classifieds, looking for someone who could read English and Urdu for their record-shipping warehouse.

And the address of that place was not very far from the university, somewhere around Lexington Ave, downtown, so Ali Gohar went there and found it. It was an EMI shipping place, and they hired him and paid him under the table, a dollar an hour. There his job was to gather and then pack orders of vinyl records and cassettes tapes of Indian and Pakistani music.

The reason they needed someone who could read Urdu also was that some of the labels on the cassettes were only in Urdu. Ali Gohar would go to school then come here and put in as many hours as he could before going back to Sufi's ultra-compact apartment. On one late October afternoon, he looked out from the rectangular basement window of that makeshift EMI storage and shipping facility at 27th and Lexington, a window which was covered with fog on the outside and years of dust on the inside, and he couldn't figure out what he was looking at in that gloomy haze. He had never seen snowfall before in his life, so he couldn't say to himself 'mushy falling snowflakes.'

He asked his co-worker, "What's happening outside, Bukhari sahib?"

"It's snowing," his co-worker replied.

That evening he walked in the snow all the way home.

Gradually that bubbly effervescent feeling of being in the northern hemisphere was disappearing, and he was walking with less awareness on the same sidewalks, taking same trains, looking at same length of long shadows, of trees, and triangular shadows of buildings at the intersections and garbage receptacles of streets. And without his knowledge he was becoming a decimal after an integer and a small gear in a big machine.

After couple of semesters, on the foreign student advisor's suggestion, he signed up for studio art and photography courses as well. He took photos while walking back and forth between his university and his job. He would take black and white photographs of light sliced between sharp shadows, of old buildings with hanging fire escape ladders. Once he took a close-up, vertically-oriented shot of the lower section of a fire escape ladder, showing a zigzag of flights of ladders, stacked one on the top of another, like a rickety scaffolding about to fall.

He also took photographs at sunset of the giant shadows of otherwise ordinary trees, climbing on the walls of adjacent buildings and peeping into windows of those buildings. He searched for new styles in which to capture the creative impressions that were popping up in his mind. He would take super-close ups of rusted metal, or the scratched cloudy glass doors of subway cars, spray painted with black strokes of exuberant graffiti letters.

Graffiti puzzled him. He could never make up his mind whether he liked it or not. But he settled for not liking it, and just decided for himself that it was an outburst of messy popular graphic art, which was unintelligible to him. He couldn't ignore it; that graffiti was everywhere, on mailboxes, in and on subway cars, on bodies of forsaken vans and box delivery trucks, and of course on city walls.

To Ali Gohar, it seemed to be some outlandish calligraphy, but still he could tell it was an expression of something that someone or a group of people wanted to say to others, and those others were not listening, but rather calling it violation of sanity. And maybe it was, or maybe it was an art form of vandalism. These are the concepts he was pondering as he photographed graffiti.

His photography professor was a young tall guy, who liked Ali Gohar's work, especially those graffiti photographs, and told him that *graffiti* was Italian word that meant 'scratching'. Ali Gohar reluctantly replied with some sort of "Humm, hann," but he never tried to dig into graffiti and its origin, which might have led him back to the pottery of Mohen-jo-daro.

He had read an article in the New York Times about this particular strip of 8th Avenue, between 32nd and 50th, called the Minnesota Strip. It was a red-light district, a young hookers' lane, full of runaway girls from the Midwest. Sometimes, he would walk around that drag of 8th Ave at night, thinking about doing a portrait of one of those runaway girls.

Like any other male they would call to him too, and lurch around him and say, "hey baby, why don't you take me with you," or "want some company, honey?" And they would look at him like they had known him forever, and say, "You look too tired, sugar pie, you need to loosen up."

But he would just walk past them, smiling sometimes, or sometimes ignoring them altogether. The soothing words and comforting gestures of those hookers reminded him of people from Shirkarpur, who start their conversations like southern grandmothers, with out-and-out love. Shirkarpuris talk like that with total strangers, calling them *'mun'a'* or *'dil-la',* addressing them with these words as their own heart. Or they would manage to engage you in conversation by calling you 'soohna' (meaning heavenly, beautiful), and then they'd say whatever it was they really wanted to say.

Ali Gohar was wandering around in an invisible bubble ball of Sindh around him. All of his references, all of his syntax, everything that he ever knew was from back home. So that invisible Sindhi bubble was his comfort. He was walking, living, and breathing in New York City, mingling with citizens of the world. But he was like those empty can hoarders who collect empty soda bottles and beer cans, which is trash to others but of utter value to them. He was trying to put new memories in old canisters, and he was carrying tons of his many old and used memories all the time on his shoulders.

So in this mishmash of school and work, materially he was living here in New York, but in his incorporeal thoughts he was living in a parallel realm. Part of that was here and a part of it was somewhere else. So in that confused, pitbulling mind of his, he never actually did those portraits he was pondering, god knows why not, probably because of Shadee.

That was his second grade class fellow who had wanted to be a physician, but instead had to follow the family trade and become a whore. During that last trip to Qamber, a couple of years back, when he had gone to ask his father for money, he had spent a day with his friends, who gave him an inventory of all that had happened since he left. One of them told him that Shadee had committed suicide by drinking rat poison. So instead of doing a portrait of one of those Minnesota Strip girls, he chose the homeless denizens of Bowery Street.

Bowery Street was downtown, close to his university and work. He took pictures at random of homeless people, some of them drunks, sleeping in weird curled positions, lying down in back alleys next to empty beer bottles, cigarette butts, and used condoms. One photograph showed two men sleeping on the ground in front of the doorsteps of a boarded storefront of a burned building. There were some long streaks of dry stains visible on ground, like urine or some other fluid that was spilled and then dried. Those two men were sleeping, dead tired, or drunk and passed out, hugging each other like two entangled lightning-bolt symbols.

The four worn-out soles of their shoes were clearly visible in that photograph. You could even see a few of the shining nail heads, and an ugly hole in the bottom of one of those soles, like an imperfect wood-knot.

At arm's length from one of those two men, there was a dog-eared and tattered old paperback copy of probably Dostoevsky's novel, though only the word 'punishment' could easily be read. It seems that the 'crime and' part of the name had been ripped from the cover of that book. But Ali Gohar didn't even know who Dostoevsky was, anyway.

Chapter 7
She Looked Almost Like Oriana Fallaci

At NYU he met Katie, whose real name was really long, Katherine Rosenstein Prince. Ali Gohar never was able to pronounce Rosenstein easily. He would try to make a quick spinning sound and end up saying, "Roseiniestein." He met her in one of his figure study classes. Katie was from Brooklyn, a New Yorker to her core. They developed a relationship which kept flirting with the term "Platonic." They never had a sexual relationship, but that doesn't mean that they never wanted to. So, it was not a platonic love, and yet it was.

Katie figured out that Ali Gohar was having problems acclimatising, especially in grasping pronunciations of words and understanding local accents. And he felt uncomfortable asking teachers and other people to repeat themselves again and again. So Katie placed herself as a buffer cushion between him and those frantically-paced others, and she slowly helped him become a modestly up-to-date citizen of this global village, a village in which there was everything else everything other than a village itself and its slow tranquillity.

In return, Ali Gohar helped her with drawing techniques, showing her how to grab a quick illusion of details and construct limbs, fingers and toes, more expressively and more lifelike, so that you almost wanted to touch the drawing board. He taught her to draw those kinds of figures in their figure study class, and explained her that jet-black and appliance-white don't exist in real life, so don't use them. Ali Gohar and Katie were both married, and they were both adults, and they both helped each other and somehow walked the walk of that godforsaken Platonic love out of sheer necessity.

Other than Sufi there was someone else who had come to receive him on his arrival at JFK airport. That person was *Badshah-Ast-Hussain,* at least, that's how he introduced himself to Ali Gohar. He was the elder brother of one of Ali Gohar's undergrad colleagues from Sindh University. His real name was Hussain

Shah, but he had replaced that with the moniker Badshah-Ast-Hussain. This moniker was a gruelling task for the pitiable local New Yorkers to pronounce, and the way they said it was just as bad as the way Ali Gohar pronounced Rosenstein.

Initially, Badshah-Ast-Hussain used to take a great pride in explaining the meaning of his assumed name, which in fact was a Persian phrase, meaning 'for all kings he is Hussain'. But then gradually Badshah-Ast-Hussain lost interest in his long pseudonym, and got tired of explaining the meaning and the whole long story behind that Persian phrase, and so finally got settled on Hussain alone.

Hussain was in his late forties, a slim man of average height, with a full head of curly black hair that he used to roll back from his forehead. Somehow nature had forgotten to encode some very important genetic information in his body, which is why he didn't have any grey yet. Other than that debacle of nature, he was a bachelor, a PhD, and a licensed cytologist, who was very much into old Hindi movie songs. He used to guess the song by just listening to the first few seconds of its introduction.

Hussain used to live in the West Side, but then he moved into the same building where Ali Gohar and Sufi were living. And Hussain became another kind of guide for Ali Gohar, sharing his prior experiences, sometimes in a comic way. Whenever they passed outside a certain jeweller on 5th Avenue, he would curse that place in Sindhi, and say *"thuka-thaee"*—spit on you—at the door, fully extending his right arm and stretching out all five fingers of his right hand.

This, in Sindhi, is a godforsaken curse. He told the story that when he arrived, four or five years back, he had worked as a watchman outside that posh 5th Avenue jewellery shop. At the time, he was also studying more to get his cytology licence, because his PhD in marine biology from England was no good here. But the reason of cursing that place was not that he was a PhD and therefore over-qualified for a watchman's position.

The reason for his curse was that, when he was hired, he was told by the owner-cum-general manager of that place to stand still outside entrance like a Grenadier Guardsman. And that general manager showed him personally how to stand still and keep staring at the other side of the street. Which Hussain understood completely, and in fact he did it exactly the way he was told in front of his boss. But when his boss went inside the store, Hussain slowly shrugged his shoulders, than relaxed his knees and tilted his head to side, but just a little.

And his boss popped up from inside and told Hussain, "You have to stand still, like the Queen of England's guards!"

Hussain said, "my apologies sir," and stiffened himself again. The boss went in, and after a few moments, damn gravity acted again on Hussain's posture, and he started crumbling. And the boss again came out, but this time Hussain noticed him coming out, and erected himself in time. But the boss was like an all-knowing god, and started yelling at him: "You were told before even you were hired, that you have stand still, and that's what you are supposed to do!"

Hussain threw a smile at him, as if that jeweller was kidding. And then, when third time the manager of that posh jewellery shop came out, he fired Hussain at the spot. Hussain protested, asking what he had done wrong. And manager said, "You were not doing what you were supposed to do!" And now he pointed his finger towards a closed-circuit camera, which was cutting-edge technology back then. Hussain was shocked to know that his boss had been watching him all along.

It was end of 1976, and Ali Gohar had been here for year and a half now. So many things had changed; this city had entered in him like a herpes simplex virus. He never caught the wrong train anymore, having now mastered this art, knowing even which end of the train was best to board, and how many cars to expect in each one. That way he not only got on the right train, but at the best point, so that he arrived very close to or exactly in front of his exit, suavely avoiding the bottle-necking rush of other passengers trying to leave.

That was the time when John Kacere—*the* John Kacere!—was teaching their figure study class. And Ali Gohar had no idea, at that time about who Kacere was. John Kacere was an average-looking man, one that you wouldn't even notice if he crossed in front of you on the street, five-seven or five-eight-ish tall. He had a long face, with long grey hairs around his profoundly bald forehead, with sunken dark eyes and hollow cheeks. And that was it.

Ali Gohar asked his own heart who Kacere looked like, and his heart said, "a bit like Ali Sardar Jafri maybe!" Ali Gohar agreed with his heart and decided that Kacere looked like Ali Sardar Jafri.

In real life, John Kacere was a hyperrealist. Hyperrealism was a brand new term then, which had carved herself out of late 60s photorealism and was like a freshly baked cookie of the arts, hot out of the brick oven of realistic painting, with that mind-filling smell of holiday cookies in which one wants to indulge.

Kacere never claimed to be a hyperrealist or a photorealist or a combination of both, but his paintings were mind-boggling.

They were long and wide, almost huge squares, of oil on canvas, close-ups of the female butt and pelvic area covered with beautiful lingerie. Ali Gohar saw one of Kacere's paintings for the first time at a New York art gallery, where the unorthodox Kacere occasionally used to take his classes. It was a mammoth cinema banner size, mid torso of a female pelvic area, and one could see her pubic hairs peeping out from under a smoke black-screen of sheer lingerie, which was still underwear to Ali Gohar because he don't know words like 'lingerie' to describe female undergarments.

His initial reaction was the word *rubbish*, but then his breath froze in his lungs for just a microsecond. Then he thought, *it must be an enlarged photograph*. He stepped up close to that painting, and the closer he got, the more complicated it became. Kacere's technique of painstakingly fine details seemed to be some sorcery that was eluding him.

There was nothing being divulged in that painting, and yet everything was in the open. One could see through to the skin, so it was neither naked nor covered. It was stunning work, picture perfect, and its subtle colours were perfectly tinted. Ali Gohar looked at the extreme corners and found that even they were flawless. The floral satin in every single dishevelled crease under her body was frighteningly real. It was overwhelming. It was beyond mind-boggling, this larger-than-life female body lying on her side, on a parallel plane.

Like the sky over a distant horizon, gently laying his head on the earth's shoulders. Ali Gohar kept looking at the painting and felt like he was being given a beating, or like someone was stretching his brain the way children sometimes stretch their chewing gum into long pink strings. Ali Gohar looked across the room to where Kacere was talking to some other students, and he saw him with new eyes. From that moment on, Kacere became somebody else to him, someone like Vermeer or Hemingway or Tolstoy, someone who could walk on water.

While he was thinking all that, Katie came close to Ali Gohar and whispered in his ear, "*He has a fetish for women's behinds,*" and walked away.

Ali Gohar didn't know what she said, but you don't always have to understand every word to get the meaning of things. He just took it for granted that Katie meant something offensive about Kacere's painting.

Kacere was a demanding teacher. He wanted to make every student into himself. And his class was a core class, so Ali Gohar had to do well in it. But where Ali Gohar had come from, you would be considered a realistic painter just by showing a rough resemblance of a human figure, and the terms of hyperrealism and photorealism had not even reached there yet.

Ali Gohar got an extra job selling pretzels, in a pretzel stand at 13th street and union square subway stations. He had gotten that job through his connection to Hussain.

The pretzel stand company had actually hired one Mohammad Warraich, an alcoholic who didn't want to do that job, but whose American wife wanted him to keep it for the sake of his health insurance benefits. So Ali Gohar was doing the job as Mohammad Warraich. And he was getting his paycheck, but Mrs Warraich was getting her husband's health insurance benefits. And Mohammad Waraich was probably getting drunk and passing out on one of those old beat-up and sagging sofas in their apartment somewhere in that all-embracing city.

Ali Gohar was putting in extra hours wherever he could, working two jobs and was still a full-time student. Sometimes, he would leave very early in the morning to go to the EMI shipping place, because they had given him the key. So he opened that basement warehouse, packed orders, took care of all the shipments, and then went to school and after that. He would do a 3pm to midnight shift at the pretzel stand and come back home looking like a worn out old rag.

But he had a strong will to earn money, not because he was avaricious for material gain, though perhaps he did have some of those greedy tendencies. But by working so hard, he was trying to do the unthinkable. He wanted to walk back into his past and erase the word *poor*, and he wanted to replace it with *prosperous*. Before him, no one succeeded doing that, and neither did he. It's not easy to mess around with your past, just like that.

Rosemary Ann, that's what her name was, but she went by Rose only, lived on 68th Street, not far from where Ali Gohar and Sufi were living. But Rosemary Ann had nothing to do with them; rather she was Badshah-Ast-Hussain's girlfriend. Rose was a nurse at New York Hospital. She was one of those nurses who have all kinds of certifications and are almost doctors themselves.

She was a tiny Italian brunette, and other than her pitch-black eyes she looked almost like Oriana Fallaci. And she somehow had managed to hold in her tiny little heart all the love in the world for Badshah-Ast-Hussain. But unfortunately this was just like any other love story.

Theirs was, after all, a story too. It had a glorious beginning, a lagging middle and an end that was as ordinary as an empty can of soda. By the time Ali Gohar met Hussain, that love story was leaving its middle and getting into its chaotic end. In fact, he saw it coming down burning in flames like the Hindenburg. Because Hussain had moved into the same building, Ali Gohar witnessed it all.

Rose used to come to their building, stand outside Hussain's apartment door, and gently knock, standing there right outside his apartment for as long as she could. She would keep knocking intermittently, always looking down the hallway to make sure no one else was looking at her. Eventually, she would get tired and go back to her world.

Hussain was always in there, but he wouldn't open the door for her. He didn't want to have a relationship with her anymore, she didn't want to throw in the towel. She would always come back, and she'd knock and call his name. "Hussain, hon, I know you're in there. Could you please open? Hussain honey!"

She'd start banging on his door, and yelling at the top of her lungs, and in her anger she'd call him all sort of names. But then, right then and there, she would regretfully apologise to him, in that empty hallway, outside his door, still yelling at the top of her lungs while apologising. From a distance, she looked like a crazy person talking to herself.

Sometimes, she would knock and bang so hard that she was almost adhering to Hussain's door, like she was hugging it, and then she would fall on her knees there. She was like a gambler who had nothing else to spend. She lay there on the floor, looking lifeless, like someone who had fallen from a great height and hit the ground, but did not die. Ali Gohar saw all that on several occasions, both leaving his apartment and coming in.

Once, Sufi was with Ali Gohar and Rose was in her trance, he looked at her, and joyfully said to Ali Gohar, "*mast thaee, Ishq lago thasee*"—*she has turned into an ascetic mendicant, has fallen in love.* Sufi acknowledged this love with a hearty laugh, "*ha-ha-haa 'ashiqah' aa.*"

And he went on, "They say it's a vine, and there is a common belief is that when love takes its root in the heart of a lover, everything other than God is effaced, but that's what I read somewhere. I personally believe that even God is erased, because if lovers are willing to erase themselves, then what difference does God make for them?"

He was elevating her, like she had reached some kinship with great lovers before her. They walked by her, and as she lay there she didn't even care to notice them, though she knew both of them very well.

Sufi's comments on Rose reminded Ali Gohar of Kackoo Mast, back in Qamber. This brought him one step closer to Rosemary Ann.

In that same period of time, she would also come to Ali Gohar and Sufi's apartment in odd hours and say to Ali Gohar, "I know he is in his apartment. Could you please call him for me and check?"

But Ali Gohar refused, because Hussain had already instructed him: "If she comes, tell her I'm gone to West Side for the weekend to see my friends there." And Ali Gohar would lie to her, but she was stubborn, she wouldn't listen, and she still went to Hussain's apartment door and said, "honey, sweetie Hussain," in her snotty shivering voice. They say love is pretty solid, but hers was like of some industrial grade.

And then she used to do the same drill of knocking and banging, and after a while, a few of Hussain's elderly neighbours heard it, and they had listened not very long ago to her yelling at the same volume but with a totally different kind of sound, when she used to have multiple orgasms and use to make exuberant, lavish, beautiful cries, like the entire universe was forcefully passing through that small space in her tiny body.

But for those senior neighbours, her moans of pleasures had been equally disturbing as her banging and yelling now. So they used to open their doors slightly and give her their half-faced poisonous looks, doubtlessly similar to those which, according to some obscure myth, God had shown to Moses for a fraction of a second, and the sheer energy of God's gaze had caused Moses to fall unconscious and toasted Mount Sinai into charred wood.

But Rose never fainted nor got burned by the old people's looks, because she had gotten stung by her own heart; the love in her heart for Hussain had turned her into living ashes. She would leave, wiping her tears with her palms and smearing her slimy snots on her face. Then she would go back to her 68th Street apartment.

Eventually, she disappeared from those hallways of Hussain's apartment. But Ali Gohar would still see her, every now and then, walking on 3rd Avenue or in those congested isles of the subbasement food market at the corner of 66th and 1st Ave. She would engage him in small talk whenever she saw him, or smile and wave from a distance like nothing had happened, and who knows, maybe nothing really did happen.

For several months, Ali Gohar was working feverishly paintings for his thesis exhibition. His style was realism, and he picked a subject he knew well.

He made four paintings: a potter, a mother with her child, two kids, and a portrait of the Sufi musician Allan Fakeer.

Pottery making has been around forever, and every culture and every civilisation have had potters. But Ali Gohar specifically wanted to paint a *Kumbhar'o*. Kumbhars are Sindhi potters; in fact it's a social class, a group of people who have been making soft clay pots for thousands of years and had even adopted their profession as their last name. In Ali Gohar's painting, there was a man crunched down, submerged in darkness. Only a very little light is falling on his face, which was otherwise covered by shadows from the rolls of his turban.

Whatever face was left there to see was of a dark tan complexion, almost brown. But there was ample light on the fingers of that potter, whose muddy hands were both pressed to the *chuck'o*. Part of it seemed to be glowing, and one could see the wetness like a mirage between and around the potter's fingers.

Ali Gohar had put special effort into detailing the potter's fingers, but still they looked conjoined, as if that clay had webbed his fingers. Maybe Ali Gohar wanted them to look like that. The position of the potter's hands was also giving the false impression that his wrists had been handcuffed. But there were no handcuffs around the potter's wrists—it just felt like that.

His second painting was a portrait of Allan Fakeer, with his signature Ajrak turban, with the starched part of the Ajrak making a Chinese fan at the top of Allan's head and a painting of two sad-looking children hugging each other. Their faces though looked like they were melting. The only things that were photorealistic in that third painting were three generic transparent plastic buttons on little boy's loose, collarless shirt.

It was summer of 1977. Ali Gohar was in his class, and the mid-morning sunlight of early July was unrolling glitters on the otherwise grime- and weather-stained glass windows of his studio classroom. Ali Gohar was working on his fourth painting, the one of a woman and her child, which was life-size. He painted that woman and her child sitting under the patchy shadows of the low-hanging limb of an old tree in the courtyard of a shrine.

The woman had a blank face, like she had never had a chance, like she was not a contender in her own life. But the courtyard in which Ali Gohar depicted her was that of Shah Latif, who always sang *hail glory to women!* And applauded and cheered their sacrifices. In fact, all of Shah Latif's heroes are women. On many occasions in his poetry, he referred to himself using the female gender.

Ali Gohar was working on the face of that young woman when John Kacere walked in studio and came to stand close behind Ali Gohar.

"You know what?" Kacere said, "There is so much in there to criticise, and I will. But I like your subject. It has your distinct accent. There is so much in there to see, and then there is a whole lot to feel."

Ali Gohar replied, "Humm; I could even smell the atmosphere of this painting, slight stench of hay with rotten soil, followed by fade distant smell of peelu shrubs." Ali Gohar paused and then said, "I've walked barefoot in that courtyard countless times. I could hear the clamour of birds, chirping and talking in all their tongues, and the prolonged coughing sounds of old devotees lying down in the nooks and corners of the shrine."

Then Ali Gohar paused again, to find right words, wanting to tell Kacere who Shah Latif was. "Every Thursday night for over two hundred years, *Shah ja'a Fakeer'a*—those are the devotees, the singers, who belong to a family of musicians—they all sing in the shrine of Shah Latif at Bhit Shah in the traditional manner created by the Sufi saint himself. Those singing sessions are called *'suma'o',* which means, a dreaming trance while still awake."

But in the end Ali Gohar failed to convey all that to Kacere, and Kacere didn't give a damn about Shah Latif either, because he still had yet to explore the big-wigs of mystic realm, like Rumi, Hafez and Sa'adi. So Shah Latif stayed inside Ali Gohar's heart, which probably Shah Latif didn't mind.

Then Kacere said, "Is everybody okay back home?"

Ali Gohar looked at Kacere with a lost look and said a weak, "yes."

"I guess you don't know yet?"

"Know what!"

"About the military coup in Pakistan."

Kacere's words should have hit Ali Gohar's ear drums with a colossal intensity, but instead he just took a sigh and closed his eyes and rolled the fingers of one of his hands against his forehead and eyes, which people usually do when they don't know what to do.

That afternoon he didn't go to the pretzel stand. He called Muhammad Waraich, who probably took care of it. He chose to have a long walk back home, taking Lexington Avenue all the way from 27th to 63rd. That was only protest he could come up with against the military dictatorship. He kept walking and talking to himself. *It's too bad that a charismatic leader is deposed.*

He was not very worried about the democracy, because deep inside his mind he had vaguely figured that there really was no democracy back home, it was all façade of democracy, like a dead corpse covered with dry leaves. He himself didn't know a whole lot about democracy, and basically that Pakistanis had not yet even discovered it. After a few days this news became hot, and the entire Pakistani community was talking about how, yes, there was a military coup back home, and the democratically elected government had been overthrown. Some local Pakistanis had organised a peaceful protest, one of those symbolic ones, in front of Consulate general of Pakistan in New York, on a Tuesday at noontime so that participants could come during their lunch breaks.

Ali Gohar was enthusiastically looking forward to attending that lunch-break protest, which was supposed to make a half-a-million strong army headed by over 178 brass hat generals of all different sorts to go back to their barracks. But then who knows, peaceful protests are peaceful protests, and once a half-naked old man of a mere 100 pounds, 5 feet tall, had peacefully asked an empire, in which sun never sets, to leave India, and eventually they did leave India.

So sometimes these droopy peaceful protests do work. And here in New York he had heard the state lottery's centerpiece slogan, "hey you never know!" So that quest of 'hey you never know' could work for the lucky strike as it did for the half-naked old man's Satyagraha pledge. Satyagraha literally means 'truth force', but that wise half-naked old man had made millions and millions believe that the meaning of Satyagraha could be peaceful nonviolence too.

So keeping those things in his mind, Ali Gohar planned to attend that peaceful protest, with this unwavering belief in his heart that his mere presence there would make things to go in the right direction, and democracy would be revived and that charismatic leader would be reinstated.

When that Tuesday came, he was supposed to be in class, but he chose to miss that class for a greater cause. He was walking in long strides on 63th to Park Avenue, and then turned south to 53rd, pacing towards the protest site, and after every few steps he was adjusting his camera strap, because amidst the fast walking his camera was hitting his elbow and it was making him uncomfortable.

Slowly logic started talking sense to him, and his romance of democracy began to wilt.

"What are you doing?" Reason said.

He wasn't able to rationalise with reason, so he never said, "It's for the greater good, for the principal of the thing. We should stand against and in front of the forces of tyranny."

But Reason had all the arguments. And Reason said, "You came a long way, from running shadow to shadow barefoot in sizzling heat on the hot salt-drenched ground of Qamber. You work for the government. What if someone sees you! What if someone reported you! Would you go back to Qamber? Would let your children run from shadow to shadow barefoot on those barbeque-hot-plate roads? Think of yourself!"

His pacing was all but gone; now he was barely walking. It was a hazy day in August, and the skies were striped with bands of empty big white clouds, rolling lazily in caravan formations, like those old folks who walk slowly because they don't have to reach anywhere important. Ali Gohar was still walking towards that peaceful protest site, but his steps were getting heavier and heavier, like he was having change of heart, like he was listening to his mind and didn't want to go there anymore.

In the median mall of Park Avenue there were trees, Ali Gohar didn't know which kind, probably they were cherry blossoms or magnolia trees, surrounded by imprisoned looking flowers, which were tired daffodils, who keep swinging their heads unwillingly in the forceful swells of air pushed by fast-moving traffic on both sides of Park Avenue. He was probably trying to find any reason to slow him down.

On the sidewalk, there was someone playing the saxophone. His everything was unwashed, and he had uncombed grey hair running in all directions, long nails filled with greasy black dirt, a ragged two-buttoned navy stripe seersucker suit, whose navy blue stripes were faded to almost white. His everything was dirty, other than his saxophone, which against all odds was glittering. People were throwing coins in red velvet belly of his saxophone's otherwise black hard leather case. And all of sudden, he stopped playing saxophone and started talking.

And talking to everyone! But it felt like he was just talking to himself, because no one was paying any attention to him. Ali Gohar was standing at a safe distance from that crazy-looking man as he started to speak.

"Imagine!" Then he yelled and shook his hands, like someone stranded on an island who has just seen a ship on the horizon and is desperately calling for help. "Just imagine, a need-based society, a world without money, thousands of years from now. You need gas, so you get gas. You need groceries, so you get food. You have toothache, so you get your teeth fixed. One thing it will do, it will minimise crime drastically. No one is going to break in to steal my couch. Why?"

"Because who is going to buy it from him? There is no money. And he can get a new couch of his own, from the couch store. Imagine a resource-based society, where no one will charge you several hundred dollars an hour, just because he is an attorney, while someone else gets paid just one dollar an hour, because he is pumping gas. It will happen from a thousands of years from now, but it could happen now! Here today, if you all wanted it! Are you listening, people, are you listening to me?"

The crazy man took a pause and rolled his dirty hands over his face and said, "Like, we didn't know about germs in the year one thousand, and there was no time as we know it, with this simple time clock then. This consumer-based society will be seen as the plague of the Middle Ages, eight hundred or a thousand years from now. Every government in the world is working on the basis of scaring their people. No matter where, it's the same. We pick our representatives on the basis of trust. Because you people are up to your eyeballs, your objective is to keep yourself afloat, pay your mortgages and bills. Just to keep a roof over your families' heads."

Then as if he were introducing himself to a crowd, the crazy man said, "I, Tom," and squarely extended his chest by folding his arms at the elbows and pushing them back.

He again said, "I, Tom, the voter, don't know what my representative is voting for in congress. And he doesn't care about me, because to him, I'm just a Tom! Tom who? And the answer is Tom Nobody. I'm nothing. But if I donate a $100 then I will get a letter of thanks, might get invitation to a dinner. If I'm a corporation and donate great amounts of money, then I could cash in my chips after elections. You are not here for yourself, listen to me, you are not here for yourself on this earth. You are here for others!"

His eyes were about to pop out of his head, but then he sat down again and murmured to himself, "But then who listens to me." Then the crazy man hopelessly bit into the mouthpiece of his saxophone and resumed playing, with an attitude that seemed to say that it really was going to take another thousand years for people to understand whatever he just said.

By then, Ali Gohar was totally mesmerised by the crazy man's speech. He had taken his 120mm box camera out and was trying to frame him in a shot. His hands were shaking like he was taking photograph of a prophet. When the man saw Ali Gohar taking his photograph, he yelled out, "fuck you!" And in that moment Ali Gohar hit the shutter, like he had taken a snapshot of 'fuck you'. Then the crazy man went back on, playing his saxophone, and Ali Gohar went back to his apartment, holding the finger of Reason like a child, and also agreeing with Reason like a child.

Chapter 8
Map of the Atum-Bom

Another year passed, but things stayed the same. He was still getting his scholarship stipend check every month like clockwork. A year ago, a military general saved the country by derailing a corrupt democracy—at least, that's what the general said he was doing. And he had promised to hold fair elections in the next 90 days, and to hand over power to the representatives of the Nation. That general had since decided to hold back on that promise of his, not because he didn't want to keep it.

He had all intentions to make good on it, because he called himself a man of God, with a capital G, which means that god with a capital G is the one true god, in which the military general placed his firm belief. In fact, the general had simply amended his promise of holding free elections in 90 days, because he wanted to ensure the accountability of politicians. He didn't want the people of his loving nation to have corrupt politicians again. And he was going to usher in a new dawn of Islamic rule in Pakistan, starting by changing the weekend holiday from Saturday and Sunday to Thursday and Friday.

Sufi pointed out, "Now Pakistan will only have a three working days week, which is going to hurt financially because the entire would is going to function between Mon through Fri. But Pakistan is going to work only Mon through Wed."

And this "Interest free banking," said Sufi, "is against the basic fundamentals of banking. It's a big scam." Sufi said this quietly to himself.

Ali Gohar said to Sufi, "But hey, he is the general, so almost a king. Anyway, who can tell a lion that he has bad breath!"

Plus, Ali Gohar thought Sufi had a tendency to overthink about small things. All these big changes must have been thought over by many intelligent people, who must have accounted for all these details like the workweek. Sufi had studied so much that he had become cynical.

Ali Gohar was about to finish his degree and return. His communication back home with his wife and his mother and brothers and sisters was all through letters. Only twice a year did he make a three-minute person-to-person trunk call to his wife at his in-laws' place, because only they had a phone. Those three-minute trunk calls used to be stupefyingly exhausting; they caused unexpected emotional reshuffling of the stagnant pathos of separation, and a tingling joy of being able to hear the voice in real-time of someone who was still poles away.

The first thirty seconds would be consumed with *can you hear me clearly?* Which would be followed by a little bit of very superficial *how is everything and everybody* for a minute and so, and then the weeping and snorting of his children who missed him, followed by alarming beeps proclaiming that the call was about to end.

He was writing letters to his wife at least three times a week, on those greyish blue aero-grams, writing inventories of his day to day life in one-page letters. Initially, they were romantic and forlorn letters, opening with, "To you, life of my heart, a greeting from pure unending eternal love to you." And then Ali Gohar use to write things that maybe Garcia Marquez was also thinking at that same time in the late 70s for his yet-to-be published novel *Love in the Time of Cholera*.

But then, over time, that romantic gentleness, that rose petal touch, that litany of love from letters of Ali Gohar kept tapering down, and it was replaced with the narrative of a souring heart to become a mere list of things like 220-volt tape recorders and hair dryers that he had purchased from Canal street and other things that he had bought for them at Macy's or Alexander's. In some of those letters, he had written entire recipes for Indian-style ground beef curry.

One of his brothers-in-law, a distant cousin of his wife, got a visitor's visa to the United States. In late 70s and early 80s, there was an invisible tectonic shift happening in societies of third world. People were making their moves by any means they could. England and Germany were already becoming saturated for Indians and Pakistanis, so they started heading towards the United States, getting visitors visa's, coming here and losing their shadow and becoming invisible. Ali Gohar's distant brother-in-law wanted to do the same, just come here and try his luck.

So he got that very important trunk call from his wife's aunt that her son was flying on a such-and-such a with the *Scandinavian Airlines* System, which was then known as SAS. Ali Gohar went that day to pick him from JFK. In those days, there was just one big terminal for everything other than Pan-American, so every other airline use to land at that international terminal.

So Ali Gohar waited there and waited there. Initially, there were a whole lot of passengers, but then there were fewer and fewer, and finally that place became deserted. Ali Gohar was standing there alone with a few pages of newspapers occasionally spinning on the floor and the occasional echoing noise of the heels of some airline crew or aviation official. Then finally his distant brother-in-law walked out, looking drawn. If he had a fair complexion, then at this moment his face would have looked bleached white. But because he had reasonably dark skin, his face was looking a pale grey.

"What happened, what took you so long?" asked Ali Gohar.

The distant brother-in-law said, "They held me, and were going to sending me back." Then he took a short pause. "But one of my bags got stranded in Copenhagen. There is no SAS flight from there for another two days, so they gave me a two-day conditional entry. They asked me to come back once my missing luggage is here, and then they want me to go back."

By then, his face had really turned an almost bleach-white, and he said, "My mother is going to kill me. She gave me thirty years' worth of her retirement savings money to buy this ticket and give me $1630 of cash."

Ali Gohar said, "Calm down. Theoretically you still have two more days to live, so why are you dying now. Let's go."

His distant brother-in-law was a young man, 21 or 22 years old. He was someone who grew up amidst domestic noises, so he was used to make his point by yelling. In those 38 hours, he called several of his references from back home, who were friends of some acquaintances of people he barely knew at all.

Three invisible young men appeared from their realm of shadowy world. Like Ali Gohar's distant brother-in-law, all three of these men were from Karachi and were children of people who had migrated to Pakistan, mostly from northern India. A big debate was going on among those three young men and Ali Gohar's distant brother-in-law.

They said he shouldn't go to claim that missing luggage, but instead join them, become invisible and disappear into thin air like the other millions of illegal immigrants. The distant brother-in-law was discussing this very serious matter with no one other than these three friends, who had been mere references to him until yesterday. He was not asking for Ali Gohar's or Sufi's opinion at all.

A prisoner of habit, Sufi poked his head into their matter and made a suggestion to these boys who hadn't asked and said something that they didn't want to hear. "You should go tomorrow and claim your missing bag. And try to explain to the immigration personnel that you came back to claim your stuff, and that you are just a visitor who is planning to stay for 6 to 8 weeks here, and then go back."

They were all looking at Sufi like he was out of his mind. Like he had just uttered some vulgar immoral obscenity. Sufi thought they were listening to him and went on to say, "Americans are very understanding people. They might listen."

One of them, who looked just a little bit like Dev Anand but himself believed that he looked very much like Dev Anand, rejected Sufi's proposal. He said sarcastically, "You your self have just used the word 'might'. It's not that simple, Sufi sahib. What if they don't understand? What if they put him on the next flight back? Plus, who is going to tell all that to immigration? He can't speak that much English, and we three are already illegal, so none of us is going with him."

What he meant was *thanks but no thanks*. So the three boys went on trying to convince this distant brother-in-law of Ali Gohar that he should not listen to Sufi sahib. Even though Sufi sahib is a legal alien and whatever Sufi was saying was probably of very high moral and logical value, goodness and rationality have nothing to do with practicality. And the ground reality was that his mother had already drained all of her life's savings into sending him here. So forget about going back to authorities. "You got a new lease on your life—come with us," said one of them.

Sufi shook his head in disagreement, and said, "I'll go with you; I'll talk to them on your behalf."

The next day, Ali Gohar, his distant brother-in-law, and Sufi went to JFK. After picking up his distant brother-in-law's missing bag, they went to an office at the airport and someone there directed them to another small room. Sufi very smoothly started talking with the person in that room.

"Hello officer, my last name is Sufi, and my full given name is Ghulam Siddique. I'm here today with this young man, because he has communication issues."

The immigration officer asked them to sit, and said, "What do you do Mr Sufi?"

"I was a research scientist at Rockefeller University, but am looking for a job right now."

The officer was shuffling papers inside a butter-yellow folder, and he kept looking at those papers while Sufi was talking. Then he turned to Ali Gohar and asked him about his whereabouts. Ali Gohar told his story. The officer checked Sufi's and Ali Gohar's IDs and asked nothing of Ali Gohar's distant brother-in-law, like he didn't even matter to him. Like the immigration officer had already made up his mind.

"You all look like very nice people to me." Then the immigration officer spread open the passport of the distant brother-in-law of Ali Gohar and stamped one of its pages with a bang. And he said to the distant brother-in-law of Ali Gohar, "I'm giving you a month stay; hope you enjoy your trip." That was the fairytale ending of Ali Gohar's distant brother-in-law's ordeal.

The distant brother-in-law then obviously started living with Sufi and Ali Gohar in that cramped East Side apartment. Calling that space an 'apartment' was always a debatable question, because really, how could Sufi call something little wider than a U-Haul truck an apartment? But then again, Sufi rented it from some management company that owned blocks and blocks of those things called apartments, and the zoning laws of the city of New York had approved them.

That apartment was made up of a bedroom which was size of a walk-in closet and a 12-feet-by-10-feet kitchen space, which Sufi referred to as the 'hall', and at the end of the hall there was a toilet. Toilet here means only a loo, a place where you could take a dump. For a shower, Sufi and Ali Gohar used a vintage cast iron clawfoot tub, with biscuit porcelain colour and chipping cracks with rusty streaks. The tub had a telephone faucet, but the lime had calcified all but three or four holes, so they didn't use that. Instead they filled the tub with buckets from kitchen sink and used it as a bath.

At the outset, in this new phase of his life, the distant brother-in-law of Ali Gohar went through the usual homesickness, and he would literally weep, missing Karachi and his mother and younger brother and a host of girls that he had fallen in love with, and become one with them, and he was missing that becoming one, which is the ultimate nirvana of love, where you in seeking your lover yourself become your beloved, and you gladly lose your existence for the sake of achieving that transforming state amidst the violent savagery of love, where your love chops you into pieces and you gladly let him do that to you.

But he was taking his time to reach that transcendent state of chopping and cutting, in which there is neither suffering and desire, nor any existential sense of self and the individual is released from the effects of karma and the cycle of death and rebirth. So his love with those girls was similar to that ultimate nirvana of being one with the one you love.

But he was still in the infantile stage of that process of reaching high spirituality, and he had only reached the physical male-female connection level so far, and he was kind of stalled at that level, and was trying hard and was taking his time to understand that part of love very well before moving to next level of ultimate love. Mostly, the distant brother-in-law of Ali Gohar was missing that male-female connection part for the time being; in other words he was missing getting laid.

They say that generally this feeling of homesickness is like influenza, and is severe for only a few days. But usually those few days are really brutal, during which time the sufferer initially burns with chills amidst a high-grade fever, then eventually overcome that state but stays rolling in bed for another few days before getting back on his feet.

There is an old saying that, "Mount Fuji is Mount Fuji as long as it's in front of your eyes. But once you move away from Mount Fuji, when it disappears from your sight, it will eventually disappear from your mind." And so the Mount Fuji made up of his memories of Karachi started fading from the distant brother-in-law's mind, and thoughts of New York City started to creep in in their place.

The distant brother-in-law of Ali Gohar became close to one of those three boys who showed up when he arrived. The name of that young man was Feroz Khan, and he was the one who thought he looked like Dev Anand. He seemed like a daredevil and an edge walker, but he was one of those who doesn't actually dare go the edge, but only slam doors hard to give the impression that they don't give a shit about anything. That's the impression he gave. He used to work for an airline in Pakistan—in fact his father was still working for that airline, and after Feroz graduated from high school his father had gotten him a job there, too.

But Feroz had other things in mind; he wanted to see the world. So he worked at that airline only for long enough to be eligible for a free ticket to New York. The moment he got his free ticket, he was mentally on his way to the United

States. But in order to get there he needed a visa, for which he applied in Karachi, and got rejected. But he already had a plan B.

He went to Luxembourg and applied for a US visa from there, and again he got rejected. After about a week, he drove to Frankfurt and applied from there, and he got rejected from Frankfurt also. He travelled to England, stayed there for a couple of weeks, and bingo—got his US visa from London. And Feroz came here to New York, the city where he wanted to be.

Feroz use to come to see the distant brother-in-law of Ali Gohar and would end up also chatting with Sufi and Ali Gohar both. Those small talks then grew in length, Feroz started spending more time with Sufi, since Sufi had been laid off from work and had all the time in the world to spend. Ali Gohar used to listen to whatever they were talking about during those small gaps in his tight schedule, working two jobs and running back and forth to his university.

Sufi would tell them—where 'them' meant both Feroz and the distant brother-in-law of Ali Gohar—things that they never believed were true. But they still would listen to him, and Sufi would whisper some of those things that he used to tell them, and ask them not to tell anyone else, because it could put him in serious trouble.

Once Sufi opened a fat book with blood red bindings, and on appearance it seemed that the book was saturated with small words and complex diagrams showing blackberry-like things splitting from one into two and then several, with descriptions like energy release, fission products (radioactive nuclei), and words like 'chain reaction'. And Sufi, still in whispers, said to them. "This is the way to make a reactor, and these are the diagrams for that reactor."

And they both looked at him with a *hello* like look, and Feroz said, "What reactor?" Sufi reacted a bit angrily as if they were both nuclear scientists who somehow didn't even know yet about a nuclear reactor, but he just said, "a reactor to enrich uranium to make atomic bomb."

The distant brother-in-law said, "What is uranium?"

Sufi hit his palm to his forehead which made a clap like sound and said, "It's nothing!"

They both looked at him like he was crazy old man, and they were probably wondering how it could be that simple to see diagrams of an atomic bomb. They used to think that Sufi made things up. Feroz would taunt him about 'This map of *atum-bom*', pronouncing it with his Urdu-inflected accent.

They never knew that Sufi had worked for the Atomic Energy Commission of Pakistan, and that they had sent him to get specialised education in physics of how to expand the mass and volume of energy. They didn't know that because Sufi never told anyone, and only a few people closest to him knew. Plus, neither of those two boys was a science student. In fact, the distant brother-in-law of Ali Gohar was a high school dropout, and Feroz hadn't been able to finish his bachelor's degree in commerce.

Feroz had his own stories to share with them, and his stories were really not his; rather they were mostly from Baray Khan Sahib, his father, whom he himself would actually call Baray Khan Sahib instead of Dad. So that Baray Khan Sahib was a religious man, who probably had looked older than his real age, a bearded guy with dark skin and a very generic face. He had only travelled once in his lifetime, when he migrated from Ajmer in Rajasthan to Karachi in 1937, even though he worked for the national airline for so many years, in the accounting department.

Feroz's stories gave the impression that Baray Khan Sahib was very much proud of his Pashtoon heritage. And Feroz also used to say proudly that he belonged to a group of Persian-speaking Pashtoons of Iranian descent, who had moved to northern India from Afghanistan. And he set himself apart altogether from the regular, dark-skinned north Indian Muslims.

Sufi would tease Feroz, saying, "How come you are an Indian who doesn't like to be called Indian, but instead you're proud to be called a Pashtoon who doesn't know Pashto—and instead you say you're a Persian-speaking Pashtoon of Iranian origin, but ironically you can't speak Persian either, but can only speak the language of those same north Indian Muslims that you don't want to be associated with!" Sufi would thus laugh at both of them and ridicule them with his sharp-tongued wit, just as they would laugh sarcastically at his uranium enriching diagrams.

Ali Gohar would hear the synopses of these discussions and in his own mind try to make sketches of Feroz's father, and ended up with an image of a calm and deep person. Ali Gohar was no philosopher, should if he had been one, he probably have thought of Baray Khan Sahib as one of those gigantic trees who never stop growing and spreading their old thick branches around them and only look up and up into the heavens, one of those trees that become institutions in their own right, who have seen everything, from soaking torrential rains to unheard of droughts, to back-breaking horizontal winds of dust storms, to see their young budding leaves falling in love with short-lived virgin dew drops of serene early morning fogs. Troubled by all that and surviving all that, for uncountable years, those trees in their robust arrogance never realise what's living under them, in their deep cool shadows. And those shadows were no doubt comforting, would never allow any other tree or plant to grow big under them. Ali Gohar wanted to think something like that about Feroz's father, though he was unable.

Baray Khan Sahib was probably one of those people who work at the same desk in the same room in the same office for a lifetime. Who in their modest living do everything possible right, following a procedure that would tell them when to wake up, when to sleep, what simple foods to eat, what simple clothes to wear, and in which government-allocated quarters to live for their entire lives, waiting for that eviction notice after their retirement.

And from Feroz's stores, it seemed that Baray Khan Sahib took his time doing absolutely everything, like one of those people who even makes the simple act of flatulence difficult. And this also because of following their procedural habits, so while sitting, if they have to fart, they first tilt their upper body to one side, then lift one of the hips with their hand, and then almost ask their fart to come out, and finally release their fart with a sound similar to someone failing to control laughter while having a mouth full of water. But those were all different ways of saying 'in love with the past'. And in Feroz's case it was not even his own love of the past, but instead his vicarious entertainment of his father's nostalgia.

One late night, in fact it was in the early morning hours, the entrance buzzer rang. Ali Gohar asked, "who is it?" Via that intercom, which was several times painted over and over and had become a part of wall itself, and which gave the impression that Graham Bell had made it himself in this very same city.

Feroz replied, "It's me—could you please open the door?" In a few minutes, Feroz and the four others were all sitting in that shoebox-sized living room of their small apartment, with their duffle bags and carry-ons. They were all here because of fear of being raided by immigration agents at their apartment, as one of their fellow roommates had been caught a day before, just by sheer bad luck. He had been standing alongside some day labourers at a bus stop, but somehow he had managed to call home and alert them to leave the place at once and go somewhere else.

It was late, so everyone cuddled on the floor and slept. Sleep can be miraculous; they say, it could drag you into her domain, and you could drift into her, even hours before your own lynching.

But those guys were only displaced and had not even a remote chance of getting lynched, so they all dropped dead asleep, like fallen tree logs in deep and untapped forests. The next morning Ali Gohar woke-up early. Everyone else was still asleep, and the air in that small apartment was filled with smell of sour stinky feet. He changed and got out of there quickly.

Katie told Ali Gohar that she had bought a grand piano, and that how difficult it was to get that in her apartment and that she had to hire a special crew who first took a big side glass window of her apartment out and then hoisted the grand piano on ropes from the roof of the 33 story building to her 12 floor apartment from the street.

That piano looked so beautiful in her small apartment, and that it occupied almost a third of her living room space. And she said that she and her husband Arthur had split, and that she was now living on her own at her new place. Ali Gohar never asked and she never said but he had a bit of an idea that what had probably had happened.

Katie was posing for John Kacere's painting, in her beautiful lingerie with black and red ribbon suspenders, stretching from her waste to her thighs, like saloon girls and prostitutes used to wear in the old west. That was not the problem; she had been posing for John Kacere's new painting for quite some time.

The two of them had been working on this project mostly at John Kacere's studio, which was his loft apartment, too. In that process, they drifted and got entangled in that funny pleasurable feeling, which always comes with strong emotional attraction, accompanied with physically touching and caressing each other's genitals, and usually that feeling is called as romance. The problem with romance is that it is innocent, and dumbfounds people to level of retardation. And because of the clumsiness of its nature, romance can't hide itself from others, and always gets caught in open. So that's what had happened to Katie in that wild, abstract state of mind, which could only be felt and has no real description at all.

On a fine sunny midday, Katie and John Kacere were making out in Katie's apartment when the clumsiness of romance joined hands with Murphy's Law, like the plot of a below-average Hindi movie. Coincidentally Arthur, Katie's husband, came back to pick up something of no value, like a damn handkerchief or sunglasses, and instead found that clumsiness of romance. That was the end of Katie's marriage.

Ali Gohar was waiting for convocation, and was killing time before heading back. In those last three and half years, Katie had come all the way from a naïve artist who used solid white and jet black in her paintings to a recognised name in the field of hyperrealism. She chose to paint the glittering chrome of head light trims and stainless steel fenders of old model cars, and somehow she hit the nail on head with full force, capturing the all the luminosity and charisma of those automobiles in her paintings. Her work was already in demand, and collectors were paying her in advance for whatever she was going to paint five years down the road.

It was June, and the convocation was in July, so he and Katie were spending a whole lot of time together. Ali Gohar quit both of his jobs and was mainly just hanging out, doing last minute shopping, buying things like a Philco two door refrigerator (where two doors means a small top door freezer and a bottom door refrigerator) and a Phillips 26 inch colour television.

Which Ali Gohar paid in full and booked from Chaudhry and Sons of Canal Street in downtown New York, but those items were going to be shipped directly from somewhere in Japan to Karachi, Pakistan. And Katie gave most of her time to him in these last few weeks. One day, while in her apartment, Ali Gohar walked towards that grand piano and sat on that black un-cushioned stool and tried to press a key.

It made a raw noise, and he was about to back off when Katie came right behind him and placed her chin on his shoulder and extended both of her arms around his, and put her petite hands on his and her delicate fingers on his fingers, and she pressed his fingers with hers to make the ivory keys of the piano sink down and create a different, pleasant sound. She kept pushing them in and out, in and out, very softly, and the piano kept sounding more and more beautiful.

A few days after that, the convocation happened, at Washington Square, and after a couple more weeks, Ali Gohar left. His distant brother-in-law and Feroz moved in with Sufi. The whole contingent came to see off him at the airport: his distant brother-in-law, Feroz, and the four other boys, all of whom were wearing tight bell-bottom pants and polyester shirts with dog-ear disco collars, and a few of them had sideburns almost to their lower-jaw line. Katie had said that she was going to come, but somehow she didn't make it.

He came back to a changed country, and he himself was a changed man. Now he had a Master's from NYU, now he had some more grey hairs and need glasses to read, now he had enough money that he had earned in the US working like a dog to buy a house in a relatively upscale suburb of Hyderabad. Now his children had since become teenagers and were ready to step into their own wildness.

The house that he bought was in the same locality where Sufi's wife and children lived, which was across the street from the Kala Board Mustafa Masjid, one of those streets that usually take a lifetime and half to cross.

It was an old unfinished damned and cursed house of a retired university professor who died of madness, and whose daughter had committed suicide in that very same house. But he bought that property in a half of a breath with all those damnations. He was an ambitious person and didn't care about superstition. He just wanted a piece of property in a white-collar relatively upscale neighbourhood.

Once, not long after he came back, Master Mohammad Alam visited him in his office. Alam was in the midst of making one of those hazy daisy crazy summer trips to Hyderabad, which he always made just to pick up his photography supplies. And he thought it would be good to stop in and see Ali Gohar. So they had a formal, father-and-son-are-both-grownups kind of chat over a cup of tea.

And Alam said out of blue, "I was looking at your *hisab*"—by that Alam meant his astrological chart. "You have got what you had to! Now it's going to be—" And he hesitated a little here, even though he normally said whatever he found in other people's charts with ruthless abandon. But he even considered saying something else before going ahead with the original thought: "You are going to be idle."

Ali Gohar replied in a tone that respected traditional values, but he was firm. "Baba, I don't believe in that. If there is any way for me, I could have reined your stars and could have ridden them, I would have!"

Alam heard Ali Gohar's doggedness, and said, "You'll be fine."

They talked a little more, but they were getting tired of each other. So Alam said, "I have to get evening train back," and before Alam could finish his sentence, Ali Gohar's chair was making noise as he stood up to say goodbye to his father.

They came out of Ali Gohar's office and slowly walked through the long corridor, which was all empty but filled with the earthy smell of dirt. Echoes of their voices and footsteps mixed in the air with the clamour of sparrows chirping were amplified in there and was bouncing back and forth.

Chapter 9
Idling for Thirty-Five Years and Counting

"That was my first snow experience," he was telling his grandson, while walking fast because his grandson was almost running on the sidewalk of Fifth Avenue, holding his hand. Kabeer was pretending that he wasn't listening to him at all, though actually he was hearing every single one of Ali Gohar's words, and dumping them somewhere in his memory, juggling them with his eager desire to see the Siberian Husky sled dog who led his team on the final leg of the 1925 serum run. They were both heading to Central Park to see the statue of Balto. This was one of Kabeer's newly found devotions, which is a small portion of that long self-explanatory instruction guide of how to fall in love.

Kabeer was checking out Balto on his perch up on a rock somewhere in Central Park. Ali Gohar sat on the grass behind the statue to rest, keeping an eye on Kabeer and also digging into his coat pockets for God knows what. Probably, it was an excuse to find that letter again. And he did find an old aerogram, which he recognised right away, because it gave him that heart-sinking feeling that people experience when a crystal glass slips from their hands, and their heart takes a plunge just before it smashes to the ground.

And there was that familiar feeling as he touched the letter. Instead of glue, Maasurar Kando's sons had used that red sticky rubbery adhesive that is used to fix punctures on bicycle tubes back home. And it was the only letter Maasurar Kando's sons ever wrote to him. And it contained very few words, all decorously formal, something like this:

"*Assalamualaikum. We are well here and your well-being is desired.*
I want to let you know that our father passed away last Friday. We kept him in the same graveyard where your grandfather, Fakeer Sher Mohammad is kept. There was a big hole at the foot of Fakeer's grave. So while there, I arranged

for two bull-cart loads of earth soil to be put on your grand father's grave too. It looks good now.

Remember us in your prayers. Mashallah.[121]"

"What are you doing grandpa?"

Hearing Kabeer's voice, Ali Gohar carefully folded that aerogram letter back up and tucked it away. "It was an old letter."

"Old letter about what?"

For a second, Ali Gohar thought about telling his grandson all about Maasurar Kando. But then he just said, "Nothing that you need to worry about."

"You should make an email account, grandpa," chattered Kabeer.

"I don't need one."

"I love you grandpa—you brought me to my Balto." Ali Gohar saw a naughty happiness glittering in Kabeer's eyes.

"Don't—" and here Kabeer hesitated, as he didn't wanted to use the word *die*, "don't leave me until I grow old, grandpa."

"No, I will not, I'll live as long as you want me to."

---

[121] *Mashallah*: 'Praise be to God'.

Story IV: Jani

Chapter 1
Pineapple of White Marble

He was born a shadow length away from Hyderabad fort, in an old and elegant mansion from a lost era, from that epoch which will never return, consigned to the dump of memory. When recalled from that memory, the mansion appeared majestic, distinct, masterfully crafted.

But was it really? He thought about it. Maybe it was an average-looking old building and his screwed up aesthetics were exaggerating its absent glory. The thing that stayed with him was a broken three-tier white marble fountain, which had a small chipped pineapple at the top, a stone pineapple, that is. The fountain was in the middle of a huge courtyard, with black and white square paved tiles, like a chessboard.

The courtyard had many well-trimmed shrubs of night blooming jasmine at each of its four corners. A long series of arches made of red brick encircled the courtyard; for some reason, long red bricks were always considered graceful. Those brick arch entrances were curtained with heavy chicka blinds made from thick dry straw, some of which were unevenly rolled up or leaning to one side or the other.

Through the archways on all four sides of that courtyard you could step onto the veranda, which had wide and square pillars between each arch, and its floor was patterned like vibrant quilts, with octagonal stars that imitated marble and parquet, one in grey, one in cream, and those eye-shaped leaves outlined in burgundy. The hallway floor was also bordered by ornate geometric tiles in royal blue with white labyrinth-like piping, like a design by Escher.

And he would follow those labyrinth lines as if they were a real labyrinth. Right after that veranda there were rooms, big rooms in a line, each with a high ceiling having two or three iron beams in the middle and floral carvings on baked clay bricks in between those iron beams. Those rooms also had colourful floors too, of their own, made up of encaustic tiles of vibrant Indian red and dull chocolate buff hues, arranged in a pattern that you could fall into and become lost, a geometric diamond pattern in several shades. This huge mansion had been converted into a private maternity home somewhere along the course of time.

He came to see his birthplace when his mother was having her third child there, and he had to stay there with her. He used to go into that huge courtyard again and again, just to see that chipped pineapple made up of white marble on the top tier of that broken fountain. He was only seven then, and only stayed with his mother in that maternity home for a few days, but he still could remember the people he met there. Maasi[122] in particular stayed in his thoughts and kept walking there in his memories, like a partially blind person who steadies himself by grasping onto the walls.

Maasi was a matron, but then she was not a matron at all, because matron is Latin for 'mother', and once was used for the most senior nurses in English hospitals, whereas this Maasi was a cleaning lady, and an old one. Her duties were changing the infants' soiled clothes, wiping the patients' bedpans, changing sheets, and getting yelled at all daylong like a peasant.

But in evening she used to put her takht-e-tavus,[123] a small wooden batten, in a corner of that courtyard, next to the night-blooming jasmines, and like a monarch she would open the treasure chests of her mind to distribute the riches of her thoughts. She would tell mesmerising stories of a brave young prince who went to great lengths to fetch the only black rose of Koh-Kaf, with the help of a Darvaish, who guided the young prince on the path towards Koh-Kaf, but warned him not to look back!—because if he did, he would turn into stone. And those never-ending stories became more intoxicating when her words were wrapped in the fragrance of the night-blooming jasmines.

He was admitted into a kindergarten, but in those days kindergartens were called nurseries. That was his second school in a short time, because he was initially admitted at the Model School's nursery, which was connected to the Institute of Education and Research, where his father was a junior faculty member. But the Model School nursery was a place of trauma for him. He could remember his father walking him into that school's corridor, which had a

---

[122] *Maasi*: this word, which literally translates as 'aunt', is often used for any female servant in a Sindhi home.

[123] *Takht-e-tavus*: 'Peacock Throne', the name of the opulent throne commissioned by the Mughal emperor Shah Jahan in the 17th century.

classroom on its one side, and on the other side there were arch openings holding a lawn with huge Java plum trees behind them. The branches of those Java trees were making a soft crackling sound from their own heaping weight. It was the early part of the day, and school was already in session, so there was a humming noise of chatter like a slow boiling.

His father was telling him that there would be colourful chairs and desks, and other kids of his age, and that he was going to hear stories of rabbits and turtles and a boy of thumb size and seed kernel which in a single night grew so tall that it could touch the heavens. They reached the nursery, which was a big room in a half-octagonal shape.

Jani looked up to his father's face with an affirmative smile, because, sure enough, there were the small coloured chairs and tables. And there was a polite old nanny, who resembled a Russian Matryoshka doll, who had a face sweet like honeydew, smiling at him. He kept a firm grip on his father's hand as they both sat down on chairs. The nanny set a few toys in front of him, and he was drawn to the abacus. He started moving those beads aimlessly, and for a fraction of a second he let his father's hand loose. When he then turned his head to look at his father, he saw that he was exiting through the door. He dropped the abacus and ran towards the door, but it was too late—his father had already left.

The nanny shut both parts of that light green door and bolted it. Jani was crying and asking her to let him go. She crouched down and simply said, "*chup*"—*be quiet*. Her face looked different now, not like the one he had seen a little while back with his father. Her pupils were protruding from beneath her stone-firm eyebrows. She grabbed one of his ear lobes and started twisting it. First it felt hot, and then a lacerating pain crawled around his ear. That was the first time he experienced betrayal, pain, insecurity, dishonesty, and all those miseries combined together which usually break peoples' hearts; he endured the full shebang all at once.

He never went back to that school. After a week, he was admitted to another school, where his mother used to teach. And that transition went off smooth as a whistle; he acclimatised. This new school had the same colourful furniture, toys, and all those Jack-and-the-beanstalk stories. But his teacher here was a very serious, quiet woman, who seemed nothing like a typical kindergarten teacher. But in those days people running schools probably didn't worry about what was typical.

One evening, after he had been in this new school for a few days, his mother told him that the next day the daughter of one of his father's long time friends would be coming with him. And his mother told him that this daughter was a tiny little doll. As he fell asleep, he forgot everything that his mother had just said, except that phrase, *tiny little doll*. And he imagined a live girl who looked like a doll, the plastic kind. he knew about cloth dolls as well, but his mother always used the Sindhi word '*guddee*' for those, and in this case she had used the English word *doll*, which meant the plastic kind. And in those days, all dolls were Caucasian with blonde curly hair. Even in that remote South Asian corner of world, all dolls used to be blondes.

The next day he was excited to meet a fair blonde doll, a fairy tale princess. The day started, and he did all the usual things with the other kids. He played with toys, sang rhymes, made drawings, but all the while he was waiting for that doll-like little girl, but no such girl arrived.

In recess break, like every other day, his mother came to buy him a treat, and she introduced him to a worried and scared, tiny dark lean and rather bony little girl, whose oil-dipped short hair adhered to her scalp like a scarf. So that was his first experience of imagining someone completely wrong. She had been sitting right in front of him all day, but he had not even noticed her.

Later, because there were so few choices until grade fifth, he maintained a crush on her, too.

His parents moved to the city of Hyderabad from Jamshoro, a university town some ten miles away. That move was devastating for him for one sole reason, which was his attachment with his *Aai*, his grandmother. In Jamshoro they had all been living together, all of his father's siblings and his grandmother.

Apparently, most kids manage to detach from their grandparents and move on with their lives. But he was a crooked one, so he got stuck, and would never be able to fill that vacuum, and a part of him stayed empty forever. The reason for his parents' move was that the school was in Hyderabad, and he and his sister would have to rise too early to travel that distance every day, because ten miles must have been an immense distance to cover in those days. So they rented a two-room portion of a house, a mile and a half away from the school. At least, that was the reason he could understand for making the move. His parents must have had some other reasons, too.

In that time, there were communal clashes between two ethnic groups in Hyderabad. Those didn't bother him; he didn't care about the communal riots, but he did miss *Aai*. Right before his parents made their move to the city, there had been some arguments between his father and one of his aunts, who was living at the time in one of the small rooms of their 'C' type quarters of Sindh University at Jamshoro. Technically that small room was just a pantry next to kitchen.

The C-quarters were cookie cutter dwellings, eight units in a row. Each unit had two rooms next to an open hall, and on the other side of that hall there was a pantry and kitchen, and in front of the kitchen there was a smaller open courtyard. At the end of that courtyard, there was a bathroom and a separate toilet room. Back on the other side, right outside of the two rooms, there was a veranda with a tiny storeroom in the end, and outside that veranda there was another open courtyard, a bit bigger than the other courtyard.

In that entire apartment, there was only one ceiling fan, in just one of those rooms. Everybody in that home, all of his uncles and aunts, were concerned about this aunt. His young uncles were proud of her, but his father and elder aunt were trying to convince her not to do something. And he was confused about why she was not eating food or drinking water, of her own choice. Then after a day or so one of his uncles, his father's younger brother, came home holding a local newspaper, which stated his aunt's name and said that she was the first Sindhi woman to go on hunger strike against 'One-unit'.

That same evening, news of her hunger strike against that One-unit was also broadcast from All India Radio's Sindhi services during the evening news, in Hiro Thakur's iconic voice. Thakur was a Sindhi newscaster with a distinct squarish diction, which made his words appear to have geometrical angles. The tone of his voice was the same colour as the pale amber light of the setting sun. He always started his news by saying, *"Hee Akashvani aa; Haunn aawahn Hiray Thakur khaun khaburoon budhahan da"*—This is Akashvani (All India Radio); you are listening to the news bulletin from Hiro Thakur. And on day he said that she was on hunger strike, protesting to dissolve One-unit.[124] Hiro Thakur said that in his Russian goose-stepping march-like voice.

---

[124] One Unit: the One Unit program, introduced in the 1950s by Prime Minister Chaudhri Muhammad Ali, consolidated the four provinces of West Pakistan into a single province. This was an effort on the part of the federal government to maintain majority, because the Bengali people of East Pakistan, whose territory was all a single province, were becoming dominant. Many West Pakistanis, however, strongly opposed the program because it meant sacrificing their own individual national and ethnic identities. Sindhi

And for a long time he tried to figure out meaning of all that commotion and that phrase 'One-unit', and wondering who was checking on her in that storeroom. Was she eating and drinking or not? Why would anyone listen to her and do whatever she was asking for? And was she trying to move this 'One-unit' from one place to another, or to get rid of it altogether?

But he was too young to understand all those complicated words, like *provincial autonomy, confederation, ethnicity, language riots*, and too young to grasp that his aunt's hunger strike was an individual's outcry trying to pierce the darkness on her own. If more people like her could unleash their hope, they could rip apart the heart of evil and shred it to pieces by the mere power of their thoughts.

That very same aunt of his taught him a small lesson of selflessness, which is that simply saying someone's name could make your heart humble. And she used to do this by adding the word *Dada* or *Dadi* in front of people's names, even people she didn't know. He would say to her, "We don't know that famous singer personally, so why are you calling him Dada?"

And she would reply, "If you stand in front of a mountain, you don't have to call it a mountain, but still it's a mountain." And she said, "hann" conclusively after that very generic example, before continuing: "That singer has accomplished so much and had given so much to culture that he doesn't need me to call him *Dada*. It's I who feel honoured to call him Dada."

At that time, he thought her to be a crazy person, but later he himself started calling people *Saeen, Dada* or *Qibla*, words which all share the same meaning.

---

people especially fought vociferously against the program, and faced dire consequences. President Yahya Khan introduced legislation that ended One Unit in 1970, and East Pakistan gained its independence the following year, becoming Bangladesh.

Chapter 2
Medium Rare, Almost Bleeding

Every summer, when schools were closed for vacation, his mother used to take him and his elder sister to Karachi to visit her family. That trip was a pleasant one, but still a cultural shock, because in a journey of merely three and a half hours, everything would change, from food and its taste, to people and their body odours, to the landscape and the smell of the air, to a language in which words would switch their genders. Karachi was a different world from Jamshoro. But he was used to acclimatise very quickly, in fact in those three and a half hours of travel time.

They would stay at his maternal aunt's grandmother's place. From that description, it would seem like she must be a really, really old person, but she was only a decade older to his mother. She worked for government, had divorced twice, and lived with her three children. She was an upstanding lady, and even in that conservative society of the late 60s and early 70s, she had not allowed the stigma of divorce to put a dent in her chromium-finish reputation. She kept everyone together, her sisters and a nutcase younger brother. Her first husband was a *Maratha*, a *Bombaiya-Babu* and a *Shobdebaz*.[125] They would say, "He could look into your eyes, and say that you were not you, and you would believe him."

Jani literally believed that Bombaiya-Babu could do that. He was a conjurer who used tricks to survive. He came to Karachi from Bombay in 1947 as an eighteen-year-old young man. He was a homeless orphan like million others, but he had been a homeless orphan even in Bombay, and had no formal education. He had worked in a roadside teashop outside the Bombay stock exchange, selling tea with his hands and listening to the conversations of stock brokers with his

---

[125] *Shobdebaz.* Illusionist.

ears.

Within a short time, he promoted himself from tea boy to *Sattaybaz*.[126] He had a bumpy start after moving to Karachi, where he was sleeping on sidewalks. But somehow he became friends with a drycleaner's employee, who would give him other people's expensive suits to wear for a day. Using those dashing borrowed outfits and his deceiving charm, he paved his way right to the floors of the Karachi stock exchange.

He started his career as a broker there, even though he had no formal education, carrying out trades on the open floors of the exchange, calling bids out loud like an auctioneer. And he made a mint of money. But successful option trading is not about being correct all the time; it's about how to salvage a falling trade. When things go wrong, which they usually do, a trader has to control the damage and rescue his trade, but the Bombaiya-Babu had not learned those tricks by then. He was an abusive drunk and bought a wrong long-call option on his own marriage and lost it all.

Her second husband was equally bad, but completely different from the first. He was a Punjabi *Jatt,* a landlord by origin, and a communication engineer by profession. He looked almost like the Soviet leader Brezhnev, with one variation, which was his misaligned left eye, whose pupil deviated to its side, giving everyone who sat in front of him the false impression that he was looking directly at them.

But he was a very sophisticated man. He was already married and had grown up children of his own, but he wanted someone to talk to, and to have a drink with, and to tell her his side of the story while rolling an ice cube with his index finger in his lowball whisky glass.

But after few years of her marriage with him, and going through several bottles 80-proof Scotch, and crying and moaning and having sex—well, at least once, because they had a boy—he came to her one day and said, "My daughter's marriage is about to be called off." This was his daughter from his first marriage. "My daughter's in-laws are from my first wife's family, and they are saying that if I don't leave you they will back out and their son will marry someone else."

Or so he said, and god knows the truth, but as a wise lady she agreed, and said, "If that's what it takes, then so be it." Probably, she figured that, if what he was saying was true, then his daughter was like her own, and if he is making all

---

[126] *Sattaybaz*. A speculator who gambles on stock forecasts.

that up, then what's the point of dragging on a soulless relationship, and they split.

So that was Jani's aunt's grandmother, who lived along with her three kids lives in a government-owned apartment in what they called the Federal B area, a communist-looking housing project. It had rows and rows of identical-looking blocks of apartments, which they called 'flats', each one standing next to its mirror reverse and then stacked on top of one another in sets of three. They were very small flats, made up of two rooms; one of those rooms had a balcony with a faulty and weak cement guardrail, which you couldn't lean on.

And for that reason no kids were allowed on the balcony. Apart from the two rooms and balcony, there was a small hallway that connected everything, the two rooms, a kitchen, and a bathroom. And in that same hallway there used to be a takht, with a slight variation. The Urdu word 'takht' could hold meanings that were poles apart, from a king's throne, to a gallows, to a simple four-legged hardwood top bench, on which you could sit or even lie down. And that third type was the kind of takht that used to be in that small hallway, on which Nana Aba would sleep every night.

Nana Aba was his mother's maternal grandfather, and father to that aunt-grandmother of his. He was a dear and loving old man, with a wrinkled face and a black lambskin cap on his head, and he had those snow-white facial hairs protruding out of his curled and wrinkled dark brown cheeks, like the tiny soft white thorns that come out of certain cactuses.

Nana Aba had been a day labourer and used to grind the inscriptions in black cement that had been filled into carved space of white marble headstones of dead people. Every day *Nana Aba* use to do that manual grinding job, of slowly rubbing of a palm-sized coarse grey water-stone onto the marble, to bring to life the gracefully carved names of otherwise dead people, sandwiched between Quranic verses in Arabic and covered with delicate trims of floral designs.

And every evening he would come back rag tired to that flat and lie down on the small hardwood-top dwarf four-legged bench that was situated in that small hall space, where everything else opened. Lying there, Nana used to tell stories, but not of fairies or brave princes. They were stories of his youth, and old Delhi, and of his paranormal experiences, and above all his romance with his own wife, whom he had been forbidden to see, because she was the only daughter of his rich and grim employer, who owned several *katras*,[127] which were prime real estate in heart of old Delhi. Those katras were three-story buildings of solid lumber, with single rental rooms lined together on each floor along a long hallway, which had a common toilet and bathroom at one end.

Nana had been the rent collector for those. And of all things that could have happened, that sixteen-year-old only daughter of Nana Aba's wealthy employer became a widow after just seven months of marriage. And Nana Aba's austere employer got his daughter remarried to Nana, on the conditions that he would become a live-in son-in-law, and none of Nana Aba's other family members were allowed to come to see him, and that he was only allowed to go see his parents and siblings twice a year.

He agreed to all of his employer's above stated conditions in half a heartbeat. And with that agreement, his employer had purchased Nana Aba, from Nana Aba himself, for his sixteen-year-old widowed daughter. But long before all those buying and selling terms, Nana Aba, as a servant, had fallen in love with his master's daughter, without her even knowing. So that Nana Aba's love story, was generic like anybody else's.

But to him it was something which kept playing, like Chopin's 'raindrop' Prelude in D-flat major, somewhere in Nana Aba's old clogged-up heart. His love story was as common as fingerprints, but then again it was distinct, too, because no two prints are alike.

Nana Aba would tell about so many other things, like how he managed to save six pennies, which he could have spent on his bus fare, to buy soft gulab jamuns, still floating in hot sugary confectioner's syrup, for his beloved wife. To save those six pennies, he had to walk miles from the factory of his grim old employer. That factory was for dyeing pure silk in different colours, and it was an additional charge that Nana Aba had to oversee.

And to save six pennies to buy gulab jamuns, he had to walk, and many times he head to bear the insults of his employer, who called him lazy. But then Nana Aba would simply laugh and say that his wife didn't appreciate his efforts to get the gulab jamuns either. She always asked him to buy her *jhumkay*, fabulous beaded dome-shaped earrings with twisted gold wires forming a filigree mesh like a hanging lampshade. But Nana Aba couldn't afford jhumkay no matter how far he walked.

---

[127] *Katra*: a separate wing of a larger complex, which is specified as rental apartments for tradesmen and their families.

Chapter 3
Agrasen Ki Baoli

Nana Aba's love stories were not the ones that fascinated Jani's young mind. The otherworldly stories were the ones that came as a stunning revelation to him, especially because his family back in Jamshoro, his grandmother and his father's siblings, never told such stories. It seemed to Jani that people in Jamshoro lived in a physical world, that is, a practical world that had to obey the laws of physics, where if you dropped a rock it would go straight towards the ground, period. But in Nana Aba's story, a gold coin could float in a pool filled with water, a pool made up of a stairwell.

Nana Aba said, "And then you know what happened? One afternoon, I was coming back from factory—walking back, trying to save six pennies. It was a steamy day; Delhi could be brutal in the middle of a summer day. On my way there was a baoli, and it was called *Agrasen ki Baoli*."

Jani interrupted, "What is a baoli?"

Nana Aba at first just repeated, "Yes, baoli!" Then he took a pause before continuing, "They are huge stairwells going into the ground. They are dug in ledges, series of steps sinking in from all four walls, like a pool with stairs going in from all sides, until they hit the aquifer." But then he summarised by saying, "Imagine a pond of water with sinking steps."

Then Nana went on. "I was tired. It was noontime, and the sun was beating my head, and then I reached Agrasen ki Baoli, the best place to rest on a hot day. This baoli was a straight flight of steps in with three side walls of red sandstone. The steps had become shabby and worn out, and tilted downwards, which made them dangerous. But people still used them with extra care. I was sitting at the top. It was much cooler there. The water level starts from ten or twelve steps down. There were very few people there because it was getting close to 1pm."

Nana then sat up on his hardwood bed, and a sparking glare blazed through his otherwise extinguishing eyes, and then he continued. "I don't know why, but even though I knew that it was time to leave and getting close to 1 pm, somehow I thought, *why don't I wet my face and run some cool well water through my hair*. I stepped down ten or so flights towards water level. I took off my goatskin cap and put it aside, and rinsed my face with cupped palms filled with cool water, which was hitting my face with splashing comfort. But then I heard the cannon shot and thought, I have to leave right now."

"The moment I grabbed my cap I saw a shining object floating towards me from left." Said Nana, "It was gold coin. I leaned forward to grab it, but it submerged and rested at just one step beneath the water level. And I thought, *it's right there, I just have to pick it up, and I know I can get her those dome earrings if I give this fat gold coin to the jeweller*. I leaned over and dipped one of my hands in to get hold of the coin.

"I touched it but then somehow because of slippery scum it slid from my grasp and fell a couple steps further down in the water. I could still see it, it was right there. But I had to submerge myself completely into the water to get to that gold coin. And I did it. The water was murky—I could barely see a yellowish gold nugget resting on some green algae on one of the steps. A frigid breath filled my lungs and a beautiful young female hand was about to clench my hand. And I remembered the 1pm cannon shot, which indicated that ominous part of day when two times meet, when the apparition beneath water comes out."

Nana Aba took a break. There was a ghostly lull in that small hallway of the federal B-area flat, until Nana went on. "I stood up and it seemed like those huge red sandstone walls were collapsing on me. That apparition was breathing in my ears, and the air was flooded with jasmine perfume. I ran towards the top, while a sarcastic high-pitched laughter kept ringing in my ears."

Sometimes, Nana Aba wanted to be left alone, maybe to make his long *dua*,[128] full of humble entreaties and supplications, or maybe to meditate on those nights in his beloved's thoughts. Lying down on that *takht*, he would remember how he used to buy gulab jamuns and never be able to buy gold jumkays for his wife whom he loved so much. And on those evenings when he felt dead tired, or so he said, and couldn't find enough energy to tell a story, Nana would give *do-anna*[129] to the children and send them out to buy candy. But usually he would

---

[128] *Dua*: prayer.

[129] *Do-anna*: twelve pennies.

summon the energy for storytelling. Nana Aba was a true confessionalist, wanting to tell his whole story to his grandchildren, in the hope that they could carry it a little farther.

Once Jani asked him, "Do you have any brothers or sisters?"

Nana replied gleefully, "No, I don't have any brothers, but I did have a younger sister. My mother died when I was two or three years old. My sister was younger than me, and she was blind."

Then Nana wanted to say the rest of it in a hurry, the way one wants to walk quickly out of a rough neighbourhood. "Our father got remarried, and had seven more kids from his second marriage. We had a mean stepmother. When I turned sixteen, I started working as assistant to a person who later made me his live-in son-in-law, so I got out of there."

Then like Nana crushed his own heart, placing it under his foot and smashing it like a cigarette butt, as he continued. "I was like a pest on someone else's doorstep. My father-in-law had made me agree that I would leave my family, and my real family was only that sister. And I agreed willingly that I wouldn't bring her with me. So I left my blind sister behind. I could only pray for her to die, because—!"

But Nana Aba couldn't offer any explanation for that, so he coughed a few times and laughed sarcastically.

Jani's mother quickly came out from one of those small rooms and grabbed Jani by the shoulder and pushed him to the side and gave him a thorny look. And then she started comforting Nana Aba, because although it looked like he was coughing and laughing, he was actually crying. Jani's mother said, "Why do you have to remember all those old things and trouble yourself. It's a big thing that you did whatever you could. At least, you prayed for her."

And Jani, standing in one corner of that hall, kept thinking that he must have done something seriously wrong to upset Nana Aba, something he was too young to understand. But whatever he had done had caused Nana Aba to cry and his mother to be mad at him. Probably, would understand it when he got older, but all he had been aware of doing was asking Nana Aba about his siblings.

Chapter 4
Kali Masjid

But then on certain evenings, Nana Aba would tell stories that were truly beyond belief, so much so that even young Jani thought that they were good for listening, but that they had nothing to do with real life. Nana Aba was kind of like Indiana Jones, but with a spiritual tweak. He was the kind of person who explored ruins and found unusual things, but for him they had nothing to do with archaeological science. Rather, they always pointed toward the divine—rewards of blessing for selfless acts and forgiveness after doing good deeds.

So one evening Nana began, "there was an abandoned mosque some distance outside Delhi that was known as *Kali Masjid*,[130] about half a day's walk away." Nana Aba always measured distance that way, in units of time. "So a friend of mine and I had the idea to go there and restore that abandoned mosque, and pray there five times a day for forty days, and clean that forgotten house of God. So Mombabu and I—" and then Nana paused a little, like he didn't want to go into any detail about Mombabu.

But he still went on and said, "Mombabu was my friend, whose real name was Syed Mannan Ali, a short-tempered man. He used to be a sub-inspector in the police, but because of his anger he had beaten one of his superiors and was reprimanded and later dishonourably discharged. Everybody called him Mombabu."

"So we reached Kali Masjid. It was not black, actually. It was just that it had a coating of dead algae that had amassed over the years on its exterior wall, which gave an impression of blackness."

Nana was saying all this like it had happened yesterday. "We stepped in. There was a triangular courtyard, of good size, with a peepal tree in it. You know

---

[130] *Kali Masjid.* 'Black Mosque'.

the peepal can get so old; they can live for hundreds and hundreds of years. Just their age alone makes them mysterious. And it was a common belief that peepal trees are possessed, also."

He collected himself and started again. "Anyway, we were there, and both of us started cleaning up the dead leaves, spider webs, bats' nests, and so much dirt. There was a small well in the courtyard, which hadn't been used for god knows how long, so it had to be emptied first, and then it needed soil and sediment erosion to open the aquifer. It took us several days to make that well viable. We were cleaning and praying and Mombabu would recite Quranic verses, and it felt to me like the archangel himself was crying out loud, speaking the verses of the Qur'an through Mombabu's throat."

"And we kept doing our deed, and we restored the sanctity of that mosque. When four or five days were left and we had nothing else to do apart from praying, we decided to plant flowering shrubs around the mosque. We dug a shallow trench to plant them in. There was village half an hour's walk away, so we used to go there every few days to get things to eat, and we also got a pickaxe and a grab hoe from a farmer."

"When we were picking up those tools, there was an old man in the front yard of that farmer's mud hut, probably the farmer's father or grandfather. He was lying on a cot and looking at us and shaking his head, saying no for some reason. But we took the tools and left on the 39th day of our 40-day commitment. I was digging a spot that I wanted to be at least knee-deep, but I was hitting some hard rock. But then when I made another stroke, the pointed tip of the pickaxe went inside a hollow part of the rock, as if it were hitting a wooden box instead of a rock. I pulled the pickaxe out and gently tapped the rock with pickaxe's pointed tip again, and again it felt weird."

"I set the pickaxe aside and tried to feel it with my hands. After scraping away the dirt and earth for some time, I found the surface of something. I yelled, *Mombabu, arrey O Mombabu!* And he came, and I told him there was something there. He jumped in and sat in front of me and we both started clearing dirt from this wooden chest with rusted iron hinges and stripes. Mombabu loosened it and we both pulled it out of its place and put it on the ground, still inside the trench. There was no lock on it, just a latch. Mombabu opened it, and it opened very easily. And it was filled with gold coins. Mombabu grabbed few. Stamped on those coins there were two idol figures."

And there was admiration in Nana's tone when he said, "probably they were Shivajee and Parvati!"

"One of them held a trishula[131] and had a crescent moon above his head. On the reverse side of those coins there was something written in Devanagari,[132] which I can't read, so I looked at Mombabu, who had passed ten classes of school. Mombabu looked at reverse side of one of those coins and murmured out in disbelief, '*Sri-Krishnaraja*'." [133]

Nana said, "Mombabu went on and said, probably name of some old king, or god knows who! Hells with what's written on coins; just think its gold "We shut the chest and brought it up into the mosque's courtyard. It was already evening, so we both decided to stay that night in the mosque. Night fell. We chose to lie in one corner of the courtyard, away from the peepal tree. Neither of us could sleep for even a moment, and it seemed like that night had decided to last forever."

"Anytime there was a slight breeze, a dead leaf would move and make noise. It felt like something was about to happen. Finally, it was daybreak. First there was only an illusion of light in the skies, but then the light kept increasing. A few stars stubbornly clung to sky, but then they disappeared too. We unloaded the gold coins into one of our checker scarves and knotted together its four ends to make a small bundle, and we buried that empty wooden chest back."

Monkey Ears asked in shock, "Nana, what happened then?"

Nana Aba replied, "We both had a whole lot of money, which lasted for quite some time."

---

[131] *Trishula*: a South Asian trident, which is a symbol of Shiva. The word means '*three spears*' in Sanskrit.
[132] *Devanagari*: the Sanskrit alphabet, which is also used for Hindi and certain other modern languages of South Asia.
[133] *Sri Krishnaraja:* Here Mombabu would have been referring not to the god Krishna but to the emperor of Mysore, during whose reign the coin might have been minted.

Chapter 5
Apollo Command Module

A couple of times during those visits, his Aunt-grandmother took them out for dinner. It was always an enlivening experience for Jani to see a bustling city and to have a taste of the speedy metropolis. On one of those evenings, his Aunt-grandmother asked them to come to her office. So his mother took him, his sister, and Monkey Ears, who was the younger son of Aunt-grandmother and just a few years older than Jani.

In the late afternoon, they all dressed up and took a bus with a route number like 5c or 6a or something to her office. He wanted to sit by the window. In Jamshoro everything was virgin clean—the air, the sunlight, even the dirt seemed clean—and so cleanliness meant monotony to him. The abundance of freshness had devalued it for him. So from his window-side seat, he would admire the toxic exhaust fumes of the city.

The roads were so wide that they looked like an airport runway, though he hadn't seen a runway yet. The most fun was when two of the buses got engaged in reckless chases there on the freeway. The drivers would swing their buses around at cruising speeds to avoid other traffic and keep blowing their deafening triple trumpet air horns, making multiple cries of *"teree papa-teree papa"*—he loved that thrill.

Every bus also had a conductor, who kept a beaten-up tough leather bag filled with loose change, and a small wooden rack in front of the leather bag to hold colourful stacks of tickets. Each stack would be held in place with a rusted heavy-duty spring. You would tell them where you wanted to get off, and those conductors, without even looking at their leather bag or ticket rack, would pick the right ticket just by licking their finger, and they would rip your coloured ticket off the stack, all the while yelling the next bus stop out loud.

Later, he wouldn't remember all of the bus stops, but the one they had to get off at was *Kandawala; Kandawala; Kandawala*, three times. And his Aunt-grandmother always would be waiting for them on the sidewalk, standing upright in an affirmative but graceful way, gathering her entire body together like the Oscar statue.

She used to take them all to some place called 'Buns Road'. Jani, like millions of others, was not aware that it was actually Burns Road, where that R is a vowel, named after an Englishman, a physician who treated the Mir emperors of Sindh in some other century.

They would walk down roads with huge peepal trees and buildings with ornamental balconies, and sections of those roads were divided into different things, like shops with only motorcycles parts hanging in and out of them, or shops selling teeth, with signs showing paintings of dentures inside and outside.

Right after that, there was a building that Monkey Ears claimed had parking on the roof, and then that building came into view and he could see that, yes, there were front ends of cars with their turned-off head lights peeping from the top. Then there was that section that was littered with books, every shop was full of books, and as they passed through there was briefly an overwhelming smell of ink and paper in the air. And after a little more walking, Buns Road would appear. There were hawkers selling all kinds of ethnic north Indian food, tikka and kab, and watery soups call *yakhni*. Their shop windows were hung with skinned corpses of dead chickens with their heads attached, which combined with the soups smells into something really acrid.

Then came that restaurant, a big hall made up of all white square bathroom tiles. There was a narrow path with a few steps leading up to the entrance. Inside there was a man sitting on stool close to the *daig*, a humongous stainless steel pot for mess cooking, which looked like that Apollo command module, the one that hit the ocean's surface while bringing astronauts back from moon, but with a collar opening at the top.

So they all entered through that narrow passage, passing close to that Apollo-command-module-like cook pot, and sat in that unintimate restaurant, which was flooded with fabric-brightener-like bluish-white light from mercury light bulbs. He had seen them before in street-lamps in Jamshoro, and one of his uncles had told him that these mercury light bulbs turn off on their own, as if they would rest when they got tired, like they had mind of their own and could think.

Even at that very young age it felt weird to Jani that two women with three children should be sitting in a place filled with blue-collar men. The budding spurs of his young rooster-like ego were bugging him. His mother instinctively knew this by looking at his anxious face, and just told him, "Everything is okay. Don't worry about the place, you are going to try food that you haven't tasted before."

He looked to Aunt-grandmother, who was sitting in front of him, with her squared shoulders, and a faint motherly smile on her face, still looking like the upper half of the Oscar statuette, like she know all about men's world and how to manoeuvre in it without getting splashed. A waiter came with a cap on his head, the kind that religious Muslims wear.

He took order politely, and then turned his back on them and shouted it back at the guy sitting at the top of the command-module cooking pot. In minutes, hot naans arrived with crispy blisters, and plates filled with a thick syrupy stew with chunks of meat and a garnish of toothpick sized strings of fresh ginger. He tried it with extreme caution after his mother squeezed some drops from a quarter of lime that the waiter had brought separately. It was unbelievable tasty, the most delicious thing he had eaten thus far in his life. He was too young to identify the complex spices in it that hint of fennel seeds and so many others, but he loved it.

In one of those summer vacation breaks, that same Aunt-grandmother of his, unknowingly or by virtue of a mistake, initiated a thought process, a chemical reaction in his mind. It was like that *pop* of chemical reaction when sodium metal hits water and it makes a small explosion. The 70s were a time of ethnic tension in urban and rural Sindh, in which the core issue was that rural Sindh wanted to become urban.

It happened one morning when Jani was there in Karachi with his mother on vacation. Aunt-grandmother's younger sister was there too, which means another Aunt-grandmother of Jani's, whom he remembered as Prophecy—that was the cologne that she used to wear, because her armpits smelled like raw ammonia and dead fish combined, but the Prophecy cologne could do nothing to hide that acetous smell. But she still wore that fragrance, and instead of 'cologne', she just straightforwardly called it a 'scent'. So Prophecy had come to visit them this particular morning, with her two sons, Rushoo and Bhaiya.

Rushoo was chubby and Bhaiya was skinny. They were roughly Jani's age, and they both had that extremely annoying quality of already being true urbanites despite their very young age. They only talked about their expensive toys, which

Prophecy kept locked behind a glass showcase in mint condition, and instead of playing with them they could only see them. However, that was fine with them because that's what they thought toys were for.

Prophecy herself was a nouveau riche. Whenever possible she tried to bring up her jewellery in conversation, and she literally would express it in terms of weight, saying, "I have two kilos of gold in jewellery." So once or twice in any given vacation time Jani had to endure the misery of Rushoo, Bhaiya and Prophecy's company.

This morning was one of those miserable ones. Prophecy was reading the newspaper, and the hot topic was ethnic tension. Jani was playing with Monkey Ears, Rushoo, and Bhaiya, and his mother was sitting, alongside Aunt-grandmother and Prophecy, around that only table in that small apartment, which served as a dining table, study table, sewing table, and whatever-else-table, but at the moment it was serving as a dining table.

Prophecy read a line from a couplet out loud from the newspaper: *"urdu ka janaza hai zara shaan se nikle"* (its death of Urdu should come out with a Jazz funeral), and then they casually kept talking, and Aunt-grandmother made a crack in Jani's thinking which kept widening. He was playing with the other kids, but children tend to listen to everything, and so he did too. And he was listening when his Aunt-grandmother said, "Sindhis are people with no self-esteem. They are as bold as brass. They have no pride, and no shame."

She had said that to her sister. But as a child of Sindhi descent, he kept listening to her, and kept playing with Rushoo, Bhaiya, and Monkey Ears, making a crane out of Monkey Ears's royal meccano-box, while Aunt-grandmother went on.

"According to official records"—that she had seen somewhere—"Hindu Mahajans keep wives captive of local Muslim Sindhis as collateral against loans, and these women even give birth to babies."

This meant that those women became impregnated by the Hindu Mahajans, but Aunt-grandmother was presuming from this unfortunate situation that the Sindhis were wilfully pushing their wives into sex slavery. And Jani keep thinking, *how can she say that, and is that true and if so?* What about Aai, his grandmother, and his father's sisters? And Prophecy wanted to add her wisdom to Aunt-grandmother's, so she came up with her own take on Sindhis: "They are uncivilised. Have you noticed the way they smack when they eat? They sound like dogs eating."

At that same moment, Bhaiya, Prophecy's elder son who was exactly Jani's age, looked into Jani's eyes as if he too had heard it and understood. Without saying a single word, Bhaiya relaxed his eyes, which gave room to a cunning smile, and Jani felt like he was being cooked, medium rare. Even at the age of ten or eleven, Jani was unwillingly agreeing with her and everybody else sitting in that room, somewhere in a two-bedroom apartment in Federal B area. Jani felt a pain like someone was finely peeling the very top layer of his skin with a very sharp peeler, so neatly that not a single drop of blood was allowed to seep up and ooze; they say that this was one of the most excruciating forms of Mughal-era torture. He couldn't rationalise her spillover anger effect and simply discount it.

And she was not alone; these years ahead would see the tipping point in the long battle of the Sindhis' right to exist. Sindhi intellectuals were yelling at the top of their lungs, protesting and trying to give voice to their ideas, but they had little political or social power, and were constantly thwarted by the big media outlets. They were like South Africans protesting against apartheid, with no newspaper writing about them, no one broadcasting their response to that general insult that native Sindhis were 'uncivilised and savage people'. They couldn't, because expressing their anger would have been taken as aggression 'against the state'.

At the age of ten or eleven, Jani could feel the insult instinctively, but he had no idea about all these legislative complexities. But his Aunt-grandmother's casual talk had sown tiny seeds of loathing on that fateful morning. He himself was not aware that those tiny seeds would grow tall very quickly, like Jack's beanstalks. She gave him a reason to find and grasp that exotic and passionate feeling called nationalism, with all its toxicity and illnesses, and he would embrace it. He would proudly belong to a culture whose history could be traced back for thousands and thousands of years—a culture his Aunt-grandmother was calling names.

Chapter 6
Jumping Like a Grasshopper

He missed his grandmother, Aai. He had such an easy, pure bond with her. Once he asked her to explain what One-unit was, and she just slapped her palm to her forehead with a knee-jerk affect, and said, "It's some godforsaken thing. I don't know myself what this darn One-unit is, my love." All the confusions of the adult world didn't matter when he was with Aai, because she didn't understand these things either.

When he first moved away from Jamshoro, he actually moved away from his father as well, for a short time. His father had stayed at Jamshoro with his mother and siblings, while his mother took Jani and his sister to the city and lived with her parents. During this time, Jani's parents lived separately, though it was only a temporary arrangement.

Couples do separate at times, for so many reasons, though there was some stigma attached to this in the Sindhi society at the time. But his parents' brief separation was not because they couldn't get along or had differences of opinion. No, there was no such thing between them. Their separation was based on different ethnicities.

His mother was not Sindhi. Her family had moved from India and settled in Karachi, then later moved to Hyderabad, where his father met her during their drawing teachers' training. She was one of the two girls in that art class. She was an urban woman—confident, well-educated, and seemed to have a future planned for herself. She belonged to a religious family, but she had her own mind, and she wanted to learn painting, and against all odds she even wanted to learn kathak dance.[134]

---

[134] Kathak: a form of classical dance that developed in northern India, blending Hindu and Islamic influences. Kathak dance in its essence is always linked to drama and

In an orthodox Muslim family like this, where all arts but especially dance were a big *No!* No with a capital N. And there were no kathak teachers in Hyderabad, so she had to teach herself, using an illustrated book about kathak. And similarly, by her own will she got herself enrolled in an art class to learn painting. And there she again broke the Sabbath and fell in love with Ali Gohar, a local dark-skinned Sindhi.

They fell for each other and got married, and she joined his struggle to climb out of marginal poverty and into the middle class. Both of Jani's parents were working, and essentially heading towards same goal. But this ethnic divide popped up in that space and time in Sindh's history. His three younger uncles were in their teens and were exposed to this viral sense of existence called nationalism.

This had oxidised their minds like toxic fungi, causing them to think of his mother as one of the enemy, even though she was living with them doing everything possible to support them. She had given up a comparatively comfortable life to get married to their elder brother.

On other hand, his mother was doing all this backbreaking work out of her own free will, because she was in love with his father. She was not supporting ten or twelve poor native Sindhis as a philanthropist. In fact, deep inside her mind she did think Sindhis were a less accomplishing, lazier, uncivilised kind of people.

So his mother's stiffness was fermenting with the younger uncles' distasteful behaviour towards her, and then one of them abused her verbally in some way, which twisted the knife. And so, his mother moved out to her parents. So those language riots had torn apart individuals on a nano level, where a five-year-old child was separated from his sixty-some-year-old grandmother—one of them too young and the other too old to understand or care about the ethnic or racial factors in the first place.

His mother's parents lived in a place called Old Campus. It was an ill-shaped colony in the middle of the city's downtown, next to the courthouse and in the shadow of a cathedral building, which was actually not a cathedral but a school. This was the one called the Model School, affiliated with Sindh University.

In fact, the whole university had once been housed in that cathedral-like building before being moved to its new location at Jamshoro. Only the

---

storytelling. The word 'kathak' arises from the Sanskrit 'katha', meaning 'story', and kathak dancers are called *kathakars*, storytellers who use a language of body gestures.

Department of Education had stayed back. Thus, this was called the university's Old Campus, and because his maternal grandfather worked for the university, he had a residential place there, like some other senior professors. When university moved, it gave the employees the option to buy those residences, and most everybody took that opportunity.

So that's where his mother temporarily moved, along with Jani and his elder sister. The house was a rectangle and triangle combined, kind of an irregular pentagon. The home was in the rectangle part, and there was a Pythagorean right triangle lawn attached to the house. So sides A and B formed the right angle, and C was the diagonal garden wall. That was the best part of the place, that teeny miniature lawn, which had a row of night-blooming jasmine shrubs alongside one wall, and a mango tree, and at the end of the wall there was an awkwardly small cedar wood double door.

There were beams forming a Z shape on of the top other crossbeams on one half of the door, painted dark grey, and the mirror image of that Z on the other side. Its height was so low that all grownups had to duck their heads to pass. There was a jasmine shrub that had grown from one side of the door and looped over to its other side.

Alongside the diagonal wall there were thorny red roses, especially thorny ones. And on its smaller straight side, which was the one attached to the house, there were some small mogra shrubs and an infertile guava tree, which never got a chance to grow to its fullest, probably because of the shadow of the high wall. In the centre of that triangle there was a lawn, bordered with half-entrenched red backed bricks in a sawtooth pattern.

Every couple of weeks, Nizam Mali, the gardener, would come and cut the grass and trim the shrubs. Nizam was a quiet, serious, no bullshit kind of a man, who would come to do his work and then tie his manual lawnmower to the back of his bicycle and leave. Jani would watch Nizam cutting the grass, pushing his manual lawnmower forward and causing small fragments of chopped grass to shower into the grass catcher. Nizam carried a sack in which he collected all the cut grass and pieces of shrub. It was seldom that Nizam asked for anything, but when he did, it was for drinking water almost every time.

Jani's uncles and grandmother had told him this, and they showed him a specific rough china cup to use if any peasant or servant-like person should ask for water. They kept the cup on a wall ledge outside the bathroom, and they gave the logical explanation that these poor people unfortunately carried tuberculosis.

He understood it well enough, but somehow that explanation was always wrapped in a looking-down sort of tone, which made him uncomfortable even at that very young age.

But despite his intuition that there was something wrong with this, whenever Nizam asked him for water, out of fear he always used that cup sitting on the ledge outside bathroom wall, though he wanted to use a regular cup. And Nizam made sure, each time he came, that he that he left that tiny odd-shaped lawn looking like a piece of Eden.

He used to play with some neighbour kids, a chubby girl and her younger brother, who were the children of some university teacher. Most of the time they would play right outside that triangle lawn, up against one of its walls, where university authorities had dumped the corpse of one of their charred buses. He and the other children liked to play hide and seek in that skeleton of a bus, the victim of a time bomb.

Years back, someone had planted a bomb in that school bus, which was supposed to go off in the middle of the day to inflict maximum damage. But somehow that time bomb had gotten bastardised or doped, and it went off twelve hours late, in the middle of night, so the bus itself was the only thing that popped and burned to ashes, so no one got hurt, or that's what people believed. In that wreck of twisted and charred iron, Jani always went for that steering wheel, which was still there—just a rusted circular iron rod, but it was there. Even some of the paddles that were once a brake and clutch, those were still there too. There was a bit of a trench there in that part of the wreckage, where he liked to submerge himself and hide from the others.

Once that chubby girl was there with him playing, wearing cylindrical pyjamas and a maroon sleeveless frock, with two straps on each shoulder and also small pink butterfly-wing-like things. And her pyjamas had no pink butterflies design, but her pyjamas did have an elastic waistband, and she wanted him to see it. In fact, she wanted him to see her—and she lowered them on her own by simply pulling them down.

His heart stopped for a moment, and another timeless explosion happened in his mind when he saw a beard-like thing between her legs. She pulled her pyjamas up and went on her way, jumping like a grasshopper. But for days after that, he kept coming back to that trench-like space in the wreckage, under the steering wheel, pushing the brakes and clutch paddles and thinking that she might come back again, and his heart would stop for a moment again, but that never happened.

Every mid-morning, Bhangis would come and clean the brick-paved open sewer line in that entire colony. Hundreds and hundreds of yards of sewer lines were cleaned every morning, manually, by this small army of Bhangis, using their wheelbarrows with their metal wheels and long spatulas and receiving pans with a long handle.

They gathered the entire colony's faeces into their wheelbarrows and carried it away somewhere. He saw them doing that pretty much every day, and he watched them, following them alongside those long straight sewer lines. Once, in curiosity, he approached a teenage Bhangi boy who was also filling his wheelbarrow with all that shit.

"What you are going to do with it?" Jani asked.

The boy looked at him and replied, "We'll eat it. Happy?"

And for a moment he actually wondered, *do they really eat it?*

But his heart was in Jamshoro. He was not happy there in the city. He wanted to go back to his Aai and his uncles and aunts. But who would listen to him? He was too young to have opinions and then express them. His maternal family members called him *'Bhonduu'* (goofy) out of love, because of his clumsy oafishness and also because he couldn't say two sentences straight.

In his mother's home, everybody took an afternoon siesta, and they forced him to nap then also. Sometimes, he would fall asleep, but other times he would escape and wander around. And because there was no one else around, he would roam about with unknown alley kids in the empty hallways of that cathedral building, that school, whose hallways felt cooler, but with the rotten smell of run-over dirt.

Sometimes, with the intention of doing a holy good deed, he and all the alley kids would go and urinate on *Hindus qabar,* the entombed grave of the person who had made this institution from his own pocket, and who had wanted his ashes to be buried there. Those afternoons were filled with screeching cries of black kite birds, which glided high up in the skies with their wings fully extended in a spiral rotation.

And all the while he was thinking that soon he would move back to Jamshoro and live with those people he loved, and who loved him. But instead, his parents rented a two-room apartment close to his school, and he moved there with his sister and both his parents. He never lived permanently in Jamshoro again.

This new place was a microcosm, a small community within another community, which itself was a part of a slightly bigger community, kind of a box within a box within a box. It was a society of its own, with its own culture and language and people. And this place had its own slang name, which was *'Kala-board-Mustafa Masjid'*—at least that's what he always heard his mother tell the taxi driver where to stop.

The Kala-board community was a small T-junction among the mass-produced rows of adjoined houses in a Hyderabad satellite town. And the people living there had given their own names to the various groups of homes around a given junction or roundabout. So this Kala-board-Mustafa Masjid community was a world of its own, the sum of the dwellings around one small T-junction.

The first family elder who visited them from Jamshoro was his father's maternal uncle, Maasurar Kando. He was the one, according to the family legend, who had helped to save his father's leg from getting amputated in childhood, long ago. But Jani was happier to see Punnu, a younger uncle who had brought Maasurar Kando, who wouldn't have been able to come on his own. Maasurar Kando was from a remote village close to Qamber and had no idea how to navigate in city, hopping buses and then switching taxies. This would have been especially hard for him, because he only spoke Sindhi, and Urdu was like Greek to him.

It was a weekend, so in the morning his mother made a breakfast of omelettes with crisp bread. He was giggling with his young uncle—whatever the uncle was saying, he liked it regardless. Unknowingly he had found that fading link, and now it was breathing again. This presence had resuscitated Jamshoro in him. His father and Maasurar Kando were eating and his father was telling Maasurar Kando that the American President had resigned last night, as if Maasurar Kando cared.

After few hours that evening departing time arrived and his uncle along with Maasurar Kando had to leave and go back to Jamshoro. And when they left, he felt again that strong abruption, that traumatic rupture, which bust hearts but is only expressed in minute snuffles and cool sighs, and his heart learned the art of missing love ones. In few hours, he recovered.

Time was frantically moving forward, always in a rush, telling him to get up, dust his pants and move on. So he did that, and tried to fit himself into this Kala-board-Mustafa Masjid community, which was only a short distance away from Jamshoro but poles apart culturally. This place was seemed to have nothing in common with Jamshoro apart from the skies, and even those were not as blue as Jamshoro's.

Everyone here was speaking Urdu, which was still a second language to him, though he knew a bit of Urdu from his trips to Karachi and visits to his mother's family in the city. But now he would be exposed to this beautiful language with all its grace, and soon he would gain mastery of it as well. There were invisible boundaries here in this place, among these rows and rows of houses, in bunches of five or ten blocks, where people had made their own communities and converted parts or entire houses into commodity shops.

Jani soon became friends with some neighbour children, eleven or twelve kids who were all siblings, and who all lived in a one-room house. Their father, Abdul Rehman Bhai, and one of their elder brothers used to make handmade riveted steel luggage suitcases and trunks, of all different sizes, made up of tin sheets. The kids were all known as *Chando Aapa kay bachay*—Chando Aapa's children. They were friendly people, down to earth. They helped everyone in that small cluster of community. Their mother, Chando Aapa, was the real driving force, an illiterate woman who nonetheless had great instinctive tools to make things work.

Her polite manner was so beautiful that it nullified her beastly unattractiveness. Then there was Rehman Bhai's mother, Fatima Boowa, who was made up of different sized circles, one on top of other: one big circle was her thorax, holding her completely deflated breasts, like sagging under-eye puffiness, on top of her stomach.

She had no neck; rather her head sat directly on her body, and her arms and legs were like circles too, because she mostly wrapped them in a circular shape around her body as she sat on a four-legged cot, somewhere in a corner. She only used her voice to do everything, usually in the form of insults, which were often provocative and creative, like the way she would angrily call to her grandson, saying, *"Aray O randi kai tabalchi!"*—*You percussionist of a whore!*

Chando Aapa and Rehman Bhai were their next-door neighbours, and right across from Chando Aapa's home there was a house that was a taboo place. No one in the community wanted to interact with that family. The head of the household Farooq Sahib, a tall, bald, and extremely agitated man, with copper-tan skin and anger that he carried at the tip of his nose. Sometimes, he would beat his wife and his grown daughters.

The house that Jani's family rented was diagonal to Farooq Sahib's home. One evening, quite late, he was sleeping with his father in the open courtyard, under a mosquito box net that was so thick that only a few very bright stars could be seen through it. And all of sudden, he heard cries, oscillating, yelling cries! Like the cries of Native Americans in battles that he had seen and heard in western cowboy movies on TV.

Obviously, his parents and his sister also heard those cries. All four of them were peeking towards noise from the ledge of the courtyard wall. And they saw Farooq Sahib's backyard, where his wife and grown-up daughters were running in circles and making those pulsating cries. At first, he thought they were doing some kind of ritual, which he hadn't yet encountered, because this was a new place where people did different things. But slowly the reality settled in that Farooq Sahib was beating his wife and daughters.

But that was not the reason why people disliked Farooq Sahib. The real reason was that Farooq Sahib had had a fight with Munchi Jee and lost. Munchi Jee was the most respected person in the community. He was the sole force who had made that Mustafa Masjid, and he was the Pesh-Imam[135] who led the prayers in that mosque's congregation.

Munchi Jee's home-cum-business was a small grocery store situated at one corner of that T-junction. When he was not conducting prayers in the Mustafa Masjid, he was there in his store, selling lentils and flour and single-serving teabags joined together in a long string, hanging from his store ceiling like grand-opening flags. And there were all sorts of other grocery items scattered on the floor in rolled-back sleeve-like sacks, things like grains and sugar, all in that one-room shop of his.

It was basically an outer room of his house, from which he had just removed a portion of the wall and inserted a concrete slab on its ledge to function like a countertop. And he had a row of squarish candy jars there, made of cheap glass with air bubbles trapped in them.

Munchi Jee always tightened those jars' rusty screw-on lids so firmly that only he could get the candy out of them. And those candies were simple ones,

---

[135] *Pesh-imam*: the word 'pesh' means present, and it is used here to distinguish between the person who is acting as imam in this specific community and the (predominantly Shia) concept of the universal imam, who presides over the whole of the Muslim community.

but still pleasurable, like silver-coin-sized sweet milk cakes or peppermint wafers, or cow's milk toffee in a red wrapper with a picture of a cow on it.

Munchi Jee was a middle-aged man, the kind of person who seemed to remain at forty for many years of life. He had barely any grey in his hair, which was curly, and he kept it combed back. He also wore spectacles, those plain round vintage-style black plastic ones. Munchi Jee looked quite a lot like Saadat Hasan Manto, though this was a deceiving coincidence, because he was actually Manto's antipole, rather like a devil who manages to look exactly like a god.

But Munchi Jee was not only one who stood out in that heavenly cluster of the *Kala-board-Mustafa Masjid.* There were others who their own personas and tendencies, moving about the place like chess pieces. One of them was Imam-uddin Bengali, along with his wife, who was only known as Bengalun Khala. They also had countless children, all boys, and they had given them rhyming names.

Everybody said that Imam-uddin Bengali had been a goldsmith back in Bengal, but in this part of the world he sold the sell milk from his water buffaloes. He had encaged those poor buffaloes in one of those cookie-cutter-houses, which was none other than his own house.

Across from Imam-uddin Bengali's home there was Kaley Maulana's madrasah-cum-carpet-weaving cottage industry, with two good-sized but primitive wooden looms and a table-top candy shop. All this was in the house along with his living and breathing home, with his wife and several kids of his own, and also kids from neighbourhood who attended his madrasah and learned Qur'an.

In return they didn't pay any fee, but rather worked on Kaley Maulana's carpet looms. And this worked like a charm for Kaley Maulana, because the young children had tiny fingers that could easily tie those delicate little knots, which greatly increased the value of hand-woven carpets.

Next to Farooq Sahib's home lived a chubby woman with a weeping face, along with her two kids. Her name was Razia Baji, and she always looked depressed. Every ten or fifteen days, a man who looked like Popeye's Bluto, would to come to her place in the odd hours of the night, in his ugly Czechoslovakian Skoda car. He was best known as Razia Baji's husband. People whispered that he was a smuggler, but Gods knows what he used to smuggle, if he really did.

In front of Razia Baji's home was Khalifah Jee's barbershop, where Khalifah Jee along with his son Bundu-bhai use to cut hair. Khalifah Jee was a short man with a generic face, like any old man of Indian descent, and a beard that always gave the impression that he hadn't shaved for a week. His son Bundu-bhai, was an ugly fellow with dark skin and a crooked tooth that looked like a thick toenail, which was always peeping out of Bundu-bhai's mouth and sitting on his lower lip.

That shop, as well as several others, were the property of the Mustafa Masjid. Khalifah Jee was also the muezzin of that masjid—the person who calls Muslims to prayer, five times a day, from a minaret of the masjid. But Khalifah Jee didn't actually climb up the minaret; instead he used a loud speaker in his signature style, first tapping twice against the microphone, which wore a paisley design scarf, with retro-style Persian pickle patterns.

Khalifah Jee probably used that paisley scarf on the microphone to prevent his spit from getting into it and ruining the mechanism, but the scarf also worked as a filter to eat up the popping, crackling, and blowing sounds of Khalifah Jee's voice, but it couldn't reduce that gurgling cough which followed his signature two taps. But Khalifah Jee's resume didn't stop there. He was also a bawarchi—a traditional chef who only cooks feasts for marriage receptions and after-burial lunches, for hundreds of people at a time. And in addition to all that, Khalifah Jee also performed circumcisions.

So that was the microcosmic new world into which Jani had landed. Everything was foreign to him; nothing was like it had been in Jamshoro. Even the dirt was not same—over here, dirt really felt dirty. But humans are wired to adapt in order to survive, and instinctively he did the same. First, he wrapped Jamshoro and placed it somewhere very secure in his heart, under the heavy rock of memories of his grandmother Aai. Then he learned *kar-khane-dari* Urdu[136] automatically because that's what everyone around him was speaking.

He started mixing with people around him, and was trying to keep a safe distance from Farooq Sahib's family, because that's what everyone else was doing. Years later, he learned the real reason why people of that urban cluster hated Farooq Sahib. Their hatred was not because he used to beat his wife and daughters sometimes in late evenings after getting drunk, and not because his political views were more liberal, or because he liked a democratic party whose

---

[136] *Kar-khane-dari* Urdu: the Urdu of the streets—with all the slang and idioms and vulgarities that come with that.

charismatic leader was a bold thinker like Farooq Sahib himself; no, those were only the smaller reasons why people of the Mustafa Masjid community disliked Farooq Sahib. The main reason was that he had been the only person who opposed the building of Mustafa Masjid on ground that had been dedicated for a children's park.

Very soon Jani stopped comparing this place with Jamshoro in his mind, because there was no comparison. The dirt was already dirtier, and the skies were different too. Here the sky appeared hazier and greyer and was cross-hatched with wires of power lines. Smells were different too; they had their own acrid fermented tint. There was only one aa-sirheen tree on the corner of his street, which did look exactly like the aa-sirheens of Jamshoro. But he ignored that aa-sirheen too, unconsciously, by using the other side of the street.

Every now and then before lunch on the weekend, his mother would give him dough and have him get it baked into flat Indian bread in a clay oven at a street-corner eatery. Everyone in Mustafa Masjid called that place 'Pehalwan ka hotal'[137] after its owner, who was an obese man like a mound of fat, who sat bare-shouldered and leaning his gynecomastic breasts against the counter, which was a wooden box. And right behind Pehalwan, on an unplastered brick wall, there were eight or ten thin black wood-trimmed glass frames, holding black and white photographs of young Pehalwan.

Each frame was hung on that wall with a small eyehook screwed in at the centre of top trim and then nailed directly into the wall. One could easily see young Pehalwan staring out at you as he gripped his ancient Indian mace in his right hand. Next to Pehalwan's hotel there was a narrow alley, which led to a back entrance of Mustafa Masjid, and after that there was one last shop space, which was Sarfaraz Hospital.

It was actually just one of Khalifah Jee's barbershop spaces, but they still called it Sarfaraz Hospital. This hospital was run by Dr Sarfaraz, who was not a physician but rather a compounder. In the old days, compounders use were the apprentices of physicians and prepared compounds of different salts, making awful mixtures, and tending the wounds of patients by changing bandages. But Dr Sarfaraz proclaimed himself as a physician and started practicing medicine.

---

[137] *Pehalwan ka hotal*: Literally 'the wrestler's hotel'. A pehalwan is a traditional Sindhi wrestler. And, in Sindh, restaurants are most commonly found in hotels, and eateries are often referred to as 'hotels' even when not attached to a hotel. Traditions of food and hospitality are very closely intertwined.

And the people of the Mustafa Masjid community trusted him; they really believed he had a healer's touch. And obviously he was helping people out of cold and flu, and coughs and fevers, and cuts and bruises. Dr Sarfaraz was a clever-looking man with puffy golf-ball-sized cheeks and both angles of his jawbones fanning out, which gave him a stingy look. But for money he was okay—his practice was thriving. Actually, he was minting money. Once he did something which almost cost him everything, and that was just because of his ignorance and increasing greed.

Poor people would come to get dextrose drips with some B complex infusion—and on this occasion he used the same intravenous dextrose drip on two different patients. What had happened was that Bengalun Khala went to his hospital to get that energy-pep dextrose drip, with its urine-yellow B-complex shot. But after few minutes she started shivering and didn't want to have any more of it.

So, Dr Sarfaraz stopped the drip, and after a few moments Bengalun Khala stopped shaking and went home. Then came Kaley Maulana's elder son, who also wanted to have that pep of energy. And Dr Sarfaraz probably rationalised his greed, thinking, what's the point wasting this almost full drip, which gave chillies to Bengalun Khala a little while ago. And probably without flushing the needle he gave the same drip to Kaley Maulana's son.

After half an hour or so, unlike Bengalun Khala, Kaley Maulana's son skipped shivering and directly went to violent convulsions. So, Dr Sarfaraz stopped that drip right away and gave him some sort of antidote, but Kaley Maulana's son became unconscious and froth started coming out of his mouth.

That news spread like wildfire in that close-knit Kala-board-Mustafa Masjid community, and within a very short time everyone was either in or outside of Sarfaraz Hospital. Those who were inside were rubbing Kaley Maulana's son's palms and the bottoms of his feet.

Meanwhile, Dr. Sarfaraz embarked on an all-night-long marathon of forgiveness prayer in that same Mustafa Masjid, trying to drag God into his own mess. A few people, who were shuttling between Kaley Maulana's son's bedside and Dr Sarfaraz's prayer site, using Mustafa Masjid's back alley entrance, witnessed that Dr Sarfaraz was weeping constantly as he prayed. By daybreak, Kaley Maulana's son opened his eyes and was out of rough waters. One of those shuttling seesaw people whispered the good news into the ear of praying Dr. Sarfaraz, and then he broke his prayer.

After that terrible incident of Dr Sarfaraz's gross quackery, his practice flourished. That incidence of malpractice worked as a feather in his cap. More people started coming to him, convinced that his blind faith in God and his hours-long prayer had saved that boy's life.

Jani walked to school every morning with his mother and elder sister. It was a 45-minute walk, and on their way they passed an intersection known as *Ponay Panch Number*.[138] In the winter mornings it had a deserted look, with only a few people bundled-up, waiting for their ride to the city. Some of those rides were mini taxis, wonderful vehicles—you couldn't call them a car, but they weren't golf carts either.

They were something in between, a three-wheeled, cartoonish black automobile with yellow stripe and a front like a dolphin's head. And these were only to be found in Hyderabad. Mostly people preferred to travel in them because the fare was cheaper. And he used to look at those mini taxis heading towards the city, exhaling thick bluish-grey smoke from their tailpipes, which dispersed very slowly in winter mornings, and he would keep thinking about how those mini taxis were going to pass the bus-stop, from which buses go to Jamshoro.

---

[138] *Ponay Panch Number*. Four-and-three-quarters.

Chapter 7
Whose Funeral Are You Crying Over?

It was all fine; everything was perfect, but somehow he was not clicking. Memories of Jamshoro were banging in his mind, like a metal foreign object banging, making an irritating noise in an otherwise smoothly running washing machine. He never shared these thoughts with his parents, but he was always thinking up ways to escape and go back to Jamshoro, to his people, to Aai who loved him. It was a constant back and forth of hope and disappointments, imagining of things and then they're not happening, which started making him dislike things, and that dislike grew into toxic feeling of hate.

Every few weeks someone would visit them from Jamshoro. Usually, it would be one of his uncles or aunts, but every few months Aai would come and stay for three days, and those three days would always be the most beautiful three days for him since her last visit. Actually, three beautiful days is an exaggeration; they used to be two and a half beautiful days and a miserable half day.

That half-day was the one right before her departure. Once, after one of those three-day visits, Aai left with one of his uncles, and he kept looking at them walking away until they reached the end of the street and made the turn towards the mini-taxi stop. And then he ran as fast as he could, climbing twelve steps and crossing two doors, to reach the second floor window on the other side of the house, and he grabbed the iron chicken-wire screen with all fingers of both hands and squeezed his face against the screen and waited few seconds to take a final look at them as they passed a distant intersection near the mini-taxi stop.

After that fleeting glimpse of them, he locked himself in the bathroom and wept for some time. He didn't want his mother to know, but she knew it anyway, because it happened every time.

Soon, she started banging on bathroom door, like she was about to break it, yelling, "Who died? Whose dead body are you crying over?" And then she would bang even harder on the door, and keep yelling, *"kis kay janazay ko ro raha hai, kambakht?"—Whose funeral are you crying over, wretched one?*

She loved him like any mother loved her child but she was trying to tie the winds and doing something different, which had never worked before in the past. But then, rolling massive boulders up the hill is not completely unheard of, either. And the boulder she was rolling was the hope of making someone love you more by force. Simply put, his mother just wanted him to be close to her instead of to his Aai.

By a stroke of luck, he and his sister got a chance to spend four or five days in Jamshoro. It was a joyous moment for him when his father asked one of his maternal uncles to drop off the two of them off at their Aai's place at Jamshoro. Meanwhile Ali Gohar was comforting Jani's mother, who had been constantly weeping since hearing from her younger brother, who had come on his bicycle all the way from Old Campus, which was the name of that cathedral-like building where the grandparents lived, after they received a trunk call.

Those were always considered a big deal, and they were expensive; and this was the kind known as a person-to-person trunk call, and it came from Karachi where rest of his mother's family lived. And the bad news that had been shared on that trunk call was that one of his mother's dearest cousins, whom she considered a sister because of their closeness, had attempted to commit suicide.

She had then died of natural causes, meaning that she did not die from committing suicide, but had died in its aftermath anyway. The explanation was a bit complicated on technical grounds. She had attempted suicide by swallowing a handful of sleeping pills, and was then rushed to the emergency room, where she regained some consciousness after gastric lavage. She had recognised his maternal grandmother before losing consciousness again, but then her lungs got filled with water and she passed away.

In the middle of all those weeping and mourning sounds, he was a bit distressed and upset, but there was a parallel thought running through his young mind, which felt more like a reward. He was enjoying this thought that soon he would be with his Aai, and because of that thought his heart was busting with giggles and joy. But even at that young age he knew he had to hide that happiness, and somehow by necessity he learned the art of deceiving.

Then after those five days, the honeymoon was over. His parents came back from Karachi, and one of his uncles brought him and his sister to their maternal grandparents' home, where the whole family was in a saddened mood. And everyone was emphasising the point that his mother's cousin had died of natural causes, not suicide. He could feel that everyone was working to convince themselves that her death was caused by the water in her lungs and not by the sleeping pills.

Then his uncle who had brought him and his sister there had to leave, and that departing farewell was as crushing to him as death of his mother's cousin had been to his mother and maternal grandmother. So once his uncle left, he too wept with an open heart, and everyone around him was comforting him, thinking he was crying for his mother's cousin.

On that Ferris wheel of life, with all its ups and downs, its swings and sudden bumps, Jani's father, Ali Gohar, got a scholarship to the United States. His father kept calling it a 'full bright' scholarship. It was a new situation, and a new thrill for Jani. Though no one was talking to him directly, he could feel that whatever his father was up to was of some value. Whenever his father was talking with other grownups about this full bright scholarship, it gave his little young mind this straightforward translation that his father was of full brightness, and that must be why he had gotten this scholarship.

Little did he know that the Fulbright scholarship was actually just named after someone, whose last name was Fulbright. But in his mind, his father had fetched a full bright scholarship for being so intelligent and bright. And the second exciting thing was that his father was going to the place where Uncle Sufi lived, who would come a couple of times every year bringing milk chocolate truffles for them.

He had never seen truffles like that before, in a box with bow and a ribbon—you would undo that bow and lift the top, and there they were, all those adorable chocolates, in square or rounds or seahorse shapes. Some of them would be filled with mawkishly sweet and syrupy stuff. The ones that Jani liked best were the fairies with wings. And Uncle Sufi use to bring for these from a place that his grandmother called *Vilayat,* which simply meant a farfetched foreign land.

There is also another meaning of vilayat, which also deals with a far-flung destination somewhere in the vicinity of heaven, and to navigate that windy, tortuous path to vilayat, one would have to follow *moula-e-kainat.* But neither he nor his simple sweet grandmother knew that other meaning *vilayat,* which was somewhere out in the heavens.

After a while, his grandmother stopped using the word *vilayat* and started calling it *New Ya-rak Amrica.* To her, New York and America were the same place, so it was up to her own discretion whether to say place 'New Ya-rak' or 'Amrica' when referring to the place where her eldest son had gone for higher education. In that small university town of Jamshoro, she imagined herself as a celebrity whose son had gone to New Ya-rak.

Sometimes, when she was sitting alone, she started singing wedding songs and putting the words 'New Ya-rak' and 'Ali Gohar' into them—who knows, why wedding songs!

Well, there is a reason. In Sindh, mothers and sisters sing wedding songs to celebrate any accomplishment of their sons and brothers. That whole thing about being a celebrity in her own mind, and the singing of wedding songs, that was all a kind of placebo happiness, and she was enjoying it, though all her troubles were still there. Her financial hardship meant that she was constantly thinking about how to pay the bills, worrying when the grocer was going to stop giving food on credit, and begging and borrowing money from her working children to feed her jobless ones.

But somehow, she still managed to steal a little time, a few moments to imagine being prosperous, wealthy, carefree, about having things like a sofa, or something similar to a china cabinet, in which she could display floral crockery that she had never had in first place. And then she would laugh about her own fancy silly desires.

His father took four years to finish whatever he was doing in New York, and then he came back. They left the Kala Board Mustafa Masjid locality and moved to an upper middle class neighbourhood, which wasn't all that far from Mustafa Masjid, but it was yet again another world. Now his next-door neighbours were not tin suitcase makers, or rug weavers, or produce hawkers. Instead, they were doctors and engineers and accountants and college professors.

One of his neighbours, who was a doctor, had a nephew called *'Bhooro'* which literally means Caucasian, though he was actually albino. Bhooro was a couple of years older than Jani, so he had elaborate stories and half-cooked answers to try to satisfy those same old teen curiosities, to find out what's under those clothes. Once Bhooro said to Jani, "There's a carnival in this area. We could go there tonight and see a naked woman dancing in the well of death."

Then Bhooro took a pause, and his eyes were glazed with the lustful joy of sin, which was one of Bhooro's elaborations. Then he said with nonchalant detachment, "But we'd need five rupees to buy tickets for both of us."

Night had just signed in. It was just after dark, twilight in fact, and he had stolen 5 rupees from his mother's purse. Bhooro was waiting at little distance, and was more worried about what would happen if Jani's mother found out about the stolen rupees and Bhooro had to take some blame. But all worries were overpowered by the excitement of the *Maut ka Kuan*—the 'well of death', the pit in which the *baazigars*[139] would spin like birds with outstretched arms on their devilish bikes.

They were hurrying towards the scouting ground where this carnival had planted itself for the past few weeks. They took a short cut through the *deviyoon* shrubs[140] towards the carnival lights, which looked like a glittering jewel. Gradually noises joined the lights. He could hear his own breath, and then his neighbour's breath, and then again his, in an alternating sequence.

When they reached the carnival, they headed straight for the Maut ka Kuan, but found it wasn't so much a well of death as a ramshackle rotted wooden pit of death. He paid for himself and his neighbour, and they were allowed to walk up a make shift staircase to a platform. Cool breezes were flirting with his neck and whispering something in his ears, which could only be felt.

Those godforsaken baazigar with their stunt acts were supposed to be the main attraction, but there were also provocative dancers and farcical interludes to gather crowds between the stunts. They would have a gramophone playing from the bottom of that well, which was made up of planks of thin wooden strips joined together into slightly arched panels, which in turn were joined to make this temporary cylindrical structure, kind of like an overgrown above-ground swimming pool, around 30 feet wide and 18 feet high, called the Well of Death.

Those dancers who were dressed up as girls—Jani didn't know, maybe they were really real girls or maybe they were girly-boys dressed up like girls. But man did they put a dynamic show. Sure it was provocative, even vulgar, but they delivered it—dancing Punjabi movie songs, dressed up in tight clothes, tight like drums, with wider open and deep necks of the shirts, where part of their breasts bulged up tightly together, those soft looking humps of deep cleavage in between, like baby buttocks.

Some of them had painted a scar on one of their bulging breasts. And they danced to Punjabi songs like *Sayoni mera Mahi meray Bhaag Jagawan Aa Gaya*. And people stood up on a platform built around the circumference of the

---

[139] *Baazigar*: a daredevil, who supposedly wins at whatever game he plays.
[140] *Deviyoon* shrubs: *prosopis juliflora*.

structure and gazed down and started clapping at the first strain of music, like they already knew that those girls were going to start spinning their hips with the swing of the flute, with the beat of the drum.

The dancers would touch their foreheads every time the word 'luck' arose in the song. And sometimes they would hang to the central pole and just move their waists, holding the entire rest of their bodies almost still. And they would look up at the audience and lock their eye with several people at the same time, while hyperventilating profusely just to move their breasts violently up and down.

Everyone in the audience thought that those girls were looking at them alone, and those wicked girls, who had been there and done all that, would even wink their eyes at them, or stick their tongue out for them, and the people standing there, even though they were poor, couldn't stop themselves from throwing coins at them.

And after a while a cocky guy came in dressed in a cowboy-style imitation leather jacket with long fringe. He had Pompadour hairstyle, which had been carefully sculpted with oil-water mousse into a full halo of hair rising up from his neck and face, forming that stuffed circular cone on his forehead. As he took centre stage, they shut the vault-like door closed.

A few members of the audience rushed down behind the back of the well, hoping to find one of those dancers whom their heart had just crushed upon, and perhaps if the price was right and they were lucky, they might buy and sell love behind those thorny shrubs. But on top of the platform everybody was leaning down, holding the ledge of the wall, and the baazigar mounted a massively altered motorbike with no exhaust filter. And it made a sudden, ear-piercing noise when his apprentice pushed the bike forward.

With a roaring burst of *'bhadeeerrr-bhad, bhad-paat; paat'*, the baazigar made a half circle in the dirt and then he climbed onto a wooden frame that was awkwardly sloped at 45 degrees, and then in a split second he had climbed onto the belly of the straight wall of the pit.

The noise was deafening as the baazigar was jostling at different heights and doing different gestures, and the pit walls were shaking like waves and making crackling noises of their own, like someone who had gotten buried under the heaping weight but was still alive, or like those old weight-lifters who managed to lift up the weight and then try to hold it there by making sounds.

And in this chaotic atmosphere among unforeseen noises, sounds and voices, someone pushed him with a stick, and he did not paid any attention. After a few moments, he again felt a stick hit him in the back. His breath froze when he realised that it was someone's erect penis pushing against his back. Fear clenched him, and he felt an eerie quietness, like real-time was snoring and leaving everything to Planck time, in which he could feel the seconds tick by in minuscule increments over what felt like an eternity.

That fast bike was now operating in slow motion, and every time it passed him with that wavy jerk, the paedophile's erect penis would hit him, and his maternal uncle's voice echoed in his mind. He could only see a set of large hands next to his small hands holding edge of the railing, and that echoing voice was reminding him of his uncle's words about *londay-baz*,[141] saying that, "they hover over lonely young boys in places like the Well of Death, where it's easy because of all that commotion and noise." And then he remembered that his uncle also said, "Push that person and run towards a crowd."

And he was gathering all the courage that he might have, and the show was in it last minutes—the baazigar was back down on the ground. And then someone pushed that londay-baz's one arm aside to say, "Let's go before it gets all crowded on the staircase." It was Bhooro, his albino neighbour, who had no idea that he had just saved him.

His heart was shaking. He was holding one hand of his neighbour and was running back to home. He did not say anything to his neighbour. Bhooro meanwhile was still worried about whether Jani's mother had figured it out about the five rupees.

Life was going at her pace, and so was he. He was growing inches in weeks and having a scratchy voice because his vocal cords were retuning themselves and getting ready to sound masculine. But his heart was still in Jamshoro.

His uncles were all artists, but which kind? They belonged to that category of artists, from whom you could keep peeling off layer after layer and still see the same essence till the core. They were artists to bottom of their hearts. He loved them all, and why shouldn't he? They taught and trained him in the vocation of a mystic craft, which was how to value and relish love, such that the more you lose, the dearer you come to the beloved. And because of their intellectual trades, most of their friends were great minds too, among them the great contemporary fiction writers, poets, and playwrights of Sindhi literature.

---

[141] *Londay-baz*: homosexual pedophiles.

One day, he was visiting his grandmother, who lived with all of his aunts and uncles on the university campus in Jamshoro. That was a holy, mystic place for him, where he always believed that he could hear every flower talking to him and that the clouds let him write his name upon them. And every pebble and rock was immaculate, prayerfully holy, like one on which Abraham stood. Everything was perfect in that university town.

The streets, skies, faded yellow walls, walking trails that people had made out their convenience when crossing through the high thorny shrubs. Those shrubs, which were called deviyoon, could be six or seven feet in diameter and three feet tall, and they had beautiful thorns, cylindrical and long, like the well-trimmed spur of a fighter rooster. But he loved them all, even that lingering sweet pain that those thorns leave in your flesh for hours after being stuck by them. He visited that place whenever his parents allowed him, on a weekend every few months.

One day, he met Ali Baba there, a middle-aged man with henna-stained red hair, which appeared thin, like he is going to go bald soon, but he never did. He had very high cheekbones and a sharp-edged chin and the kind of caved-in wrinkled cheeks typical of chronic smokers, and hazelnut eyes, and a natural smile with sarcastic tint, but that was deceptive—it only seemed sarcastic. Whenever he saw him, Ali Baba would say to Jani, *"Hay dhan nehaar—hay dhan nehaar!"*—*Look at me, look at me!*

And then Ali Baba would talk to him like he was an adult, and he kind of liked that, though he had no idea that this middle-aged man with henna-stained hair was the George Bernard Shaw of Sindhi literature. Ali Baba had secured that place for himself even that long time ago, when Jani was just twelve or so.

They went on a long walk together on one Sunday. The university was closed, but they kept roaming the streets, walking up the hill to the library, and tall eucalyptuses were making noises, like they were having hot arguments with the leash-less winds of Jamshoro. Ali Baba was narrating to him the concept of his new television movie, in which, to his astonishment, Ali Baba said he would be playing the lead role of the hero.

He interrupted and said, "But I'm just a teenager!"

And Ali Baba replied carelessly, "My hero is a young kid too."

And he was completely taken in with this awesome idea of being the hero of a movie, while Ali Baba was narrating those tiny, bitsy, lilliputian details of his story. He was already signing autographs after success of that movie, and at the same time agreeing with Ali Baba by nodding his head in quick succession, while Ali Baba was telling him, "You are going to pull a chain to blow the whistling horn of a locomotive engine in a long-long-short-long blast pattern, to indicate that a fast-moving train is approaching—a train that you will have taken from the train yard—"

Jani was a little lost in the storyline, but moving along still, and he didn't want to interrupt Ali Baba, who was still going with the flow, "—where this hero's father is a locomotive engineer, and by spending whole lot of time with father he had learned and knows how to operate a steam locomotive. His father had taken him on test runs and even asked him to pull this lever and turn off that knob, so he knows about those three pressure metres, with dazzling needles, shaking like they're suffering from Parkinson's disease."

"And there's a long cranking lever right above that inferno, which he is going to push towards the right and steam will be released, and the locomotive is going to make its first long '*chuuu-co*' and move forward."

And then Ali Baba said, "we are going cut that shot and show the fast-rolling wheels of the engine throwing sparks off the grinding metal, like you had jacked up the steam in anger."

His eyes were locked on Ali Baba, and Ali Baba didn't have to ask him *"Hay dhan nehaar—hay dhan nehaar"* this time, because he was all consumed by Ali Baba's story telling. Ali Baba said, "And a feudal lord's son who always teases him is there in his father's convertible American car with tailfins"—Ali Baba did not remember the make or model, but that was okay—"and challenges him to have a race, in which that feudal son is going cruise in his father's American convertible and while the hero will race steam locomotive on tracks parallel to the highway."

And he got lost in the light pistachio-green colour of that convertible with the tailfin, which actually was a feature that Ali Baba had not mentioned, but he was assuming it on his own. And Ali Baba noticed the distraction, and said with a frown, *"hay dhan nehaar!"*

And Ali Baba continued, "This young skinny bare-shouldered boy in khaki shorts is going to lean out of the locomotive canopy and make gestures with arm, challenging his opponent to come on and drive faster, while the locomotive is exhaling tons of smoke and persistently heading towards the railway bridge, which we're going to show from the locomotive's perspective, like a big metallic rectangle frame, which normally isn't possible for people to see, with all the charred black smoke deposit of years at the top centre of the bridge."

"And the locomotive is going to enter the bridge, beating the convertible of the feudal lord's son. And the moment the engine reaches the bridge, we'll cut the shot and switch to the reverse perspective from a mounted camera on top of locomotive, showing that convertible car lost in heavy thick smoke."

And he asked Ali Baba, "How do you know all about the locomotive engine and its inside valves, knobs, and levers?"

And Ali Baba replied, "Because I'm that boy." As they walked back home, Ali Baba was still telling him about the climax of that television movie, in which he was supposed to play the lead. But somehow that movie got lost, or slipped from hands of time, or got ripped apart in those hot arguments between the tall eucalyptuses and the leash-less winds. But he always remained Ali Baba's pick for that lead role.

He was in his fifteenth year of life, at that point of divergence that happens in so many lives, where you turn around on a dime and willingly leave your childhood behind forever. And you move on, because you are tired of it by then, and you are eager to let the sweet sap of your youth to rise in maple of your body—and you find yourself in the spring of your life.

Chapter 8
Tiffany Bow

It was an October day and he was representing his school in a painting competition. But he saw her there. She was unbelievably beautiful, with a smile that spread and got lost in the dimples on her cheeks. She was trying to restrict her laughter by covering her face with her delicate hand, placing her fingers on her lips, but then that was triggering her eyes to smile with equal intensity. And with all that immense beauty, she didn't need that complex hairstyle, which looped sections of her around one another like a floral Tiffany bow. He knew her; she was the daughter of a renowned painter, one of his father's friends, and she herself was a promising young painter. He had already seen her earlier that day, but now he was hoping to talk to her.

First, he had to focus on the task at hand, which was to paint something on the theme of disability, because that particular competition was in accordance with an international day of recognition for disabled people. His own painting came from a very simple impressionistic thought, which was a beaten and wounded human figure in lemon yellow, surrounded by dark and dirty colours, with a brightness rising from the figure's head and glowing in the darkness.

It did not take him long to depict that on the art paper. When he was finished, he got up and reached out to her on the other side of the aisle to ask for a number 8 or 10 washing brush. It was just an excuse to talk to her, and even though he was whispering, a proctor showed up and told him to go back to his designated area or else he was going to be disqualified. So he apologised to the proctor, and told her that he'd return her brush once he was done—though he actually didn't need that brush, or any brush, because his painting was finished anyway.

He came back to his seat and waited for the proctor to announce closing time so that he could go back to her and return the brush. Up until that moment he was pondering that fragrance she was wearing, unable to describe to himself the value of that fragrance. It was like a pinch of mystic frankincense burning on the simmering heart of a restless ascetic monk.

Once the time was up, he approached her again to return brushes, after just dipping them in plain water and wiping them to give the impression that they been used. She took them back with a silent smile. He saw her flawless beauty again, and desire began budding in his heart. It was mid-afternoon, and he left that big auditorium, hoping to see her there again when he returned in the evening for the prize awarding ceremony. As he rode his bike back home, he never stopped thinking about her enchanting presence and her intoxicating fragrance, which had filled that entire auditorium and the entire atmosphere and beyond.

The prize ceremony was set for seven that evening, but he deliberately came back early to the auditorium, which was completely empty now. He could hear echoes of his own footsteps in there. He had come to catch any remaining bit of her fragrance, but there was none left. It was all gone; all he found there was the damp smell of an empty basketball court.

The influenza of romance had invaded and had reached farfetched corners of his being, and that illness of love was aching in his heart. He was at that ripe age of fifteen and ready to dive into the state of mind where vice of anxiety won't allow you to sit or stand or rest in any place; you become humble or edgy for no reason. Flames of love had engulfed him like a wildfire; he became a charred tree. And serenading bells were echoing in his mind.

He saw her once again later that evening, and once again she was emitting that warmth of glowing beauty, so much that mirrors would have been unable to reflect her image without breaking themselves into pieces. As she walked in, her long curly locks of hair were swinging and bouncing from their own weight. She wore an off-white dress with golden squares, as if Gustav Klimt had sat there and painted those golden squares on that dress just for her.

She occupied Jani's mind; rather he had given her his mind to occupy. She settled in his mind like a free-running measure of mercury, coating every nook and corner of it. Ceaseless thoughts of her kept rolling in his mind, like droplets of fresh dew rolls on the waxy surface of lotus leaves, never breaking their roundness. Her mere existence was over-filling the universe of his mind, like a rescue air cushion that opens in a small space. Like William Warfield holding onto the note on that word 'along', all the way at the end of 'Old Man River'. Like the echoes of Sohrab Fakeer's voice filling the predawn horizons, bouncing between notes and then holding a single note with *O-Rano-Rano-O-Rano*.

Rano was a folklore hero synonymous with pulsating, throbbing love, and his anguish and agony was elevated to heights of ecstasy. So, despite his dyslexia, and his being last in everything, and his feeling of nothingness, his young and cajoled heart wanted to be close to her, and he wanted to give her that pulsating, throbbing heart of his for keeps, which was oozing with nothing but *Rano-O-Rano*.

After that October evening, he found someone in his school who lived in the same colony where she lived, in a stand-alone bungalow under the shadow of one of the four minarets of Hyderabad Eid-Gah. And he would go there every almost every evening to visit that friend that he had just made out of thin air, who just happened to be her neighbour.

A whirlwind winter was approaching, where passion-mania-obsession seemed to him like his first name. And the poetry of songs that he had never understood before started revealing itself to him on its own, and his fanciful factory of his own mind also started conjoining words together into phrases.

Ameer was the name of that classmate of his, whose home was right across from hers. There were two trees there, a gulmohar and an amaltas.[142] Amaltas are like weeping willows, but their flowers are a burning bright yellow when they bloom, which happens in the sizzling heat of July. They too crave for monsoon rains to come, and when they do come and soak those bunches of hanging flowers, they swing in the amaltas's branches like chimes with no sound.

Between their homes, he used to stand in the shade of that Gulmohar tree, looking at her home, not even noticing that he was stepping on the achingly beautiful flaming red flowers that the Gulmohar had let fall to the ground. Ameer had told him that the last window belonged to her room's, so he would gaze at that tightly-shut milky glass window for as long as he could, presuming that she was in there.

Sometimes, when a light was turned on inside, the milky glass would emit an ivory white glow, which gave giggles to his heart. Anyone in her home could have turned on that light, but he always assumed unquestioningly that it was she and only she who turned that light on.

My heart is burning, my heart is an open book, and my heart is filled with you. Then he thought about his statement, which was a bunch of clichés like regular white socks with grey toes.

---

[142] Gulmohar: *Delonix regia*. Amaltas: *Cassia fistula*.

"Why don't you just tell her that you like her, that you love her?" His heart asked him.

And Jani replied to his own heart, "Isn't that too generic?"

And his heart responded in a flash, "Love is generic. Everyone does it, and everyone thinks that their love is different from others. But I think it's the same, like the sky. Billions of people see it for themselves, but it is always pretty much the same generic blue sky."

Chapter 9
A Mass Panic of Thoughts

He was crossing that lonely, bridge-like road. It was a thin asphalt-paved string, built on a stagnant and waterlogged swamp, with bloated dead fish lying on both of its salty banks. He looked eastward at the smoke-exhaling chimney of the cement factory. A desire, a hazy stampede, a mass panic of thoughts overtook him. And his heart whispered in his ears, be that, as it may…and so it began.

A couplet started taking shape in the nebula of his mind. By the time he had crossed that thin stretch of road past the foul-smelling and translucently pinkish swamp and had begun climbing up *Umeedan-bharyo* Incline*, that couplet had assumed its shape, and he had become a poet.

He was young, deeply in love, making paintings and writing poems and vertiginously trying everything that he was told not to do: drinking moonshine with the street name 'Bum-bat' (a mispronunciation of the word Bombard), smoking cigarettes, and hanging around with hotheaded, silly boys at odd hours.

But Hyderabad was all heart then, motherly and tolerant. Its evenings like beautiful assassins, from whose hands you begged to be killed. He would go with those hotheaded friends in the early morning hours to a taboo place called Khadra Gali,[143] which was tucked away in a back alley very close to Hyderabad's old market tower. They would go to a vintage teashop there, a clamorous place that somehow managed to harness its chaotic noises into a kind of orchestration. Jani could occasionally hear the sweet sound of Lata Mangeshkar's voice singing, "*lag ja galay…hum…hum-mum…*" and falling into a luxurious humming before

---

[143] *Khadra Gali:* 'Transgenders' Lane'.**Umeedan bharyo Incline:* Umeedan bharyo incline, is a steep curved uphill road circumventing, rather carefully finding its way around a shrine of a saint called '*Umeedan bharyo*'. Which literally means 'wish-bringer from Ether'.

returning to finish the Raja Mehdi Ali Khan's intoxicating couplet, then humming again.

But it was Madan Mohan who had made that song unbearably sweet, like he had chopped and diced and then minced his heart to fill those scores, which sounded soothing even at a high volume. That place was flooded with blindingly bright light streaming from small hanging stainless steel triangular lamps, enveloped in a purplish-blue-grey metallic smoke of all sorts, cigarettes, burning flash of tikka on charcoal embers and charred corpses of those eternally crazy, light-loving moths.

All the transgenders would gather there, dressed up in women's clothes in shocking colours of tight cheap polyester. They would clap their hands and shamelessly calling out vulgarities. *"Tujhe khol ka dekhaoon kiya chiknay?"—Should I spread for you, you sparklingly hot, sweet boy?*—as they pointed first toward their groin and then motioned with the same hand to whoever was looking at them for a little longer.

Jani would sit with his feet up on those long wooden benches, which were situated in an unlikely but somehow workable position over the thin walls of a fast-moving open sewer channel. There he sips that gooey tea that was so sweet that it almost tasted bitter, from those dirty chipped and cracked white rough china cups.

But the conversation in that company was mainly about violence, and violence meant fist fighting or beating someone with a field hockey stick or whipping them with a bicycle chain. And the second topic of conversation was a more hidden one; they would bring you in little later once you become a trust worthy. And that topic was the heart-throbbingly pure, virginally holy love of one of those moonshine drinkers for his neighbour's daughter. That part of the conversation was spoken in whispers, focusing on how to let her know that this guy with his scarred face, calloused knuckles, and tobacco-stained teeth also carried swinging daisies in his heart for her.

He was managing his life in completely separate compartments within his mind. His urban street friends were in one slot, and then his class fellows who were ethnically diverse in another, and in another were his literary friends, who were purely Sindhi and mostly staunch believers in non-violence. And he was switching between these lines like a vintage telephone operator switching male and female jacks to connect people. His street friends had no idea who Archie was, or that, 'Total Eclipse of the Heart' was sung by Bonnie Tyler.

Whereas his class fellows had not tasted paan[144] with bitter chewing tobacco, much less the head-spinning combination of ingredients in 'Chaayso-number-Raja-jani-Zafrani', nor did they know how to ask for nihari gravy twice from a grumpy waiter at a roadside eatery. And neither of those two groups had any idea that he also mingled with poets, intellectuals, and writers, who talk about Nikolai Gogol and transcendental aesthetics and Indian parallel cinema, dropping names like Satyajit Ray and Shyam Benegal as if they knew them personally.

Sometimes those worn-out Sindhi intellectuals would talk about unexplainable theories and philosophical approaches which regarded "the existence of the individual as a uniquely lonely experience in a hostile and indefinite universe." And they would regard human existence itself as inexplicable, stressing freedom of choice and responsibility for the consequences of one's actions. And then some of those intellectuals would curse God, too.

Jani was a very bad student in school, but it wasn't for lack of curiosity. At this fertile age of 15, he met a Darvaish geologist who opened limitless doors of information for him. That geologist was an amateur astrologist too, who had once pointed his finger at a star and told him, "That star—you see?—is probably not there! It has probably died or destroyed itself. But its light is still coming, because that light had to cover the whole distance between you and that star." And for the first time he felt personally related to a star, to a breath-taking object from those alluring night skies, to a cosmic being.

The geologist was the neighbour of one of his class fellows, a class fellow who was filthy rich. His father worked for a government department that built bridges, and he used to take bribes, like everyone else. That was the culture then: opportunistic people were vultures, waiting for you to die. That culture is gone now. Now they eat you alive.

When he told his friends from school that he had met this beautiful girl at the painting competition, and that she had spoken to him and now he was pursuing her, a small race started, like "It's a mad-mad-mad-mad world." Behind his back all three of his close friends from school secretly jumped into the same pursuit.

The class fellow who was the Darvaish-geologist's neighbour wanted to have a better grip on the situation by eliminating Jani first. So, he asked his chauffeur to run Jani over with his father's official truck. The chauffeur, who had been with his father for ages, such that he was essentially a family member and had raised

---

[144] *Paan*: a preparation of betel leaf with areca nut and sometimes also with tobacco, chewed for its stimulant and psychoactive effects.

this boy from his birth, replied, "I'm going slap you so hard that my finger impressions will stay on your face for days."

So then this particular classmate turned to his neighbour, the Darvaish-geologist, and asked him to eliminate Jani. Instead of dismissing his naivety outright, Darvaish-geologist showed his interest and wanted to see the person he was supposed to run over. That's how Jani met Darvaish-geologist for the first time.

Chapter 10
Darvaish-Geologist

Darvaish-geologist was a man of average height, with a broad forehead and unmanageable, silky hair. He seemed to have gained fountains of knowledge by enduring gruelling times in his life. They became friends, and Jani started spending most of his after-school time with Darvaish-geologist, who was like someone pouring water on chalk, giving cognition to this dehydrated mind, which was starved for knowledge. That knowledge was coming from all four corners of knowing, from Kalidasa Shakuntala, to Alpha Centauri, to lines like:

he committed suicide,
by jumping off of the Moon

In Gulzar's prose poetry. And the moment when Neruda blesses his hung clothes:

I wonder
if one day
a bullet
from the enemy
will leave you stained with my blood
and then
you will die with me

And if that was not enough, Darvaish-geologist use to shock his mind by saying that a straight line never existed, there was no such thing as a straight line—we just can't see its curve, where it bends. And this unbelievably beautiful knowledge was driving him out of his mind, but he loved it. Darvaish-geologist also had an uncle who was called '*Doodh-patti*'.[145] He had a real name of course, but they called him Doodh-patti because once he made a single cup of tea out of a quart of milk, by boiling it and stirring it for hours.

Doodh-patti was a retired clerk in the revenue department, but his passions were classical music and nationalism. He would come from Shikarpur to see Darvaish-geologist's mother every now and then. Doodh-patti was gaunt and had a thin grey film of oil and water soaked hair plastered on his head.

And whenever Doodh-patti was in a good mood, he would start talking about Hindustani Shastriya Sangeet,[146] picking any raga and then verbally dismantling that raga, whereby he would examine the components of virtually every single note and reassemble it all back again. Doodh-patti once told him that all seven pure notes have their own gods and a point of origin, a chakra, in the human body.

Originally, every note was the sound of a different animal, like the note 'sa',[147] whose full name was Shadja, was a peacock sound according to Doodh-patti. Doodh-patti went on and defined all the different notes for him, but he got so lost in note 'sa' that he didn't pay attention to the detailed description of the remaining six notes.

Nationalism was Doodh-patti's other passion. He loved his people, his literature, his land, and the ways his forefathers had lived for thousands of years. He was the kind of patriot one who identifies with a culture. He would recite a litany of resources of Sindh being abused by others, and then illogically jump to radical solutions about them. But his similes were always poetic, and nothing was black or white, everything lay somewhere in between taking its first breath and giving its last.

But it was not Doodh-patti alone who wanted to ignite his anger for not getting his rightful share. Rather, there were millions of Sindhis who shared Doodh-patti's thoughts. Above all, three of his uncles were staunch supporters of Sindhi radical nationalism.

One of those uncles told him once, while stretching his arm towards the setting sun and opening all of his fingers, as if to grip onto the sun like a dial,

---

[145] *Doodh-patti*: tea with milk.
[146] *Hindustani Shastriya Sangeet*: classical music of North India, as distinguished from the classical music of the south, which is Carnatic music.
[147] *The note 'sa'*: in the Indian classical scale, the notes have the names sa-re-ga-ma-pa-dha-ni, equivalent to the Western solfège syllables do-re-mi-fa-sol-la-ti.

that he could then move his hand slowly clockwise and set the sun himself. And the same could be done counter-clockwise at predawn to make sun rise. But Jani kept thinking to himself, *if I move dial the other way around, would it stop sun from setting or rising?* But he didn't ask his uncle that question, instinctively thinking that his uncle might not have its answer. Instead, he kept slowly moving his fingers clockwise until had sun had sunk all the way down below the horizon.

"Time is a marvel. It's a river whose two banks are internally separated—maybe that is a cliché. And there are bridges of all different kinds over this river, weak and strong, big and small, beautiful and hideous, made up of ice or even of crumbling sand. But they all bring those disparate banks together! It's stale and tasteless, but that's what time is," said one of his art teachers.

That complex statement soared above Jani's head like a high-flying jet way up in deep blue skies, leaving a streaky trail of white cloud. He could only say to himself, "Time is like a person?" But it didn't bother Jani a bit; he just dumped all that knotted gibberish into one of his memories slots to untangle some day in the future.

Years back that same teacher had been his father's teacher too, but after retiring from that job, just to make his ends meet he had started working at Jani's school on contract. And instead of training art teachers, now he was teaching arts and crafts to kids in sixth to eighth grade. His name was A.K.B Shaikh, but everybody called him Shaikh Sahib. He seemed a lost man, almost a walking skeleton, with caved-in cheeks, sunken eye sockets, and grey hair as old as he was, combed back without any fuss, lying on his scalp all day long, the way he set them in the morning.

Shaikh Sahib always wore a double-breasted suit, even in Hyderabad's blistering May heat. Shaikh Sahib was like his grandfather. Jani didn't have any apparent skills, other than drawing things differently from how others did, so he ended up in Shaikh Sahib's art room a lot. Shaikh Sahib was also one of those crucial people during that stage in his life who had treated him as an adult, such as asking him to take a seat in his office and then offering him tea.

In one such meeting, Shaikh Sahib started talking about someone who had frozen to death. Shaikh Sahib said, "He got angry, and left the comfort of his palatial mansion on his estate, and kept roaming on trains, a journey to death. He got off at a country train station, and kept sitting on a bench there all night long, at that remote Russian railway station, which later was only known as the place where he died."

As Shaikh Sahib was telling him this story, Jani was continuously watching a glass paperweight that was sitting on Shaikh Sahib's office table, which looked like a crystal ball but with air bubbles trapped inside, resembling a shower of tiny flowers. Then Shaikh sahib asked him, "Do you know who I'm talking about?"

"No, I have no idea sir," he admitted in a resigned tone.

Shaikh Sahib said, "You will," without revealing who it was. And Jani wanted to know who had died that lonely death, but he didn't ask. Shaikh Sahib simply started sipping his tea again. Shaikh Sahib's office was a long cylindrical room with an odd, column-like window at each end, and Shaikh Sahib's lackey would open both of those windows each day. Jani kept looking at the Scarlett-O'Hara-red bougainvillea flowers peeking their heads in through the window that was right behind Shaikh Sahib's shoulders. Those red bougainvilleas looked like they wanted to see him.

Chapter 11
Wrinkled Photograph of Tolstoy on the Wall

Years after that day, he went with his uncle Punnu to Karachi. He was his father's younger brother, but only ten years older than Jani. Punnu was opinionated and abrasive and spoke with a cutthroat rawness, that joyful literary arrogance, like young bridegrooms who have yet to spend their wedding night.

Punnu was already a short story writer and budding playwright working in television drama. He was in his twenties, but he had already started to make his mark on modern Sindhi fiction by then. He had a sharp-edged style, like those red and yellow flaming stickers that rebel bikers place on the jet-black tanks of their custom-made Harleys.

Punnu took him to visit one of his writer friends who lived in a small apartment that had two rooms and one bathroom, a kitchen, and an ill-shaped space in between called a hall. Those apartments were packed one on the top of another like a honeycomb hive. Punnu could find the key to the apartment two flights of stairs up, hidden in a crack in the wall.

Punnu opened the front door. It was dark inside, though it was the middle of the day. They went into the bedroom and slashed open some curtains, allowing a weak brightness to crawl in like a hunched old man, because even behind that curtained window there were other buildings dividing the light. It was just enough light to make the dust visible on the curtains.

The walls of that room had once probably been painted some kind of green, which had by now turned into slimy wet algae colour. In that room, there was a twin bed, high above twin bed there was a cockloft, stacked with books, piled haphazardly on top of each other.

Some of those books had tattered edges and looked dog-tired, like they had been roughed up, and others had cracked spines, like they had been thoroughly interrogated. It looked like whoever had gone through those books had squeezed as much out of them as he could.

On one of the walls there was a wrinkled photograph, which had tried hard to be straightened, but once wrinkles like that set in they don't go anywhere. That picture was stuck to the wall with four small pieces of black electric tape. It was a portrait of a sad-looking old man with a long white beard, gazing resentfully to his side.

Punnu told him, "That's Leo Tolstoy." Jani had never seen a picture of Tolstoy before, though he had heard the name a lot, especially his *War and Peace*. Many of those things he had heard about Tolstoy were spurious factoids, like how he had been nominated 13 times for a Nobel Prize but never won, and that he tried hard but failed to get a bachelor's degree.

But despite those confusions, Tolstoy was still Tolstoy in his mind, and the moment Punnu told him this photo was of Tolstoy, the room was transformed into something beautiful in his mind. Those slimy dark green walls started glowing like flawless turquoises. The lack of light didn't matter anymore, and the piles of exhausted books with broken spines now seemed to have the faces of jolly drunks. Those dirty curtains didn't change a bit and just remained dirty, but he was able to ignore them.

After a few hours, Punnu's friend came home, a short middle-aged man with Beethoven-like hair, and a set of huge beautiful eyes like a bull's, and a handful of drooping moustaches. After looking at Punnu, he burst out with one of his signature laughs in his bass voice, with unusually long pauses in between the laughs, making them almost sound artificial. Loud Laughter also had a name, a common name like anybody else. But Jani chose to remember him as Loud Laughter.

It was the early 80s, and ideas were getting bigger. Michael Jackson was doing his moonwalk dance—that was one of the things that Jani would talk about with his non-literary friends. But here in this company there was no room for moonwalk chat. Punnu and his writer friends would talk instead about the effects of Indian parallel cinema or the revival of street theatre, and used to take name of some Hashmi guy, a playwright cum director cum communist who had revolutionised theatre on streets of Calcutta.

Where his actors perform as a power loom by joining hands and moving to and from, while doing that in a discreet way, they take off clothes of another actor who acts as a common labourer or machine operator, in their intellectual discussions, while Jani listened in.

Loud Laughter was a reserved man, consumed with thoughts. Several ideas were always running in his mind at the same time, like he had a dual core processor. Loud Laughter didn't have a whole lot of friends—or at least, that's what Jani thought, but again he could be wrong. Loud Laughter was doing many things to support himself, to pull the whole bandwagon of his life, which included a younger brother whom he had raised as his own son, an old retired father, and a widow aunt back home.

That back home of his was a serene and heavenly place, tucked in the middle of the guava orchards of Larkano. In summer, when winds would blow from the orchards to the village, that sweet thick guava fragrance would fill the air, so much so that one could almost see that sweet smell in the air like ticker tape confetti in Broadway victory parades.

He was writing short stories just to invigorate his aesthetics and was getting no money for it. He was also writing television dramas, which had the advantage of making him a celebrity of sorts, and more importantly he was getting paid for that work. But he wrote them so rarely that he had to keep other jobs as well, including some that he hated. He worked as an assistant to a lawyer, and he also taught the Sindhi language to inner city kids, who were least interested in learning it.

And Loud Laughter preferred teaching over being a lawyer's assistant—but not because it was a noble profession, or because he was teaching his native language to inner city kids who otherwise wouldn't know the language of that land where they lived. No, those were not the reasons. Loud Laughter liked teaching because it gave him chance to be in close proximity of some female teachers, and some of those female teachers got really close to him. And that wrinkled photograph of Tolstoy on the wall of Loud Laughter's room bare witness a whole lot.

Chapter 12
A Writer Who Rode to Rob a Train

Once, after they had become friends, Jani asked Loud Laughter, "How did you end up in this city?"

Loud Laughter looked back and laughed, leaving such a generous smile on his face that his big moustaches had to part to accommodate it. And he said, "I was a fugitive, running away from being prosecuted."

"Why? What had you done?" Jani asked with unabashed curiosity.

"I robbed a train!" He said, and then he laughed his signature bouts of solo laughter, which had a beginning, a body and an echoing conclusion. Then he said, "It was during the language riots of 1972. I was a freshman at Larkano College. We were getting news only by word of mouth that native Sindhi in the cities were being robbed and murdered by Muhajirs."

"Why just word of mouth?" Jani asked.

"Because almost all the main newspapers were in Urdu. A few were in English. And of course, those Urdu newspapers were owned by people who migrated from India. So they were biased, and they portrayed Sindhi people as savages who were snatching the rights of the Muhajirs."

"And were we snatching their rights?"

"No—we were just asking for ours!" Loud Laughter said.

"So what were we Sindhis doing for that?" Jani asked, with a hint of his own cocky nationalism.

"I don't know! We were voiceless against the people who controlled all printed media. But still, if I could go back, I would not have gotten on that train."

Loud Laughter's face was drained by now, not a shred of happiness left, and his big eyes were looking even bigger and deserted. One could see strands of brown and pale mustard threads in the now expanded pupils of his deep-set eyes. Loud Laughter shook his head, like he wanted to tell his own conscience, *leave me alone.*

Then he spoke again. "In those days, Ghulam Shah was an office-bearer of the Jeay Sindh[148] chapter at Larkano College and I was sympathetic to that movement. One day, Ghulam Shah, came to me in college, and said, we should set the score even. And I just went with that thought. Ghulam Shah said, 'We'll take revenge for the blood of our innocent fellow Sindhis against these *Mackar'a!*'"[149]

Loud Laughter paused, and then went on, "Ghulam Shah's words were so pleasing to my ears that I answered with boiling rage, '*yes, we should!*'"

Then Ghulam Shah said, "Just the two of us are not enough. Could you get someone else that you trust?"

"How are we going to do that?" I asked.

He said, "I'll let you know—you just find at least one more person."

"So I turned to Malak'a," said Loud Laughter. Malak'a and Loud Laughter were friends, and not just any kind of friends; rather they were inseparable, complexly entangled in each other like two pubic hairs, curled into each other impossible to separate. Malak'a and Loud Laughter had grown up together in that same village which was next to a canal and surrounded by guava orchards. Malak'a had dropped out of high school and never gone back, because he got married at a young age. In fact, Malak'a became a father at fifteen.

But his quest to learn on his own brought him leaps ahead, and he would become a writer, too, later on.

Loud Laughter said, "I asked Malak'a and he just replied, 'I'm in.' Then we both went to Ghulam Shah's room in hostel, and Ghulam Shah revealed his plan. He said, 'There is a train that goes to Quetta daily, carrying Mackar'a from Karachi. It briefly stops at Larkano, and then it won't stop for another two hours. We'll board that train tomorrow night, and once it leaves city limits, we'll do it."

Loud laughter said, "Me and Malak'a were looking at Ghulam Shah and trying to listen not only with our ears and eyes but with every part of our bodies. We were so charged up and eager that tomorrow felt like an eternity away. But finally the next evening came. It was winter. I remember very clearly, because all three of us were covered up completely, including our faces, with long grey

---

[148] *Jeay Sindh:* a student nationalist group formed by the Sindhi intellectual G. M. Syed, with the intention for Sindh to secede from Pakistan to be its own nation, Sindhudesh.

[149] *Mackar'a*: literary translation is swarming locusts. But is a bias racial slur, used by indigenous Sindhi's for people who migrated from different parts of India to Sindh after 1947.

shawls, like the other common people. We were waiting in a dark portion of platform. Ghulam Shah brought us two very hard farmer's walking sticks, shoulder-high. And he had a *tamancho*,[150] too."

"The train came, and there was a little commotion as people got off at Larkano, and a few boarded, too. But Ghulam Shah told us to wait in the dark, so we kept waiting till train started to jolt. And then we thought we might be hallucinating, and maybe it wasn't moving at all. But yes, it was slowly, slowly moving forward. And Ghulam Shah said, 'Wait—let her pick up some speed, and then we'll get into the last cars.'"

"The train started gaining speed, and it seemed like we'd miss it. And Ghulam Shah started running towards it, and we followed, all of us managed to get into one of its third-class cars. My heart was about to wet my pants! I had never been in that situation before. Anger was gusting like crazy in our minds, so much that we couldn't even hear that thin voice of our hearts, asking us not to do something that our hearts thought was wrong. But we said, damn our hearts! The train had left city of Larkano, and by then there was only darkness outside."

Loud Laughter paused and reluctantly said, "and kind of inside too. Malak'a couldn't hold it in anymore, and yelled out, *bhala tunhunjee runa khay*![151] And Malak'a, swung his fat farmer's walking stick, which made dull cracking sounds as it hit people's limbs. And I followed Malak'a, like a knee-jerk reflex. We were hitting people mercilessly, and they were crying and begging and apologising, without ever having done anything wrong. *'Maf kardo Bhaiya! howa kiya?'* Some were saying. *'O-bahi, O-bahi, Khuda kay leya.'"—Forgive me please, brother. O, brother, God have mercy.*

"Malak'a was beating them and shouting curse words," said Loud Laughter. "And Malak'a's curses words were falling on my ears, like the cheers of a soccer coach to his players' ears. And we kept beating their heads like drum, pummelling them. I saw Malak'a's face—it was red like raw flesh. And my own face was burning, and my ears were hot like a toast right out of a toaster."

"There were also women and children in there, but we were sparing them, leaving them alone."

Loud Laughter took a pause and then said with emphasis, "We, means me and Malak'a. All of sudden I heard the cries of a woman, and then children. I

---

[150] *Tamancho*: a homemade breech-loading single shot handgun.

[151] *Bhala tunhunjee runa khay:* literally, 'watch out for your woman'—a curse phrase of warning in Sindhi.

looked back and saw that Ghulam Shah had snatched an earring from a little girl's ear. She was crying in pain and fear, and her ear was bleeding. And an older woman, probably her mother, dropped to Ghulam Shah's feet. But then she quickly sat back on her seat, covering her another teenage daughter behind her and trying to take the remaining gold earring from the younger daughter's other ear, in a frenzy. She kept repeating, *'Sab lay lo Bhaiya, sab lay lo.'*"—*Take it all, brother, take it all.* "And then Ghulam Shah roared, *'Phuryoon!'*"—*Let's rob them.*

"Before this, Malak'a and I hadn't realised that that robbery was the real objective." And here Loud Laughter's voice cracked, but he cleared his throat like it was just an intrusion of phlegm. He was a proud man, one of those who wouldn't cry even if the sky fell. He continued, "People sitting there start handing over their valuables to us, watches, gold rings, cash. It was so much that we couldn't even carry it.

"So Ghulam Shah spread his shawl and made a bundle out of it and tied it. Then he pulled a red chain hanging from the ceiling somewhere in the middle of the car. Nothing happened at first—the train kept going at full speed. But after a minute there was a huge jerk, like the train driver had slammed on brakes. Ghulam Shah jumped out, and we followed, and then ran for miles in the dark, until we reached the rail station in Mahota."

Loud Laughter said, "we boarded that train as revolutionaries, but we got off the train as thieves." Then he stopped. Probably, there was nothing else for him to say. His own confession had ripped his face to shreds.

Jani told Loud Laughter, "Hey! 'a writer who rode to rob a train' isn't a poetic phrase!"

Chapter 13
A Romantic Account of Death

It was during the part of his youth, which everyone has, when everything looks easy and anything is possible and post-puberty bombardments of hormones are ready to push you off the cliff in that go-getter's mode, that Jani got interested in Che Guevara. Hey, the flu of revolution infects everybody at some time or other in life, and Jani was not immune to it. And it was Che Guevara who enticed him, especially the way he died in Bolivia, fighting his enemy till his last breath, facing them head on till the very end, with his wide open and unapologetic dark puppy eyes, which, they say, were still glittering even after Che was killed.

Of course, his image of Guevara's death was comprised of what local Sindhi comrades had told him, which was probably 5% factual and 95% a romantic account of death, tied up in sheer Sindhi leftist love for Che. In this account, an asthmatic, lonely Guevara was fighting with the thousands of Bolivian soldiers who had besieged him, and the fatally wounded Guevara kept on fighting.

And in the end, Guevara was resting his back against a generous trunk or broad chest of a tree, probably a shaded cedar, one of those laurel-like cedar trees of Bolivia. And Guevara held his head high, even though his chest was turned into a punched-hole strainer by the multiple bullet rounds. Some of the tips of those bullets had penetrated into the cedar's trunk, while other parts of those bullets were still lodged in Che's body.

Other than that, Che was an asthmatic, the rest of the story fell into the category of the 95% sheer love of the Sindhi comrades for Che. But no one cared, because it was *revolution*, the kind that ends by choking and drowning in your own crimson colours of bloody romance for revolution itself.

In Sindh, revolution was viral, and it only had a romantic part, without any downside. And he was swamped with that electric, beautifully arresting thought, like the first time in early adolescence when you fearfully deny the existence of a deathless and eternal god—and in result, nothing happens. You walk away unscathed—actually, feeling good. And this fetish of revolution could win you a kind of immortality, like your name being tattooed on the chest of time with a heart-shaped halo, wrapped in a ribbon.

He started with little things, like chalking anti-government slogans on the boundary walls of government buildings. It was kind of graffiti, but then not really, because graffiti is a form of art, whereas these chalkings were just a mode of communication. They were outcries of the people that the newspapers had refused to publish, so the people, in their desperation, had to print their own headlines on the city walls.

And then he started attending secretive late-night meetings for the select few hardy ones among them who had made their mark by taking bigger risks, like chalking the demands for a separate state on walls of courthouses, or pasting posters on the walls of the police superintendent's office.

And it was in these selective meetings that certain nationalist leaders who had disappeared underground would reappear to whisper fiery speeches. There was one particularly spellbinding orator among those nationalist leaders, a clean-shaven dark-skinned man with talking eyes and a deep and dark booming voice so crisp that you could practically see its edges. He was known as a shepherd of narrative prose. He used to be a Pesh-Imam with a long traditional beard who had led Muslim prayer congregations five times a day.

But they say he had a change of heart and initially got interested in Maulana Abul Kalam Azad, who himself was an unconventionally liberal orthodox of his times. So Maulana Azad bugged Pesh-Imam's head for a bit, but then he started mingling with Sindhi fiction writers, who were a notorious crowd, as almost all of them were communist and some of them atheist.

And Pesh-Imam, a believer, had a head-on collision with reason. His new comrades filled his mind with the noisy crickets of reason and logic, who kept crying freedom in his head all the time. And that Pesh-Imam became leader of a nationalist movement.

When Jani saw him in that meeting, Pesh-Imam had already become chairman of the party. He was saying, "Close to 44 million people without a leader—and the irony is that all the leaders we have ever had in Sindh were revolutionaries who ended up killed by the oppressors—all the way back to Rahib!"

Rahib is what the King Priest of Mohen-jo-Daro was called locally here: he is that ancient palm-sized bust statuette of a bald guy with a bearded face eyes peacefully closed, showing an utter calmness. But he had been assassinated! Of course, it would have been some five thousand years ago, so this was nothing more than a poker bluff, but hey, anything goes in politics and revolution.

Pesh-Imam went on, "Sindhis are in a deep pit. They have wallowed in this social dilemma for the last several thousand years—and in the last thirty-five years many Sindhis themselves have been complicit in the mutation and debasement of their own culture at the hands of the Muhajirs."

Pesh-Imam was a fire-spitting orator. His initial training had been to sell God, but now he sold revolution. And he was always scanning the meeting attendees with his eyes while his words were coming out of his mouth like gushes of water out of a broken fire hydrant.

He was saying, *"Ehay dhariya panhageer"*—these alien refugees—"they settled in urban Sindh but made no attempt to adopt anything belonging to Sindh or Sindhis. Instead they displayed their extreme distaste and chose to keep themselves uncontaminated from Sindhi culture.

"Muhajir politicians go on television news networks and say that Sindhis are savage people and that they Muhajirs are bringing culture and civility to them, like culture and civility is a readymade canned food that they picked up from the shelf of a utility store and are now offering to deprived Sindhis as a gift—who then are expected to open the can of this generous gift and gulp all that ready-made culture and civility down with gratitude."

Pesh-Imam was declaiming his message like there was no tomorrow. "Some Sindhi intellectuals have crawled out of their pits and tried to acclimatise with the urban intellectuals, but time and time again these Sindhi thinkers find themselves alone, on any small or big issue associated with Sindh or Sindhis. The Muhajirs always step aside precisely when their help would be most needed, which is tantamount to going against the Sindhi cause."

And the things Pesh-Imam was saying were kind of making sense to Jani, and everyone there was agreeing with him, which added to the sense that he was convincing. Most of the people gathered there were underprivileged and felt that they were deprived, which probably they were.

Plus, Jani had his own grudges, and personal venom is so sweet, the kind that you nurture inside, somewhere tucked very carefully in your heart. The seeds of unrest that Aunt-grandmother had sown in his mind were not any ordinary seeds—these were Jack's beanstalk seeds, which kept growing in his mind, reaching high into the heavens of Pesh-Imam's hatred and onward from there.

"For decades these urban 'civilised people' have been reshaping Sindh in their own terms, and using words that I would expect to hear from my doctor rather than my neighbour. Whenever I hear the phrase 'interior Sindh,' I always think, 'then where is posterior Sindh?' Are we a nation or a specimen being dissected on a table? And now, these Muhajirs still haven't made any effort to blend in with the local culture and community."

And then Pesh-Imam made the obvious comparison of the Sindhi-Muhajir problem with the Israel-Palestine conflict, and he also compared Sindhis to the Native Americans who had been forced to live on a small reservation while their whole wide land was taken over by colonial Europeans. Pesh-Imam did say all that.

Life kept moving forward like she always does, and so did he, enjoying these newly discovered vernal and youngish years of his life. He kept mingling with those nationalists. But Sindhi nationalism was like combustion engine, which makes lot of noise, takes too much energy and produces too little motion. Plus anyone could attend those meetings no question asked, and anyone could leave that movement at any time with no penalty; there were no strict oath of allegiance.

That made Sindhi resistance movement quite liberal, or virtually fictitious—at least that's what Jani felt. Because that was the time Jani became aware of Bobby Sands, who died for his principles. And he also learned from his uncle Punnu about one Panagoulis, who was a poet but was known for the torture that he endured in detention for a failed attempt to assassinate a dictator.

In addition, there was a barrage of resistance moments in surrounding countries, movements with long names that were usually called by abbreviations like LTTE or GNLF or CPI(ML), and these were all spinning like colourful tops in Jani's mind. All those long names like Communist Party of India (Marxist-Leninist) Liberation—that name itself carried everything but the kitchen sink.

And he learned about stubborn creative people like Safdar Hashmi, who came up with a street play protesting against corporate greed. Hashmi's characters sat on the ground and joined their hands and feet together and moved their limbs in a cyclic motion, giving the impression of a machine producing something. But in fact those actors would take off each other's clothes and strip one another bare naked, while constantly moving their hands and feet in that cyclic motion.

And at the same time, he was running along the parallel track with the Sindhi separatists, whom the government called anarchists. And he was enjoying that ride, listening to the loud claims of those self-proclaimed rebels, watching their disobedience, hearing them decry their oppressors. Jani was like those small town kids who run alongside military convoys, cheering them on just for fun, without any knowledge of what they had done, or where they were heading. To him, they were liberators.

Chapter 14
Magnificent Ray of Divine Truth

He was a soul-trotter, sightseeing inside his own life, travelling widely around his surroundings. He loved poetry, he loved painting; in fact, he loved the whole packaged deal of cognitive activities, as well as the sheen of glittering praise in which that package is wrapped.

He too wanted to say something, but there was rumpus in the creative arena of Sindh and every seat was taken. He had to come up with something new, something transcendent, a kind of double-entendre to catch their ears. And he was searching for that idea, like those poor children who scavenge trash all day in the hope of finding something of value. There he came across resistance, whenever he had thought he found something. It always turned out that it wasn't actually a new gadget, but hey! Ayaz, Neruda, Faiz have already been fiddled with it.

And in this garbage dump of life he was picking through so many hated relics of his childhood, where he had been torn between the two halves of his family. And stumbling over this debris always reignited his own anger, and he kept wondering how the Muhajirs had managed to take control of everything, and he tried to rationalise, and then he would circle himself back into silence.

He was arguing within himself, thinking *I'm a racist!*—but at the same time, *surely it is a moral imperative to work for the legal rights of millions of indigenous Sindhis*. And he unwound these thoughts further, thinking, if the Sindhi people don't have good education at the dawn of the twenty-first century, then we have to hold someone responsible…and round and round Jani's thoughts continued to whirl.

At this time, Sindhi society was going through yet another restless syndrome of tossing and turning. A popular prime minister whose name had become synonymous with the word *democracy* in Pakistan had been overthrown a few years ago. He had been literally dragged to the gallows and hanged by a dark military regime led by General Zia-ul-Haq, a man whose name means 'magnificent ray of divine truth'.

That slain prime minister had been a charismatic politician, a brilliant statesman and spellbinding showman. He used to address public rallies wearing a loose cloak shirt with rolled up sleeves like a common man, yelling at the top of his lungs, unaware that his yelling was tearing apart his thin voice.

But still, with that croaky voice, he would deliver galvanising, moving, almost haunting speeches. He would inspire the masses to cross the Rubicon with him, and people were in love with him, and would have been willing to jump into any river of fire with both feet.

When he invoked, "This nation will become ironclad!" The people would reply, *yes we will!* "Will you work hard, will you fight for it, and will you die, for the sake of your nation, will you die?" And thousands of voices would erupt together like echoes of roaring thunder bouncing in the ravines of the Grand Canyon, *yes we will, yes we will, yes we will!* That was how he used to be with the common man.

There is a legend from when he had met President John F. Kennedy for the first time at the White House in 1963. They said that JFK was so impressed that he said to him, "Too bad you are not American, because if you were, I would have appointed you to my cabinet." And he had responded humorously, "President Kennedy, that is very kind of you, but if I were American, I would not be in your cabinet but would be President of the United States!"

But that was that. He got executed, and then the military was ruling with its usual iron fist, driving combat tanks, and parking them in public squares. They were rounding up everybody who was anybody, from career criminals, thieves, black marketers, and bribe-takers on one side, to everyone who was trying to make any noise at all, on the other side—student and labour union leaders, journalists, intellectuals, poets, communists.

The military was publicly flogging them with lashes in sports stadiums and school playgrounds. Multitudes of the same crowds who had been willing to even die for their now slain leader from not very long ago were coming in droves to see these public floggings.

Jani and Punnu were curious, too. So they went to see one of these humiliations of humanity to quench their curiosity. It was a festive gala, thousands of people were there that hot summer day. The clamour of noise was so high that it was impossible to hear each other. Some people were holding over-sized black umbrellas to shade themselves from the punishing rays of sunlight which were poking onto their heads like spears.

Some of those unfortunate black umbrellas had faded into light grey, having seen barely a drop of rainwater in their lifetimes, instead of only being baked under the sun. Hawkers were selling cheap sugary cold drinks. Some were selling sliced cucumbers with a pinch of salt and wedges of sweet watermelons for people to keep hydrated in hot weather.

People were carrying their children on their shoulders so that the little kids could see clearly. It was a place like a softball field, fenced with posts and rope. In the centre there was a wooden frame making a huge X, tilted downwards a bit, as it was on an easel.

There was a small VIP enclosure that was shaded with a canopy and chairs for those very important people to be comfortable.

There was live commentary coming over loudspeakers. The commentator announced the names of the condemned who were about to be flogged. All that vociferation of crowd now diminished gradually, a leisurely decrescendo, as if all that noise were on hydraulics.

It was sizzling, so hot that Jani could smell heat in the air, which was reeking metallic, like the smell of pennies on your fingertips on a muggy day.

Then the first of the condemned came out on the grounds with a few policemen. He was a middle aged, chubby dark-skinned man whose hands were tied with rope. His shoulders were bare, and he was wearing dirty white pyjamas[152] and also a white cap which appeared a little whiter than his pyjamas. He was looking confused and pale, but that paleness had turned his face grey, probably because of his complexion.

Policemen were dragging him toward that makeshift wooden cross in the centre of the field. The commentator was announcing the man's crimes, which were selling inferior goods, stockpiling daily use commodities, and black marketing. The announcer went on into details: "This guilty man is accused of mixing impurities in daily food items, such as mixing dry papaya seeds in with

---

[152] *Paayjama*: though the English-speaking world has adopted this word to mean a comfortable two-piece outfit for sleeping in, the original use of 'paayjama' in South Asia refers only to the pants. The word came to Hindustani via a Persian word meaning 'leg-garment'.

whole black peppers and husks of black chickpeas in bulk black tea and ground red brick powder in with cayenne pepper."

The policemen were busy strapping the condemned man onto the St. Andrew's Cross. Then they loosened his pyjamas and pulled them down, revelling his rear. The flogger was a tall and scary-looking man standing at a little distance, some ten or twelve steps away from the strapped prisoner. He was preparing his lashes, moving his whip in the air so fast that it seemed he was cutting air into pieces. That whip was a long thin bamboo stick soaked in oil.

Each time the flogger sliced the air with the whip, it made a spine-chilling sound. Then the flogger started running toward the strapped man, holding the whip, which he slammed against the prisoner's backside with full force, making the prisoner to cry out loud, "*Hai ray*" (—*Oh my!*), which was heard loud and clear on the speakers, because there was a microphone placed strategically very close to that cross so the audience could hear the cries. There was a pin-drop silence. Only the circling crows up in the sky were making their harsh *caw-caw! caw-caw!*

After five lashes, during which he made horrible cries for forgiveness, that prisoner fainted. The on-site doctor examined the prisoner and halted the flogging. The commentator announced that the prisoner would receive his remaining ten lashes on some future day.

Then the second condemned man was announced, and the commentator said, "This prisoner is worse than the previous one. He invoked unrest in society and encouraged people to question the authority of the government of our beloved President General Mohammed Zia-ul-Haq." Then the commentator yelled, "*Murd-e-momin, murd-e-haq!*"—*Man of belief, man of truth!*

Almost the entire crowd all replied, "Zia-ul-Haq, Zia-ul-Haq!"

Jani said it too, along with the crowd, half-heartedly out of sheer fear. Jani looked at Punnu, who kept quiet and did not join others. The commentator continued, "This wretched person insulted Islam and the unity of this beautiful country and its brave armed forces."

In the midst of all those announcements, the policemen brought in a short thin man with a full, untrimmed beard. He looked shaken, but was walking straight, and somehow he was able to carry his head solidly on his shoulders. He looked stressed but not scared.

Or maybe he was scared but just because Punnu whispered in Jani's ears, "I know him, he is a medical student and a Sindhi nationalist," Jani might have perceived that the man wasn't scared, just because of that.

They strapped him and flogged him. Jani was expecting that this nationalist would sustain the lashes as if they were rose petals, and that pain would not move his muscles. But damn life is real, and that nationalist was after all a human, so he did cry out and moan, but also managed to say "long live Sindh" in a frail voice after that first lash. The organisers quickly turned off the microphone to shut out his voice.

After that, no one could hear his voice or his cries any more. No doctor came to examine him after the first five or even ten lashes. They went on and lashed him fifteen times. In the end the policemen dragged him away, as he was unable to walk on his own. The salt-drenched earth of that place was so hard that his dragging feet couldn't even leave any marks behind on that ground.

Punnu told Jani, "We should go now." Jani followed and they slowly walked away.

"What harm could he have caused?" Jani asked. "He was just an individual. Why would a government want to punish him?" He paused and then asked further, "And why was that announcer saying he was worse than that other guy, who was mixing trash in food?"

"Because, for the government, he is worse than a petty thief," said Punnu. "He can think! and thus he is a thought! Thinkers like him, could make the government crumble. In our village they say a single ant can kill an elephant if she manages to get into the elephant's trunk." Punnu caught his breath.

"They are dreamers," said Jani.

"No, they are not. They are committed people," said Punnu. "They want justice for their fellow countrymen. You know they don't bend their knees to bow, even at the gallows. They are made up of some kind of wood that even hell can't set fire to. These people"—and Punnu was still talking about the nationalist who was just flogged—"they are a cognitive idea, a thought, like a gospel. How can you bend, or break, or beat an outcry, a belief!"

Punnu went on supporting his rational. "Just as nothing comes for free, so neither does freedom. But things can be purchased by money, and the price of freedom is what you just saw—pain, suffering, shame, and even life for those few who won't bend or bow. They pay for the freedom of all."

By now, Punnu and Jani had walked further away from that crowded event, so they didn't have to speak so loudly to hear each other. Punnu went on pontificating about those who mattered to him.

"A few months ago, agencies"—and the word *agencies* usually means military intelligence—"tortured and killed a leftist named Nazeer Abbasi. It's a sad piece of news, but I'm not telling you because he was tortured and killed."

Punnu shook his head. "No, but because he told them before any torture during the initial interrogation, 'Yes I'm a member of the communist party of Pakistan, what else you want me to tell you? I have nothing else to say.'"

"There is a notorious army colonel nicknamed Billa, who has a reputation for breaking enemy spies. He started beating Nazeer Abbasi, and Abbasi asked that colonel to stop." Punnu took a pause like he was about to say something important. "And Nazeer Abbasi said to that colonel, 'My name is Nazeer Abbasi! Now you go ahead and try to make me say my name again.' They tortured Nazeer Abbasi for six long days. In the end, they killed him, but people say Nazeer Abbasi never even repeated his own name again for them."

By now, Jani and Punnu had left that dreadful place way back. It was early evening, and although the winds were still cooking hot, there was a hope in the air that it would cool down to a bearable warmness before too long.

Chapter 15
Back under the Gulmohar

He still would go and stand under that gulmohar tree next to the lonely minaret. But not just to see a shadow on milky glass any more. Now he would wait for her to sneak out and come and meet him. Like Jani's, her real name was also as ordinary as Jane Doe. But no one called her by her real name. She was known as Chia to most everyone. That was a name her father gave her, the name of a Sindhi bird even tinier than a hummingbird.

And she used to come out of her home to meet Jani, in those gloaming semi-melted evening skies of Hyderabad, which turn velvet blue after holding fiery Salvador Dali sunsets. She would sneak out with the help of one of her sisters, who vigilantly looked out for her and kept an eye on time. And she would let Chia slip out briefly, to step into that curve, that fractal time, so that she could go and, interlude outside of linear time, to meet Jani. What could be called a moment of absolute bliss.

Where love transfixed time, and time came into a trance, and started whirling like Darvaishes of Rumi, and time forgets to go anywhere and keeps circling around that sheer aesthetic of plain old love. At least, that's what it felt like to those in the throes of love, who somehow managed to stretch those winks, those tiny fragments of time, into multiple lifetimes, and to live several lives in those split seconds, discussing the affairs of their hearts, who are already consumed with each other.

So both of them, there, under that Gulmohar in those fleeting moments, would hold each other in a tight jam, so close that their breaths effortlessly could change hands to enter into each other's bodies, and he could easily see even in that frail light her eyes and those widened pupils, circled by rings of brown hazel fold irises.

He felt she was asking for his image to dive fearlessly into her deep eyes, windows to her soul. And she was quietly looking at him, like her eyes could not see him enough. And there, holding each other, she wanted to say and hear back those same rundown and beaten up words, which always felt brand new to those in the crush of love.

"Say you love me!"

"I do! Yes."

But she insisted, "Then say it!"

"I love you."

"Say it for me again!"

Who knows how such powerful emotions could be reiterated in this many words that they kept saying over and over again, as the gulmohar bore witness. And that gulmohar probably had gladly done it. In fact, if it was in its blooming season, that gulmohar could have dropped a few of her blushing amber flowers on them.

Though she only walked ten or twenty steps to meet him under that gulmohar, those few steps were considered great leaps in Sindhi culture for centuries. This was a social taboo. In her case, it wasn't just a transgression of young romance, but she was also breaking the shackles of religious hierarchy. Because she was born to a Syed family, who belong to the Shia clergy of Islam, people who are direct descendants of Imam Ali, whom the Shia consider the true successor of the great Mohammad.

Though Jani's family had advanced on the social ladder, he was still, after all, a commoner. He was an offspring of the indigenous people of Sindh, who basically are Bheel, Kohli, Menghwar, and he didn't carry any blood lineage to connect him to any shining stars of religion. And he had zero regrets about it.

In fact, he would brag, "I'm a direct descendant of a little known Fakeer who lit literally used to roam around in the dusty alleys of faraway lands and beg on narrow streets of unknown towns, next to a great river, and I'm proud of him!" Other than that statement showing his stubbornness, nothing had changed at all. He was still considered a commoner offspring of nothing more than barely advanced enough *Homo sapiens* who could walk straight. Whereas she was still an heir of Ali, the peerless lion of God, and a true successor of the great Mohammad.

So he made the parallel in his mind, comparing theirs with that wildly eccentric romance of Vincent Van Gogh with Kee, his cousin. Jani had read that

Vincent had once tried to visit Kee in her home, but was barred entry by her father, who claimed she wasn't home. Jani wasn't sure if it was true, but in his memory, Kee's father was a priest. Anyway, Vincent kept pleading with the father, knowing that Kee must be there at home, and the father kept refusing.

So Vincent decided to prove the intensity of his love by sticking his hand in the flame of a lamp and crying out, "Let me see her for as long as I can keep my hand in this flame!"

But this excruciating pain was entirely in vain, because it only convinced the father that Vincent was a madman. And then Kee felt insulted by the suggestion that her lover was crazy, and she rejected Vincent coldly.

So Jani sometimes felt like he was Vincent standing up to the cruel priest, but, of course, he only wanted to be like the Vincent of just before the flame and lamp episode. He totally didn't want Chia to be like the priest's daughter, and she was not.

Four years had passed since Jani first met her. It was the mid-80s and they both were attending university, the same university where Jani was born and his Aai still lived with his uncles and aunts and his grandfather, Master Mohammad Alam, who had permanently moved there not long ago. He had come from Qamber, a dusty town that Jani had visited a few times, once when his great-grandmother died, and a couple other times too.

Sometimes, after class, he would take Chia to meet Aai, who would call them "O muhanjee lalun je jori."—*Oh you my pair of rubies*. But his grandfather wouldn't always recognise them, and he would greet them very formally, like those good-hearted old folks who have forgotten pretty much everything, and only remember how to be kind with total strangers.

Somewhere along the way between the faculty building and the residential colony for university employees, there was a burial site, more of a memorial, which was also a pedestal for the winds of Jamshoro to do the tango every evening. It was a dome, but not like one of those onion-shaped domes in the Kremlin—it was more like an ample bosom, standing on seven matchstick-thin pillars.

Those thin pillars held up the dome and also served as a kind of honour guard for the two graves. Those graves were constantly gazed down by the sacred Quranic verses, which were carved in cement and then painted in bone-dry white, or rather broken-heart white, inside the rotunda. But it was that perfect ratio of saturation to brightness, with a cool undertone of sky blue colour in the background of that rotunda, which silently held the lines of those godly verses, sacrificing its own existence and becoming almost unnoticeable, just to enhance those holy verses, allowing them to run on and on in their unending spiralling circles, and symbolically revealing the story of an infinite God even to those, who couldn't read the Arabic.

There were also trees outside that mausoleum, and most of those trees were eucalyptuses, which burned all day in Jamshoro's merciless heat. But every evening, coolness would spread through the winds and turn the charred air into ethereal, almost other-worldly cool breezes, and the leaves of the exhausted eucalyptuses would sway in symphonic love over the graves of those two people who had fallen in love.

They had chosen to spend their lives together, but had been separated when one of them died first, but the other followed soon after, and they were reunited for eternity, and placed here in an open shrine, where the winds of Jamshoro do a tango every evening for them.

Jani and Chia used to go and sit on the stairs of that enshrined tomb.

Chapter 16
Winds Avoiding Him

He could see small spiralling cyclones of sand as he drove through the barren land. As he crossed over a bridge, he caught sight of Sindhu, which was now shrunk to a mere puddle that you could easily jump over in a single leap. He was thinking about the *bundhun,* the blind dolphins of the Indus, which had been named an endangered species by Prince Philip some thirty, thirty-five years back.

He hardly believed that the Prince would have even thought of them a second time since then; and maybe even that first statement had been issued by his staff and not him. And why should a dummy monarch spouse care for a fish, when we Sindhis, the people with whom the bundhun had lived for thousands of years, were doing nothing for them. Since this river had dried, the whole city gave an impression of a slow-simmering garbage dump from a distance, and the irony was, if you got up close to it…it was still a simmering garbage dump.

He was coming back after eleven years. For eleven long years, memories of this beloved city adhered in his mind the way nails stick fast to a nail bed. Once this was the city of winds, where fragrance floated in its brick paved drainage lines. Every evening, young poets used to roam around its back alleys to bathe their romantic imagination in that fragrance that rose from the drain water of affluent neighbourhoods, forming seductive couplets about the delicate bodies of those women who used to bathe in perfumed water.

Once they had called it the Paris of India. Long ago, an emperor had come here and saw three hills next to a roaring river, and he built two gigantic forts, one with baked red bricks and the other with clay mud walls. He made the city his capital and he slowly fell in love with her. His son named her Hyderabad, after the title of Ali Mola.

This was the city where he was born and grew up, where he had come to his senses and had walked for the very first time, and fallen and stood up again, and tasted ice cream for the very first time, and fallen in love, and lost his senses for the very first time. But that was then. Now he was here to sit in front a pile of dirt and try to talk to the soil, because a few days back Aai died. Who knows the reason—it was probably old age, or a bad heart, or she got tired.

The bottom line is that she died. He heard the news from his elder aunt, the one he called Adi Wadee. Her real name was Zaibunnisa, but she had several names—his father used to call her Zaybull, and some people used to call her Nisa, though those who did were all long gone by now. Anyway, Adi Wadee told him that Aai's last breath had left her so quietly, the way the loose end of a kite string can sometimes slip and escape unknowingly from the kite flyer's hands.

Adi Wadee said she had been hospitalised for some heart issues. The doctors had tested her and said that she had a weak heart. There Adi Wadee took a pause and then said, "*Janal'a,* these doctors call themselves *dil ja dakter'a,** but they don't know anything about hearts. Those silly doctors said she had a weak heart!"

Adi Wadee went on, "We were in the cardiac ward, and the doctors said they wanted to keep her for one more night. It was late. She asked for water, so I gave it to her, and then she asked for a chikoo!"

Adi Wadee's hopelessness was apparent from her face, like she wanted to stop the earth's rotation and then spin it in reverse to go back in time, just to give Aai a Chikoo (*commonly known as sapodilla, sapota, chikoo, naseberry, or nispero is a long-lived, evergreen tree native to southern Mexico, Central America and the Caribbean*) for one last time, but instead of all that she just said, *"muo chikoo ba kaana dino maanus."*—*I couldn't even offer her a darn chikoo.*

After a nasal sigh, Adi Wadee continued, "She told me to forget about the chikoo and asked me to sleep beside her in the hospital bed. So I slid in, and we were lying there, and her head was leaning on my shoulders. And Aai said, I have to tell you something, and I replied, I'm listening, Aai, say what you want to say. And she changed her mind and said, I'll tell you tomorrow."

Adi Wadee's voice was still full of that anxious curiosity. "I said, tell me now, but she only said, hmm mm…I will tell you tomorrow. Then we slept."

"The next morning, the EKG guy came and Aai was still sleeping. I helped him to place those leads. After a few runs, he left everything there and ran to get a doctor, and in a few moments that room was full of doctors and other staff, and they were doing all sorts of things. I was standing in a corner, and after a few moments everyone kind of slowed down. But my heart was jumping like it was going to come out of my throat."

Then Adi Wadee looked at Jani and said, *"Bus Janal'a."*—*That was it*. And after a long pause, Adi Wadee said, "I wonder what she was about to tell me."

That evening, he and Adi Wadee kept talking about Aai. Then Adi Wadee asked him to rest, so he lay down and kept looking up at the dull light of a distant bulb and those baked red clay ceiling tiles clenched together in iron teardrop girders.

The next morning, he walked alone. Adi Wadee wanted to come, but he needed to go on his own. It was very early morning, but sky was already a clear, bleached blue. There was no residue of last night there. Everything was wrapped up; every single star was gone, even those big stars that usually hang around for a little longer.

Only illusions of the comforts of the previous night lingered in the air, and he knew that reality would soon slap him like a hard blowing wind. He was walking with heavy Atlas steps, carrying the burden of his memories, which was possibly heavier than the weight of the entire world.

His conscience had saddled him with the punishments of Prometheus and Atlas combined, where he not only had to carry the burden of memories, but also that heart was being constantly eaten by an immortal raven of guilt. He felt guilt that he had been dispassionate towards his Aai, aloof towards that person who taught him how to walk and smile, and laugh and love, and say words wrong, which she used to correct, and even how to wipe his butt as a child.

And in the end, she taught him how to snuffle and cry alone, and she placed the pain of love in his heart, like a master chef who very delicately places a small piece of hot burning amber in the middle of a steak, just to give it the flavour of smoke.

But he kept walking towards the university burial ground, which was an oasis of a place, a cluster of eucalyptuses in the middle of a bed-rock of sunbaked limestone. He was walking on irregular pathways like designless human palm line, meandering around those countless devi shrubs at bordered the path. He didn't want to reach to her burial side ever; he wanted that path to be endless.

On some level, he was enjoying that heavy Atlas drag, that punishment, during which he kept randomly flipping the pages of memories in his mind. The way Aai used to celebrate her accomplishments, which he then used to think were none, zip, nothing! And he is never able to understand why Aai believes that whatever his father, he himself and his other uncles and aunts had achieved, it's all her success.

But now when she chose to become a feeling, someone who is always around you but, you could only feel their presence. Aai was the McQueen of cars story, someone who had the heart to stop and turn around just before the finish line and lose a winning game to help lift someone else who had fallen. But life had denied victory to that tricky cheat who was not victorious of hearts and just had the piston cup.

He was so lonely at that moment in time that it felt to him that even the gushing winds of Jamshoro were ignoring him, trying to avoid him completely as they passed by, like they too were siding with Aai.

Aai had never gotten mad at him, but in the end she did refuse to speak to him on the phone, and she died a few hours after that, not leaving enough room for him to wiggle and make up with her. In the midst of those thoughts, he reached the burial site, and figured out that it was the fourth grave behind his grandfather's grave, towards the east.

There was no gravestone yet, but he saw the dry roses spread over a small dune of dirt. Mercilessly the sun had baked those red roses into a purplish blue, like the sun had suffocated life out of them. He sat near the foot of her grave. He wanted to say something, but his mind went blank, like there was nothing in there, and nothing really meant nothing.

After that long void, the first thought that came into his mind was, *This is not Aai.* Ai was vibrant and warm, emitting piercing rays of love. But this—this was a strange cold pile of dirt. This was not Aai.

He came out of there carrying a living thought of her, and saying to himself and to that Aai thought, *We will never go back there again.* The same winds that a little while ago had pretended to ignore him now messed up his hair, like they were saying, *we are friends again, we're cool.*

Chapter 17
Stupid Monologue

A young cousin of his, twenty-three years younger than Jani and even a month younger than Jani's own son, asked him to come to a student gala at the Department of English literature. This cousin was the son of Jani's uncle Punnu, who was the same Punnu as always, though he had become ill by this time, and it would be terminal, though maybe he didn't know it yet. But Punnu was as curious as always, seeking out all those funny things in life, in death, and pretty much in everything in between.

Jani and his cousin and Punnu arrived at a multi-storey stand-alone building on a lot that had been a barren piece of land back when Jani left, twenty years ago. The place was buzzing that day, overflowing with raw awkward jejunity. The hot March afternoon was dripping from their foreheads and dribbling down their tender flushing cheeks, and their shaved faces emitted a greenish tone of sheer youthfulness. And he could see his own forthcoming tomorrow in their faces.

A desire crawled through his mind, dragging this thought with her: *why don't I talk to them, they'd probably listen!* And a monologue started forming in his mind, which started with, "I'm sorry, I really am, sorry that I have done nothing, absolutely nothing for you, for my own tomorrow. I left 20 years ago to the western hemisphere to sell my abilities in return for a better life, which basically meant things, material things like cars and a house and other comforts. If that's what a better life is, then I got it, I got it all, and for that I'm very grateful."

"But over a period of time, I lost a big part of me. I lost my ability to appreciate selflessly. I lost my ability to find time to sit in the shadow of a tree leaning back on her trunk. I lost my inability to hold the hand of a loved one for the last time and say this lie with all my honest heart, that 'it's okay—you're gonna be fine.' I lost myself."

"My heritage was too bulky for me to carry it from here to there. Plus, where I went they have their own beautiful culture and heritage, so there was no room to keep my past there. And I chose to become a no-one with a whole lot of things. So I learned the hard way what they mean by that expression, 'penny wise pound foolish.'"

"What I'm moaning for now was never part of the deal, neither had they promised it nor did I account for that part in my hasty acceptance twenty years ago. I wanted things made up of valuable materials, and I never cared for that part of me which got lost. So here I am—partially successful, positively aged, and unable to go back to fix what I had broken."

"But I'm willing to share that experience of mine with you, and with all honesty, whatever I say is going to sound like hackneyed, overused phrases for some of you, rhetoric for a few others, but may be it will make sense to just one or two of you. So I will cut to the chase, which is about how to improve the quality of life of an individual. But first, take a moment and think about what 'quality of life' actually is."

"It could be an indicator of general wellbeing, for an individual or the entire society. As a term it is usually associated 'standard of living'. But the two are not actually the same. The standard of living is basically equal to the wealth and job holding ability of a person in a society. But *quality of life* does not require monetary assets. You could find a middle-aged and penniless person sitting utterly contented in the shadow of a tree, filled with some unexplainable joy. So the standard of living and quality of life are different things."

Then he gazed out at their faces, from his imagined position as orator, and he felt he might have started to bore them by getting into the nitty-gritty of social sciences and economics. So he abruptly moved onward in that imaginary speech, and jumped to the next thought. "But now forget about that standard-of-living and society baloney. I'll come to the core issue, which is how to make a common man well-off."

"There are a few options. One is that we could try perfect medieval alchemy and start converting a substance that's 10% gold and 90% lead into 100% gold. But the problem is that the right ratio of alchemy is always the one that you have not done. In other words, it has not been perfected for thousands of years. In organic chemistry, you can't mix lots of trash with some good stuff and expect it all to become good stuff. So, the odds are against us."

"We have to think about trade, 100% indigenous trade. You become the buyer of your own goods. You buy and you sell and build the economy from ground up. Say, hypothetically, we are 44 million people. If every one of us spends one extra rupee every day, it would add 16060 million rupees to our economy annually. But the key is that buying and selling has to occur among us, in between us."

"Trade works on very simple principal. You need a buyer and a seller, but the problem is that the buyer has to have the resources to buy, and the seller has to offer a product to sell! We can't buy because we are poor, and we know that, but do we have something worth selling? See, the mother of the whole problem is the economy. It was economy that made the great empire of Rome, and later it was the same economy that destroyed Rome."

"Rome was flourishing thousands of years ago. For example, Romans were buying things as simple as frankincense resin from the Arabs, and just that trade alone was making the Arab economy boom. But then something happened, and the European economy took a nosedive—because of external forces—and then came the Dark Ages, and all things became dull; all the spices were gone. But we can learn from that lesson. We don't have to go through all that again—we just have to find something that we could sell to others or to ourselves just to break that stagnant quiet of hopelessness, just to initiate that ripple effect, which needs a jolt of kinetic energy."

Then he took a pause and inhaled deeply, his gaze fixed on the crowd, obviously in his imagination.

"So what is the commodity that we have to sell? We have nothing! We are dirt poor!" He again took a brief pause, and in his imagination everyone was listening to him, all those youths, every single soul. And in his same imagination he told himself, *At least they are quietly looking at me, they are listening.*

"But then," his mental oration continued, "we get into all those problems that I already mentioned."

Actually, he hadn't really mentioned them, but in his head—that head inside his head—he thought he had. "Like identifying petrol or gas as expensive. Everyone knows that—that's the problem. And how to make it cheap! That would be the mother of all answers. Well, I don't know how to make gas cheap. The best thing would be to stop using it altogether."

"But I do have a suggestion for the problems of Sindh. How about air? We sell air—it's free and it's abundant and the atmosphere is full of it. But then, it's free for all, so who is going to buy something they already have for free? But we can convert wind and sunlight into electricity. Sell the sunlight and wind—as energy. Don't look at other people to solve your problems. Get your own grip on it and strike it down!"

He took a breath here, in that speech within his mind. A few of the imagined faces in front of him wanted to smile. And he went on, "Don't look at the government. A government should not provide for everyone, and a government should not pamper 44 million people. Each one of you is the government now. Tell me what you can do for the guy sitting next to you. And if you don't have an answer to that question, then think what you can do *as the government* for the person sitting next to you."

"We come to know that a great number of us literate people don't actually know much about politics or economics. In fact, social scientists, economists, and political scientists are all agreed that the voters know very little about politics and economics—and the worst thing is that all of those scientists think it doesn't make any difference. In other words, a democracy is for the people, of the people, by the people—but those people don't necessarily have to understand it."

"We are in a deep hole, and the first thing that we have to do is stop digging. Get the best possible education wherever you can get it, and then come back and do whatever it takes to make it happen. Sell energy. Make your own corporations. Make small, individual contributions, because cumulatively they become substantial. Say any thousands of you contribute a thousand rupees each to form a limited liability corporation. The initial capital of that company is going to be one million rupees and you'll all be stakeholders in your own corporation."

"And with that company of yours you can start a small power grid, somewhere in the deep interior of Sindh. Why in the deep interior? Because it is so needed there that it would be very easy to maintain, with very few hoops for you to jump through. Provide them with that much-needed electricity for way less than the government, who can't provide any decent service in the first place. On a small scale, it's going to be easy to maintain—and it will be reliable, 100% indigenous, and eco-friendly energy."

Someone stood up in his imaginary audience and yelled, "It's too good to be true!"

And another one said, "He's just barking, we don't want to listen to him." And someone else said, "He is a CIA agent!" And another: "Why don't you come back and try living here with us again!" And another: "He's a selfish traitor—he just came back to deceive us!"

In his imagination, he tried to escape that wild crowd. In reality, he simply walked out from that gala with his young cousin. But he was still in the world of his imaginary speech, which he was now judging to be incoherent. Plus, now he was thinking that he hadn't accounted for those blood-sucking feudal lords and tribal leaders who would never allow these kids to do something that in the deep interior, and meanwhile the ethnic renegade thugs wouldn't let them do it in the cities—so it was really a poor speech, and a stupid monologue.

Then he figured that, instead of agitating himself by giving a speech that he didn't know how to give in the first place, he should write a poem or two on this mess.

Chapter 18
Seven Days and Six Nights

It was already the fifth day of his week-long trip. He only had seven days and six nights, and half of a day got lost somewhere in the time difference. It was an evening and the winds of Jamshoro were the same, blowing in their ears, shouting at the top of their windy lungs.

Jani and Punnu were lying down on four-legged cots under an old mango tree in Punnu's backyard. Mango trees usually didn't grow very tall, because their wood is soft and breakable. But this one did get tall, and the winds of Jamshoro were forcing its trunk to make crackling sounds.

Jani said to Punnu, "This tree is making weird sounds. We should move our cots a little to the side."

Punnu didn't reply and kept lying there on the cot with his both eyes closed, as if that mango tree had assured him of not falling on them.

Jani said, "You know, the story of my life is the story of someone who doesn't do anything but only dreams of doing everything. Those desires of mine kept adjusting themselves along the way. When I was young, I used to imagine winning an Oscar or two, and a Nobel Prize at the same time, and giving my acceptance speech. Actually, I used to think that acceptance speech all the way though."

Punnu's eyes were still serenely closed while responding, "But you did well, got what you wanted…and as for those prizes, Gandhi and Tolstoy never won a Nobel Prize, but they are still Gandhi and Tolstoy. And Sartre never wanted one."

Jani pressed on. "But now in my mid-forties, my daydreams are a little different. Now I keep thinking about changing the whole economy of Sindh, and dividing its resources between its people better than even Karl Marx could have suggested, without any bloodshed."

Punnu said, "That you can do. But you will not do it, because you are just entertaining your conscience. You got tempted and you left Sindh. But you got what you were looking for, so it's okay—no regrets now. Sindh and its people have been surviving for thousands of years, they'll still live."

His eyes were still closed. The trunk of the mango tree was still crackling of its own heaping weight. Punnu always said whatever he really thought, even if it was razor-sharp. He was notorious for that, and Jani knew it, too.

"What happened to that novel that you have been working on for over twenty years now?" Jani asked him.

"It could grow up to four hundred chapters," said Punnu. Now he lifted his head and opened his eyes, and then rested his face on one of his hands with the help of elbow, still lying down but sidewise now. "Though I have just finished twenty-five chapters so far. This novel of mine is not going to be a popular novel like my last novel. I don't expect it to be popular! Instead, I am working on this novel like a vocational craftsman. It's a painstakingly slow and detailed depiction of an orphan who grew to become a middle class man. The story in the late 1800s against the backdrop of rural Sindh, in fact of India. My protagonist was born in same period of time when Gandhi was born."

"He's a middle aged man carrying his nine-year-old wife on his shoulders, whom he had purchased for very little money. It's early morning and the sun is rising and that soft light is reflecting in tearful eyes of that obscure girl."

Punnu kept talking about his masterful development of characters and their surroundings around a dusty small hamlet next to an oddly shaped lake. "But I'm enjoying writing it," he said, and then his voice shivered, and a glaze moved across his eyes. He was trying to hide that, and Jani went on pretending that he hadn't seen it.

Then he started talking about another section, like he had learned it all by heart, like that whole damn novel was tap-dancing in front of him in his mind, even as he lay there on his cot. "...*She removed a third of a brick from that hole of dry mud wall and sunlight started gushing in with throbbing intensity, and her parrot kept saying Haq Pak Allah, Haq Pak Allah after her...*"

"And here's another piece," said Punnu. "And I have seen this with my own eyes, but I'll have it in my novel, too...*It was a rare torrential downpour, with dark clouds jammed together, which gave way to a deluge that could have sunk*

Noah's boat. There was only one ber tree in our courtyard. When sparrows started dropping like rocks, from that old ber tree on the ground, Mamoo Khawindino ran with a knife and an empty canister and started slashing their throats and throwing them in that can."

He then said with deep resign and sadness, which he had probably carried with him all those years since that day, *"We ate them."*

Then he said, "If I am ever able to finish it, this is going to be a classic novel."

It was a winter morning. He was awake but didn't want to come out of bed, so he cuddled into a soft blanket. He rested his head on the ledge of the window, there inside their rented condo in northwest New Jersey, somewhere alongside Schooleys Mountain Ridge. The folds of the blanket around him were holding in his body heat, which he was feeling every time he moved a little.

Chia came into the room holding a tray with tea for both of them. It had all the accessories—a teakettle with a lid, which was covered with a clean kitchen cloth to hold the steam in and make the tea strong, two empty cups and a single spoon, a can of evaporated milk with holes punched in it. The moment Chia lifted the lid from the kettle to stir, the whole room was filled with the smell of richly brewed black tea.

While pouring and mixing the tea, Chia said, "Kabeer has not replied to any of my emails, nor did he send his cell number from Africa."

He didn't reply to her question. He kept looking out at that winter morning. Outside their window there were a couple of condo blocks in a stepladder formation, as that whole development was carved willy-nilly onto the steep side of that mountain, and one could see tall trees completely stripped of their leaves, going all the way to the top of the hill. Probably, he didn't know what to say. And she didn't say anything else to him.

Eventually, Jani stopped staring out the window and let out a "humm…" and then a sigh. "Whatever I say, you are not going to like it! But I'll say something anyway. I don't know why he hasn't responded to your emails. Maybe he is too busy, maybe he doesn't have the internet, maybe he doesn't want to! You pick your choice and I'll rephrase it with the answer that suits you."

Chia finished mixing sugar and milk into the tea and gave him his cup. "Talking to you is like talking to a wall," she said. "I don't even know why I do it."

Jani took a first sip and felt the caffeine of that black tea run into his system, the way that nowadays they illustrate digital data running through fibre optic cables at lightning speed. Now he said, "Listen, I read a quote someplace, that only we humans cling to our children forever. No other species of animal does that. After a while, birds let their chicks fly away, never to come back again. Other animals let their cubs walk out of their lives after the first few years, forever."

"You are full of rhetoric," said Chia.

Jani took another sip followed by a "Humm…"

It might look from the outside as if their relationship had entered into that phase where people become unaccommodating of each other's habits, and say things like "Why do you always squeeze a toothpaste tube from the middle?" But actually, that's not how they were. They still felt that curiosity to go explore the unfound nooks and corners of their existence, of their bodies, their souls, their minds. So no, they were not tired of each other yet. That's only how it might appear from a distance.

Chapter 19
He Who Used to Manufacture Time

Jani came to know that Punnu had become ill. But then again, he hadn't really been well for decades, almost for quarter of a century. His illness was kind of a wound that had healed long ago, but which still had to be treated as an open gash. Because that is what happens when a vital organ of someone else's body is borrowed and then domesticated in your own body, and your own body never quite accepts that foreign object and keeps rejecting it. Even though that organ is basically cherishing your body and keeping it alive.

So Punnu used to get himself checked into hospital in Karachi from time to time, where they somehow used to tune him up, and then he would keep running fine till the next tune-up.

So, Jani thought it was one of those hiccups. But then Jani got another call from back home: "This time it's serious. You better come."

For a second everything became a blur, dim and then opaque. His heart took a plunge, like an art lover being told that someone had shredded the Mona Lisa. He jotted off a few emails to his office, asking for some emergency time off, and then he got himself to Jamshoro.

From the outside, Punnu looked fine as always, but he had become less involved if not mute. Rather, Punnu was looking at those few days as if they were any other ordinary days. It was a mutual understanding between Punnu and Jani that a handful of water can't be preserved by squeezing the palm tight. So without saying goodbyes, those real ones, Jani left again. And, after a few weeks, the one who used to manufacture time seemed to have lost interest in time and run out of it.

Days after that, Jani called and spoke with Punnu's wife, who said, among other things, "You and I have lost the mutual interest of our conversation, with him being gone; there is nothing much left for us to talk about."

After a few useless comforting words, which could only hope to erode the pain, Jani asked her, "What happened to that novel that Punnu was writing for almost twenty years? He told me"—and Jani's voice became a bit emphatic—"That he had written twenty-five chapters of it and that it could grow up to three or four hundred chapters."

She responded in her utterly calm manner, "He had only actually written the first three chapters of it. And they were published in some monthly journal twenty years ago." She took a pause. "If there were four hundred chapters of it, they were in his imagination. He took them with him. That novel is now gone forever."

Life is in the small things—that's an old adage, but it was true for Dhayani, or one could say she thought big of small things. Meanwhile, for Jani, manmade mechanical objects were always the objects of admiration. He liked big airports, moving walkway belts, interstate jug-handle-loop exits.

But in the end, he tried to listen to those birds who sing in several different voices. He was never a birdwatcher, though, preferring to have accidental encounters with nature, rather than travelling around the world to find it, or sailing the blue sea and then waiting for the whale to pop up, which some people will do without even looking at the whale, their eyes fixed instead on the screens of their digital cameras.

He would just go walking, like he did one day, along the banks of Musconetcong River, in the shadows of Schooleys Mountain. He sat there in a remote area, thinking to himself that perhaps no one had ever visited it before. There were fat trunks of trees, mostly sycamore and ash, extending their branches way in, hanging down over the river, slowly moving up and down like they were heaving with the weight of birds' sounds combined with green leaves making a gentle swish.

The water was giving the impression that it was moving very fast, though it was not. He could see unadulterated, crystal clear water appearing muddy green, because of algae on the top of the riverbed rocks, and the cardinals were calling out ("birdie-birdie-birdie!") like brat teenagers, winking and whistling at the same time. And the ravens were caterwauling like *bundhun*[153] and spoiling all those beautiful unwritten woodwind scores with their voices like ruptured beeper. And the common yellowthroats were making their *wichity-wichity-*

---

[153] *Bundhun*: blind dolphins of the Indus.

wichity sounds, constantly breathing beauty back in to the soundscape, with the help of the northern mockingbirds, who were the master conductors, and could repeat phrases with all syllables in one pitch before moving flawlessly to a new sound flawlessly, calling out their *chewk-chewk-chijjjand-chijjj* and *chew'hew-chew'hew*.

But actually, he couldn't identify any of them, nor could he differentiate who was who. He could only feel that those beautiful sounds were disappearing in the branches of trees like something falling down an elevator shaft from a great height. And he saw three big ill-shaped boulders, two close together and one a slight remove, all half-submerged in the dancing waters of Musconetcong River.

Those boulders were half-covered with different shades of algae, from bottle green to parrot green, and then higher up a dark mustard colour and a dirty muddy green. They reminded him of his very dear, middle-aged, bald headed, fat, type-two diabetic friends, who had spent 40 years with him. It was as if those friends were standing here half naked in the knee-high water, with their hairy and bulging tummies, and they were asking him, "How do we look?"

And without any hesitation he replied to those boulders, "You look beautiful."

He knew it wouldn't make any sense, but he went on and initiated a conversation with the Musconetcong River. "You know what," he started. "There is a river, and it's still my river, a lion of rivers."

Then he took a breath with a sigh, and said in a deep, slow voice, "A big river…"

Then his eyes popped open, almost bugging out of his head, and his cheeks had to give way for a smile to spread.

Then he swallowed, and with that vanishing smile he said, "But that river is dying now."

He threw a flat chipped rock, which skipped several times before sinking, even on that wavy surface of the Musconetcong River. And he kept talking to the river, without even realising that an old man was sitting across the way on the other bank, showing a young boy how to throw his line. Now he saw that child, who giggled, probably thinking he was just a crazy old man talking to himself.

Story V: Kabeer

Chapter 1
"If You Are Sad, You Go Hug the Tree, You Go Fit!"

The chopper was coming down very slowly. He watched people grow from barely visible specks to action figure size and then bigger and bigger. There was a circle down there, slightly brighter from the rest of the barren landscape, which was a sort of helipad. The windsock sleeve at the top of the pole there was playing in the wind, barely inflating, like an enfeebled old penis who tries hard to get erect but fails every time.

The chopper was getting even slower as it neared the ground. A cloud of dust was rising, as if the dirt itself were making room for the chopper. Soon, he could see nothing but spiralling dust outside his window, but then he felt a jolt, which confirmed that she had landed. After a few minutes, he and the others came out of the chopper, whose rotor blades were still ruthlessly slicing the air. He ducked his head down and ran to a safe distance from that violent noise.

He felt everything was different here, from smells to noise to the air. He was breathing a thick jet fuel exhaust blended with a dry earthy smell. The Burundi ground was all red soil and the skies were filled with dirt.

There was a woman waiting for him there, who was young, but that kind of young who appears old. They shook hands.

"Welcome. I'm Tunishka, and I'm team leader here." That must have been what she said, but she said it in such a thick eastern European accent that he had figure out the meaning of the entire sentence by working back from the word 'leader'.

"Kabeer," he nodded in return. He threw his backpack in the rear of the appliance-white, UN-type vehicle and hopped on the front seat. Tunishka started the motor. "Is diss you-r farst trrap?" She asked.

This time instead of nodding his head he said, "Yes," and artificially cast a smile onto his face, which the seasoned Tunishka ignored, like she knew all about those fake smiles. And he kept staring at the small bullet hole in the windscreen, which was surrounded with long streaking cracks that looked like the frozen first moments of the big bang. As the Jeep was snaking its way forward on the dirt roads, he reluctantly kept watching Tunishka's tough hands as they loosened and tightened their grip on the steering.

They reminded him of Aai's fingers. He had vivid memories of her, though most of her memories had been transplanted into his mind from his father. Aai was his father's grandmother. In fact, that's what he called her in Sindhi, 'Baba-Dadi', which means 'father's grandmother'.

He was not even four when he saw her for the very last time, but he had heard so much of her that it was as if she lived with him. He had seen photographs from when she was in her prime, which now appeared orangish-brownish-yellow toned. But his mind had classified that photo version of the twenty-something Aai as a completely separate person from the Aai he knew, the old woman with cheeks caving in.

The latter was the real one for him, vivid in his memory, weakened and barely breathing, with a weathered and wrinkled dark face, which might have been young and beautiful once. Even at that age she was still glowing with the warmth of her motherly love, the love that doesn't need any co-signer, any assurance. You just trust it, because it is there, like a plush satiny comforter of love that you could jump on as a child with your full force, assuming that you are not gonna get hurt, so that was his Baba Dadi. All these thoughts of his great grandmother rolled in his mind in a fraction of a second.

Tunishka interrupted his thought-weaving process, saying in that same thick accent, "Why did you come here?"

He looked at Tunishka, but she was looking straight ahead at the dirt road. He said, "Do you want to hear a poetic answer or a factual one? Here, I'll tell you both. I think I've lost something of great value in me. I came here because I want to find that. That's the poetic answer and the factual answer at the same time."

"We are almost there," Tunishka said. They were arriving at the base of his mission with Doctors without Borders. It was a generic building with cinderblock walls and a wavy tin roof. There was a covered porch extending all the way to the end, with several rooms on its one side and barren land on the other side with sporadic shrubs. He glanced at the beautiful setting sun that was wearing an amber scarf of evening clouds around his neck. That sight gave him some comfort, like seeing someone he knew.

Tunishka showed him to his room, and he dropped his stuff onto an old wooden study table. After the requisite orientation activities, he returned to settle in. And the room felt a bit familiar too. Of course, it was nothing like his room in New Jersey, but he had seen some rooms like this in Hyderabad and Jamshoro.

This one was a box room made up of four walls with an iron door and a ceiling of tin sheets. One of the walls had a window with two iron shutters, and there was a single metal bed with an algae-green bed net, part of which was rolled up a bit like the valance of a theatre curtain. He threw himself on that bed, and his landing there caused all sorts of crackling noises.

He didn't know when day had appeared, but it was the next day for sure, and early. They went to a nearby village to revamp a burned out clinic, which locals said had gotten destroyed by a militia army of one of their own local lords. It was a temporary medical post with a military green canvas roof propped up on sticks, using one of the original mud walls of the old clinic, now badly charred.

Part of that wall looked like the inside of an old fireplace. There was an overwhelming smell in the air which had everything in it, a medicinal odour of sun-baked shrubs, mixed with bad breath and human perspiration, combined with the acrid smell of the ankle-deep pond of stagnant water nearby. But there was also an unexplainable hint of lavender in that air; God knows why.

They were there to start with very basic treatment, mainly to help with malaria, so they were unpacking their supplies, fever-reducing medicines, anti-malarial tablets, thermometers. The villagers had realised that someone had reopened the clinic. An old man came holding a young girl by the hand. A staffer called out, "There is some one here!"

"Bring him in," said Tunishka. "Let's see what we can do."

"He has a girl as well," said the staffer.

"Bring her in; we'll look at her too."

So the old man brought the girl in, and the local staffer helped them to figure out what symptoms she'd been suffering from: fever, vomiting, and other signs of malaria. But it wasn't just guesswork—Kabeer's team had testing kits, so in a few minutes it was properly confirmed that she was positive for malaria.

They gave her treatment and sent her on her way—a successful first case for Kabeer in this war-torn corner of the world. Really it was a completely ordinary experience, but he was trying to add meaning to it in his own mind, remembering what his father used to say, that, "even the longest journey must begin beneath one's feet"—not knowing that he was quoting Lao-Tzu.

There were four doctors on the team: Tunishka and Kabeer and two others. One of them was a British Indian trauma surgeon, and the other was an American paediatrician who'd been doing this kind of mission work for the last ten years. He was a tall man with a receding hairline and questioning sad eyes like Tagore's, with brown circles around them. He was a haggard and quiet person, with a burned out and fucked-up look.

They say thousands apply every year to join Doctors without Borders, but very few come back for a second mission. American Paediatrician was on his fourth mission already. From the look of him, Kabeer would have guessed many more trips than that—but even four can be too many. That's four times lowering himself into the burning hell of history in the making, into a world of perpetual emergency and of being constantly on call.

The other doctor was Indian by descent, and he was dark in complexion and slight in stature. He didn't want to leave, but didn't want to stay either. He had been a trauma surgeon back in England, but was working here as an obstetrician, doing C-sections and correcting vaginal fistulas and trying his damnedest to treat abused women with high-risk pregnancies, and failing to save a large number of them, and listening to the agonising stories of those who were surviving.

Initially, he was just hearing them mere as sounds and voices, but little did he know that the acid of sadness had found its way in from his ears to his mind and had gotten settled in a bloody corner of that already cluttered and messed-up heart.

He was an extremely edgy man, who couldn't stand carnage, but ironically had placed himself right in the middle of it. He couldn't stand to see people dying, but people were dying every day in his hands. He was constantly picking fights with the others, saying, "I didn't sign for this, this is bloody rubbish," and then making graphs in thin air with both hands, trying to explain his own threshold of pain through invisible peaks and valleys.

With one hand held low, he would show that he could only take so much pain, and the other hand much higher would show Tunishka's threshold. And he would say, "I'm not like you! I can't take it!"

This was the situation that Kabeer had come into. But he found ways to adjust to this calamity, using smiles and small talk to carve out some space for himself in this thick emotional gunk of his team members. In principle, everybody had come here to give something back to humanity. But he had already hit rock bottom—he didn't have anything to give. He wanted to be on the receiving end. He was looking for hand-outs of peaceful repose from humanity itself.

Work was intense and never-ending. He began to realise that no one could help him in this place—it was a sink of sorrow, a black hole of misery. But then he would also look at Tunishka and the American paediatrician, who had both been working here for years, but they still were able to laugh and smoke cigarettes. *You'll settle in soon,* he told himself. *It's only been a few weeks.*

On his days off, he would go walking aimlessly around a village close to his station. That village seemed abstract to him, like a surrealist painting, with its huts made up of thin, dry sticks and mud. Some of those homes had an entrance door, just one door, or made up of light blue metal sheets with a white UN logo on them.

There was one door he saw that had its UN logo all the way down at the bottom, where it had gotten bent and twisted and dirty beyond recognition. Those metal sheets had once been 40-gallon drums of some sort, which had then been cut and straightened into rectangular metal sheets. The people living behind those doors were no doubt natives, wearing their traditional wraparound dresses in shocking colours, but the shocking colours had long died from those fabrics, and had become faded and worn out. But all this wasn't what made the place abstract to him.

It wasn't that, nor was it even the old and tattered denim overalls that some of the kids wore, on whose stitched-on labels he could still make out the faded words *Oshkosh B'gosh*. The abstract part was those big baobab trees, which were like huge, fat, and nearly cylindrical Greek columns, rising straight in the sky, with proportionally very small branches and even smaller leaves all the way at their top. Those thin baobab branches also mimicked the several arms of the goddess Durga, who seemed to be holding leaves in all her hands and extending them in all directions.

It was a silent, subdued early evening, so quiet that the silence was hushing in his ears, the way silence usually talks in whispers. Kabeer was sitting alone in that same room with the window having two iron shutters, and a single metal bed with an algae-green mosquito net, part of which was still rolled up like a theatre curtain. And that old man's casual words were there in the room with him, too.

He had met this old man out on his wanderings in the village, and he had spoken to Kabeer in a melodious but unclear Pidgin English. Kabeer couldn't understand a lot of what he said, but some of it had stuck with him, something about baobab trees, and it was coming clearer now that the silence was whispering it back to him.

And these words were bugging him now, a frenzy of whispers in his mind, anxiously asking him to give them voice. His intuitions reached out to grasp the hand of conscious reasoning. His face turned warmer and then flushed completely, and then he felt a little tremor in his hands and his emotions started spinning in the blender of his mind. And all this finally triggered his mind to spill out a chain of thoughts. Kabeer didn't think of it as poetry—he just wanted it to make sense.

Now he could hear his pen making scratching sounds on paper leaving lines of many shapes, which were in reality the words of his poem about the baobab tree. The old man had told him in his Pidgin English, "If you sad, you go hug the tree, you go fit!"

What the old man meant, as Kabeer understood it, was, "If you are sad, really sad, you go and hug this tree and tell her to take your sorrow. She'll let you pour all of your sadness into her. Then once you release your arms and let go of her, you'll become free of sorrow. She'll take your sadness."

But there was something else here, too, that came into Kabeer's poem. It went like this:

You can pour all of your sadness
into me; said the tree.
But be very careful,
because I'm filled with pain,
filled with so much so pain,
to my limits,
that every branch,
every single tip of my leaves
is soaked in the sadness
of so many others,
who came before you.
So when you pour your sorrow
into me,

be a little careful.
I don't want you to hurt yourself
and spill my sadness
back into your heart.

His short poem ended and so did the scratching sounds of the nib of his pen against the paper. This small act of creation gave him some happiness, but his day of work had made him deeply tired. He pushed the poem aside, where it would stay for a while and then slowly get mixed up with other scrap papers and finally get tossed in trash, like so many of his prior poems, which he never kept nor remembered, never thinking they were even worth calling poems.

He curled up on his bed and let sleep envelop him.

Life was going on. He was doing whatever everyone else was doing there, treating the sick to heal them of their illnesses. But the mechanics of healing are a gruesome process. It starts all red and hot and inflamed, and then comes the oozing, the tenderness and throbbing pain, then a warm discomfort, and then it discharges with foul-smelling pus.

American Paediatrician usually kept to himself, but one afternoon he started talking to Kabeer while smoking a cigarette on the hospital veranda. He took a puff and then with same fingers that were holding the cigarette he pointed towards a simple signboard, which read 'Emergency Hospital' at the top, and underneath 'Free of Charge—No Money'.

American Paediatrician murmured, "That is the only thing I like about this place. Just those five last words on that signboard." He paused and sucked in another deep puff. "It took me 22 years to make up my mind. I raised two kids and was married and was a doctor in the system, a member of the industry, like all the others. And after a while?" American Paediatrician threw out his cigarette butt, and before turning to go back inside, he said, "Healing the sick should be a passion, and passion can't be industrialised."

American Paediatrician left, but Kabeer stayed behind on the veranda looking out at the beach, which wasn't all that far away. He appreciated the soft but sad beauty of the light of the sunset, which was forcing itself to be recognised over that beach that was littered with thousands of empty cans and soda bottles, which the ocean had spit out upon it at high tide. But if you managed to avoid that ugly reality, the beach could look like a grumpy intellectual who wanted to deny the brightness of setting sun, reasoning in favour of the wet grey and silver-white sand.

The sky was lit with transparent layers of light tan, fading silver, and amber orange. The ocean reflected the same colours, only a bit darker, and there was a glossy sheen on the sand, where the waves were seemed to be reciting the same couplet again and again. In the distance, there were also a few palm trees that had tilted their heads away from the beating coastal winds. They had moved their branches toward the land, looking like protesters raising both hands to protect their heads from police baton beatings.

After few weeks he was moved, along with Tunishka and American Paediatrician, to another emergency hospital in another country that was some five hours flight time away. The situation was the same—the misery and hardship and lack of resources—but over here there was no abstract surrealist village nearby with an old man sharing poems in pigeon English, and no baobab trees who would invite you to hug them and release all your troubles.

On his days off, he would go with Tunishka to an enormous slum. It was a peninsula, or really just a lump of land off the Atlantic coast. It was a no-go zone for all the staffers, but Tunishka would go there anyway. It was a toxic dump of decaying humanity, over 70 thousand souls, camped in a space of less than a quarter of mile, all sharing six makeshift community latrines.

The first time he went to West Point, which was the name of that slum in Monrovia, he followed Tunishka through alleyways which were also people's homes, walkways in which women were cooking and kids were playing and people were sleeping, all at the same time.

Tunishka was walking fast, squeezing through, dodging people, and politely saying, "pardon," "excuse me," "thank you sir," as she pressed through that labyrinth of virtually nothing. She brought them into a comparatively wider opening, a kind of rectangular courtyard in the middle of those tin houses, which Tunishka called 'zinc houses'.

She started talking to a few women at random, with a sudden smiley high-pitched, "Hi, I'm Dr Tunishka, from the emergency hospital!" And then she threw on a smile, which really looked natural, and she continued, "Do you know about the MSF hospital in town?"

Some of them said, "yes," and Tunishka urged them to come there if they needed any medical treatment, explaining that it was completely free, they wouldn't have to pay anything. Those women were dirt poor, but were still uncomfortable with the idea free treatment. They kept trying to find the hidden price of the free treatment in the offer, as if Tunishka was a hoax.

Kabeer unwillingly had to agree with his father that sorrow, pain, poverty and shame are your desperate lovers; they love you with all of their being and want to sacrifice their everything to you, and they follow you for your entire life out of their utter love for you. But the problem is that all they can offer you is themselves, only sorrow, pain, poverty and shame!

Thinking about that riddle of his father, Kabeer left Tunishka trying her best to explain to those *chary* women that prayers are always free, and what MSF was doing was kind of like that. He made a gesture towards Tunishka with his hand to tell her he was going to walk back to their truck. She nodded in agreement, and he started walking back, but he took an alley that led not to their truck but to the banks of the Saint Paul River, and what a sad-looking river it was, a slow moving body of liquid filth.

Its banks were completely covered with trash, mainly all sorts of empty plastic bottles, and there was a latrine out ten or fifteen feet into the river, connected to the bank via a pathway made up of a scaffolding of long single planks of wood. The latrine itself was a squarish frame standing on bamboo, and its four sides consisted of rusted tin sheets, within which people would squat and directly defecate into the river named after a Saint Paul.

He was standing by those riverbanks in the middle of all that trash, when he heard a "quack! quack!" To his astonishment, there was a white duck waddling there. Actually, she was not white at all, but rather completely dirty and stained with streaks of used motor oil. But there she was, with her several chicks, roaming around with her clumsy swaying ass. That duck gave him a frail reason to smile. There in her carefree swagger was all the resilience of life.

Almost four months of this mission had passed. It was like trying to stop the bleeding of the stinky guts of dying humanity with his own two hands, and having to do that while his own experience was still raw and dripping. And then something happened that was as random as that proverbial butterfly of chaos theory, who flutters his wings in one place and gives birth to hurricanes on the other side of the planet. And that was that he saw that Médecins sans Frontières was now asking for volunteers for a flood relief mission to southern Sindh. And he didn't know if it was a sudden compulsion or maybe he had been looking for this opportunity all along—but he decided to go.

Chapter 2
Dying Freshness

And soon a small aircraft was lifting him along, as if he were retracing the influence of that theoretical butterfly from the Atlantic coast of Africa back to the land of his own roots. After several stopovers and three plane changes he reached Karachi. It was the middle of monsoon season. It wasn't his first time going there, and not even his first time seeing the monsoons. And when he got there, he didn't go to the MSF quarters, but instead chose to stay at the home of Babli Mama,[154] one of his mother's cousin-brothers.

His real name was long, like all his mother's other male family members, a combination with nouns and adjectives and other syllables and preferably some title too, all thrown together, but he could never remember it all. Anyway, everybody just called him Babli.

Babli Mama was a wacky fellow, an opinionated married man and a flower child, a hippie. Over the last twenty years, Kabeer had watched Babli Mama inhabit a number of different looks. When Kabeer was about 10 or so, and visiting Pakistan for the first time, Babli Mama was a young man with a long slim face, with silky hair that he used to comb frequently with fingers of both hands. He had been single then, and his banking career was growing like bamboo at the time. Plus, he was an amateur radio jockey, hosting an oldies show on 90.1 FM.

But that was 20 years ago. Things had kept changing, like they usually do, and so did Babli Mama. He put on some weight, and his baldness increased, and he became the head of some division of financial products that multinational banks offer, but he still kept hosting his radio show. And yes he got married, but

---

[154] It bears reminder here that the word '*mama*' in Sindhi refers to a maternal uncle.

he also kept being unfaithful to his wife, Doctor Aunty, and there were also some rumours that he used to beat her at times.

And now, at the airport in Karachi, Kabeer was seeing him again after seven or eight years away, and Babli Mama was again another man. He had quit his bank job and was working as a consultant now, and he was still doing his FM 90.1 oldies show every evening. He was looking 15 years older than his real age because of his beer belly and horseshoe baldness, but his love was unchanged. He gave Kabeer a gripping hug and then patted both his cheeks, as if he were a little boy again.

They left for Babli Mama's place. It was somewhere in Clifton, which is Karachi's upscale area, close to the beach, with streets named after Persian names. It was not the Boat Basin, but Kabeer called it that anyway, because he had his own set of memories of the Hudson Boat Basin and the cafés of West 79th street.

Clifton was the relatively safe and secure part of the city, though nothing is completely safe in Karachi. Some areas are taken for granted to be safe, probably just for the heck of it, and that shoreline was one of those.

"How is everything?" Babli Mama asked.

Kabeer said, "good" without really thinking. He knew that Babli Mama lived on the other side of the city, so it was going to take a while to crisscross the town. It was night and Babli Mama's car was cruising on a 3- or 4-lane elevated highway, with wavy sporadic peaks followed by dips. There were bright orange road lamps, which were arming over and covering almost a third of that highway top, and because of the thick humidity, the orange and yellow glow from those lamps was making virtual pyramids of light. And there were also usual billboards, most of them showing pretty women wearing colourful linen, which was called lawn here, the same word as a grassy lawn but a different thing entirely.

"How are your mother and that crazy father of yours?" asked Babli Mama with a laugh.

"They're still kicking," Kabeer replied lightly.

"In your email you wrote that you are going to work with flood relief project! That is great."

"Humm, it is," said Kabeer.

Kabeer kept looking at those doubtful early morning skies, where a thin brightness was trying hard to peak through at the horizon, but one could still see a super-size moon slowly dragging its feet like an old diabetic on those rapidly brightening skies. By the time they reached Babli Mama's home it was still aurora, and the air was wet but cool, with a bleachy smell, a combination of dominating pollutants and dying freshness.

There were distant sounds of maybe seagulls and early morning sparrows and other noises of life itself, but then there was an eruption of several *azaans*[155] at the same time, one after the other, overlapping each other; they permeated the atmosphere, overpowering every other sound.

He was so tired that he slept for hours, in that white villa that belonged to Babli Mama. It was a modern home whose architect had hinted at a vernacular style, with rough edges that tried to echo the exteriors of mud huts. But the whole block was full of these cookie-cutter assemblages, so the attempt to capture the nostalgia of indigenous architecture quickly fell flat. Only Babli Mama's house had four palm trees in its front yard, because Babli Mama was an artsy guy, after all.

Inside the house, in the main family room, there was a painting on one of the walls, and there was a light purplish and beige rug right under that, like it was placed especially for someone to stand on that beautiful rug while looking at the painting and all its vibrant colours. It showed a bouquet of triangles, like graffiti in a vase, which instead of flowers looked like tools and yet your heart wanted to believe that they were flowers.

It was an explosion of colours that Kabeer couldn't have named, all those burned siennas, glowing oranges, luminous greens, and flat cobalt blues, spread on the canvas the way a child would make a rollercoaster out of dynamic arcs circling and circumventing straight rod-like lines. On one of those frilly lines, the artist's name was written in a cursive script; the first name was legible as Ahmed, but the second word was so smushed that it had all turned black.

Kabeer had wanted to come here because it soothed him, without any reason. He felt strangely at ease with the loose end of his roots. He liked this mirage that everyone was always kind. Whatever Sindhi he could speak, they would always reply back, and Kabeer liked that one language monotony. And that language was his own preference, because he only mingled with his parents' families and their friends.

---

[155] *Azaan*: the call to prayer, sung from the mosque.

He had deep affection for this place and its people. But then he had hated it equally, for some shitload of reasons, one of which was that super formula, the story of his first love and betrayal, which rose and went down exactly the way those stories always do. But apart from that crashing romance, he had grown up always feeling close to Sindh and its culture, and he liked that benevolence, that spirituality. He started listening to Alan Fakeer and to the guy with the henna-orange hair and beard, who was Sohrab Fakeer, but Kabeer couldn't ever remember his name. Still he loved listening to the *'Mystic hymn of Latif'* as sung by Sohrab Fakeer, playing it from his phone, just relying on the expression of the voices to understand the poetry.

Part of Kabeer's inclination towards all this was his father, who carries on his own art of storytelling. In Kabeer's childhood days, sometimes, in the frigid New Jersey winter evenings, while driving back from his twice a week karate class, his father would start translating some weird form of ornamental Sindhi that was playing from the car audio.

It felt to him like someone was crying while the others were playing music to accompany the cries, and his father kept doing his crude translations of it for as long as he could before Kabeer would beg him to change the CD and play the Spice Girls instead. But his father would keep translating, and Kabeer would become angry, saying, "I don't understand it! Whatever this man is singing is not the Sindhi that you and Mom speak!"

And his father would continue replying, "It is Sindhi, but it's in an old dialect. It's not difficult at all. Here, listen—" And then his father would translate it word for word, stopping and rewinding it, and ruining the whole beauty of the *'Bhit ja bhatti'* in the process.

Jakee munjh jhaan; so taray tagay tohanjay;
Lutaf jee Latif chway to wath kamee kaan;
Adlain choothan aaoon na; ko pearow kaj fazal jo.

Whatever there is in the universe, It all keeps floating because of you.
Glory is all yours, said Latif,
You are the domain of pleasure.
I know I'm a sinner, but please let me go, (pretty) please,
Because you are bounty and you are grace.

Somehow those crude translations of his father's stayed in him, and it gave him a weird feeling, like that he knew something very unusual. Like he had a key of some sort that might open a hidden chamber in him, if he could ever find the door to it.

Now things are changed, he himself is changed, he is a fresh physician, who just pop out of the box, and thirty-one years old broke-up three times for sure including that bare knuckle first romance of his with his cousin, who was five years older than him, and wasn't serious about him, but rather narcissistically liked being loved.

The second was his Gujarati girlfriend from senior year in high school, who dumped him after finding out that he was screwing other girls, including her own friend. At that time in his naivety, he was thinking that he could walk around displaying his stone-carved muscular body to appeal to average girls and his diverse chest of knowledge to the nerdy ones.

And what might they find inside that mental treasure trove? For example, all about the six-sigma performance rating of the Mumbai *dabbawala*[156] phenomenon, where close to 5000 mostly illiterate folks would pick up a quarter of a million lunches, distribute them, and then bring the empty tiffin boxes back, with 99.9999 percent accuracy.

This meant only one incomplete delivery in 6 million transactions. He used to love narrating that last sentence of his statement and trying to end it with that statistical drama of 99.9999 percent accuracy. The Mumbai dabbawalas had actually been doing their job with that same accuracy since the 1830s, but Forbes magazine had just made a big thing out of it.

Or sometimes he used to explain Kant's transcendental aesthetics at that unripe age of 17 or so years, but somehow he managed to pull it off to attract the girls. He would mix in bits and pieces that he had heard from his father with some of his own research, but he still took some liberties, narrating the transcendental aesthetic the way he wanted.

Like, "It's the realisation that space is not something that we learn from experience. That is, space itself is not verifiable because it is instead required for there to be any experience of the outside world. Any representation of something outside of me must be a representation of something in space."

---

[156] *Dabbawala*: literally 'box-bringer'—a lunchbox deliveryman. The box itself is also called a 'tiffin' box.

Right at this juncture of his statement, when he felt that the cross-questioning might start, he used to throw in something which had nothing to do with Kant at all, by saying, "Kant said God is not complete!"

When his subjects out of their astonishment asked, "What do you mean by that?" He would explain, "God is limitless—and if God is limitless! Then he is still expanding. So he is not complete—right?"

Then he would hum a little and start up again. "Take a cube. It has six sides and eight angles, and we know it is complete because we explored it. Has anybody explored God yet? No! Then Kant was right."

Kant never ventured any such argument, but it worked on Kabeer's young listeners, most of whom were nerdy girls who wore thick vision glasses and didn't shave their facial hairs.

Apart from those soap-opera-like half-cooked romances, there was something else, a little thorny, a little achy, that he kept locked up in his heart. Probably, it was that relationship which stirred his mind and gave calluses to his thoughts, but again, maybe not.

But now he was here, living the agony of getting everything and still feeling deprived with the pain of the unknown, which makes you nauseated, and you grope and stretch and never hurt enough, and he wanted to get rid of that feeling. He wanted to find that fucking bliss, that euphoria, all those different definitions of Nirvana that his father would always go on about.

His father used to tell Kabeer's American friends that contentment was a relative term, and that in the villages of Sindh he had seen people sitting crunched down in the shadow of the thorny old babur trees, people who probably had less than five dollars to their names. But if you asked them, "How are you?" They'd reply, "Fine!" Smiling with their eyes and lips. He wanted to see those people who are old and sick and poor, but still fine, and really happy.

Chapter 3
Solid-Looking Body of Liquid

The next morning, he reported to the Doctors without Borders clinic, somewhere in the old part of the city, which was serving as the main flood relief operational centre too. It took him 25 minutes to half an hour to reach this place from Babli Mama's home.

That epoch of 25 to 30 minutes of time, brought him to an eerily familiar place. Yesterday it had taken him close to 15 hours and three flight changes to reach Karachi from northern African coast, but today, it was only 25 to 30 minutes. He was anticipating it, so there was no shock, but still the size of that slum was mammoth.

He had read about Karachi's Orangi slums while he was still in Africa, and he had learned that it had beaten out that the even infamous Mumbai Dharavi slum from *Slumdog Millionaire*, and this became darkly comic notoriety of a slum got glorified by celluloid and somehow stayed in his memory.

Over here things were a little different. There was a doctor who was in charge of this clinic, and there was also a girl who was overseeing relief camps in towns that had been particularly devastated by the floods. That doctor was an Irish guy, with a shaved head and an Iranian style beard, and wearing a white safari jacket when Kabeer met him. He was very busy, but he managed to introduce Kabeer to Uzoo, whose real name was Kainat Arzoo, but she just went by Uzoo. She was the girl taking care of the flood relief effort.

Uzoo seemed a young girl, but she had a professional background in sociology and community work. She was an urban post-9/11 Pakistani girl—one of those who wanted to stand out. She wore a loose, plus-size mega tunic length blouse over blue jeans, and flashy ballet flats with a big bow on the toe, detailed with decorative nail head studs. And she covered her head with a floral-print hijab with vibrant blue hibiscuses and a pearly white background.

Her heart-shaped face would peek out from under this hijab as if out of a scuba diving hood. She had an olive complexion and big eyes, and when listening to you, her eyebrows would very slowly take the shape of curled arms, or of the curved bows of Hun archers, which made it seem that she was unhappy, but would keep nodding her head up and down in agreement.

She took Kabeer into one of the rooms and got straight down to business. "We have three camp locations that are ours," she said, "and two camps of another NGO that we are helping. They're for flood affected people all along the right bank of Indus—Kashmore, Sukkur, Shikarpur, Larkano, and Dadu." Then she looked up into Kabeer's eyes and said, "there are close to three hundred thousand people, in those five camps alone."

Kabeer was just listening. In the past few months, he had seen hell—how much worse could this be? Uzoo took a sigh. Looking down at the ground, she said pretty much to herself, "We'll do it." Then she told him, "We have two more days before we go back to the camps. A team of local volunteers are in there working 24/7. You are going to help and train them."

He called Babli Mama to be picked up, and then, without letting anyone know, he stepped out of the emergency hospital, against his own better judgment. The Orangi slum is not a place to roam around, but he did it anyway.

Out here in the open, the smells got stronger, that stench of ammonia combined with humid dust, on a buzzing street full of people. Most of the children were wandering half-naked, wearing only knee-length shirts that had gotten stained and re-stained until they turned into a grey unitone. It was bleak. There was no vegetation.

Those kids were playing by the side of a runnel of filth. They called it Ganda Nala,[157] an indescribable stream of filth, maybe 20 or 25 feet wide, but in length it goes as far as he could see to either side. That filthy Nala had a sorrowful look to it as if it had been gang raped. Nothing was floating in it; it was an almost solid-looking body of liquid, with a grey crust on the top, and other waste was peering up from underneath, making it all look a bit like the top crust of a banana crumb muffin, except that it was grey.

But then below that toxic crust, it had everything else possible in there, all sizes and sorts of plastic shopping bags, empty plastic containers, all manner of trash. There were fat black rubber pipes running across the stream, probably

---

[157] *Ganda Nala*: literally, 'dirty stream'.

carrying water. He noticed a concrete slab bridge over the stream, where plastic bags and other trash was making its way onto that bridge, and the whiteness of the plastic was mimicking early autumn fog that rises from streams. That false mist of trash crept upward and was lurking almost at the top of the bridge.

The Musconetcong River came into his mind and his heart stopped for a moment, like he didn't want to force this comparison onto that river and the way in which, somehow, on early October mornings, fog would find its way to her stone bridges. The Musconetcong had a bridge that was a perfect half a circle of stones, and, very rarely, when the river was still, from a distance one could see that bridge with its reflection in the water as a perfect full circle.

One of those black snaking pipes on the Nala busted suddenly, and a flock of sparrows that had been hiding in that trash fled in all directions. Kabeer realised he should go back to hospital now, before he got lost. He started walking back, and something that he had seen somewhere on Facebook or YouTube came into his mind.

It was a report of two little boys from somewhere similar to here, who would swim out into the open sea a ways in order to catch crabs from a swamp at a muddy island, and then swim back before high tide to sell those crabs to support their families. He was still thinking of those children when he reached back at the hospital, where he found Uzoo again in the hallway.

"What are you doing?" She asked. "I thought you were gone."

"Just waiting for my ride."

Uzoo said, "Come join us—we're having a project meeting about how to supply fresh water to these"—she scrambled to find the word, and like she had discovered one, she said, "urban growths." She probably hadn't wanted to say slums.

"What am I gonna do in there? I'm a physician."

"Just sit and listen," she said. And she led him into a room with a table a several chairs. It wasn't a proper conference room, but something like that. The hospital director Irish-Gut-with-Iranian-Beard was sitting there with two other middle-aged men and a woman. Both of the middle-aged men were wearing suits. One of them was a chubby with a double chin and a loose necktie knot. The other one was just smiling. Kabeer took a seat.

The woman started the meeting off. Kabeer was trying to think of someone she resembled, but he couldn't find any one that he could relate to her with. She had a long face and retro-like curls, and teeth that seemed crowded in her mouth. She wore a long stole that rested on both shoulders.

"There is lack of water supply all over Karachi," she began. Then she took a pause and hummed, blinking behind her thin-framed glasses, like she had said all this several times before. She rolled her lips over her tongue and then carried on, saying, "Today about 665 million gallons of water come daily into Karachi."

She again took a pause, followed by a prolonged aahhhh sound that was not yet a word, and then said, "And we have just completed a study, together with government officials. We work closely with them; we know a number of them very well," she again prolonged that same aahhhh, "…and we found about 242 million gallons of water were siphoned daily from the bulk mains, from huge pipes, 24 inches to 72 inches in diameter, and this bulk supply constitutes…" and she dragged here like she wanted make sure in her mind that she was coming up with the right number, and finally said, "forty one percent of the entire supply, generating 50 billion rupees annually. It's a huge operation," she distorted her voice to emphasise the word huge, "done by an organised group of people, who have very good connection with the politicians, with the police, with the military, with the powers that be."

She smiled. "So in Karachi we've got a parallel governance mechanism which supplies daily use water through tankers, a black market of fresh water supply." She went on talking about those numbers.

Kabeer was keeping quiet, looking at her like he was listening, but he was really thinking about how wrong he had been about today's Pakistan. In his view a person like her should not survive; she should be neutralised, to use that creepy euphemism for killings. And here she is being director of some experimental housing project for poor, and she is openly kicking everybody's asses, from military to politicians to police.

His cell phone vibrated in his pocket; it was Babli Mama. He got himself excused and whispered gently towards Uzoo, "I'll meet you here in two days," and stepped out.

Instead of sending a driver, Babli Mama had come to pick Kabeer up himself. Babli Mama's car smelled of some mixture of a fine French fragrance and pot. They drove past narrow streets with tin-roof shacks made up of concrete blocks, and then all of a sudden they were amid the city's old Victorian limestone buildings. But these also looked extremely dirty, neglected, some of them painted with solid colours right over the limestone, in white and ocean blue.

Most of them were completely altered, with additions made of concrete blocks protruding from the main facades of those Victorian mansions; some of them had air conditioners hanging out of their windows, mooning their fat asses.

It reminded him of those modern photographs of New York City that showed distorted images of the old buildings as reflected in the mirror-glass panels of the new skyscrapers. The buildings in those photographs might have been ordinary office blocks or apartments, but their reflections in the shiny glass panes rendered them beautiful and mysterious, with their melting geometrical shapes and watery colours. The shots look more like abstract paintings than architectural photography. But here it was reversed.

The people had converted beautiful limestone structures into ugly dwellings, like those merciless criminals who abduct children and then chop their limbs to make them crippled or pour hot boiling lead in their eyes to make them blind, so that they could become effective beggars in the villains' employ.

He thought of those children when he saw these buildings, whose elegant limestone facades with floral carvings had been expanded with plain cement blocks. Some of their balconies were covered with sign boards showing dentures, and something written in Urdu, which he wasn't able to read, but he assumed those bold strokes probably announced the dentist's name, and the smaller writing must say something like 'get your dentures here.'

But after a few moments, the landscape changed again, and they were driving through a series of flyovers, which expanded to a wide 4-lane road, bringing them to a part of Karachi where there were high rise buildings with names carved on them like Horizon Towers and 70 Riviera.

All along Babli Mama was talking to him on different topics, and he was engaging in that conversation at the same time as all these thoughts of the urban orgy of those old buildings were processing in his mind. Babli Mama had turned out to be a staunch patriot, one who has developed a keen interest in Pakistan and in its founder. He had even chosen a full portrait of Jinnah to be his own Facebook profile picture, with the quotation, There is no power on earth that can undo Pakistan. And right under the word Pakistan were Jinnah's black lace oxford shoes, the perforated ones with the glittering sheen on them.

Babli Mama also wanted to see a change in the country's system. And he also blamed the Western world and particularly the United States for most of Pakistan's troubles. And part of that might be true, but Kabeer also remembered how his father had explained that most of Babli's distrust of the United States could be blamed on Madeleine Albright, because apparently Babli had been refused a US visitor visa twice during her tenure as Secretary of State. Jani would laugh about how much more radicalised Babli Mama's views had become after those consecutive rejections.

"Things have changed," Kabeer said.

"No," Babli Mama replied with a smile. "You have grown wiser." Babli Mama glanced over at Kabeer. "Look kid, being touchy with the past is real."

Kabeer interrupted, "You mean nostalgia?"

But Babli kept on. "And things do really change, they break, they age, they die!"

Kabeer interrupted before Babli Mama could get into any of that intellectual crap. He had had enough of that growing up as the only child of someone who had his own intellectual axe to grind. "Babli Mama, let's go see the people of your town tonight," Kabeer said.

Babli picked the sentence up right where Kabeer had dropped it. "All right, after my show, we'll go, but I just wanted to say one more thing."

Babli Mama was talking in a frenzy. "By 'things have changed', you meant to say that bad things are happening here. But look, it's not all bad. It's an organic soup of good, bad and ugly. There are between 18 and 22 million people in this city, and that number keeps rising, so yes, things do change, constantly. Old people die, young become old, the unborn take birth—you want to hear more?"

"No," said Kabeer.

"Okay," said Babli Mama. Then Babli Mama said something that was like an eighteen-wheeler breaking through a red light to come crashing into you. "You want to get laid?"

Kabeer never expected this, so first he let loose some spontaneous, shallow laughter. Then he said, "Are you nuts? And no I don't want to get laid, I'm an idealist utopian, Mama! I need to go through the whole fucking nine yards before getting laid."

Babli Mama said, "Fine just asking." So that's Babli Mama, a guy who wrote articles for the Tribune, a regular radio broadcaster, resident of Clifton, ambassador-at-large of something or other, and screwer of whores.

Chapter 4
The Rest of the Journey Was Dust Grey

They hopped a convoy of four SUVs, heading north towards Dadu. The last noticeable thing he saw before leaving Karachi was a huge array of colourful bolts of fabric hanging from a tall network of erect bamboo scaffoldings, vibrant yellows, reds, oranges, turquoises, with dark browns and purples between them.

"What's that?" Kabeer asked Uzoo.

She answered without even looking up at Kabeer, just scrolling through email messages on her cell. "It's an old *dhobi ghat*,[158] but now they dye white cotton bolts there."

That was last of the colours; the rest of the journey was dust grey. Soon, they were passing through a semi-industrial area, with sporadic shacks, and occasional people who looked like oily rags, walking across two lane interstate highway.

Uzoo said, "Did you notice that everything is grey outside?" which actually Kabeer had not noticed yet. She explained, "It's because of several cement factories in this area, with little to no pollution oversight."

He didn't reply, but just said, "Um-hm." And he thought of late-night episodes of Law and Order on TV, and how there would usually be law firm ads during the commercial breaks, with grim statistics about mesothelioma. Inside his mind, Kabeer was speaking to those people who looked like rags, people who were living and breathing under that dusty grey death, telling them that he could only feel sorry for them, and that's it. 20 million people are affected by floods, 800 thousand flood victims suffering right now, but no one was going to even think twice about mesothelioma, which was going to take twenty years to kill you.

---

[158] *Dhobi ghat*: a part of a riverbank where professional launderers wash clothes by hand.

The car had a weird smell, and the air conditioning was blowing pretty hard, so the smell was coming at him in bouts. It was a smell of coffee beans and strong vintage perfume, the kind that is usually unavoidable anywhere in the proximity of the fragrance booths of Macy's in holiday season, followed by sour layers of body perspiration that seemed to have kept happening and drying one on the top of the other on the same clothes.

Uzoo started going into detail about the ugliness of the situation, and she was throwing all different numbers, she was telling him that the resources were either limited or non-existent, no diagnostic tools, hard working conditions, on and on.

Kabeer kept saying, "Um-hum" alternating that sometimes with, "I'm listening," as he stared outside at that vast, barren landscape of rock. He looked over at Uzoo and said it outright, "I like what you're doing."

"Alright," she replied casually.

When they eventually reached Dadu, it was as bad as he had expected. In this one location there were more than a thousand people taking refuge. Tunishka's words came into his mind: "In emergency there is nothing personal or professional—it all gets blurred! You have to make your own lines." There were so many people there, volunteers and local help in addition to the scores of flood victims.

Kabeer said to Uzoo, "Let's have a walk around this camp; I just want to get the feel of it."

What it felt like was a train wreck. There were mothers holding their infants in their laps, but the limbs of those kids were soft like Jell-O, and their eyes rolled back in their heads. There were also men holding sick kids in their laps and carrying them on their shoulders. At one spot, they all gathered around Kabeer and Uzoo. They didn't know Kabeer, but they had seen Uzoo before, so the women started pulling at her and touching her to get her attention, and they were all speaking at the same time in Sindhi: "*Amari O amari!*" And another: "*Toon dacktarayani aan.*" And another, trying to bring her child in front, "*O aama, hay muhanjo nandharo.*"[159]

It was a clamour, and Kabeer said to all of them, "*Sub khay deesoon tha.*"— *Everyone will be seen.* There was a brief shocked silence, from all those women, including, Uzoo, who never expected a reply in Sindhi from him.

---

[159] "*Amari... nandharo.*" The Sindhi spoken here translates to:
"Oh mother!" (where *Amari* is a particularly reverent term for 'mother') "You're a lady doctor!" "Oh mother, this is my little boy."

So he started examining children there in the open, literally on the ground. Someone got him a beat-up but still robust-looking blue plastic Jerry can to sit on, one of those thick rubber ones, and he asked some volunteers to help the patients form a line. The first patient he saw was an incoherent infant. On auscultation, he heard rattling and crackling sounds in his abdomen, followed by bubbling on one side.

Upon percussion of the chest there was a dull *thud*. He just wanted make sure it was pneumonia. In that fraction of a split second, he gathered everything he had learned about diagnosing pneumonia with just a stethoscope. And yes, there was a rumbling sound, like the engine of a steam locomotive, making its long slow departure, followed by the distant lob-dub, lob-dub, of a restless baby heart.

He said to Uzoo, "If I'm not mistaken—which I know I'm not—then we need ampicillin and gentamicin for these kids, and a whole lot of it. This one," he nodded toward the one he was examining, "has pneumonia. If it spreads and becomes an epidemic, then the children in this camp will start dropping like flies."

Uzoo turned to one of the other team members, an active and eager guy of about twenty-some years, and ask him to go and get the medicine from town. Kabeer kept examining kids. Most of them were suffering from severe malnutrition, coughing, feverish. After what felt like a long time, over an hour anyway, that young man came back with five boxes of antibiotics. Five boxes meant fifty doses—for more than five hundred sick kids. Kabeer looked at that young man and asked in Sindhi, "Why so few?"

"Saeen, this was all I could get from Bhan," he answered, meaning Bhan'nan jo Shahar, which the town closest to the camp. "If we send someone to Dadu, we'll get more."

"What's your name?" Kabeer asked.

The young man replied, "Roshoo Gopang," but then he corrected himself and said, "Sibt-e-Najaf Gopang, that's what my father named me, but everybody calls me Roshan Gopang, or Roshoo."

Kabeer thought to himself, Roshoo must like his real name, Sibt-e-Najaf, and that's why he took time to explain all that, like maybe this is the only thing he has to be proud of in his life so far. And he wanted to share that with a stranger, in the midst of mayhem. And Kabeer was also trying to grasp some disconnect that he was perceiving in this situation.

Before embarking on this task, from the other side of Africa, he had heard a podcast of Morning Edition or some other NPR news show. They ran a small sound bite of a Hillary Clinton speech, in which she was telling the world about this flood, in her sombre voice saying, "The enormity of the disaster is hard to fathom. This flooding had already affected more people than Indian Ocean tsunami, the Haitian earthquake, and the 2008 Pakistan earthquake combined."

And this speech had mobilised sixteen people from his organisation alone, and the UN Secretary General was asking for hundreds of millions of dollars for the relief effort. And he himself had come here from Karachi in a convoy of four or five SUVs. And here was Roshoo, who had walked an hour to get lifesaving medicine for dying kids and could only get fifty doses from some place called Bhan.

These things were all popping up in his mind, in that parallel mind-world we all live in, where we speak aloud to ourselves, in which we all have the power to hire and fire everybody, even God sometimes.

Eventually, more medicine came from city or somewhere, enough to serve as a preventative drug for the kids in this camp. In these few days, he made infant check-up his top priority. Every three days was shuttling with Uzoo between camps at Shikarpur, Larkano, Dadu, and Karachi. He still couldn't fully conceive how these millions and millions of people could be displaced and lose everything; whatever little they had owned had been swamped in floodwaters. But still it was normal somehow, where normal means the skies had not fallen.

Roshan Gopang was sort of in charge of that camp in Dadu, and he had a genuine desire to help. He also had some feelings for Uzoo. Whenever he saw her, there a watery glaze would appear in his eyes, and outer edges of his both eyes would relax a little, like a kind of smile. That wet glaze in his eyes reminded Kabeer of something he'd seen in a painting by Rembrandt, called 'Old Man in Military Costume'.

Rembrandt had even painted a small pink tear gland, in one of his subject's eyes. But he had not just remembered that portrait, because of that sad moistness in those eyes. But because it was also known as 'formerly called as portrait of Rembrandt's father'. So those were the kinds of eyes that Roshan had for Uzoo.

Here on the lip of chaos, at the outbreak of disease, where millions were forced to live on levee tops, on those thin elevated strips of endless dry land, with vast bodies of stagnant water on either side, where every kid on examination, turns out to be severely malnourished or dehydrated, where half of the population is ill and suffering, it seemed that Roshan Gopang had chosen to fall in love anyway.

He had fallen in love with this goddess of artificial intelligence, because that's what Uzoo was—almost a machine, a city girl, with her signature colourful hijab, who couldn't speak a single word of the language of those people she had volunteered to help. But it was her choice, to go finding money for them, running between city and camps, at times holding and hugging scores of sour-smelling women with their soiled, barely breathing infants. And she, who was a no-bullshit kind of person, metaphysically in this processes, her whole heart had become so big, that probably there was no room left for a vagina in Uzoo.

Why was she doing this, Kabeer had no idea. He could only hazard a wild guess that maybe in one of those dark scary nightmares of her childhood, Uzoo had found a safe refuge in the big heart of a philanthropist. Apart from all that, she was Urdu. Well, she belonged to that urban population of Sindh who spoke Urdu and were called Muhajirs. But Kabeer called them Urdu in his own mind. So Uzoo was one of those city girls who wanted to make a difference in the lives of those who had less in this world.

By now, Kabeer had started to get the hang of living in unease. He was slowly getting used to this busted bubble of life, and it seemed normal to him now. It was all monotonous, checking sick children, giving them medicine that might prolong their lives, and then listening to the complaints of those poor people, which have to do nothing with him, and having no way to help.

Those laments would all come pouring upon him the moment he asked, in Sindhi, to be told the child's name. And then as he was writing down the medicines on the small sheets of scrap paper that he had for this, the child's caretaker would take this as a cue to tell their whole story in those thirty seconds—all of it, all the same, all sorrow, all misery.

One young man of olive complexion started yelling in this moment, in a mixed language, Sindhi and Urdu combined. The poor fellow was probably doing that thinking that it might make his cries a little more audible, a little different from the others. He had a short boxy beard with moustache, and he was so thin that one could grab on to his clavicle like a door handle. But he was angry, and kept saying, "*Hum ghariboon ka yeh hal hai daikho, Traparo lat gayai diwaron kay neechay.*"[160] And he went on, "It was late at night. The flood entered

---

[160] "*Hum ghariboon... ka niche.*" "Look at the state we poor people are in. Whatever little we had got buried under the collapsed mud walls."

and washed everything away. Whatever is left is buried under collapsed mud walls. No one helped—can't you see our condition? We are in the rain under open skies, and our kids are writhing and wailing. Is this wreck, life?" He didn't even pause between the words 'wreck' and 'life', he just said it and dropped the whole payload.

And Kabeer kept telling him, "everything is going to be fine," with the point-blank certainty in his heart that nothing was going to be fine, and that olive-skinned man was going to suffer even more.

In the evening he started taking short breaks, just to try to think about something else, or not to think at all. He would walk across the levee, smoking a cigarette, hoping to find a quiet space, but there was none. And why would there be a quiet space? There were scores of people on that unending levee, of all different ages. There were children playing, carefree and busting in giggles, others were bogusly crying. There were old women talking to themselves, oblivious to the world, and even if you looked them straight in the face, they wouldn't care; they would still keep talking to themselves.

Then there were also worried looking middle-aged men, and a few hungry and sad looking bulls, whose carts had canopies over them erected on wooden sticks. And there were a number of red Russian-made tractors, which looked like those invincible vintage Soviet weightlifters who never lost a match. The tractors were dragging hayride trolleys filled with household things, including some weird stuff, like orange and blue plastic iceboxes and washing machines.

On one of those evenings, Kabeer looked into the distant horizon at the breath-taking blue skies, a kind of blue that made him want to say "blue-blue-blue" like in a song. Those skies were laced with shredded clouds, and the setting sun's cosmic rays had turned those clouds into pure gold at the horizon. A little higher up they were still bleached white in streaks, giving way to a robin's egg blue and then transparent sapphire, a crystalline look. But then those clouds split into small amber orange lumps and became sluggish, like they were not going anywhere.

An old man was sitting crunched down almost at the edge of the levee. He was playing with a child who was wearing a stained and dirty shirt that reached down to his knees, without any pants underneath. The kid seemed demanding and obnoxious to Kabeer, but the old man didn't appear bothered at all; in fact, he was enjoying the child.

Kabeer felt an urge to speak to him, without any reason. Maybe the old man's affection towards that child reminded Kabeer of his grandfather, or maybe not. But he went over to him and lowered himself down and sat beside him. The old man squared his shoulders and craned his neck.

"Keyan aahyo?" Kabeer asked, translating the English 'how are you' overly directly into Sindhi.

The old man replied in affirmative tone, *"Khush chakno bhalo."* And after half a breath of pause he returned the inquiry, asking *"Tawhan khush aahyo?"*

Kabeer wanted to know the old man's story. So he asked him simply, "What happened?"

The old man looked at Kabeer and said, "What happened, what?" Then he threw out a sarcastic laugh that felt like cough, and continued, "The flood came and swept everything away."

Though Kabeer had been hearing this same story with slight deviations for days, he wanted to know this old man's version of it, so he poked him on, saying, "Tell me."

"The flood waters came in and everything drowned," said the old man. "All of our livestock, even my pair of white bulls were swept away. But I saved my grandson by carrying him on my shoulders and walking all night through chest-high waters."

Then old man looked at child and a screen of viral happiness spread over his otherwise gaunt face, on which dismay had carved permanent frowns. The old man went, *"Biyo cha budhandain sahab'a, malik ja lakha thora ain."*—*What else do you want to hear? God is merciful, sir.*

And for the first time Kabeer wished he had some magic secret of the universe. He had once read a book that suggested that everything was connected and that the power of imagination could actually make things happen. He had read it a long time ago, but suddenly he wanted its wisdom to work today. In that book, the author tells how her old dog had gotten loose, and she and her daughter kept wandering in that hilly forest all day to find him.

Then they came back, imagining that the dog was with them, and they put food in his bowl, and envisioned that he was eating it, and then hearing tiny bells like he was running in the hallway. And then the daughter imagined that her canine companion was sleeping beside her. And the next morning they saw a hand written flyer nailed on a tree, which said that someone had found a wandering dog, which could be claimed at such and such a place.

So Kabeer lit a new cigarette and then tried, in his broken Sindhi, to explain this phenomenon to the old man, though he himself was starting to have serious doubts about that everything-is-interconnected hypothesis. All the while he was taking frequent puffs and blowing smoke sometimes to his right and sometimes to his left like a novice smoker.

He took his time to go through that dubious story and explain this positive energy thingy, which could turn imagining into happening, and that maybe the old man could get his pair of white bulls back by virtually imagining that the bulls were with him. The old man kept looking at Kabeer and said, *"Saeen, toon charyoo aa cha?"*[161]—*Sir, are you crazy?*

Out of awkwardness Kabeer dropped his cigarette butt, which rolled down the levee slope and sizzled before becoming extinguished in the stagnant waters. He stood up and said, *"Chang'on bhala,"* which was again an over-direct translation of "all right then."

The old man replied in a firm voice, *"Mashallah saeen, bera'ee-par."*—*God's word is sure; keep floating.*

Kabeer looked at the sky, which had turned all dark by then. All those lumps and streaks and shredded clouds had turned grey. There was very little brightness left in that sky; most of it had turned dim and gloomy. The levee had become comparatively quiet. The clamour of those kids had died down, like they had been functioning on solar energy. And he walked back, past the flickering lanterns hanging down from bull-carts.

He felt the buzz of his phone, and saw there a text message from Babli Mama, "Just want to say hi."

"I'll be with you in few," he texted back. It was so hot and humid that a person would need three or four showers daily, which was not possible, so he was becoming use to perspiring and letting it dry. He was living an antediluvian life, like everyone else around those campsites. There was no lustre in this raw, acrid stench. It was completely different from what he had imagined.

Like while reading and imagining that King Salman has seven thousand armed men mounted on their horses at his castle, you never factor in the stench of shit and urine of those horses alone inside the castle walls. Years back, in his childhood days, his father told him some about Nepalese city probably

---

[161] The honorific title 'Saeen' conveys more respect and reverence than the word 'sir' does in English, so prefacing the question this way would remove any potential sense of insult.

Katmandu, or may be some other Himalayan city, which had only three elevators.

And that whole city, or maybe nation, was kept in the dark, away from the modern world, by its emperor, who didn't want his people to have knowledge—the gift of knowing. And he remembered seeing an old issue of National Geographic that had broken the story of that city. There were a number of photographs of vintage buildings, with carved wood plank fronts, and some of the pictures showed the high peaks of the Himalayas peeping over them, like a close-up shot of a person with big head looking out over tiny toy houses. At that time, it was all desirable and enticing. He wanted to see that city that had gotten tucked away in forgotten times. And those pages of National Geographic magazine, with those period-piece photographs, used to emit a synthetic smell of ink, and the pages adhered together such that you had to peel them apart every time.

But in real life there was so much grinding and friction. It felt to him that he was getting close to that feeling, which his father always talked about but had never achieved. It was to go and sit anonymously on the steps of any obscure shrine for rest of your life and never talk again.

He would say to Kabeer, "You should sit preferably on the lowermost step of an obscure shrine." But then, his father was a romantic idealist clunker, so Kabeer hadn't thought much about it. But now he felt he was starting to understand it somehow.

He thought this could be a virus-like thought which was corrupting his head—he didn't want to give up everything yet. For years now, he had been debating that million-dollar question in his head, that one that so many others had tried to answer, about the meaning of life. Kafka's answer was, "It ends." Kabeer would always change that to, "It's nothing," instead of "It ends."

So it's nothing—but nothing should have something in there, emptiness maybe! Does emptiness have a mass? Kabeer felt overwhelmed and said to himself, "What an abstract fuck, this stagnation is getting onto my nerves," and that he should go to the city, for a change.

And he would go back for a few days in Karachi every few weeks, with Uzoo. And those few days would feel like his time off, because there were so many national and international helpers here, Japanese, Dutch, French, and tons of locals too, all trying to pitch in. There were several huge camps being run by everybody from compassionate goodwill hunters, to NGOs, local governments, religious fanatic groups, Hindu devotees, and of course Uzoo's organisation. He went with Uzoo to one camp that was being run by the city of Karachi, which looked like a pretty sophisticated operation. City officers were keeping track of all the details, of how many meals were dispensed, who was getting which medicines, and how much and when.

They were doing all this through their own database, stuffing their laptops with everybody's information, logging it in their system. Every family living in that camp was numbered and registered.

After several trips from inner Sindh to the city, Kabeer started to figure out, that in this natural catastrophe, the poor people who had suffered the most were the most unwanted ones in the city, and are forgotten in camps, alongside Dadu, Shikarpur and Larkano. This was because those poor people were least important for even for their own representatives in the elective government.

Those elected officials were also the feudal lords of their cities, in Dadu, Shikarpur, and Larkano, and they didn't even consider the poor villagers to be a necessary part of their voter bank anymore. For several decades now, those lords cast votes on behalf of hundreds of villagers in their territories without even asking them. The villagers were only important to those feudal lords in so much as lords need humans to reign over. But every few days they would appear in their official capacity to visit those camps and hand out few hundred Ajrak shawls, and have their photos taken with big smiles, and those poor people would smile for the camera, too. But those ajraks weren't much help to these people who needed food, shelter and medicine.

And in the city there was all that tidy software, keeping tracks of those victims, those clueless people. The city employees were tallying them one by one; just to make sure they all were accounted for, so that when the time comes, they should all go back where they came from. Because if these victims found their ways out of the camps and started finding odd jobs and chose to stay there, then that could change the demographics of the city, or if not actually change them, it could potentially initiate an undesirable shift. The cities of Sindh were governed mainly by people of Uzoo's ethnic background, mostly Muhajirs, but they were not at all like Uzoo.

Rather, they were Uzoo's antonyms, those elective representatives want to have their own piece of cake and eat it too. Instead of joining together to help the needy ones, they all seemed to want a piece of the action. A lot of them were vultures looking to capitalise on the calamity. And there were conflicts of interest clogging up the works, like certain American concerns that didn't want Islamic fundamentalist organisations to do anything with flood relief, and so instead of channelling resources towards the victims, they were working harder to block the help of those fundamentalist organisations.

And the media was involved, too. "There is a class system among those news channels' reporters," Uzoo told him, when the two of them were in one of those city camps, and several teams of TV reporters were roaming about.

Kabeer replied, "That's true everywhere. A CNN or MSNBC anchor is a celebrity as compared to a local channel 9 news reporter." A team of Sindhi news journalists popped up, and wanted to interview Uzoo. All their questions for her were about numbers and statistics, like how many meals, how many vaccines, how many doses of medicine given, how many affected victims are there.

It felt to Kabeer that they didn't have anything to ask. But Uzoo answered them all. And although they were from some Sindhi news network, the interview was not all in Sindhi. That was another thing that Kabeer had observed here, a strange daisy chain of languages. Sindhi television networks interviewed city people who couldn't speak Sindhi, so they would reply in Urdu, and Urdu news channels would interview people who preferred to reply in English, and occasionally some foreign news team from CNN or BBC interviews people would interview people in English and then hear responses in Urdu or Sindhi or some other local language.

That evening, for the first time, Uzoo said, "let's go for dinner—my treat." And so they got into Uzoo's car, one of those fuel-efficient compact ones that spiral around the city roads by the thousands, all looking alike, though they have different makes and models.

She took Kabeer to a restaurant in the lobby of the Karachi Marriott, which had a familiar epicurean smell of the gourmet coffee joints of New York City and the food courts of European airports. They sat comfortably at a table with a starched white cover and a small beautifully carved copper candle lamp. The candle inside that lamp was flickering and light was escaping from those openings, which could be called the discarded space between the carvings, the space that whoever designed that lamp didn't wanted there.

In the one corner of that restaurant, there was a small stage and someone was sitting crouched down was playing live sitar. That sitar player looked worried and appeared not to be enjoying what he was doing. Uzoo had already ordered food, and soon the aromas of charred beef tikka and spices were making room for themselves, pushing that gourmet coffee smell aside, like someone impolitely elbowing space for himself in a jammed elevator.

"I want to create a non-governmental organization of our own; they call them NGOs here," said Uzoo.

Kabeer said, "I'm listening," while dipping his beef shish kebab into yogurt dressing, savouring the moment of indulgence. At the same time, he was struggling to keep thoughts of his mother at a bay. She was a staunch vegetarian and had given up eating meat long ago, replacing its presence in her life with two bumper stickers on her car's rear end, one of which read, *choose life over death, kindness over killing, go vegetarian*, and the other one, *Tree-Hugging, Liberal, Feminist, Animal Rights Activist, and I Vote.*

So while Uzoo was elaborating her plan, Kabeer was indulging his food, which was not overwhelmingly tasteful but was nonetheless elegantly served, and that gourmet coffee smell was still enslaved there in that restaurant, and the sitar player had gone, probably for a break, leaving his sitar lying down in the middle of the stage. That sitar looked like a tired intellectual who decided to recline to straighten his aching back during a coffee break between his lectures.

Uzoo was saying, "You are going to be the CEO. We'll register it in the United States as a non-profit. With your being a US citizen, we could get donations and charitable funding from there as well. Then Uzoo dropped the cotton napkin from one of her hands and reached and grabbed Kabeer's four fingers in her hand and squeezed them. Kabeer felt the softness of her moist warm hand."

Kabeer was trying to figure out whether a professional meeting should include a gesture involving the soft warmth of a moist female hand, and several thoughts were spinning in his mind: *why she was getting personal, is she trying to lure me into something? But she herself is a philanthropist, so maybe she really wants to help.* So he took the plunge, he went for it, and in fact he loved that moment. Somewhere, back there in his mind he thought that Catholics believe that most people who commit suicide regret it after they jump. So he would have some time to regret it, if he had to.

Uzoo still holding his four fingers, like they were her own, whispered intimately into his face, "What do you say?"

Being a person who read the instruction manual of everything thoroughly, Kabeer said, "I have to think it over." Then he added, "But it seems like it's not a bad idea."

The sitar player came back and resumed playing, some Indian movie song. His face still had that unwilling look of a day labourer who hated his job. The candle was still flickering and emitting light from those tiny openings which were not part of the lamp's design, and Uzoo was squeezing his four fingers at irregular intervals, but by now those four fingers of Kabeer's hand had become equally warm, as if they were of Uzoo's. They sat there for little longer, and finally drank that damn coffee whose smell was making all that fuss.

Kabeer could feel that somewhere along the way that evening an irreversible change must have had happened in Uzoo's and his relationship, a change that would never allow things to go back, that kind of change which can convert warm milk into curd.

Late that evening she dropped him off at Babli Mama's place. He went inside and found that Babli Mama was not back yet, though his car was parked in garage. An unexplained uneasiness compelled Kabeer back outside and he started walking down the sidewalk. Thick ocean winds were blowing into his face, and those four palm trees outside Babli Mama's house were making their presence so much so felt that he had to look up and see their leaves shaking like pom-poms in restless cheerleaders' hands.

He lit a cigarette, bending over to make a cup out of his two hands, putting his back against the ocean winds. When he exhaled his first puff, the fast winds snatched the smoke right out of his mouth and ran away with it, like they wanted him to quit.

He kept thinking about that unusual evening, the way her common brown eyes had the utter calmness of autumn skies. Her hijab was hiding her every single hair, but exposing her forehead completely. He had looked at her face with fresh eyes, and noticed her delicate cheekbones and her burnished copper complexion, and that plump lower lip of hers which had a wet sheen, probably because of her lipstick, and a beautifully carved nose with a cute pinched button tip, leaving an impression of some tiny chiselled marble square on it. Every now and then she threw a shameless hardy stare into Kabeer's eyes, like she was asking him to look at her, and look at her good.

While he was in clamour of those thoughts, a car stopped at Babli Mama's entrance, and Babli Mama got out of it. Kabeer had walked far enough away that by the time he walked back, Babli Mama had already said all his entire goodbyes to whoever had just dropped him off.

Babli Mama saw Kabeer and said, "Kay-Bee, what are you doing out here this late? You're not supposed to walk around late at night; someone could have snatched you. This is a wild city now." Then he squeezed Kabeer's shoulder in a joyful manner and said, "Let's go in."

Kabeer was eager to talk. Already as they were walking inside, he said, "Listen, the girl I work with wants to make a charitable organisation." Babli looked at Kabeer with mixed look, like he wanted to know more, so Kabeer continued, "She wants me to be the CEO!"

"So what's the biggie?" Babli replied. "I myself am an ambassador-at-large, where is the fire in there, kid? What else?"

By now, they were in that hall where the Ahmed Parvez painting was hanging on the wall. And Kabeer knew that Babli Mama was going to jump on it, but said it anyway, "She also wants me to register it in US so that we can get charity and donations from there."

And sure enough, before even he finished his sentence, Babli Mama said in a gentle but loud tone, "She wants to use you! Screw her." And then Babli Mama laughed a shallow single laugh, "Ha…"

But he was not comfortable talking to Babli Mama about that. He wanted to talk to Ben.

Chapter 5
Guy with No Glitter

Ben Olsen, a deviant covered in a benign wrapper, had been his friend since kindergarten. Now he was living in San Francisco trying to do something in the IT industry. He hadn't succeeded yet, but he would soon, or that was the common wisdom between Kabeer and his other friends. Because Ben always got what he wanted, from straight As to higher SAT scores to Persian girlfriends to acceptance at the University of Southern California to his FB profile picture with the porn star Ron Jeremy, and so much more in between.

For Kabeer, Ben was an oracle; to him Ben was that cocoon, which enables the butterfly to grow its wings. Kabeer wanted Ben to tell him what he already knew; he wanted Ben to buy in into Kabeer's idea. He just wanted to hear from a peer, "Keep doing whatever the fuck you are doing, dude."

After a day off, Kabeer went back to shuttling between their three campsites by the left bank of river Indus. He had chosen to stay back, although the humanitarian organisation that initially bought him here had handed over their relief operation to the local government and completely scaled their flood relief work.

Now Kabeer was working independently with Uzoo's NGO. And the work was immense, but he liked that he was helping, though it was sort of like a punishment from a Greek myth, emptying an ocean using only a mesh strainer.

Months passed. A new year and a new February had arrived. It was not really cold, not like the cold-cold of the Northeast, but people were still bundled up here, in their traditional shawls that they wrap all around themselves. Passing through rural Sindh, Kabeer sometimes even saw men wearing shocking pink shawls.

He had called several times but, as usual, Ben didn't reply. Kabeer realised with irritation that he probably wasn't going to reply now, after four months.

Having given up on Ben, he turned to another friend, Sid. Years back, in high school days, only Kabeer's father call him Siddhartha, and would always remind Sid that this was Gautam's real name. And Sid always replied, "Mr Abro, my name is not Siddhartha. It's Siddharth Johri." And his father would simply reply, "It's the same."

Sid was a quiet guy with no glitter. He was a kind of a rope bridge with beat-up wooden pegs that could take you to other side, if you really wanted to cross. And, as Kabeer expected, Sid picked up on the third ring. Kabeer noticed that the bell from Pakistan to the US was weird, like it was ringing inside water, and in pairs of two frequent rings followed by a longer interval, like the irritable calls of some bad-tempered old frog.

"Hey-yo!" Sid's voice came. "Where are you man, what's up?"

After a few hi's and hellos, Kabeer went straight to the core and regurgitated everything in unusually long sentences, so long that he had to stop at times and say, "hey Sid!" And Sid had to confirm by saying, "I'm here, keep talking," and Kabeer would continue his long sentences.

When Kabeer finished, Sid said, "It seems you like the girl, dude. I don't think you're interested in being the CEO of a non-profit."

Then one of those pauses came, which neither of them wanted to break, but finally Kabeer broke it with a disappointed, "That's it?"

"What else you want me to tell you?" Sid said. But Sid knew it was his turn now, so he went on with his own semi-monologue. "Yo, I've known you since forever. You left that paediatric surgery fellowship, even though it came with a guaranteed six-figure salary. You never showed any interest in your parents' business. To me you were always that free soul of a wild tree, which got caged in a machine's body. By leaving all this behind, you got your freedom, man. Now why the hell you want to entrap your soul back in that same old crappy machine?"

Sid's words were heavy, and they went straight into Kabeer's heart; like a salt carrying vessel, which if sinks goes straight to, bottom of ocean. But Kabeer wanted to wind up that talk on a lighter note. "You are getting literary, dude. I guess NYU's creative writing class worked."

And they talked about some unimportant things, and finally Kabeer said, "Thanks brother, later then." And Sid returned some similar goodbyes.

Sid cleared away all that smoke. Now there was no dilemma left in Kabeer's mind; he knew that the journey was his. So he kept floating on the currents of time and waiting for things to unwind on their own.

Now his main objective was to educate local team members, who then could train the masses. Every few weeks he and Uzoo came back to the city for a few days. She had already formed that NGO and named it HELP, "Health for Every Loved Person," unusually long and pitiful name, but that's what she named it, and Kabeer became its CEO.

He rented an apartment in Babli Mama's neighbourhood. So now, he was living in Karachi, a genetically mutated city, a city with virtually no philanthropist left in her, a city whose habitants only ask for more from her, a city whose feverishly burning forehead has not been touched by any healing hands for a long, long time. A heavy-hearted city, where no one chose to run his fingers through her windblown tousled hair.

Chapter 6
Crowbar Clanging Noise

Occasionally Uzoo would invite him to her home for dinner. Hers was a single family house in the neighbourhood of Karachi called Gulistan. Kabeer didn't know the meaning of *Gulistan;* to him it was just another word. But it means garden, and not just any simple garden, but something poetic, like a land of roses or a place where fragrance and flowers live side by side. But it was just the name of that locality, which was no different than any other part of the urban periphery, which is neither metropolis nor suburbia.

Which had all the pollutants, the chemical air filled with exhaust, piles and piles of trash decaying and waiting to become ashes to ashes, dust to dust, around that heartlessness of a city. People would buy a piece of land there, which also came with a free piece of sky, but they didn't care for the sky and clung only to the land. That place was rows and rows of small houses jammed into each other from both sides and having conjoined backsides, spanning over streets after streets. People would build them and then live in them for their lifetimes. In most cases, those homes represented everything that they had made in their lives.

Uzoo's home was also one of those, for which her father had probably swapped his entire productive life. There was a waist-high box hedge, squarely trimmed and holding a tiny front lawn, not bigger than a king-size mattress. Right after that there was an iron bar door with repeated geometric designs of shamrocks, clubs in playing cards. Due to many thick coats of paint, that poor iron door couldn't even make a crowbar clanging noise when banged.

Inside, Uzoo's mother would examine him thoroughly every time he came, seeming to be trying to scratch Kabeer's surface out of her curiosity to find out what material he was made up of. She would do that very delicately, and in her own mind presuming that Kabeer had no idea what she was doing. "How many siblings do you have?" She asked him once.

"None," he replied, and he felt that his answer pleased her.

That vaguely reminded Kabeer of a poem that his father used to read him in Urdu, and after reading it his father would try to translate its meaning, or rather dissect that poem for him anaesthetically, and show him the bloody guts of that poem the best he could, to make sure that Kabeer understood everything it had to say.

It was a poem about a blind small-town junk-and-scrap dealer, who tells his story of gathering dreams. You could say he ran a sort of search and rescue operation for dreams, those dreams that are dead tired, falling apart, broken beyond repair, scattered throughout the cloisters of city. The city dwellers themselves were unaware of the dreams, but that blind junk-and-scrap dealer would roam there night and day to gather them. He would put them into the hellish inferno of his heart to burn away their impurities. Then he would sand them to smooth away their old bumpy dents, so that their details could come back to life and their faces start to glow again, and their lips start to gleam, like those of cocky young grooms.

Every morning the blind junk-and-scrap dealer would take his haul of reconditioned dreams to the city square and sit with the other street hawkers hoping to sell their wares. He would make loud street cries: "Buy my dreams, buy my dreams, these golden dreams!"

People would approach to inquire about his dreams, cautiously with their doubts, like they knew all about dreams, like they lived and breathed dreams and were appraisers of them.

When midday approached and no one had bought his dreams, out of desperation, the blind junk dealer would cry out even louder, "Take them for free! These are my golden dreams; take them for free."

When people heard the word 'free', they got more scared and distanced themselves even farther from the blind junk dealer and his dreams. They started murmuring in each other's ears, "Who wants to buy dreams from a blind junk dealer? And who knows what these dreams are made up of! Who wants these unsure dreams, these reconditioned old dreams. They might cast magical trance, and they might stupefy us."

And those buyers all dispersed from there. The poem was even longer and had some much more in it, which Kabeer doesn't remember all. But he could imagine Uzoo's mom among those suspicious buyers, who thought they knew everything about dreams already and didn't need that blind scrap dealer. Uzoo's mom was annoying, but she cooked very tasty kababs, so Kabeer would eat her kababs and allow her to scratch him to see what he was made up of.

Kabeer found Karachi to be grandiloquent and bombastic, but at the same time it was a place in need of a Mother Teresa. It had its own stuffy mugginess in the air. It had its own culture, its own architecture, its own elegance, but it was dilapidated and literally in shambles, having been overtaken by the malignant tumours and abnormal growths of cubical apartments, which were nothing more than four walls and couple of windows and doors.

Their front sides were scarred with exposed and leaking sewer lines, like pockmarks left by chickenpox pustules, because these hideous apartment complexes had been built by upstart contractors. God knows why they were even known as builders and developers—probably all their ugly constructions were developed on multiplications of greed.

But despite all that, he liked it there. A few days into this new CEO gig, which he was juggling like a street performer, his phone rang with a call from the US. He didn't recognise the number, but he answered anyway.

Obviously, there was someone on the other end, who greeted him and called him 'doctor' and used his surname. After some pleasantries, that person said, "I work here in Washington DC with our congressmen who are members of the congressional Sindhi caucus. It's great that you are doing that work in Sindh. Let me know if I can be of any help."

Kabeer said, "What could you do?"

The lobbyist answered, "We can help you to get aligned with direct funding towards your 501(c)."

That flew right over Kabeer's head. "What's that 500 something that you just said?"

"It's your non-profit; we call them 501(c)'s, because that's what they are. And as your organisation is registered here in the US, it is entitled for funding." After a small pause, the lobbyist said, "You don't have to worry—we could do it for you, for a small fee."

"Thanks, let me think," said Kabeer.

"I have your email, I'll send you the details," said the lobbyist and also repeated Kabeer's exact email address letter for letter, just to confirm it was right. And before letting Kabeer go, the lobbyist did a little more encouraging talk, like a dash of cinnamon on top of a creamy latté.

Kabeer didn't mention any of that to Uzoo for a few days. They were in Dadu and had launched a new campaign to fight viral Hepatitis. It was not actually a fight against Hepatitis, by any account; rather that was just the name of the campaign to test people and tell them whether they were already positive for Hepatitis B or C or not. But then the campaign would help by telling those patients how to prevent spreading it among others.

Roshan Gopang was working with them in the campaign as well. There had been a shift in his demeanour, in his persona. He had become more comic, letting others laugh at him. One time, alone with Kabeer, he was being hilarious in that self-deprecating state, saying, "I'm a dick of rags," as if he had found a way to whip the bare back of his own soul in humiliation. He was punishing himself by letting others laugh at him, and that was okay with him. He had somehow found the way to junk his ego.

It was like Roshan had accepted it, like he had said to himself, what's the point of saving just my heart alone, when my whole existence is ablaze? Or maybe he was isolating the damage in his heart by throwing onto it a blanket of self-bashing. And when even that caught fire, in the heat of deep affection, he invited others to step on it mercilessly with him, to help him suppress his want.

He would still look at Uzoo from the corner of his eye, whenever he could and for as long as he could. If she was talking to someone or doing something, he would always wait as long as he had to so that he could ask her some question he had been saving. In that waiting, Roshan Gopang would live lifetimes. It lasted until she was done with whatever she was doing, or finally noticed him standing there.

Apparently, Roshan was in charge of running day-to-day errands in the camp. One thing that he did was to read a local Sindhi newspaper every morning, though there must be several other newspapers, but it seemed that there was only one Sindhi newspaper that everyone liked to read, just this one particular newspaper. Kabeer found lots of amateur but full-time journalists circling around camp trying to find a story.

Amateur meaning that they had hands-on training as journalists, though a great majority of them were actually supposed to be schoolteachers. But they didn't teach children in schools, because most of those schools actually didn't exist; they were ghost schools, and these were their phantom teachers. Most of them were poets, and some of them were short story writers too.

They were much more interested in literature than journalism, especially Russian classics. They all loved Tolstoy more than Shakespeare. Actually, none of them that Kabeer met had actually even read short stories by Tolstoy, let alone *War and Peace*, but they loved him. And their other favourite was Gorky. They all fell in love with him after reading a translation of his novel, *Mother*.

The guy, that Sindhis really fall in love with, is Gorky.

One of these journalists at the Dadu camp was a young man named Sarang, who was littered in today's dirt but buzzing with promising tomorrows. He wore a light pink dress shirt and khaki pants, and he had a striped messenger bag slung over his shoulder, its belt-like strap crossing his chest. In other words, this fellow Sarang looked like a hybrid between a Wall Street intern and a Bengali Maoist from the late sixties. He was enthusiastic about Western journalism and wanted to know if Kabeer read the Wall Street Journal or the New York Times or watched CNN?

"No," answered Kabeer, "I'm not really very fond of news journalism, and I rarely pick up a printed newspaper. But yes, I do read articles; sometimes from the New York Times. But I don't watch television news at all, and haven't for some time now."

Sarang was clearly a bit disappointed by Kabeer's answer, but he pressed on nonetheless and showed him a picture on his cell phone in which he was shaking hands with an old white man. Kabeer didn't recognise the man. "It's my picture with Ted Turner!" Sarang exclaimed.

But this also didn't help Kabeer, who still looked puzzled. "Sorry, I don't know who he is."

"He is owner of CNN!" Sarang cried, with an astonished *hello*-look.

Kabeer apologised and tried to comfort Sarang for his own ignorance of the topic. "I'm sorry; I really don't know who owns CNN any other media outlets. I really don't. I just know that one Murdoch guy from Australia. I know he's an old man who owns something like half of world's biggest media outlets, and that he is a conservative and I'm a liberal, so I instinctively don't like him."

At this point, Kabeer felt like saving face a bit by showcasing his other knowledge for Sarang, so he kept talking. "I like celebrities from two thousand years ago, people who changed course of history by simply giving away wisdom, and that was their tool. Like ability to awaken one's consciousness—" Here Kabeer tried to say the word '*bodhi*', which means 'To wake up'. It came out as 'body' when he said it, but he was able to make his point nonetheless. "—that's where the words Buddha and Buddhism came from."

Then Kabeer paused and made sure that Sarang had not lost his footing, before continuing, "A man named Siddhartha developed philosophy of awakening, sitting under a tree. Nowadays young people find wisdom sitting in their parents' garage. I think Siddhartha could have done that in his parent's garage too if his parents had had a single-family cookie cutter house somewhere in Southern California."

Kabeer smiled a little, letting his point of view seep into Sarang, who was trying hard not to like Kabeer's idea of comparing present day innovators with mystic philosophers of another millennium. But Sarang failed to hide his admiration for Kabeer's abstract thought.

Kabeer barged onward. "Some of these new guys even succeeded in compressing a whole lot of knowledge and wisdom and holding it inside a palm size glass inside an aluminium box frame half of size of a deck of playing cards."

"Why don't you just say iPhone! Instead of saying all that," said Sarang.

Kabeer went on, "But it's great that you had a picture taken with CNN owner."

That seemed to satisfy Sarang. "What you are doing here?" He inquired.

The question could have sounded confrontational, but Sarang intended it politely. Kabeer took it as, "What brings you here." And he answered, "Helping people in need."

"Say something more than that," prodded Sarang. "Elaborate it. Your answer is too short and kind of generic."

Kabeer thought briefly, as if cherry-picking among juicy words in an effort to concoct a cerebral sentence. And he looked at into Sarang's eyes, and simply said again, "Helping people in need."

But then Kabeer started to get edgy. "Why does that seem simple to you? And if it is simple, so be it. Why it should be complex. I really want to help people in need. Great stories are very simple, don't you know that! And if you don't, then you have to start over. A wise man once said, literature is brilliant illiteracy."

Sarang interrupted, "I just wanted to know what brought you here—isn't that a simple question?"

"I'm chasing after myself, and I'm running away from myself too. The part of me that is running away thinks he'll get something, someplace, somewhere.

And the me who is after myself… wants to tell me that it's here, it's now, this is it!" Then Kabeer looked at Sarang and said, "Did you get it?"

Sarang very calmly said, "yes I did, and sorry to say that it felt to me that you actually don't have enough to say. And you are repeating what other people have said, putting it a little differently, I guess? And you comparing Gautam with Bill Gates? I don't know much about them. But I think you don't know either."

Kabeer felt trashed by Sarang, like he'd been found out. Sarang wished Kabeer goodbye and walked on, in search of his breaking story that might one day put him alongside someone like, at first Kabeer thought of Anderson Cooper or Chris Matthews, but he knew that they usually didn't come to this messy part of the world. And so he thought of Christiane Amanpour, who usually did come here, but he didn't remember her name and simply imagined her long face.

Uzoo was excited when Kabeer told her that some lobbyist had called him from Washington, DC wanting to help getting funding for their NGO.

"That's great!" She said. "How it's going to work?"

"He'll do some work for our NGO, and obviously he'll charge us a fee for his services."

"Wow, we'll be able to do so much more with US funding!" Uzoo was already looking forward.

Kabeer showed his reluctance. "Money doesn't come for free. We have to do something for those who are going to give us money. If nothing else, they'll at least want a photograph taken of us receiving a giant bath-towel-sized check from them."

"So what!" She said. "I'll do that, don't you worry. Just send that lobbyist an email thanking him, and introduce me, CC it to me also. I'll get in touch with him from there on."

Things were intertwined, mixed up crazily in this cosmic event, where heavy elements were getting into weak elements, possessing them, penetrating them without asking. Weak elements were forced to lose their identity and become compounds.

Kabeer was trying to find something, but he wasn't sure what it was. Maybe it was that deep serenity of static peace of that holy man with no home, who had charmed the Buddha so much that he gave up his wife, his son, his wealth, his throne, and his kingdom, all to become a holy man with no home. Or else he wanted to be like those CEOs of multibillion-dollar investment banks, who travel all the way to the foothills of Himalayas, seeking blessings of from a present-day holy man with no home, and ask to be blessed to become even more successful.

The present-day holy man with no home would ask the investment banker to sit and catch his breath. Once the banker is settled, the holy man offers for him to come and sit across from him on the ground. There is a very low, raw-surface wooden table between them, almost like a square bench.

There the Holy Man places a small cup in front of Banker and another small cup in front of him. And, uncharacteristically, Holy Man slowly starts pouring hot herbal tea into his own cup first, instead of the Banker's, and says, "This tea is a healing tonic, but it's very hot, so drink it slowly, and let me know when to stop."

He starts pouring tea into Banker's cup, before continuing to speak. "What were you saying earlier, when you came here, that you wanted?" And he was still pouring that hot herbal tea into Banker's cup very slowly.

Banker wants to harness that moment, wants to squeeze as much as he could out of that short time alone with holy man with no home. Although Holy Man is pouring the tea very slowly into Banker's cup, it is only a matter of time until that cup is filled to the rim.

Banker tells Holy Man that, "I came to see you, from afar," which Holy Man already knew, and that, "my mother was a cleaning lady in Staten Island and use to sweep office floors all night long. My father was an auto mechanic and a heavy drinker."

Those are painful realities, and Holy Man knows about sufferings of life and is listening and nodding his head, and he keeps pouring hot tea, and Banker's small cup was filling.

Holy Man says, "What you want from me now?"

"I worked tirelessly. Wiped dinner tables, then went to Princeton, then to Yale. I came a long way from Staten Island. I started an Investment Bank."

By now, his small cup is almost filled to its rim, and Banker says, "I want you to bless me so that my bank becomes one of the top investment banks, O…o, o, stop, stop…please stop…" Banker is panicked, seeing his cup overflowing. Hot tea is spilling into Banker's lap and burning him.

Holy Man with No Home stops pouring tea and says, "This herbal tea is very hot, but it's good, it has healing properties. But it can burn too. Your cup is full, my child, there is no room for more in there. You have to empty it first, before you desire to fill it again."

Holy Man stands up and gives his blessings to Banker, and then goes on his way.

Kabeer knew that all of this was cooking in his mind. He had reached a fork in his path. Very few people come to these crossroads. And of those who do come that far, even fewer will take the turn toward static serenity. Most of them will choose the other path.

Chapter 7
"Physical Inventory of Giggles and Acrid Sadness"

Almost a year had passed and another monsoon came, bringing with it another devastating flood. The carnage was the same—thousands of villages were swept away, and a quarter million already displaced people were once again displaced. But the foofaraw was much less than the year before.

Kabeer was still shuttling back and forth between the camps and Karachi, where he had rented an apartment to call some place home. On one of those transient afternoons, he was lying on his bed and looking at the ceiling fan, which was running for while, then picking up speed, and then dying down, and this sequence was being repeated again and again, because the power was going out and coming back on of its own free will.

That was another phenomenon he has gotten used to in Pakistan, which was called load-shedding of electricity, which meant that the entire nation got electric power on rations, in increments of eight hours on, then eight hours off, or some other proportion of hours on to hours off. People had started living around those schedules; they did everything according to the power outage schedule, like cooking and eating dinner before 7:59 pm or finishing their Facebook status updating or Skype video chatting before that same 7:59 pm. And at exactly 8:00 pm, darkness would engulf them, and they moved into an antiquated epoch with lanterns and candles.

Kabeer felt like this country was always in a sort of time machine, with eight hours in the brand new millennium followed by eight hours of medieval times, and the population was perfectly adjusted to it, having no other choice. People just kept dragging on and living with the load-shedding.

In everybody's life, there are moments that feel completely wasted. Everyone experiences them, mostly without sharing them with others. Those are the moments when people thoroughly see things. So he was going through that idling void of time, looking at things that are usually ignored, gazing emptily at the ceiling.

Harshly washed pale afternoon's sunlight was filling that room with woes of passive sadness. It was giving almost investigative detail to them. He thought to himself, that it was probably at this time of day when Newton's apple hit the ground. He was doing the same kind of observation in that moment of time, looking at the wavy flaws in the ceiling plaster, which was mimicking the surface of a still body of water.

And he was looking at the dirt, rather disciplined dirt, which had accumulated on the slicing edge of the ceiling fan's blades and that ceiling fan was making noise every time power came back, like a bad transmission slipping second gear at a traffic light. And then he thought, Newton had changed the world with his observation, and meanwhile he had just observed imperfections in the ceiling plaster and some dirt on the fan blades, and he said to himself, *what the fuck, I'm going nuts*. He was craving to see someone from outside of this same miserable life that he was coping with at the camps.

His phone made a whistling notification to tell him "there's a text in my belly." He checked it and saw the words of Babli Mama: "What's up kid, where have you been keeping yourself?" And that message contained for Kabeer all worldly pleasures, a marijuana-like. He called Babli Mama.

"What's up?" Babli said.

"Nothing. More of the same old shit," Kabeer replied.

Babli laughed a loud, "Ha…live a little, kid!"

"Yup, you're right," Kabeer replied, without meaning it.

"Hey listen, I'll pick you up around eight. There is an exclusive gig. You'll forget all about New York"

Kabeer said, "Okay."

"Wear something devilish," Babli suggested.

"Are you taking me to see the Antichrist? I don't have cheeky clothes."

"Okay, okay…Just wear something trendy, and see you at 8."

When Babli arrived, he said, "I'm taking you to a party where there are gonna be models, girls of course, and Columbian cocaine, and filthy rich folks, and goat-grown hashish from Darra."

Kabeer said, "Mama, I can understand that you probably know that the girls there could be models and the people could be filthy rich. But how the hell do you know that the coke is from Columbia and the hashish is goat-grown? That is preposterous."

Babli replied casually, "Okay, I don't know if it's from Columbia or not, but I say it anyway, it adds to the value, specification does that."

Kabeer gave him a funny look, but Babli carried on, "I always use random numbers instead of round numbers, like February 29th, 1963 for a specific event from past or 2187.32 for any fictitious amount. It feels more authentic."

Then Babli looked at Kabeer and said, "Doesn't it?" And he kept looking at him like he wanted Kabeer's endorsement. "You should do that too."

Kabeer rolled his eyes and said, "What if 1963 wasn't a leap year?"

Babli said, "Wow! I have never thought that. Thanks. Next time I'll not use February the 29th at all."

Then Babli Mama asked, "How is your father these days?"

"Don't know, I haven't spoken to my parents for a long time."

Babli said, "Your dad was into arts and stuff…"

Kabeer replied "yes," a one-word answer to show he didn't want to talk about it. Babli said, "I have one of his oil paintings, but it seems that he never clicked."

Kabeer still said nothing, staring at the back cover of one of Babli's CDs. Babli said, "So what's he doing now?"

"You really wanna know, huh?" Kabeer replied edgily. "He is an okay painter, an okay prose poet, and a story teller who is never able to make up his mind, trying to find new angles on that same old beat-up fucking love story. Probably, at this very moment he is running around with his old-fashioned leather laptop bag, which doesn't have a laptop inside but instead is filled with handwritten scrap papers, most of them covered with those stories from an era long gone. He used to make me read them."

"No one meets with no one in his stories, fucking old, pathetic mediocre tragedies set in times before electricity, in which a lover would have to ask his beloved to meet him behind some big sand dune, way past the slippery edge of the river bank of their village, on a moonless night. And then instead of making love, his characters, who are simple country folk, start talking about reason, which I think my father takes directly from Kant and Schopenhauer."

"And then in the next generation, the guy asks his lovers to meet him at the end booth in an Iranian restaurant, which were called family rooms, closed with dirty curtains. In those secluded booths, instead of getting into each other's pants and having sex, his characters would cry and weep and make plans about how to end their miserable lives and how crappy the damn world is."

"And on the top of all that, my father doesn't make those more educated city people talk about philosophy, which would actually make a little sense. But my father doesn't do that. And then the following generation guy sends an SMS to his lover, so that they can see each other for the last time at the departure gate, something like B17 of terminal 4, just to say, 'that's it then,' like two business partners who just couldn't agree on the numbers so their almost-done deal went sour."

"So that's what kind of stories he writes, and they don't even fall in the genre of short stories; they're semi-biographical accounts that he thinks are proper short stories, and keeps sending them to Granta and the New Yorker hoping they'll publish them. But after eight or nine months they send him regretful emails; *'sorry, your story is not suitable for our magazine.'* Here is the best part—that my father, thinks that it's the loss of Granta and the New Yorker that they haven't published his masterpieces in their journals."

"I keep telling him, Baba I read somewhere that nowadays 93 percent of the editors who sort through new submissions at those literary magazines are under the age of 26! They are half your age—the crowd that you have to appeal to is half your age, and you are too old. You have to reinvent yourself or give it up."

Kabeer gasped and continued as if he were talking to his father. "At your age, writers are already!—are already established! They don't write any more; they become big names and they usually just screw around and make love to their admirers who are twenty years younger than them, and want to become writers themselves."

"But he doesn't listen." Kabeer paused for a minute and then repeated more slowly, shaking his head as if he was talking to himself, "He doesn't listen."

Babli said, "He is weird."

Kabeer paused again and then said, "But I love him, you know! I think he keeps taking, his life's 'physical inventory of giggles and acrid sadness' in his stories!" And after another moment, he asked Babli, "What is this Iranian restaurant thingy anyway?"

Babli said, "I don't know exactly. That must have been even before my time. But there used to be some Parsi joints with very good cheap food, and the middle class used to go there, I guess. But that's all gone. That damn middle class itself got melted. There is no middle class in this society now, and there are no Iranian restaurants."

After a few more turns on the road, Babli parked his car outside a mansion, a huge villa in one of Karachi's posh areas. It looked like a Greek revival kind of plantation mansion from one of the Carolinas, probably South Carolina.

They entered through a gate that looked like a modern sculpture, made up of wide sections of imperfect raw wooden planks, stacked one on top of the other, finished with a high gloss varnish, which transformed its impurities into beauty, amplifying the wavy veins and dark knots of the wood into something that makes one want to stand and look.

Inside the gate there was a swimming pool, which was hugged by a wide terrace. Then there was the house, an exaggerated miniature of a Roman palace, with a wide hall with a vaulted ceiling and a floor paved with marble. One side of that hall was all French glass windows facing the pool.

The hall was congested with people and was coughing loud music. To Kabeer it seemed more like noise than music, making people yell to communicate with each other, and when the DJ was scratching and cross fading discs it felt more like he was sodomising the disc's ass with the sharp needle.

But there was fun, too, as lots of people met Babli with hugs and cheers. Every now and then the lights were fading to make way for dismal and red and green strobe lights, which created illusions of people's body parts being frozen in mid-motion.

Babli Mama shouted in Kabeer's ears, "There are going to be people here who smell like designer cologne, and then there are going to be people here who smell like they are carrying dead rats in their arm pits." Then Babli caught his breath and said, "Everybody is here, whoever could afford the entrance fee. The guys with dead-rat-armpits pick fights, so be careful."

Kabeer nodded his head in acknowledgement, and then Babli took him to the bar. They were serving German ales and Russian vodkas, alongside Scotch whiskeys, and all the other crap. Babli said, "carry on," and left to mingle with the crowd.

Kabeer ask the bartender, "Do you have Coors Light?"

The guy shook his head *no*. "Heineken or Budweiser?" He offered.

"Heineken, then."

The bartender said, "Gud choiss sir," in a thick South Asian accent.

Kabeer sipped his beer and started wandering around the place. It was unintentional, but his gaze kept getting caught by and then locking onto the flashy bodies of young girls, and some of them were very pretty—maybe those were the models that Babli had been talking about. There were also some aunties[162] there who were even flashier than the young girls. All that mix of people was dancing hysterically in the middle of the floor.

Freezing illusions of red and green laser, on those people, were showing them stoned in awkward position for a fraction of second. Than DJ start messing with the song 'Believe' by Cher, and one of the aunties got really carried away and started shaking her body so hard that one of her breast scooped out of her deep scoop neckline. Kabeer was enjoying it—he knew it was artificial, but it was damn good. He already had a couple of beers.

Suddenly, that old man popped up in his head, the one who had rescued his grandson by carrying him on his aging shoulders and walking all night long in chest-high flood waters. He was like, in that state of mind where you could open an inner door and come outside of your own self, move around and see yourself from the outside, and time, which used to click in clocks and now usually flips on cell phones screens, stops and becomes as mute as fish, and you move into some other kind of time. This time doesn't move or click at all, but becomes almost stationary, like a vase that you place on a countertop, which will stay there until you move it and put it someplace else.

Babli appeared and asked Kabeer to come around with him so that he could point out the people who mattered to him. One of them was a tiny young woman with a sharp little chin. Babli looked at her and murmured something to himself in Urdu, which kind of rhymed. It turned out that this was the granddaughter of a slain ex-prime minister. In fact, Kabeer had heard the name of this slain prime minister so often in his life that it felt to him that that this slain prime minister must have been the only prime minister that Pakistan probably ever had.

That girl was dancing a bit, but cautiously, like either she was shy or had too much weight of family pride on her shoulders, which was restraining her from moving freely. Somehow, she still managed to look feisty, independent, confident, kind of like an Alice in Wonderland who was looking for a way out? And Babli translated words that he had rhymed earlier, with this regrets that the

---

[162] In South Asian parlance, the word 'aunty' is often used for any woman who is over the age of 35 or 40, and often distinguishes married women from unmarried potential brides.

translation was nowhere close to the beauty of the original Urdu couplet. "Have you gingerly seen her eyes, Faraz, they look like eyes of those, who sleep with eyes open, or of those up all-nighters who don't sleep at all." Than Babli took a pause and said, "I'm going to say the original again." And he repeated:

"*Uski ankhon ko kabhi ghor se daikha hai Faraz;*
Sonay walon ki tarah jagnay walon jaisi."

Babli was happy as if he were reciting his own poem though Kabeer still didn't understand a single word of it.

Then there was a middle aged satirical novelist who was wearing checked cowboy shirt over pink jeans. He was moving around with open eyes, maybe trying to find his next plot in that crowd. He was making an illusion of mingling, but carefully keeping himself sterile, like someone wearing thick rubber gloves and plunging his hand into a gutter to find a precious ring, managing to keep the shit of that gutter from soiling his hand.

And there was a middle-aged woman there. The sight of her might have provoked some scornful reaction, and in his mind he was on the verge of slotting her into that category of anxiety-ridden, bitchy, overweight, depressed women who loudly complain and unnecessarily make scenes in expensive restaurants, shouting that their food is good or bad or just cold.

Or to that other type of old women who don't understand the art of aging gracefully, who can't get over the feeling that aging is a curse, and who try to get into their daughters' clothes just to end up looking pathetic. Rather, she looked to him like someone who knows that her time has passed, and sadly her time had indeed moved forward, leaving her behind.

And so also Kabeer's gaze left that middle-aged woman behind, and soon landed once again on that aunty-like woman, who was wearing a plain sapphire blue sari. Kabeer looked at that woman's back, watching how its central curve appeared from under her blouse and disappeared again behind her sari rolls, just above her perfect hips. Babli said she owned some of the original works of Sadequain, Ahmed Pervez, and Zain-ul Abedin! Kabeer said, "And who are they?"

Babli replied just as Kabeer expected, "They are like Picasso, Van Gogh, and Monet of Pakistan." Kabeer gave her a fresh look as a patron of fine arts, and all of sudden, she start looking more beautiful to him for no good reason.

Babli again retreated, and a young man with perfectly shaped eyebrows came close to Kabeer and said, "You want party! You want party, more-more party! I will tell you something!" And he was moving his head in inquisitive way like he has more to say but ran out of words.

Kabeer remembered Babli Mama's warning about people with dead-rat-armpits. That man kept lurking there for a while, and then moved on to sell his goods to someone else.

Outside that hall, past those French windows, there was that pool. Its surface was languidly calm, very slowly heaving up and down like the chest of a peacefully dying person. And all of sudden, one of those French windows opened with a bang. Someone ran out and jumped into that pool with a splash, violating its calm and sleeping surface of that sleeping pool. And then there was a series of splashes.

Now it felt that they all were ripping off the clothes of the earlier calmness of that pool. And then there was mayhem, there was laughter and there were tee-hees, people were diving into that pool and splashing and jumping, submerging and then emerging, gasping for air with their eyes closed, some of the women coming out of pool with their thin clothes laminating to their bodies, revealing their erect nipples.

And then that granddaughter of the dead politician came out of the water, and the moment she emerged, the satirical novelist started clapping slowly, like a symphony had just ended.

Kabeer was brimming with thoughts and a budding desire to think something poetic. *So much life!* his mind started. *No! No...a see-saw...or no, start with 'rollercoaster'...Or how about wow! Or Haa...*Then he sighed and realised that he wasn't going to come up with anything poetic, because the booze was working, unwinding his words.

On their way back from the party, Kabeer said to Babli, "Tonight it felt that, even though it's less than a hundred miles away, our camp is in the past, in another millennium!"

"Why is that?" Babli asked.

"Why what?"

In echolalic speech from within his mysterious cloud of booze Kabeer said. "At bank of Indus, on one of her unending levees, it was the later part of the day, are you listening?" His speech was slurred. He was swallowing, maybe because of dry mouth or overflowing heart. "There was a sharp sting in that afternoon setting sunlight, in those receding floods, I saw!"

Kabeer said with frowning brows, "an ultra-malnourished kid with his distended stomach, like a basketball was in his tummy. He was walking there carelessly, though he was probably dying slowly on the bank of the Indus. But since we had stopped there, a few other kids and a woman gathered around our van. The woman was that kid's mother. I asked her, what happened? Like it was her fault. And she said, 'we don't have food, so our kids eat mud.'"

"I thought she was being sarcastic!" Kabeer continued. "So I asked her, 'why don't you feed him?' She didn't reply to my question. Instead she just pulled up her shirt with both hands, in anger and hopelessness, showing her breasts. And she pulled on them several times and then opened up her hands to show her dry and empty palms. Then she just said, 'We have nothing, saeen.'"

Kabeer sighed loudly, the way drunks do to avoid throwing up, and then said, "The sky doesn't fall; the earth doesn't rip apart; virtually nothing happened, Mama! And she was not being sarcastic; kids are really eating mud, less than a hundred miles from here."

"It's not that simple," said Babli.

"Why not?"

Babli replied with audible frustration. "Because people are stupid, and politicians here are not politicians, they are assholes!"

Kabeer was still light-headed. "And why are they assholes?"

Babli went on, "Because there are no politicians here; we only have heartless feudal and urban thugs instead." And then he muttered, as if just to himself, "I don't know why I'm saying all this." And again to Kabeer, "Forget about this place, go back to where you came from. Nobody is able to fix this world ever. that's why those wise guys keep coming periodically, every few hundred years. Trying to align people. But people are full of shit, of their own will. They don't listen. So don't you worry, just let it be! Just go back."

"Mama, even if I go back all this is coming with me! I can't get rid of it now," said Kabeer.

"Well here we are at your place. Go get a good night's sleep."

Kabeer received several follow-up emails from that Washington-based lobbyist, asking him to come and present his non-profit organisation to USAID and others, including a few members of Congress who might be able to get him grants and donations. Uzoo made a whole power point presentation, in fact she had it made by professionals, with dramatic statistical graphics showing vertical bars and colour wedges of pie charts, divided into alarming reds and peaceful green and god knows what blues and yellows stood for in them. But it was all to show goal vaccinations achieved and spread of diseases controlled.

"What we need for what we're doing is immense," Uzoo said to Kabeer. "We'll do as much as we can, but I know it's not gonna be enough."

There was a new project site that Uzoo and Kabeer were working on. They wanted to expand more and reach into north-western Sindh, close to Larkano. They were trying a mobile unit this time, which instead of staying at one stationary location could visit several places in and around Larkano area. Roshan Gopang was handling all the logistics and communication with people in those areas, spreading the word ahead that a mobile unit was going to be in their area. And he was making arrangements for the teams to stay in the otaaks of wealthy landowners in that area, in case the team couldn't always make it back to the Larkano base.

"What's an otaak?" Kabeer asked Roshan during one of their briefings.

"Hmmm…otaak is…" Roshan was trying to find a simple explanation. "Otaaks are private guest houses. Everyone in villages and small towns of Sindh has their own otaak."

Kabeer quickly Googled it on his phone and found that 'Otaak' is the name of a band. So then he spelled it *otak* with just one A, and this time came up with a Chinese cake made from fish meat. So he texted Babli, who replied with a series of messages.

"An otaak is a guest house. It could vary from a single mud room where common folks invite their guests and offer them simple food and have long chats. People also host cultural gatherings in there with Sughara. They are usually old men, those 'been-there-and-done-that' and 'have-seen-it-all' types of individuals. They come and recite oral traditions that they have learned by heart, and when they unfold their series of words, those words, those unwritten incantations turn into magical spells. If they could be written down, those tales could grow to fill volumes."

"But an otaak can also be a lavish farmhouse with captive peacocks roaming within them, and even in captivity displaying their breath-taking feathers and making ugly cries, obviously enslaved. But otaaks are not only used as guesthouses. They can also serve as courts where feudal lords can mediate disputes among their community. Some of those lords make irreproachable decisions that could be presented to any legal auditor. But then, most of those lords try to secure their terror and give awful judgments; they make innocent peasants defecate and then eat their own faeces in front of their entire community on legation that those poor peasants made a joke about that feudal lord in neighbouring village."

"And other than those gross acts, which are a disgrace to humanity, they can also use their otaaks to host festive dinners with *mujra* dances performed by prostitutes. The mujra comes from the classical Indian dance kathak, which was patronised by the Mughal emperors, who were great lovers of the fine arts."

"In Mughal courts, a kathak dancer, usually a very pretty young courtesan, would tap and stamp her feet rhythmically and engage her whole body in the music performed by a percussionist and singer, who usually sang a *thumri* or *khayal*, songs about immortal love or Lord Krishna or some such. Lord Krishna was different from other gods because he was very human too, and he did things like steal butter and run after pretty girls."

"Coming to appreciate the South Asian praise of immortal love is like developing a palate for aged blue cheese. Listening to a thumri from a master singer used to be a spine jolting experience. They sing about the hopelessness of love, and in that poetry they beat the shit out of their own hearts, calling their hearts useless scumbags."

"But those classic days of the art form are gone. The kind of mujras that get performed nowadays in otaaks are purely exhibitionist, performed by poor girls, who are trained to shake their breasts violently up and down or sideways and spread their legs and crouch and stoop almost at the verge of exposing their genitals. And then those girls talk dirty with the person in the audience who throws most money to them."

In the end, Babli wrote, "Is that enough info kid?"

Kabeer texted back, "Thx."

So, between Roshan, Google, Babli, and the give and take of his own thoughts, Kabeer finally figured out what an otaak is.

Chapter 8
"Qalandar! Mast Qalandar. Qalandar, Lal Qalandar!"

Roshan had been handling many of the camps' affairs with confidence lately. And Kabeer noticed another kind of change in Roshan—it seemed like he had made peace with the entire damn universe, like he had found his place in it.

On one of those twilight evenings, after a day's work at the Dadu camp, Kabeer and Roshan were back at their resting place, which was a dilapidated school building. Its roof had already caved in, but the arched veranda stubbornly held what remained of its structure. Kabeer liked this ruination, thinking that it had a good energy.

Kabeer said to Roshan, "You look content…which is great! But, are you okay?"

Roshan who was sitting on ground with his back against one of the mud walls, in which tiny fragments of hay in the mud plaster were shining like gold flakes in setting sun light.

Roshan craned his head like any simple country boy, taking Kabeer's question to be the cue he had been waiting for. And he launched into his story.

Roshan told Kabeer about someone there, a Hafez, who had been Roshan's elementary school teacher. Hafez had noticed some helplessness in Roshan's bearing, so asked Roshan, "What is troubling you?"

"Nothing, I'm fine," said Roshan to Hafez. And Hafez had looked at Roshan and wisely said, *"Aaba! Daayian khaan ba kaay Chuda goojhaa!"*—*Cunts are no riddles to midwives, my child.*

After a bit more prodding, Roshan revealed to Hafez that nothing seemed to be working for him. He wanted something but he didn't know what. He wanted to be close to certain people, he wanted to have things that he always dreamed of. In other words, he was looking for his chance in life.

"You only want!" Hafez said. "Did you ever think of giving something?"

"I have nothing," Roshan sighed.

"Everybody has something to offer. You haven't thought about it hard enough. Offering doesn't have to be of monetary value. You could offer a tear!"

Roshan was looking at Hafez with his mouth a little open, like he wanted Hafez to explain it a bit more. Then Hafez said to him, "Because you don't have a firm belief. You need *Hidayat*.[163]"

After a few days, Hafez asked Roshan to come with him to pay homage to Qalandar in Sehwan.

Roshan was telling Kabeer all of this, and Kabeer was listening waiting for some enveloped superstition to unravel in Roshan's story.

Roshan said, "Hafez was telling me all about Qalandar, though I knew it already. Qalandar Lal is one of those saints who had reached the invisible throne of *Vilayat of Mola-e-Kainat, Imam Ali ul Murtaza, Shan-e-Panjtan Pak*. Qalandar reached such a pinnacle of glory that he lived in the realm of *La-makan*. He could freely travel between the seven skies and could reach seven layers deep into the earth's core at the same time."

"He already knows what's in your heart," Hafez had told Roshan that day. "You just have to reach out to him."

On their way to Sehwan, Hafez said with great firmness, "Tell me! Thousands of pilgrims have been visiting Qalandar every year for almost a thousand years now. Do you think that all these people are all crazy, that they're coming here for nothing?" But Roshan could only keep looking at Hafez in astonishment.

It was an hour and ten minutes' bus ride from Dadu. They reached the shrine at mid-morning. Roshan had been there countless times already, since his childhood days. Those same fields were on both sides of the road that he had seen every time on the way to Sehwan. The morning sunlight was blindingly bright, so he couldn't see much of those fields, but whenever their bus passed through rows of trees, he could see glittering light piercing through between the branches.

And as they arrived he could see that familiar golden dome of the shrine, squared between those same four blue minarets, which always appeared thin, covered by a halo of dust and the rest of the dusty dwellings of Sehwan. Those

---

[163] *Hidayat*: holy instructions.

humble dwellings were flocking around shrine, like they were the shrines of less enlightened but loyal disciples of the saint. There was a tall Alam Pak of Mola Gazi Abbas Alamdar, and a couple of cell phone antenna towers, which were even taller than Mola's Alam. But probably these scientific things had to do nothing with religious relics, so it was ok for those antennas to be taller.

On the road leading to the shrine entrance, which had turned from a road into a crowded walkway, there was someone dancing a *dhamaal*—a dance of ecstasy in a state of trance, an optimistic euphoria, a spiritual merriment, kind of like diving into the black hole of your soul, your own inner being, in hope of being sucked up, and to travel across in that mystic universe inside you, just to see a glimpse of Mehboob Saeen on the other side, that side where the divine light lives.

It was a young man wearing a red polyester skirt, and he was shaking his head violently, with a broad grinning smile. He was dancing and throwing his head and body and somehow balancing them. Every time he shook, locks of his hair fanned outwards, turning his sweat into small misty jets. His face was all red and glistening with his own perspirations, his eyes were rolled back. His mouth was open and saliva was dripping; there was a satisfaction of overdose on his face, like he was having the elation of a lifetime.

There was also a drummer following that young dancer, pounding his drum with a thin drum stick, which was making irritating shrill pitches like someone mercilessly beating your eardrums with a thin hard straw.

Droves of people were following them, like they had nothing else to do. The air was filled with a clamour of different smells, dry rose petals, camphor, cheap incense that actually smelled like horse shit, sour body odours, some of which were really acrid, mixing with the subtle smell of fine dust in the air. There was no need for Roshan to notice all that, it was all usual, ordinary, everyday life. The only thing that Roshan noticed today was the blood oozing from the muddy feet of that ecstatic dancer.

Legend has it that Qalandar himself was *jalal,* kind of a mystic bipolar. In Arabic, 'Jalaal' could also mean something like the fiery glory of an inferno. They say that in the days when Qalandar lived in flesh and blood, he was a grumpy and angry man. Once it happened that some wicked people captured one of Qalandar's most beloved disciples, and they killed him and chopped him into pieces. Those wicked people then mixed small pieces of Qalandar's disciple's flesh with regular meat and gave that meat to every house in the town of Sehwan, and the people of the town began cooking it. Then, Qalandar called to his beloved disciple, and even though he was physically dead, he could still respond to the calling of his master.

Every small piece of his body flesh started flying out of the cooking pots of the people of Sehwan and piled up in front of Qalandar, in the pure obedience of a disciple to his master. Angry Qalandar in that state of jalal grabbed a clay bowl that was in front of him, lifted it up slowly, then turned it upside down and smashed it on the ground. And so goes the legend that the entire city of Sehwan first rose up, then turned upside down and they say it got smashed back on ground like a cherry pie hitting the wall.

In the shrine's courtyard, everything was the same. There were the same crowds of people, pilgrims, and beggars who had been there for generations. Hawkers selling their special quilted caps made from small triangular black, white, green and red patches sewn together. Some other hawkers were selling shocking red, electric blue, and fiery orange *ghana* garlands of Qalandar.

"What's gaa'na?" Kabeer interrupted.

Roshan found himself clueless, as if Kabeer had just asked him what air is, or water, or fire, or earth; or even more, it was as if he had just asked, *what is ether*?

"Gaa'na is gaa'no!" And so Roshan made up an answer, trusting it to be basically true. "It's a blessing garland made up of strands of twisted artificial wool. Though the individual strands of wool are weak, they work together to form a strong bond, and they connect those pilgrims with Qalandar. For a little price, people can buy a band of bright strings to wear around their necks. It adds a little colour to their otherwise dimming and dull lives."

"And maybe by wearing those garlands people metaphorically dump all of their worries into Qalandar's backyard—with this self-assurance that they are getting cleansed by Qalandar's mystic charms, getting scrubbed with the detergent of his spirituality."

Roshan took a short pause and with astonishment replied like he really got a good example. "You could say this erases all of their junk files from the USB drives of their minds, creating new space in there, for them to make it all cluttered with worries again in the future." And by that naïve explanation Roshan, defined *ghana* almost perfectly.

In Sehwan, there were vendors sitting next to their mountains of roasted chickpeas and mountains of pea-sized white sugar balls and smaller mountains of misri—lumps of crystallised sugar, shaped like Superman's nemesis crystal. But in this part of world, misri was used in religious offerings; Lord Krishna was especially fond of it. Probably, Qalandar liked it too; maybe that confection could sweeten his grumpy mood. Other venders were selling flower garlands and long algae-green *chadars*—shawls with Quranic verses inscribed in real golden threads, for those who could afford them.

They also had cheaper green scarf-sized pieces with Quranic and Persian script printed in silver or golden ink, for pilgrims to buy and spread on Qalandar's mausoleum. Others were selling huge pots of cooked rice pilaf for devotees to buy and feed the poor as an offering to Qalandar.

This was routine for Roshan. He had only come here to please his elementary school teacher. But then, there was a frail wish there too in his puzzled mind, which somehow wanted to believe in Hafez's mystic theorem.

They sat there all day in a remote corner at the back of the shrine. Many others were there too, men, women, and children, old and young all sitting there under a makeshift canopy.

One woman who was sitting there in the centre suddenly placed both her hands on her knees and then started throwing her head up and down. Her hair made whipping sounds as it hit her back and then the ground, back and forth. In her trance she was crying, "Qalandar; Mast Qalandar!"

Roshan confessed to himself in his heart, "She is possessed by a jinn."

Women around her were taking their veils off from their heads and spreading them across their arms, presumably so they could catch as much as possible of Qalandar's blessings from heavens. And the woman in the trance kept shaking her head and saying, "Qalandar! Mast Qalandar. Qalandar, Lal Qalandar!"

There was an old man sitting there also who was just rocking back and forth on his hips. And was weeping, but his tears were disappearing in his grey beard, which seemed to be holding his dignity together.

Roshan and Hafez stayed there all day, and Hafez kept telling Roshan that he'd get a *bisharat*—a good sign. He will communicate, Hafez kept saying, just look for the good news.

All day, passed as usual, and finally Hafez said, "Let's go." It was early evening; there was a fatigued generosity in the pale light of the setting sun, which was taking on yellowish-orange tones, mixed with looming sadness. There were the normal sounds of a countryside town, with birds chirping, mostly sparrows making a big fuss of their evening commute back to the trees.

There were the annoying truck and bus horns, loud Hindi songs playing in *hotal'a* tea shops, and all of the day's heat had sucked the moisture from the dirt into the air, making the dirt lighter and dustier, so that it was rising up and forming a stagnant cloud, hovering just above the ground.

Hafez and Roshan boarded a bus and headed back to Dadu. On their way back, Hafez asked Roshan, "Did you feel it?"

"Feel what?" Roshan asked.

"Put your right hand in right side pocket of your kameez—but before doing that, say, 'dum-madad baraee-paar,' loudly."

Roshan did that with inexactness, feeling certain that there was nothing in his pocket. But then the fingers of his right hand fingers touched upon something like paper. He took it out, and yes indeed, it was a folded piece of paper.

Hafez sitting next to him said, "*Qalandar Jee chithi thaee.*"—It's Qalandar's personal letter to you.

Roshan opened it. There were saffron letters of some language that Roshan had never seen before. Hafez said, "Fold it back, you fool, you don't have to read it. You'll go mad trying to understand it. Just soak this letter in water and then drink it."

And surely Roshan dipped Qalandar's chithi in a glass of water, and when the script started disappearing, and the water was took on a pale hue like there was turmeric in there, he gulped.

Roshan ended his story. After a long period of quiet, when Roshan still said nothing else, Kabeer asked, "Is that all?" And he kept looking at Roshan's face in stupefaction, trying to grasp within Roshan some trace of that fading distinction between fact and superstition.

But Roshan said nothing. He just peacefully closed his eyes, still leaning his back against the mud wall. But those tiny fragments of hay were no longer shining like gold, as the sun had set now. There was an unexplainable calm on Roshan's face, which gave the slightest impression that he was smiling, as if he had found that good energy, while he half nodded his head with his closed eyes, appreciating something that he didn't have to look at.

Chapter 9
Is That the Place?

One of the mobile units that their NGO was setting up was for the town of Shahdadkot. There was nothing great about Shahdadkot; it was just another dusty Sindhi town, dragging its feet through its unavoidable life. But that mobile unit also had to stop serve Qamber on its way to Shahdadkot. The name Qamber gave Kabeer's heart a feeling akin to the drop on a rollercoaster ride. He had heard a lot about Qamber from his father and grandpa, whom he called *Dada*.

In Qamber, the mobile unit was stationed on the dirt grounds of a high school. Because of Roshan's good planning, there were hundreds of people, mostly children and women, already waiting there. The mobile unit was only for Hepatitis screening, but these innocent people thought it was for every cure. So there were people who were suffering from toothaches, and elderly people with fully mature cataracts, and kids with cleft lips. One old man came to Kabeer and showed him three fingers of his right hands, which were fused together in a half-closed formation, due to an old injury or severe trauma. Kabeer looked at him and said, "What?"

The old man said, "Fix them."

Kabeer said, "We are here for Hepatitis screening. Plus it's next to impossible to revive atrophic fingers." In slang, Kabeer explained to the old man that the muscles of fingers had dried.

"Baqi dak'dar chajo aan!" The old man said—*What sort of a doctor are you, then!*

Roshan cut in and said to the old man, *"Chacha, saeen daktar'o aa; ko khuda'o thoree aa, tu ta ko charyo; aan, chaa?"*—*Are you nuts? Yes, he is a doctor, but he is not God.*

Kabeer said *sorry* to the old man. Then the old man cheered up and said, "Okay, I'm fine. I thought, no harm checking." Then the old man smiled and went on his way.

Then there was a middle-aged man wearing spotless moccasins with metal hardware and grey pinstriped trousers and a starched white shirt. Though he was standing on the dirt, somehow he was keeping himself from getting dirty. He stood out from the rest of that milled and soiled crowd, and he was standing literally apart from them as well. He approached Roshan and said, "I want to meet the American doctor."

Roshan pointed to Kabeer and said, "There he is."

The man seemed disappointed. He probably had expected someone Caucasian. But he recovered quickly from that shock and asked Roshan to arrange a private meeting with the doctor. He also told Roshan that he was the grandson of the elders of Qamber.

And when he met Kabeer in private, which actually meant fifteen feet away from the main uproar, after all that fuss and display of grandeur, he got straight to the point. "Could you get me American-made Viagra, you know the original one? The ones they sell here are fakes."

Kabeer just looked at him. Then the man on his own said, "its fine if they are difficult to get, don't worry." He hung around for a short while, instructing the locals to help do things. Kabeer looked over at him every now and then. He did have a special gift of walking in the dirt without getting himself dirty. And after a while, that man disappeared in his white Japanese car.

All day, he kept seeing patients, and unfortunately turning most of them away without helping them, because they weren't there for Hepatitis issues. And all day this thought kept bugging him, that he wanted to talk to some who knew his forefathers, someone who could assure him that, *yes, your forefathers are from here*. But then he was wondering why he was so obsessed with the idea. They lived in this town. So why be melodramatic about it?

The fact of the matter was that they had lived here and then they left this for a bigger city. And a few years back, his grandfather had come back here, for probably for the last time, to sell their family home, and now there was nothing in Qamber that they could call theirs. Other than that, that they were from Qamber.

That evening before heading back to the Larkano base camp, Kabeer told Roshan with a slight hesitation, "This is, I guess, my town. My grandfather was born here in a mud house built by his grandfather."

Roshan said in astonishment, "*Wah saeen wah!*"—Wow! That's great. "Do you know where they used to live here?"

"No I don't know," said Kabeer. "In fact, this is the very first time I myself am here. When I was young my grandfather use to tell me stories of this place! But those were like adventure stories. In which he used to play marbles with boys, and once he lost all of his marbles, and was left with only one fat trigger marble. But from that last remaining marble he started winning and gained all of his marbles back. He even won some marbles from his opponents. And in those stories he used to climb onto rooftops and run after loose kites, to snatch them first, before the others, and that he almost lost one of his legs doing that."

Roshan seemed even more astonished. "Saeen, it seems like your grandfather loves you."

"Yes! He does," said Kabeer, and then just to himself, "…yup." After a moment, he looked back to Roshan and said, "I think they said they used to live behind a school. It might be possible they lived behind this very school."

Roshan said, "Let's check it out. But we shouldn't stay here for long. You could get kidnapped. Already hundreds of people have seen you here today." He paused and then said, "You understand what I'm saying."

Kabeer nodded his head in a yes.

With Roshan at his side, Kabeer ventured outside that school ground, stepping into memories that were not even his. He was not aware that it's always a risky business to walk into memories, because usually people want to reopen them right from where they left off, they want to go back to see themselves as a careless youth being baptised in their first teenage love, and to find initials of their name alongside someone else's initials in a heart shape, roughly etched onto the trunk of some tree that has long been cut down, and those people are more interested in seeing see those other initials that have nothing to do with their name.

Or else people want to see old streets, and sniff the smells, and listen to the sounds, which have changed, just like those memory seekers themselves. But Kabeer was trying his luck on borrowed memories, so he didn't have to fear that heartbreak.

Outside the school walls everything looked awfully sad, all covered in a muddy screen of fine talc-like dust. Even the poor trees were covered in that dust—each leaf had that fine coating. There were electric poles with complex meshes of wires, which looked hopelessly entangled, like convoluted theories intended to boggle the mind, but actually those wires were still functional.

The shadows of the autumn sunset appeared longer than usual. Kabeer was trying hard to find those feelings in his heart that he had read about in books and seen in movies, where people weep tears of joy and feel fulfilled by returning to their place of origin. But he was having no such feelings of overflowing happiness. They passed through a narrow alley where crying live chickens were jammed in iron cages, and next to that place someone was pressing clothes out in the open, with giant primitive press-iron on an ironing board the size of a dining table.

Part of the alley was roofed with something like of greyish-green rag, a kind of material that was probably once a tent fabric. That alley was snaking in, leading them toward downtown Qamber. Kabeer was amazed to see that this place looked like it was from the era of Jesus, like the streets of old Jerusalem, which he had seen in documentaries on the History Channel.

But in those documentaries you don't smell acridness of blood as you pass by the poultry shop, or the constant foul odour coming from dark rotten soil in the open sewers, and you don't see the fruit flies slow flying through the heavy atmosphere filled with fine dust, lit by the in the sickening pale glow of the setting sun.

As they walked through the bazaar, Roshan stopped to ask all the shopkeepers if they knew Ali Gohar, Kabeer's grandfather, and if they could point them to Kabeer's ancestral home. And the answer kept coming back no. They emerged into a different part of town, where there was a paved road and street was much wider, but everything else was the same as in the alley. The shops were all pretty much closed here, though there were few lorry trucks being filled by labourers with sacks of grain.

An older man was sitting in there getting one of the lorry truck loaded. Roshan ask him his question, and the man asked back, "Who are you?"

"I have no relationship with him," said Roshan, and then pointed a finger towards Kabeer, "But this is his grandson."

The man looked at Kabeer and said, "At least shake hands, saeen!"

Kabeer obliged a bit sheepishly and shook hands. The old man said, "I don't know your father, but I do know your grandfather." And then he said to himself, *"Ali Gohar, saeen, mastar Mohammad Alam, jo puto...balay!"—Ali Gohar, the son of schoolmaster Mohammad Alam...Wow!*

And the old man seemed to have nothing to say, but he went on anyway. "This is the old grain market." Then he pointed out towards a flickering light and said, "That is a tea shop beside construction site of bank. That bank is being built on the land which used to be their house!" Then old man took another pause, like he was disappointed and almost angry. But he just looked at Kabeer's face and said, "That was your house, but that house is levelled. There is nothing left there of your father's."

They said some kind of thanks and took their leave of the old man, walking towards the flickering light of the teashop.

Kabeer was thinking to himself, the beauty of this place is all gone, if there ever was any. Is this the place that my grandfather's grandfather built? This is garbage, piles and piles of rubble. He felt like this place had been left behind somewhere in the Middle Ages; it seemed so old, so uncanny. He didn't want to have anything to do with it. Just being there felt difficult to him; it felt like that monumental task of learning how to walk again, for an amputee.

But then a part of him wanted to see the place where his family started from. They reached the teashop, which was just a straw canopy standing on Y-shaped sticks, with two raw wooden benches underneath, and a clay stove with a big pan of brewing tea and a dipper.

Roshan and Kabeer sat on one of the benches. Roshan asked for tea, and a man there immediately produced two teas and a few slices of pound cake on a rusted tin cookie jar lid. Roshan, being a countryside guy himself, initiated a conversation. "What are they building here?" He asked, though he already knew that it was probably a bank.

The tea vendor seemed pleased as he replied, "This is going to be new location for national bank, and bank manager is letting me stay here."

Then Roshan jumped to the core question. "What was here before?"

The tea vendor simply replied, "Nothing."

So Roshan said, "Nothing means what?"

"Saeen, this was a ruin. I've been here for over thirty years. I haven't seen anyone or anything living in there, other than a ber tree. Every few years one of the owner's sons used to come and say that they were going to build a shopping strip, and ask me to move my tea stand from their wall, and threaten me with court orders, and then they use to disappear. This place was a waste dump. *Heroieene*[164]* used to go in there and smoke. The roof was caved in, walls collapsed. The only living thing left in there was a *neebhagi*[165] ber'a saeen!"

"That ber tree, alley kids use to throw rocks at her, every year when she bore ber-berries. But the construction crew cleared all that debris and cut out the tree and threw her trunk out here, next to my teashop. I chopped it into pieces for burning in my woodstove."

Kabeer had never heard of any ber'a tree from his father or his grandfather, though his father used to talk a lot about different trees, some tree blooms with tiny tentacles, like an old fashion shaving brush, and that the out of this world fragrance of those blooms. His idealist father used to claim, even while still alive that, "those trees outlive them" including him. So Kabeer had never heard of any ber tree from his father or his grandfather, so he had no idea what the tea vendor was talking about.

The thought came in to Kabeer's mind that may be they were at the wrong place, but at the same moment his phone started shaking in his pocket. Nowadays, these phones have this kind of childishness—they keep ringing or vibrating until you shut them up or listen to them. Kabeer looked at it and saw an email from the lobbyist. "Hi, just wanted to talk with you about a possible meeting for you with our friends here in Congress to work on getting you some donations and maybe grants. The time slot that I have open is six weeks from today. Please contact ASAP, if you are interested. Very best."

Kabeer put the phone down, finished his tea, and said to Roshan, "Let's go!"

---

[164] *Heeroine*: heroin addicts.
[165] *Neebhagi*: Ill-fated—literally, 'snake-bitten'.